There are

THE SEARCH FOR

JEWEL ISLAND

Tulku: Book 1

R.N. JACKSON

www.rnjackson.com

Cover by Ben Jackson.

To my daughters,
Lucy, Annabel and Phoebe

With our thoughts, we make the world

—Buddha

PART ONE

GATLEY HOUSE

APRIL 28TH 1986

1

DOMINOES

Well, it was me who flattened my English teacher's nose.

I'm not proud of it or anything. But I will own it... sort of.

He'd said something about Dad, and I'd stood up with a screech of chair-leg. Twenty-five expectant faces turned and silently peered at my scowling face.

I am not a fan of the limelight.

Heat rose inside me, making my face burn. Mr Blakely tried to back-pedal. But you can't unsay stuff, can you? Once you drop your coin, it always hits the bottom.

Teachers were supposed to let me out of class to cool down. That was my understanding of 'The Agreement' between Mum and the headmaster anyway. But Mr B clearly hadn't received the memo, because he tried to follow me out of the classroom, which meant he was in exactly the wrong place when I slammed the door.

There was a howl of shock from the other side.

I winced and came to a shuddering halt a few feet down the corridor, picturing Mr Blakely's nose spurting blood all over his comfy leather shoes.

I took a breath and thought about 'The Agreement' and what breaking it might mean. Surely the headmaster would accept this was an accident. I mean, it was violence. But it was violence against a door, not a person. There were witnesses and everything.

I had to sort this. I would own it. I would apologise. Admit to losing my temper, offer to get the nurse. Be the better person.

Straightening my shoulders, I made my way back to the classroom. Muffled voices from the other side of the heavy wooden door got louder as I approached. I couldn't make out everything that was being said, but I understood the tone alright—scandalised and shocked.

I gripped the handle, closed my eyes and whispered the mantra Dad had taught me whenever I froze: Feel the fear and do it anyway, Esta Brown.

Deep breath.

I pushed. The door opened a creak. One voice rose above the others: a girl's high-pitched whine.

Just two words.

But they were enough to turn my stomach to molten iron again. I let go of the handle as if it had bitten me, turned on my heels and stormed off down the corridor. The imaginative little nickname I'd been given rang in my ears.

Depresta Brown, Depresta Brown, Depresta Brown.

I shoulder-barged a fire exit and headed for a space near the P.E. storage room.

It was the only spot this side of school without classroom windows overlooking it. It was a space where you could sit in silence. Let the heat cool.

But not today.

Two boys were hunched over something, whispering to each other.

I came to a stop six or seven feet away from them, flattened myself against the wall and wiped my face in case either of them looked round. I wasn't crying. I don't cry. But anger makes my cheeks go blotchy.

One of them—the shorter of the two—was holding the blade of a silver key between his forefinger and thumb, and they were both staring at it like it was some kind of alien artefact.

'It's dangerous,' the taller boy said.

I was still shaking and boiling on the inside, but I recognised them both, and despite everything, a tiny, calm, rational part of my brain couldn't help wondering what these two were doing together.

The tall one was a sixth former called Graham. He wasn't much for uniform. His school shirt was untucked, the end of his unworn tie trailed out of the front pocket of black drainpipe jeans, and he wore a pair of battered trainers. The other boy could hardly have been more different. Simon Taylor. He of the permanent tan, piercing blue eyes and straight blond shampoo-commercial hair.

I'm no social expert, but even I knew this was an unlikely team.

Simon eyeballed the sixth former with all the seriousness of someone planning a bank robbery.

I should have edged away, left the boys to their game and found a hedge to crawl under. Instead, I stayed. Why, I don't know. Maybe it was the weirdness of seeing a geek and a posh cool-boy talking so intimately. Maybe it was the way they both stared at that key. Or, perhaps, some part of me already knew what it opened.

'Come on, Graham,' Simon said. 'No one else'll come with me. And you know the place.'

Graham grabbed his satchel from between his feet. 'Absolutely not.'

I braced myself to run, sure one of them would see me now. But Graham was stalling. He was making to leave, but his feet were rooted to the spot. Trust me. I know that feeling. I've not always been the storming-off type.

'I thought you wanted to come to the party?' Simon said.

Graham seemed to deflate. He let go of his satchel.

There was a pause while they contemplated the key again. A bird sang away overhead; a P.E. teacher's distant whistle answered it, signalling the end of Games.

Graham tapped the back of his head against the wall. 'You're actually going inside?'

'My dad's going to knock it down. So he has access. Which means…' Simon shook the key, so it looked like a wriggling fish. 'I do too.'

Graham adjusted the strap of his satchel.

It was almost 3.15. Home time. I needed to move. Leave the school grounds, go somewhere no one could find me. Usually, in times of crisis, I would make my way through Fletcher's Field to the gate by the old house, just to watch the place for a bit while I calmed down. But there was something about that little wriggling key that made the sweat prickle against my forehead.

I sidled forward, drawn to it, not bothered about them spotting me anymore.

'You scared?' Simon whispered.

'Course I am. The place is a death trap.'

'That's why I need you to go with me.'

'I can't…'

Simon pocketed the key, which was—weirdly—a relief. The sort of relief you have when a high-pitched electric buzz you weren't fully aware of suddenly stops.

I inched closer still.

'We go in, mooch around, then leave. What's the harm?'

'What's the harm?' Graham hissed. 'You never heard of Charlie Bullock?'

Charlie Bullock?

My brain clicked like a cog in a machine. Before I knew what I was doing, I peeled away from the wall and opened my mouth. 'You're going inside Gatley House?'

Simon turned and blinked at me as if I'd appeared in a puff of smoke.

I stepped closer, my heart hammering away. But I'd started talking now, and apparently my mouth didn't want to stop. 'Gatley House,' I repeated. 'That's what you're on about, isn't it?'

Simon seemed to collect himself. 'You don't know what you're talking about.'

I glared at him with complete certainty. 'That's where they found Charlie Bullock,' I whispered.

The brief exchange of glances between him and Graham told me

I was right and, if anything, my heart galloped even more quickly.

They had a key to Gatley House. They were going inside. And honestly, right then absolutely nothing else mattered. Not 'Depresta Brown', not Mum, not even Blakely's bent nose.

'I'll go with you,' I said.

Simon raised an eyebrow. 'What makes you think I'd let you?'

I folded my arms.

'I don't even know who you are,' he said. 'Why d'you want to come to my party?'

'Who said anything about going to your party?'

Simon blinked. Normally a boy like him wouldn't even consider speaking to a girl like me. He was fifteen, same age as me, but he might as well have been a different species. His clothes were new, his hair neat and tidy. I doubted his skin ever experienced teenage grease, let alone spots. I half-expected him to ask Graham to translate for us.

He didn't. He smiled. A smile that grew on his face like a line of ink crawling along blotting paper. His teeth shone white and straight behind his lips.

I didn't know whether to smile back or shrivel up.

Graham broke the spell. 'You're Esta Brown,' he said.

Simon's smile faded. He looked at Graham. 'As in Richard Brown's daughter?'

I felt myself shrink. But I forced myself to glare back at them both, my green eyes—one of the few things Dad had left me—darting from one to the other. 'You can't stop me from coming,' I said.

'My dad would,' Simon said between his teeth.

'Not before I told him about your key.'

Simon considered me for a second, his jaw clenching beneath his perfect skin.

I held my breath.

The bell for end of lessons chimed. A door banged open, and the tangle of first years spilled out into the Quad.

8

Simon broke eye contact first. He shook his head and turned to leave.

'Wait!' I said, grabbing his arm.

He brushed my hand off, and he and Graham headed towards the widening stream of students. More bodies exploded out of the doors, barging into each other. One of the smallest ones knocked into Graham, who staggered and swore. His satchel swung upside down, and something slipped out and was lost amongst the scramble.

I stood and watched the class fan out as they went their separate ways home, or to the corner shop, or the park, or wherever normal kids go after school. Graham and Simon stood out like giants among them.

I glanced down. A Star Wars magazine sat crumpled and torn on the concrete. I bent down and picked it up.

'Esta?' Mr Blakely's muffled voice drifted over from the fire exit I'd left open in my haste. Concerned eyes looked at me above a folded, bloody tissue he held to his nose.

I did that.

We watched each other for twenty long seconds. Then the next wave of kids piled out of the P.E. changing rooms, and I allowed myself to be carried away by them.

I did do that, I thought, but some of the blame lay elsewhere too.

People say the universe is just like one big row of dominoes. You ever heard that? You push one tile and it flattens the next, and the next. And on and on in an unbroken, clattering sequence of causes and effects. But I think maybe there are hundreds of intersecting rows, and they're all clattering off each other. And sometimes, at a four-way roundabout, people's noses get flattened.

2

SINCE WHAT HAPPENED

Backstory. I know. Yawn. Give me a couple of pages, though.

What was the deal with Gatley House? Well, no one had been brave enough to venture inside the place for almost two years. Not since what happened.

Charlie Bullock had been wandering about the place all alone when she'd fallen through the floor. Spent two days lying in a creaky little cupboard room beneath the stairs. Two days lying there with her back broken and her mind in pieces, jabbering on about invisible people and a valley with mountain peaks tipped with snow.

Crazy story right? But what's it got to do with me?

The man who found Charlie was my dad. And he was the town hero…

For about a week.

People had already started asking questions. Obvious ones like: why didn't the police find her first? Why did it take a regular bloke to do the job they failed to do?

But then there were other questions. One in particular was: how could Charlie have fallen, broken her back, and then found her way to a spot underneath the stairs all by herself?

There was only one explanation. Someone must have moved Charlie after the fall. And it wasn't long before people started putting two and two together and reaching five.

Who could have moved Charlie other than my dad, who found her?

What was he even doing wandering around Gatley House in the first place? Had he been searching for Charlie? Had he known she was there all along?

Even though the police "eliminated him from their enquiries", the whisperings and gossip about Dad carried on for weeks.

It's a small town.

Dad didn't exactly work hard to shut people up. He was never the same again. He spent days away from home 'researching' material for some upcoming museum exhibition, and when he was home, he spent hours in his room scribbling in his notebooks, barely eating anything and almost never speaking to Mum or me.

Then, a month after finding Charlie, he just… up and left.

He left our house in the morning and never came back. He abandoned everything: his research, his passport…

Me.

Disappeared without a trace. No explanation, no goodbye note, no clue.

Ever since, I had known, I mean known, that if there was an answer to why he left—an answer to where he might be now—it was inside the walls of Gatley House.

Simon Taylor was going to break into Gatley House this evening. What did it matter if he didn't want me to come?

I would go anyway.

3

FEEL THE FEAR

Fletcher's Field was the last bit of green space in my town. Really, it was just a few acres of grass surrounded on three sides by housing estates. The fourth—the western side—ended at a high wall and then Wilmslow Road, which took traffic through the town and on to Manchester Airport.

Gatley House stood near that wall.

Streetlights from the main road flickered through the branches of the trees as I approached. I couldn't see the house huddled between them, but I could feel its presence, like sensing the edge of a cliff in darkness.

A security light caught my movement and flicked on. It cast the surrounding ground in shadow and lit up the outlines of a bulldozer. The field was like a First World War battleground. This whole area used to be green fields, but machines had been clawing and gouging it up for months for the new airport road: an ugly stripe carving the town in half. "Progress" they called it in the local paper.

I pushed through the gap in the hedge, stepped over the muddy track and stopped—as always—at the gate. Beyond it, skulking between half a dozen trees was the old, three-storey building. Bare branches from both sides wrapped around it like bony fingers.

Ever since Charlie Bullock's accident. Someone—the owner, or maybe the Council—had nailed boards over the front door and every window. It had made the house look blind. Over winter though, one of the boards had peeled away from a second-floor window. Now distant street-lights winked invitingly off the still intact glass.

I shivered and blew out a long breath. The chilly air turned it to steam.

A voice hissed from the other side of the gate. 'Who's there?'

A yellow spot of torchlight flicked on twenty paces away, zigzagging closer, getting brighter and then catching me dead in the eyes.

'I knew you'd come.'

I ducked out of the beam.

'It's me, Graham,' the voice said.

I said nothing. I'd only ever watched the house from this side of the gate. I never thought I'd ever actually cross over. From this distance the house was nothing more than a picture in a frame. A story in a book. You know, something you can dip into and then walk away from.

The torchlight sparked off the twisted spikes wrapped around the gate.

'It's now or never,' Graham whispered.

I closed my eyes. *It's now or never.*

That's what Dad had said to me about three years ago as he took me scrambling up Crawley Rock. He'd been meaning to take me the whole holiday and on the last day, while Mum was packing, he did. I remember standing on the top, shivering, looking down at the waves, something like fifteen feet below.

'It's now or never, Est.'

He'd flashed a wild grin at me. 'You have to feel the fear and do it anyway.'

Then he'd pulled of his shirt and jumped, whooping all the way down before smacking into the cold, grey sea. I stood there, heart in my mouth, watching, as he smiled and waved at me to follow. I stood and watched as that smile slowly melted into disappointment before he gave up on me and swam to shore by himself.

When he left us, part of me wondered if it had nothing to do with Charlie Bullock, or Gatley House. Part of me wondered whether it had more to do with that look he gave me. I used to carry a mental image of his disappointed face like a scar carved on the inside of my skull.

'Watch the barbed wire on your way over,' Graham said, pointing the torch at the gate.

I shook the memory from my head, swung a leg over the top slat and leapt to the ground. I pulled the rolled up Star Wars magazine I'd saved from earlier from my back pocket and handed it him. 'Here.'

Graham cocked his head. It was a strange thing to do. Like he was trying to see me from a different angle. He took it the magazine off me, tucked it into his belt and smiled. 'Come on. Everyone's here already.'

I walked behind him as he led me up the driveway towards the looming shadow of the house. It was bigger, more real, on this side of the gate. I concentrated on the satchel Graham carried over his shoulder instead. I'd heard his dad was a soldier overseas, but Graham didn't look the military type to me. He was more interested in geeky stuff. I'd seen him in the school library reading science textbooks and of course there was the Star Wars magazine.

A girl's voice sneered from the other side of another sudden beam of light. 'What's she doing here?'

The beam moved from Graham to me and back again before clicking off and revealing three outlines.

I recognised one of them even before my eyesight recovered: Hannah Pritchard. She was squeezed into a denim jacket and jeans and had a perm so stiff it might have been a wig. Even in the dark, you could see her permanently blood-red lips pucker up as she sucked on one of her disgusting menthol cigarettes.

'Depresta Brown, what a surprise,' she drawled, blowing minty smoke in my face.

I waved the cloud away, resisting the urge to cough. 'What's Hannah Piranha doing here?' I whispered to Graham.

The girl snorted and turned to her two friends. 'I'm just here for the show.'

I stared her down. Or tried to. She was a good three inches taller and wider than me. Her lips flickered into an unpleasant smile that reminded me of the barbed wire.

'You haven't got a clue, have you?' Hannah said. 'You turned up to see if we find any more bodies I bet.'

'Where's Simon?' I said, ignoring the sniggering of Hannah's mates. Now I was finally on the other side of the gate. I wanted to get a move on before I lost my bottle.

Hannah placed a hand on my shoulder. 'Time to find out if all the stories are true eh, Depresta?'

I shrugged her off me.

Hannah pointed with her cigarette to the corner of the house where tree trunks stood close and straight like the bars of a giant cage.

Graham whispered into my ear, 'Simon said there's a way in on the side. There's a window, then some steps to the first floor.'

'Are you coming?' I asked.

He glanced back towards the gate before answering. 'Yeah, course.'

The other kids stared as we nudged between them. One boy wore a hoodie; the end of his cigarette wobbled like a star in the blank space where his face hid. Next to him was another face I recognised: Kev. A scrawny skinhead who'd been expelled from school last year and now hung around the school gates trying to sell the rest of us dodgy stuff. Proper little businessman. What was he doing here? Were they all planning to break in?

It felt like an invasion.

I mean. This was *my* house.

'I know you,' Kev rasped. 'You're the daughter of that missing bloke aren't yer?' His teeth were buckled like old piano keys, and he needed a shave. I tried to move on, but he stepped in my way, blowing out a cloud of smoke. 'I bet you know the full story, don't yer? Better 'n anyone.' He held three fingers up at me. 'Three people dead.' He raised his little finger to make four, then poked my forehead with them. 'You'll be next if you go inside.'

'Charlie Bullock didn't die,' I said, ducking away.

'I wasn't talking 'bout Charlie,' he replied. The boy with a shadow for a face broke into coughing giggles.

I bit the inside of my mouth to stop unwanted tears.

I didn't cry about Dad. That was my main rule. I didn't cry about him in front of people. Not Mum, not my teachers, and especially not these idiots.

I thought about turning round and running away. Was I ready to do this? It was still early. I could sneak home before Mum got back from her meeting. I'd be asleep under my covers before she climbed the stairs.

The others laughed, but they were chewing fingernails, hoovering up their cigarettes, not one of them closer than twenty feet from the house. That's what kept me from running. Behind all the mean laughter, I knew fear when I saw it.

I thought about Crawley Rock—If Dad were here, he wouldn't hesitate. My dad was fearless. And it's time I was too.

*****

Simon Taylor was crouching by a fallen branch, staring at a small basement window set low in the wall of the house. He wore fancy jeans, a button-up shirt, and polished white leather trainers. Hardly the gear for breaking into a haunted house.

I glanced behind to see if Graham was still with me. He'd stopped. The glow from the streetlamps caught the edge of his face; the rest of him was a silhouette.

I took a deep breath and headed for the wooden panel that covered the basement window.

Simon stood, brushing dirt from his jeans. 'Your mum know you're here?'

'Does your dad know *you* are?'

'Your dad—' he started.

'What about him?' I snapped a sizzle of electricity racing up the nape of my neck.

'That why you've come? Cos of him?'

The electricity frazzled and died. He was just poking. It's all anyone talked to me about. Except people never actually used words. They did it with their eyes, whispers, nudges and grins.

But they knew nothing. Just because someone goes missing, it doesn't mean they're dead. That's what the *law* says. Mr Blakely should have known that. Might have saved him a flat nose.

I took a step toward the house. 'So? Are we going in or what?'

Simon followed. 'Do you believe the stories?'

I flexed my fingers to stop them from trembling. When I reached the panel, I nudged the heavy padlock with the toe of my shoe. 'Depends which stories you mean. You got the key?'

I didn't want to discuss any "stories". I'd heard enough of them from the Hannahs of this world. They mainly involved ghosts and rattling chains of course, but more than a few involved unpleasant speculation about what my dad had been doing lurking around in an abandoned house the night he found Charlie.

I'd come up with plenty of my *own* stories while standing on the other side of that old gate.

'I'm talking about what happened *before* Charlie. About the couple who used to live here.'

'Why don't you just unlock the window?'

'Scared?'

'What are you? Ten?' I said. But I was way past scared. I didn't know what I was hoping to find. I didn't know what sort of answers there would be, rotting away inside those walls. Part of me, the part that listened to the stories, the same part that stopped me from climbing over the gate all this time, didn't *want* to know.

He showed me the key, then crouched, rattled it in to the padlock and twisted. The padlock clicked. Simon glanced up at me, then pulled. The wooden panel creaked open on a rusty hinge, revealing the decaying remains of the original window frame, the pane of glass long since smashed out. A damp, stale smell of soggy newspapers escaped from the darkness below.

I turned to look for Graham. He was a couple of paces away, staring towards Hannah and her friends. He might as well have had the words: "I'm outta here" printed on his t-shirt. To be honest, I didn't care much who came with me. I just wanted to get inside. Get it over with.

'I heard whoever owned it before went mad,' Simon said, licking his lips. 'Full-on Psycho. Killed his wife. Buried her in the garden somewhere.' He pointed the torch in the direction of the lawn. The light disappeared into the murk that lay thick behind Hannah and the rest.

Shivers crawled up my arms. 'For God's sake. Let's just do it,' I said.

The torch flicked off. Simon swore, banged it. It flicked back on again. He shone it into the basement. Shattered glass sparkled like a thousand tiny eyes. 'They found him in the house weeks later,' he whispered. 'Can you imagine?'

The torch blinked off again, leaving lava-lamp-blobs sliding across my vision. I knew the rest of the story:

The old man screwed a meat hook to the ceiling of one of the first-floor rooms and took out the floorboards. A week later a deliveryman with an acute sense of smell and an over-developed sense of curiosity found his body dangling from a rope.

I pictured the old man swinging away in his lonely house. *Is that what drew in Charlie?* The ghosts of the past? Is that what drew in my dad too?

My dad worked at the museum. He collected stuff. In my better moments, I told myself he broke in that night to do some research on local legends. That kind of thing would appeal to him.

I stared into the black hole of the window. It stared right back at me with a blank, dead eye. Acid burned in the pit of my stomach and curled up my throat. I swallowed it down. *Feel the fear, Esta.*

There was nothing for it. Simon and Graham might be wavering, but I couldn't back out now. I pushed my feet through the gap and edged my way in, avoiding little shark-fins of glass embedded in the wooden frame. I took a last breath of fresh air, pushed myself off and landed inside Gatley House with a crunch of glass.

4

Monsters in the Wardrobe

When I was seven, I used to wake with night sweats, screaming about monsters in the closet. Dad used to open my wardrobe and shine a light on the hanging clothes. 'Look. Nothing scary in there, Est,' he'd say. 'The monsters in your head are always worse than the real ones.'

My breath stuttered; my hands shook as I struck another match. Its tiny flame danced pathetically in the dark. Simon followed me. His torch made the room spring into life around us. Shadows stretched and slid over walls to my right. To my left, concrete steps led up to a door.

The wall was cold against my palm, the plaster smooth as skin. I climbed with shuffling feet, my shadow getting fainter as I reached the top. I turned. Simon was pointing his torch at me from the bottom.

'What are you waiting for?' I hissed, but he just stood there staring up at me. 'Don't be such a scaredy cat.'

Behind him, the basement window was a square of pale yellow. Graham's leg poked through.

Simon swung the torch at it, 'Watch out for the gla—'

There was a ripping sound, a yelp and then Graham landed in the basement, stumbling into Simon and sending the torch to the floor. Ridiculous, child-like voices came out of the sudden darkness: 'Something bit me,' Graham complained.

'Get off me!'

'Where's the torch?'

I looked down from the top of the steps, shaking my head, as the two shadowy outlines of the boys separated.

They were ruining everything.

I'd waited for *a year* to come here and now I was inside they were acting like little boys. This was just a game to them. Nothing more than a silly dare.

From up here I suddenly thought I knew what Mum must feel like looking down on her wayward daughter; why she sometimes glared at me and stamped her foot in frustration. I almost did it myself. Instead, I turned away from them and faced the door. An ordinary, plain one. It might have been any old door, leading to any old room.

Except every jangling fibre in my body told me this one would open up... *secrets.*

I whispered my dad's words back to myself. 'Nothing scary in there, Esta.' Took a steadying breath, and pushed.

The door creaked outward into darkness. A chilly breeze teased my hair. A sickly smell slithered up my nostrils.

I struck a match, cupped it with one hand and held it out.

A landing.

The elongated shadows of my fingers stretched along it. Strips of paper hung from the walls like writhing snakes. The flame wagged.

The breeze sighed. The match flickered out.

I glanced over my shoulder. The boys were on their knees, searching the floor for the torch.

I rattled the matchbox: not many, but I wasn't about to scrabble around in the dark with the boys. So I clenched my fingers in to a fist to stop them shaking, then lit another match and stepped through the door.

The floorboards creaked under my weight. I thought of Charlie and shuffled towards the wall where I thought the boards might not be rotten enough to collapse under me. The creaking they made brought another image too, one I could have done without: an old man swinging in a room without a floor.

Cobwebs caught in my hair and tickled my neck as I came to a corner in the landing. There was a whiff of sewage. The hallway was a bit brighter here. It continued on for twenty-odd feet and ended at a boarded window, which let in faint orange street-light. The wood was rotten and a knot of twigs had squeezed their way through a gap in it, as if they were prising the thing open. Trying to get inside.

Halfway along the left wall was a patch of shadow that I guessed had to be the staircase going up to the next floor. Opposite that, on the right wall, was another door. It took me fifteen slow, sliding steps to reach it.

I liked this door even less than the last one. A foul smell sneaked through the gap under it. I touched the handle, trying not to imagine all the things that could be making the awful stench. *The monsters in your head…*

I twisted the handle and pushed. It didn't budge. I pushed again. It was jammed or locked shut. I released the handle, turned my back to the door and leaned against it, my shoulders melting with relief. *Maybe the monsters in the closet don't want to play.*

The staircase opposite snaked darkly upwards, switching back to the landing above. I thought of Dad climbing it. *What were you doing here, Dad? A grown man breaking into an old house?* I didn't believe he'd been looking for Charlie. I remembered the distant look in his eyes in the weeks before he left. He had been obsessed with something even before finding Charlie. He'd stopped going in to work, always had his head in those indecipherable books that filled his office. He'd found Charlie in a room under the main stairs. *But the police found your footprints upstairs too Dad. What were you doing up there?*

A voice whispered out of the semi-darkness right next to me: 'Esta?'

My heart skipped, and I instinctively swung the back of my hand in the direction of the sound. I connected with something bony. The voice gave a satisfying yelp.

'What did you do that for?' Simon moaned in his cockney lilt.

'Don't creep up on me then. Where's Graham?'

'Is that the room?' Simon said. A circle of light appeared against the door.

'You found the torch?'

'Yeah, but the batteries are low.'

'Switch it off then,' I said, trying to keep my voice level. I really didn't like that door. No. It wasn't the door. *It was what might be behind it.* The idea of Simon finding a way to open it made the hairs rise on my neck. Part of me knew damn well what was behind that door. I thought of the dark shape of a body swinging from the ceiling. 'It's locked,' I said.

The torchlight wavered but didn't dim. The circle of light shrank against the door as he moved towards it. 'You think,' he whispered, reaching out for the handle, 'that's the room where she fell?'

I grabbed his arm. 'You can look if you want, I'm going upstairs first though.'

The torch flickered and died. I heard Simon rattling it.

'No,' Simon whispered in the faint light from the window, 'I'm coming with you.'

It got darker as we climbed, but the smell improved at least.

'The torch,' I whispered when we reached the top. 'I can't see a thing.'

He banged it against a wall until it coughed up a beam that struggled through clouds of dust. Something glinted at the end of the hallway, a single bright eye staring back at us. Simon's hand wobbled. So did the eye. I took the torch out of his limp grip. 'It's the light reflecting off a window, stupid. It's boarded from the outside. Come on.' I gritted my teeth and made a show of striding up the landing, but my pace slowed with each step, until I stopped about half way down. Something was wrong. I shone the torch at my feet. The landing here was firm underfoot: stone, or paving or something. Not like the sagging floorboards downstairs.

'Esta?' Simon whispered from behind me.

I shone the light up and along the walls. No rotting wallpaper here. The walls were smooth, painted in two thick stripes ... and something else. Something that resembled Graffiti.

'It's freezing,' Simon said, blowing into his hands.

His words barely registered. I was studying the marks on the wall. I placed a finger against them. If it was writing it made no sense to me. But it wasn't scrawled on like regular graffiti—it was more like a row of strange symbols.

'They look foreign,' Simon whispered.

'They're so neat,' I said, squinting at them.

'Look. Can't we do it from that window?'

I frowned. 'Do what?'

'Shine the light. Then everyone knows we made it.'

'Who cares what everyone knows?'

'That was the deal.'

'What deal?'

'For the party?'

I stopped and faced him. I'd forgotten this was all part of a dare. 'You think I'm walking around here so I can go to a party?'

He shrugged, 'I dunno. That was the dare. Why not?'

'If it's your party what are you doing up here?'

He paused for a second. 'I just wanted to see…' His voice was low and stuttering, 'For myself.'

Simon was a rubbish liar.

'Its history and…'

I pointed the beam further along the wall while he spoke, frowned and raised a finger to my lips. 'Shh.'

The graffiti wasn't just writing. There were pictures too. Faded and cracked, but you could make out details in the thin beam of light. Images of people. Here, a huge belly. By its side, a muscular arm and a fist gripping what looked like a weapon: a sword, or a dagger maybe. I traced the torch up the arm. A head. Fierce glaring eyes, teeth bared in a horrible snarl.

'Jesus!' Simon hissed at my shoulder. 'This must have been what Charlie saw.'

I shone the torch at another image. A dark figure standing on one leg, a pointy tongue poking out of its mouth.

'I've seen stuff like this before,' I whispered.

'Who paints their walls with monsters?'

'My dad collected art for the museum.'

'Must have been the guy who hanged himself,' he muttered. 'This is how he decorated. I told you he lost his mind.' He tugged my arm. 'Come on, this is creeping me out.'

I ignored him and shone the light further along the wall at another image. This one was of two figures: a woman sitting in the middle of Lotus petals. She was dressed in silks and jewels and smiling. Next to her: a man with blue skin and long black hair. He was smiling too, but I didn't like the look of it—it was a smarmy smile. A Hannah Piranha sort of smile. This must have been some old art collection my dad had discovered. No wonder he'd been so obsessed, I thought with relief.

'What about down there?' Simon whispered.

'What?' I turned away from the pictures on the walls.

Simon pointed back the way we'd come. I swung the beam down the landing. It stretched out beyond the pale orange glow from the stairs. The torch stuttered. I tapped it against the wall like I'd seen Simon do. It turned off.

'Bugger,' I whispered into the sudden dark.

Simon grabbed my arm. 'What was that?'

I rattled the torch. 'I don't hear anything.'

'Shh. Are those voices?'

'Settle down, it's probably Graham. How do you make this thing wor—?'

A deafening crash cut me off, echoing against the walls, making my ears jangle. Simon yelped beside me. I slapped my hands to my ears, almost dropping the torch.

Then just as suddenly there was an equally deafening silence as if someone had flicked a mute switch; just the sound of blood pumping in my ears and Simon's shallow breaths.

I lowered my hands and, inexplicably, the torch flickered back on. Simon's face was a pale blinking moon in its light. 'What the hell was that?' he whimpered.

'Graham?' I suggested hopefully, training the light back towards the stairwell. Darkness dissolved the trembling beam.

I inched forwards.

'Maybe he got that door open.'

There was another crash. A clattering of metal, and a grating noise like the sound of heavy furniture being dragged across a hard floor. The type of sound that makes you grit your teeth and squeeze your eyes shut.

Simon shoved me to one side and made for the stairs. 'That's not Graham!'

I stood, frozen to the spot, listening to the waves of sound, *feeling it* under my feet, the floor vibrating.

There was a brief pause, then another noise, a deep, rhythmic *Boom, Boom, Boom*.

If it *was* Graham, then he'd found a couple of baseball bats and was playing drums on the walls.

I ran after Simon, the torchlight arcing back and forth ahead of me.

Before I reached the stairs, the noise shut off again, plunging everything into another sudden and complete silence.

I skidded to a halt.

The torchlight cut through the darkness a couple of feet ahead of me.

In its weak halo, there was an outline.

My voice trembled. 'Graham?'

The shape, not much taller than me, seemed to… Did it move? I couldn't tell, I was too busy swallowing down my heart, which was trying to climb out of my mouth.

The torch blinked off.

A second passed in the darkness. Or maybe it was a hundred. My limbs locked. My eyes fastened on the silhouette. Was it a figure? *Was it even there at all?*

I don't know what compelled me to do it, but I took a shuffling step forwards, and slowly reached out. I stared at my hand as it inched closer to the dark unmoving shadow, like it was being drawn in by a magnet.

An icy breath of air brushed my fingertips. I watched in dumb horror as they touched the edges of the shadow.

The torch sputtered. I gave it a cursory shake. It turned on and off. And then again, and again, flickering faster and faster, until somewhere between the flitting pulses of light and dark, the distinct impression of a figure emerged.

My heart stopped.

Off: Darkness.

On: A face. Lines etched into its skin as if engraved into wood.

Off: Darkness.

On: Eyes like bowls of fire reflecting electric light back at me.

Off: Darkness.

A sound behind me made me spin round. The torch beam steadied, flooding light over Simon's squinting face.

'What's that?' he croaked

I turned back. My heart moved into a deep disco thump which was so powerful it made the torch shudder in time.

No one there—just an empty hallway. Except, right in the spot where I'd seen the figure...

'There's a door,' Simon whispered.

5

THE HOOK

I moved forwards, eyes fixed on the door. 'There was someone here,' I murmured under my breath. 'He must have come from—'

'Atchoo!'

Simon's sneeze made me drop the torch which clattered against the floor. 'God's sake!' I hissed, picking it up.

'Sorry,' he said wiping his nose on his sleeve. 'Dust allergy.'

'I saw someone.'

'Thought you said it was Graham?'

'I thought you ran away?'

'You had the torch. What do you mean you saw—?'

I placed a finger to my lips and leaned in to the door. No noise from the other side. I placed a hand against it. The wood was freezing.

I shivered. But I could feel sweat collecting on my forehead too.

'What if it was a tramp?' Simon whispered behind me. 'Or druggies?'

I considered him, standing all still and straight with his back against the wall and his face as stiff and pale as the cold custard they served at school. He didn't want to be here, he didn't *need* to be here. And yet here he was.

A thud from the staircase made him jump. The soles of his trainers actually left the ground. I pointed the torch in the direction of the noise. Another thud.

Footsteps. Definitely footsteps this time.

The light blinked out again.

I shook the torch casing, patting it hard against my palm. Dark shapes lurched out of the stairwell, shadows danced on the ceiling. Simon backed up against the wall. I flung out a hand to stop him from running away and felt his chest, warm under his shirt. His heart was having its own dance party under there.

Torchlight waved against the walls. Graham's voice hissed, 'That's foul down there.'

He reached the landing, torch swinging one way and then the other.

Simon's heart trembled under my hand. I searched for his eyes in the gloom and held his frightened gaze. I knew that look. I knew what it felt like to be behind eyes like that, the sort of fear that nails your feet to the ground and makes your brain freeze, so that no matter how much you want to jump, you know you'll never ever budge.

But seeing that look in someone else's gaze somehow calmed me.

'Take a chill pill, Simon,' I said.

Graham's voice rebounded against the walls. 'There must be dead things living off dead things behind that door. Simon? Is that you? What are you two doing in the dark? Am I interrupting something?'

I swiftly moved my hand away from Simon's skittering chest.

A powerful beam sliced through the darkness as Graham reached the landing. 'I heard a noise. You OK?'

'I thought that was you,' Simon said, finding his voice. 'What were you doing down there?'

Graham pointed the light in our faces. 'Getting a better one of these. Anyway, you found anything?'

'I thought I saw someone go in there,' I said, pointing to the door. 'But I dunno,' I shrugged. 'Maybe not.'

Graham gave no response.

'I said—'

'No, I heard you,' Graham said. 'You saw her?'

'Saw who?'

Graham handed me the torch then reached into his satchel and pulled out a black box, 'The ghost. You know, the woman?'

'Yeah. Wait. No. I saw a man. Or not. Simon's torch was kind of flickery.'

Graham wasn't listening, he was busy opening the lens cap on what I now realised was a camera.

'What are you doing?' Simon said.

Graham glanced up from his device. 'If she's here, I'll need evidence.'

I shone the light at Simon who could have been nailed stiff to the wall, by the looks of him.

'Esta, give Simon the torch so he can shine it on the door. This doesn't have a flash, so stay still until I've taken a picture, OK?'

'I thought you couldn't take photos of ghosts,' Simon mumbled as he took the torch off me.

'Esta,' hissed Graham impatiently, 'Get the door.'

I swept a gaze over him and Simon, checking if they had their feet planted. It wasn't likely, but there was a chance this was all a trick. Satisfied they weren't about to make a run for it, I stepped back to the door.

Graham held up three fingers into the edge of the torch beam. 'Ready?'

I nodded.

He curled his ring finger down, 'Two.'

The handle of the door was *cold*.

Graham dropped his middle finger: 'One.'

I inhaled a lungful of freezing air, twisted the handle, and pushed.

*****

The torchlight cast my shadow along bare floorboards. Heavy looking curtains hung over the window opposite.

Graham slid past me, the camera held to his chest with both

hands. 'It's freezing in here.'

'Wait,' I said, 'what if this is the room Charlie fell through? Be careful.'

Simon sent a beam from corner to corner through cobwebs and clouds of floating dust. 'It'd be locked up like the other one if it was dangerous,' he whispered.

A breeze chilled my ankles as I followed Graham inside.

The room was empty from what I could see, which wasn't much because Simon, torch in hand, made a beeline for the curtain.

'Keep it still,' Graham hissed.

Simon ignored him, pulled the curtain aside and pointed the torch out of the window. I waited in the dark while he signalled to the others. After half a minute he was still waving the torch back and forth against the glass.

'Hurry up,' Graham whispered.

'They aren't there,' Simon replied.

'What?' I said, making my way carefully across the floor to him. 'Maybe they got bored.'

'No. I mean. *Nothing's* there.'

I joined him, parted the curtain and peered outside. It was dark. The reflection of my face stared back at me. I leaned my forehead against the cold glass. Nothing. 'Maybe someone blacked out the glass?'

I took the torch from Simon and directed the beam down. The window wasn't blacked out. I could see outside, but we weren't looking out at a field. The ground was flat and smooth, roughly the size of a school playground. Opposite, about fifty feet away was the outline of a long two-storey building with a sloping roof.

'You seen that before?' I whispered.

'No.'

I pointed the torch left and right, but it picked nothing else out. No trees, no other buildings, no street lights. Just emptiness. Like looking over the edge of the world.

I remembered the unboarded window I'd seen from outside,

then tried to do mental gymnastics figuring out how we'd twisted and turned around the house. 'This must be the back of the house,' I said.

'It can't be.'

'Why not?'

'Because the house backs out to trees and then the road. We'd see streetlights from up here.'

'Maybe there's been a power-cut…'

'Oy!' Graham hissed from the other side of the room. 'I found something.'

I swung the torch towards his voice.

My heart skipped a beat.

Graham stood facing us, his features bleached white. Standing behind him in the darkness was a hooded figure.

The beam juddered in my shaking fingers.

'Don't point it right at me,' Graham complained. I steadied my hand; the figure behind him shrank away. I breathed again. Just his shadow against the wall.

This place was getting to me. There were too many shadows, and that man I'd seen—*probably seen*—still spooked me. Not to mention the monsters painted on the walls.

'Point it down there,' Graham pointed to a low table. On it was what my Gran used to call *bric-a-brac*, the sort of random stuff that cluttered up a church charity stall.

There was a click and a rattle as Graham wound on the reel of film.

'Here,' I said, handing the torch back to Simon and walking towards the table. The objects sparkled as I got closer and when I slid a finger along the table top, it was cold. Frowning, I lifted my finger up. It was wet.

'What are they?' Simon whispered behind me.

'I bet they're his things,' Graham said under his breath, lifting the camera for another photo. 'Just where he left them.'

'They don't look that old,' I said.

'They're covered in dust,' Graham said.

I brushed a silver cup, the frost melting on my fingertip. 'It's not dust.'

Graham gave me a sceptical look over the top of his camera.

'They're all in threes,' Simon said, tracking the beam of light along the rows of objects. 'Look. Three cups, three necklaces, there's three of everything.'

Other frosted metal trinkets sparkled. Spoons, plates, bells, bowls, and, leaning against the table, a long bony staff. 'All neat rows,' he said.

'Like a museum,' I murmured. *Like some kind of collection.* I recognised some of them from Dad's sketches of Indian artefacts. Ancient objects for his display. There was no doubt what he'd been here for then. But what was he doing? *Studying* them? And why were they still here? Wouldn't he have taken them to the museum?

Graham bagged his camera and picked up a knife. He held it to his eye and blew along its curved blade, sending ice crystals scattering.

'What are you doing?' Simon said, pointing the torch into Graham's face. 'I don't think we should touch them.'

Graham replaced the blade. 'It's only old junk.'

Simon directed the torch at me—blinding me for a second—then at the table again. His fingers stretched out, caressing another one of the knives. He picked it up and turned it over, studying it before putting it down. Something about the act made me hold my breath. I shivered at the deliberate way he put the knife back. The tip of his tongue touched his top lip as he picked up a large hand bell with an ornate handle. Like a kid in a sweet shop. *Not a scaredy cat now are you, rich boy?*

'What if they belong to the man I saw?' I said, but my voice was hollow. I was as drawn to the objects as Simon was.

'They belong to my dad now,' Simon said rolling his wrist. The hand bell he'd picked up rang, causing the skin on the back of my neck to crawl. Graham didn't seem to notice anything. In fact, he'd lost interest in the objects and had walked over to the curtain.

Simon smiled. A relaxed smile. The smile you make when you've found an old toy you used to play with years ago.

That rhythmic beating started again then. It was fainter inside this room. It could have been a plane coming into land, or a truck bumping along the road. Or the thumping of blood in my ears.

'Come on,' Simon whispered, tugging at my arm. 'Hear that? My dad'll flay me if he finds out I nicked his keys.'

Simon—still holding his hand-bell—and Graham headed to the door. But I didn't move. *Dad had been here. He put those objects on the table.* It didn't occur to me then that the police would probably have removed any objects when they searched the house after Dad had found Charlie.

Whatever. If I left now, I suspected I'd never come back. Simon would lock the window shut and in a couple of weeks this whole house would be rubble.

'Give me a sec,' I whispered. But the two boys had already left. The shadows in the room closed around me. The drumming noise slowed into a faraway rhythm—like the beating of distant helicopter blades.

A floorboard creaked behind me.

The dark must have been playing tricks on my ears as well as my eyes because, along with the fading drumming,—*in time with it*—there was the murmuring sound of voices.

A breeze blew against my ankles. A whisper, as silent as silk, travelled with it.

Simon's torch, the one I'd dropped before Graham had joined us, flickered on again. Its dull yellow light picked out an object that gleamed in the middle of the table.

I reached out and closed my fingers around a hard, curved edge. I lifted it, fascinated. It was sturdy and fit perfectly in my palm.

A movement behind sent prickles crawling up my neck.

I slipped the golden object into my pocket.

The torch switched off.

Creak.

I froze. Listening to the dark.

Esstttaaa... the breeze seemed to whisper.

'Dad?' I whispered back. The word blurted out of me of its own accord. It was a stupid thought.

But the breeze replied: *Essttaaa...*

The torch flickered back on. 'Dad? Is that you?'

I backed towards the door, bent down and picked up the torch, sweeping the beam around the room: floorboards, bare walls, the hem of the curtain trembling in the chilly breeze. *Stupid thought.*

Out on the landing the drumming and chanting was louder. Quicker. Whatever it was, it was close, because the floor, the walls, the ceiling were shaking with it. An overwhelming urge to get the hell out of there gripped me. I closed the door behind me with a *click.*

Graham and Simon were already down the first set of stairs. I hurried after them, with a horrible sense I was being watched tickling the back of my neck. When I got to the top of the stairs, the feeling was so strong, I had to look behind me. I shone the torch on the landing.

The door I'd *definitely shut* was now wide open.

I leapt down the stairs, heart in my mouth.

Esssttaaa... hissed the breeze.

I jumped the last step and bowled straight into Simon, who lurched forward into the door opposite.

This time it swung wide open.

Simon gripped the door frame. The torch tumbled out of my hands, bounced once then dropped into the gaping hole where the floor should have been. In its flickering light, the line of a rope hung from the centre of the ceiling. And there, glinting in the light, swung the cruel curl of a meat hook.

PART TWO

THE ORB

6

BIRDSONG

I barely remember how we got out. Just shadows and scrapes and silent swearing. Even in the dark, we must have given off waves of fear, because Hannah, Kev and the other one took off over the gate without waiting. We did the same and collapsed on the other side into fits of nervous giggles.

Graham had taken a couple of 'souvenir' snaps of us, then stuffed his camera away in his shoulder bag, made his excuses and headed off along the track. That left Simon and me alone by the old gate, staring down at the bits of metal we'd lifted from the table. I recalled the deliberate way he'd chosen his hand-bell, no sign of the fear that had turned him stiff just before, and had wanted to ask him... I don't know what. Something about why he'd chosen the bell. But the question died on my lips and we'd stood in silence for a minute or so before he freed a blonde lock of hair from his eyes with a practiced flick of his head and, without saying a word, turned to follow Graham and the others into the darkness. I'd taken one last look at the house, then slipped away too. Back through the hedge and across Fletcher's Field, my heart pounding like a hammer being dragged over corrugated iron. And all the way home, the wrinkled face of the old man seemed to stare back at me from every shadow.

By the time I was back home, the apparition had faded and my rational brain was trying to put the events of the evening into shape. It had been dark, I'd been scared and fear makes you see things, doesn't it? I'd definitely heard that somewhere. *We'd broken into a scary house, we got freaked out by shadows and creaky floorboards and... that's all,* I told myself.

But another voice whispered, *Charlie Bullock* inside my head. And no matter what I told myself, the face of that old man kept creeping back into my sleepy thoughts.

Keys rattling in the front door jerked me awake. I held my breath, waiting for the sound of steps climbing the stairs. When they came, they were light and careful. Mum, back from yet another meeting. She stopped on the landing outside my door. I pictured her, standing in silence, listening, breathing.

I stared at the door, waiting for it to open. Knowing it wouldn't. She always stopped and listened, but never came in. When she finally moved on, I breathed a sigh of relief, made a tent of my sheet and reached for my single battery torch and one of Dad's note books.

We didn't talk about Dad much anymore. I mean he was *mentioned,* but after a year of conversations, which tended to swing from disbelief, to hope, to despair in a matter of moments, I think Mum had had enough. Now she resorted to smiling and patting my arm whenever I mentioned him. I soon took the hint and clammed up too.

There's safety in silence. That was the policy. I definitely got the impression that 'talking about Dad' was a dangerous pastime. A bit like jumping off a rock into the sea, I guess.

I once heard Mum sobbing to someone on the phone when she thought I was upstairs in bed: 'It's the not knowing that kills me...'

It's the not knowing.

So exactly a year after Dad left, Mum stopped crying and started filling boxes instead. The odd one every few weeks, left outside for the bin men to collect.

One time I got up and watched as they lifted it and tipped out Dad's shirts, shoes, books and papers. All spilling into the jaws of their truck.

It was a gradual theft. One box after another. My memories of Dad evaporating like clouds in the sky.

Why did she do it? She never said. But that's when we stopped talking. We spoke to each other of course, but we stopped *talking* the moment Mum started throwing my Dad away.

There was one box I wouldn't let go of though. It was a box he had filled himself a few weeks before Charlie. Mum had found it in his study and handed it to the investigating officer. The police gave it back after a few months and since then, I'd kept it stored in my room.

Dad used to write books about travelling when he was younger—before Mum and me—and he'd filled this box with all sorts of stuff from that life. Tattered books, maps; an old letter knife, photos from India, Japan, China, Tibet, and a cardboard folder filled with typed notes. Articles he'd written about the things he'd found in the Himalayas. Adventures he'd had before I turned up in his life. At the top of it all was a battered leather-bound book filled with poetry. Some of the pages were ripped out, but he'd underlined one poem in red ink: *'Defeating the Devils'*. It was probably wishful thinking, but sometimes I wondered if he'd left all this stuff—the photos and the poems—for me. His way of telling me why he went away.

Dad used to say that poetry was one thing that made sense of the world to him. That it didn't hide from the dark bits, it shone a torch on them instead. Just like the monsters in the closet.

The book fell open at the usual place. I whispered the lines to myself:

Defeating the Devils

You cannot defeat the devil with hate,

For his hatred is too great.

You cannot defeat the devil with fire,

It only fuels the devil's desire.

You cannot deceive his devilish eyes

For he is the master of disguise.

Whether a bishop or merely a priest,

There's only one way to tackle the beast.

'Pity his cries, pity his rage, pity the talons, pity the claws, pity the monster that is pained by its scars, that hasn't a care, but is tortured by kindness and bitten by sweetness and bound after all

By love.

I closed the book. I couldn't bring myself to read anymore. On the front cover he'd scrawled, *'Against all available evidence, poetry suggests the world might be something other than an interlocking chain of disappointments.'*

I thought of his face staring up at me from the sea that time on the rocks, waiting for me to join him, full of enthusiasm. I remembered looking down at my shivering legs. I had tried. I had *tried,* Dad. I had almost jumped. I *would have jumped.* But I saw the sparkle die in his eyes while I wobbled on the rock. Watched disappointment pull his smile away from me as he swam to the shore, alone. *Is that it, Dad? Is that why you left? Was I one of those chains of disappointment?*

Before I went to sleep, I inspected the object I'd taken from the table in Gatley House, turning it round and round in my hands. It was like the graffiti I'd seen on the walls. Alien but at the same time somehow familiar. A thin golden rod roughly five inches long with a lump in its centre and five spokes that closed at each end like the petals of a flower. Kind of like an ornate mini golden dumbbell. There were no moving bits and no part of it seemed to serve a purpose. Something about its symmetry gave it a sense of balance, though. I decided to call it 'The Orb' and went to sleep staring at it.

That night my dreams began with a blur of flowing gold. I had the not unpleasant sensation of floating high over fields, lakes and streams. A chocolate-box landscape that stretched far away to a horizon dominated by a towering snow-topped mountain. As I approached, the slopes of the mountain transformed into an old weather-worn face. A pair of eyes twinkled at me out of the darkness.

When I woke the next morning, I was still wearing my uniform, and my teeth were depressingly furry. My hand went instinctively to the Orb. It wasn't as golden as I'd remembered it. In fact, lying there on my bedside table, washed in the grey morning light, it seemed a little older and a little more worn. My eyes crossed a little as if it was slightly out of focus. I rubbed them, yawned, then picked the thing up and dropped it in my blazer pocket.

I almost tripped over Mum, standing in the hallway fully dressed, as if she'd been there all night just waiting for me. One arm was folded around her chest, the other held up a slip of paper.

'This is important,' she said, her eyes hollow with sleep—or lack of it.

I glanced at the opened envelope with my school's crest stamped on it.

'Culter,' she said simply.

I blinked. 'What?'

'You didn't tell me about Mr Blakely.'

'Oh,' I sighed. The slammed door. The yelp. I closed my eyes. 'That.'

'Apparently his nose isn't actually broken, which is probably why we're meeting Mr Culter and not the *police*.' Her voice raised to a high pitch with that last word.

'It was an accident,' I murmured looking up and concentrating on the artex ceiling. Dad had done that. He'd stood on a board suspended over two rickety chairs, spreading the gooey plaster with an outstretched arm. I'd have been ten, and I had thought it was like wedding cake icing.

'Why didn't you tell me?'

'Because you weren't here to tell,' I snapped. 'You were at one of your meetings, like you always are.'

'You're not taking anything, are you?' Mum asked.

I lowered my gaze to hers, 'What do you mean?'

'Drugs.'

I rolled my eyes. 'You've got to be kidding?'

'Seeing anyone or something?'

'Mum!'

She shrugged, confused. For a second I felt sorry for her. She hadn't signed up to be a single mum. When I was born, she'd had a husband, a functioning parent of her own, and a sister fussing over her. Then her sister moved away, Dad left, Gran fell ill, and just like that she'd lost her whole family.

But then, I didn't ask for this life either.

Satisfied I wasn't on drugs or pregnant, she let me into the kitchen, switched on the radio and poured milk into a bowl of Rice Krispies. 'Eat. You look like you'll blow over in the wind. What did you get up to last night?'

I thought about telling her what I had found. But she wouldn't understand. Mum and me were like opposite poles of a magnet when it came to Gatley House. I was drawn to it. She was repelled by it.

'Esta?'

'Nothing,' I mumbled, trying to remember the question. 'Homework.'

'It's terrible,' she said after a moment.

I frowned, spoon half way to my mouth. What had I done now?

'The accident in Russia,' she said.

I let out a silent breath of relief. 'What accident?'

'A nuclear power plant blew up, apparently.'

I swallowed a mouthful of cereal. 'That doesn't sound good.'

'They're saying the radioactivity might go into the atmosphere. Up into the clouds. Coming down in the rain.'

'What's to be done?' I said. What did it matter? Russia was so far away, had so little to do with us. But since Dad left, Mum was always trying to fix impossible problems.

'It's just… wrong,' she murmured. 'Rain's supposed to *give* life, not take it away…'

I swear, I wouldn't have put it past her to go on a march to change the weather.

We cleared the dishes and cups. I washed, she dried. We did it in silence, listening to the birds singing and the planes coming in to land at the airport.

I'd read in one of my science textbooks that birds aren't actually 'singing' at all. They are more than likely warning other birds or cats off their patch. A fact that made me wonder about other stuff too. How some things seem one way, but they can really be the opposite. I thought maybe that was another reason Dad liked his poetry. I got the impression poetry understood that.

I stared at my reflection in the window above the sink, mulling over last night. I concluded that the old man I'd seen had just been a shadow; a trick of Simon's stupid flickering torch; my overactive imagination filling in the gaps.

The monsters in your imagination are always worse than the real ones. Right, Dad?

Those monsters on the walls and the floorless room with the hook in the ceiling would give anyone the creeps; no wonder they broke Charlie's mind. *What if they broke Dad's too?* I thought with a chill.

Mum stroked the tea towel and gave me a pleading look, her voice softer. 'Why don't you come with me to see Gran after school? We need as many people as we can get and it'll be good for you to get out.'

I emptied out the water from the basin. Stray Rice Krispies swirled into the plughole. 'What does it matter? She doesn't even know who I am anymore.'

'She does, Est. Somewhere deep down, she does. It's just the stress of everything—what with the airport road and...'

Another plane rumbled overhead, drowning out the rest of her sentence. When it had faded, she continued, 'We can stop them, you know? If enough of us make a noise, we can stop them from knocking it down.'

'You're such a hippy,' I said, drying my hands on the towel Mum had just folded. 'This isn't the Seventies anymore. You can't get in the way of progress. They aren't going to stop the road because of a bunch of old people.'

Mum gave a heavy sigh, clutched her car keys in one hand, then grabbed an armful of rolled-up posters. 'They aren't just old people, Esta. It's your Gran. Dad's mum. And yes, if we fight for it we can stop them tearing down her home.'

I shrugged. Even I knew the situation was more complicated than that. She might as *well* be demanding the rain not to fall.

'You know there's a boy in your school whose father is in charge of this?' she said. 'Taylor, he's called. It's one thing when developers from outside destroy a community. Quite another when they're crooks in your own town. Have you seen what they've done to Fletcher's Field? And when it's done? There'll be a hundred trucks piling through this town every day. It makes me sick.'

She stared at me with a fierce expression, challenging me to speak. But I was picturing Simon clambering out of the basement window, racing down the drive with his hand-bell clanging away in his fist. Had he seen something too?

'Evil wins when good people do nothing,' she snapped after a minute.

I nodded a 'maybe', and she stormed down the hall. 'Don't forget the meeting with Mr Culter!' she shouted, wrenching open the front door. As she slammed it behind her I heard her mutter, 'Such a waste.'

I didn't know if she was referring to me or to the planned bulldozing of Gran's nursing Home.

The house fell silent.

Just the fading engines of the landing plane and the twittering of birds in the garden.

7

THE CULTER ULTIMATUM

I sat in the headmaster's reception room at morning break, hitching my skirt down a couple of inches to cover my knees. Yesterday had been a nightmare. Yes, I'd slammed the door, but how was I supposed to know he was right behind me? I winced at the memory of the sound of wood on soft flesh; the howl of pain. I imagined the blood spouting out from Mr Blakely's nose. *Dominoes…*

The reception was like a dentist's waiting area, except with school yearbooks instead of glossy magazines. Photos beamed down at me of smiling students, slim and tall. Crisp shirts tucked into well-ironed skirts and trousers, tightly knotted ties, orderly hair. Gleaming shoes. My own scuffed leather ones dangled against the faded pink carpet. I ran fingers through my limp brown hair, gathering it into a ponytail using a rubber band from my blazer pocket.

Mr Culter made you sweat, that was his thing. He wasn't a shouter; he was a *starer*. His voice was soft as sponge cake, but when he got angry, he could stab you with his dagger-grey eyes. He was the sort who shook his head at you in kind-hearted sorrow but kept a row of wooden canes in a glass case on the wall above his desk. Hitting naughty kids was still legal in the mid-eighties.

I stared up at the happy, perfect students on the wall. Their happiness seemed so… effortless. I shivered. I'd be happy too if the world would only let me.

'Esta.'

The door to the headmaster's office opened. Mr Culter stood in its place, a tall, immaculately dressed beanpole of a man. He stared down his long nose at me with a mixture of pity and disappointment. 'Come in,' he purred. 'Take a seat.' He stepped to one side to let me in. Mum had apparently taken a break from protesting because there she was, sitting in a plastic chair facing away from me; not even looking round when I squeaked inside the room to take a seat by her side. I glanced at her. She had a crooked smile that was so thin-lipped it could have been cut into her face with a bread-knife.

I looked at the display case of canes and gulped.

Mr Culter brushed his lapels, sat down opposite us and laid his hand on a pile of exercise books—*My* exercise books—stacked on the big oak desk between us, each one torn and covered in graffiti. 'Esta,' he said, his voice soft and fatherly.

I refocused on the collection of canes above his shoulder. Dad used to walk me past School on the way home, telling me stories about his time here when he was a kid. 'Always getting in trouble,' he'd say with pride in his voice. 'But. If you break the rules, you got to accept the consequences. If you ever have to make the choice, Est, the wider ones hurt, but the thin ones sting like a bee.'

Something reflected in the glass of the display case. I blinked. The old man's face from last night seemed to stare back at me. Lips moving, forming a word…

I blinked again, shook my head and re-focused on the headmaster. His lips were moving too.

'… hope to gain from this behaviour?' he said.

When I didn't answer he sighed and repeated what I guessed was a version of the question he'd just asked. 'What do you want, Esta?'

I glanced at Mum, she was sat upright, eyes down, staring at my books on the table.

I looked at Culter. He wanted to know what I wanted. So I told him.

'I want my dad back.'

There was an uncomfortable silence. You know, clocks ticking, the sound of adults thinking…

Mum broke it. 'Esta you have to—'

I didn't let her finish. I knew the line. Had heard it a hundred times. 'I don't want to move on,' I cut in. 'I don't want a new life. I want the old one.'

Mum's voice grew stronger, 'Esta. Face facts. It's just me and you and Gran and—'

'Mrs Brown,' Mr Culter said, before she could continue. He'd already probably heard enough of our bickering. 'I can see that things are difficult. But you understand the seriousness of this situation? There are rules and... consequences if those rules are broken.'

Mum readjusted herself and returned her gaze back to my books. 'Yes, of course.'

'Mr Blakely would have been within his rights to bring charges against Esta for what she did. It was a reckless and aggressive act.'

'But it was an accident...' Mum began, then tailed off.

I shuffled on my chair, straightened the hem of my skirt again. You didn't argue with Culter—even parents weren't supposed to argue with him.

I stared at my books again.

I had tried at school. Honestly I had. I'd be working quietly in class minding my own business and then someone would look at me funny, or worse they'd *say* something and I'd feel the heat form in my belly and then surge up to my face as if some fisherman were hauling up a burning hot eel through my innards. The classroom would turn a dark red. My stomach would squeeze itself into knots and I'd struggle to breathe. I'd want to get out. Push everything away. And that's when things usually went pear-shaped; *literally*, in Mr Blakely's case.

We waited in silence. Mr Culter breathed through his mouth. He swallowed, making his Adam's apple roll up and down. Eventually he opened my English book, revealing a double-spread piece headed: 'A Living Local Hero'. It was the best thing I had done at school. I'd even used a ruler to underline the title. I blinked at the carefully written words, the stick figure of my dad next to Gatley House. I'd drawn it the way it would have been before the place had been boarded up. The way it would have been when Dad found Charlie.

'When Mr Blakely spoke to Esta about her work,' Culter said, 'He wasn't fully aware of the circumstances regarding your husband.'

I massaged an eyelid which had started to twitch. I remembered the hushed silence that met Mr Blakely's comment. *'That's good, Esta, but it was supposed to be a* living *local hero, love'*. The classroom had turned to black ice. I barely remember leaving. Just slamming the door.

I ground my teeth. I wasn't going to run out of Mr Culter's office.

Mum sniffed. 'So, what happens now?'

I stared at the desk.

What had I done?

I knew the deal. I'd been flirting with it for months. If I was kicked out of school, we would move to London. Mum had told me 'countless times' that the only thing keeping us in our house was Gran and me. If Gran was evicted, and I was expelled, then there'd be nothing to keep us here.

We'd leave.

I didn't much care about school. You end up in some school wherever you live. But if we left Gatley, if we left *home*, then that would be the same as giving up on Dad.

And I did care about that. I cared about that a lot.

Dad *was* alive. No one believed me, but so what? I'd been inside Gatley House now, and I *knew* there was an answer. I wasn't going to leave. I *couldn't* leave now.

Mum rummaged around in her bag, pulled a fistful of tissues from it and blew her nose.

Mr Culter removed his glasses.

I wiped an eye with the cuff of my shirt.

'Miss Nuttal,' the headmaster said. 'The Chair of governors, has expressed concerns about Esta's mental health…'

Mental health? What was that supposed to mean? I could see the same question flitting across Mum's face too.

'… but before we explore that, I'm inclined to give Esta a final chance to prove herself.' He stared at me with those dagger eyes of his. 'If she can manage to get through until the end of term without further incident. Control her temper. Avoid violent outbursts.'

'Of course,' Mum said with a gush of relief. 'Esta you can do that, can't you? We could try meditation or yoga.'

I gave her a pained look that was supposed to say… *Yoga? Seriously?*

'… but, Mrs Brown,' Mr Culter continued, 'these are baby steps. As I've said, there must be consequences to her actions. And so, if she can make a positive contribution to the school or the community—something visible. Something to demonstrate her change of attitude—it may persuade Miss Nuttal to delay further action.

'I have spoken to Mr Blakely. He agrees with me and I therefore thought it fitting he suggest something for Esta to do.'

I shared a glance with Mum.

'In just over two weeks, we run the summer term Community Celebration assembly where we celebrate the achievements of students in our community. This will be Esta's opportunity to show us how committed she is to the school. If she demonstrates her willingness to conform to the rules, if she gives me something to reward her for, then I'm certain Miss Nuttal and the other governors will look upon that kindly.'

'But…' I started to protest.

Mum placed a firm '*shut up*' hand against my thigh. 'Thank you, Mr Culter,' she gushed, 'we'll think of something.'

Mr Culter replaced his glasses and pushed the pile of exercise books across to me. 'Esta. I do want to help you. You've had it harder than most. But I can't help you if you keep getting into needless trouble.' Then he dismissed me from his office with a flick of his hand.

Bewildered, I stood and silently picked up my books. Without looking at either Mr Culter or Mum, I left the room.

The corridors were empty and the squeak of my soles echoed as I made for my lesson. I stared at the scrawled message I'd etched weeks ago on to the cover of my Physics exercise book:

You lose.

The law of gravity is a lie.

The Earth sucks!

The meeting with Culter soon faded into the back of my mind as the prospect of lunch—and a possible reunion with Simon—approached. I couldn't stop thinking about the look on Simon's face when he'd picked up… no, when he'd *chosen* that hand-bell. That look had been bugging me. It had been a mixture of excitement, fear and… *greed*.

For some reason, Simon had *wanted* that bell. Just like I had wanted the Orb-thing. And there was something else. What had Simon *really* been doing in Gatley House? Just for a dare? I didn't think so. He wasn't the type. So when the lunch bell eventually went, there was only one place to go.

Simon occupied a geography classroom during lunchtime. Him and his little club of chosen ones. I made my way there, after staring at, then rejecting, a grey-tinged burger in the dining hall.

I paused outside, peering through the window in the door. Closest to me, a group of boys sat on a table watching a card game. At the back, Simon's blonde hair flashed through a crowd of girls. He was sitting down behind a desk, scribbling notes on a pad. The girls—all cross-legged and short skirts—looked on, pouting and shaking their heads in mock disgust at something Simon was saying.

My stomach clenched, and I wondered which was worse: walking in here or the haunted house?

Probably here.

I entered, holding my school bag in front of me as a shield. No one paid me any attention as I made my way across the room, sidling past the crowd of boys, waiting for Simon to look up.

Someone lost the card game. They were playing 'raps.' If you lost you had to cut the pack to see how many times you'd have your knuckles 'rapped'—hard—with the pack of cards. It was a brutal game loved by psychopathic boys. I pushed forward for a clearer view of Simon, certain he'd drop everything when he saw me.

Hannah Piranha's immovable perm blocked my view. She moved aside so I could see Simon writing what looked like a list of names for his upcoming party. When she noticed who I was, she whispered, 'You're not on it if that's what you're thinking,' and nudged me away.

Simon paused his writing and glanced up. I tried to smile, but my insides twisted and I winced at him instead. I raised the fingers of my hand in a pathetic wave.

'You bottled it, Detesta,' jeered a voice from the circle of girls.

I realised I was biting my lip and released it in self-disgust. I shifted my bag to a shoulder as six pairs of eyes bored into me.

Simon was supposed to smile and ask me what I wanted. I'd imagined him taking me to a private space to talk about last night.

He didn't. Of course he didn't. Popular boys like him couldn't be seen talking to girls like me... that was one of those unwritten school rules, you know that, right? Some people's dominoes are just too far apart to touch.

His blue eyes gleamed storm-cloud grey for a moment, then he went back to his list. I was left with a cold emptiness and a hard elbow from another one of his girls. A boy yelped behind me as someone cracked the cards against his knuckles.

I backed away, jabbing my hip against the corner of a table, too embarrassed to say anything. I'd rather Simon had told me to get lost instead of the silent dismissal he'd just given me. Was it even a dismissal? Did he even see me at all?

Hannah peeled herself away from the group to place a pale, nail-varnished hand on my shoulder. 'You wouldn't know anyone going,' she whispered before leading me away. 'It'll be full of couples snogging and having fun. Normal people. Not your scene at all.'

I looked back at Simon over my shoulder. He murmured something to a chorus of giggles.

'Whatever you think happened last night,' Hannah said, edging me out of the door, 'he's miles out of your league.'

The others whispered to each other. One laughed. Someone muttered, 'Depresta Brown.' Another shushed her.

Hannah clicked the door shut behind me.

I spent the rest of lunchtime replaying Simon's distant gaze, suffering the memory of that stupid finger wave. My bottom lip tasted of salt from where I'd bitten it.

With nowhere to go, I paced the corridors, a boiling disgust rolling inside me. I mouthed swear words and slammed doors behind me as I went, hoping at least one would rip from its hinges.

By the time I barged my way outside, my hatred had turned inwards, searing through my veins with its poisonous words: *Worthless, stupid, self-centred little girl, to think anyone would ever notice you.* As if the universe was actually paying any attention to me.

I stared out at the school playing fields full of kids. Hannah was right, too. Why did I think I even vaguely mattered to Simon? All we'd done was wander around an old building together. Why did that mean we should be bosom buddies all of a sudden? When he had looked at me, it was as if he were trying to place my face. *That is how low I am on his radar.* I drifted through chattering collections of students until I reached the field.

No, the universe—at least this part of it—revolved around Simon and his impending party.

Before Mr Culter's secretary had summoned me to his office, I'd been in Dr Harkness' lesson. He'd been telling us about comets that morning. He said they were wanderers in space. Every other large object in the solar system orbits something else bigger than it. Comets aren't tied in the same way though. They meander around the sun on their own solitary course. With that in mind, I made a beeline across the playing fields, ignoring the girls gossiping in little groups, boys chasing balls over the grass, a gaggle of smokers huddling behind a bush. It was all just physics, and despite Culter's warning, I didn't feel much gravity pulling on *me* at all. Nothing to drag me back, nothing to orbit; so, like a comet, I slipped away through the hole in the fence.

8

GREEN GABLES

The cracks between the paving stones slid between my feet as I put distance between me and the school. There was heat in the sun, so I pushed my ankle socks down to the top of my shoes and loosened my tie. Planes drum-rolled in to land overhead, a lawn mower buzzed in someone's back garden. There was a fresh scent of newly budding spring flowers and the first cut of grass. And beneath it, something else. Something greasy and smoky: maybe fumes from the planes overhead, or diesel from the trucks digging up the fields over the main road, or... I gazed nervously at the cotton-ball-clouds and thought about what Mum had said earlier about radioactivity *coming down in the rain*. I wasn't sure exactly what radioactivity was, or whether it smelled at all, but it wasn't good. I was sure about that.

I kicked a stone and watched it skate along the curb. All this time I'd been watching, waiting and imagining from a distance. And all the time those pictures, those objects, had been sitting there. I had been inside Gatley House now. I'd seen what must have attracted Dad to the place. It explained a lot.

But it didn't explain why he'd left mum and me.

What if I had known sooner? Would that have changed anything? Would it have brought him back? I didn't think so.

I'm convinced Mum didn't know I visited Gran after school. Gran would never have remembered to tell her of course and, by the way they smiled, the nurses knew not to say either. She was old and frail, but after Mum, she was the closest thing to Dad I had. And anyway, there's something about talking to a person who has, for very good medical reasons, no motive, no agenda to push on you. I could tell Gran anything and it was like throwing a pebble into a lake—a couple of ripples and then gone. Or at least, that's how it seemed. It's what I needed now. I needed to unravel everything in my mind and there was literally no one else I could tell.

Green Gables Nursing Home was on an arrow line between the airport and Fletcher's Field. It was a red-brick, detached house, with green window frames, probably built at the same time as Gatley House. Except this was lived in. Lived in by *real* people, I mean.

I walked up the neat gravel drive and raised my finger to the bell.

The door opened before I could ring.

An old man stood there with an ancient leather suitcase in one hand. The whiff of stale tobacco clung to him. White hair hung over his ears in ringlets. He had a raggedy beard and moustache, which masked a long, thin face. He squinted at me through a pair of smudgy glasses.

'Carol?' He said. His voice was reedy, like he'd hardly used it in years.

I thought he was talking to someone behind him at first, but he took a step towards me and said the name again. I looked down at his feet. He was in slippers.

I was about to call for one of the nurses when the old man's free hand shot out and grabbed my arm. I tried to jerk away, but his grip hardened and he dragged me close. 'Carol?' he asked in a rasping whisper. His breath smelled of cough syrup.

I panicked and leaned back hard, trying to get away from the old man.

'Carol?' he repeated and let go of my arm.

I fell backwards on to the drive, my heart pounding. The old man took another step and leaned over me, lifting his glasses to his forehead. His eyes were watery, but intense, like melting ice. There was something familiar about them. Not the colour, more the shape of them. Quick as a hawk, they flicked to my right. I followed his look. The Orb had slipped out after my fall. I shoved it back in my blazer pocket and looked back up at the old man. His face was even paler than before, his mouth open in surprise. The hand he'd used to remove his glasses was pointing shakily to my blazer pocket.

I lay there in silence for a moment, pinned to the gravel by the intensity of his gaze.

'There's a change...' he said, his voice suddenly much stronger, his finger now waving somewhere beyond the drive. 'Can you feel it?'

I didn't respond or move a muscle. The guy was delirious. I didn't know if he was dangerous, but his eyes had a crazy edge to them.

'Did you see her?' he hissed.

'I'm sorry?' I said, trying to push myself up. Get away from those eyes.

'Did you see?'

Thankfully a woman's voice bellowed from inside: 'Harold!'

A stout, middle-aged woman in a white nurse's uniform came out of the door. 'What are you doing, you old codger?'

When she saw me half-lying on the ground, she gasped, nudged the old man aside and bent to help me up.

'Oh dear, Esta, love,' she said, brushing me down. 'You're all right, ducky. Don't worry about him. He's been funny all morning. Driving me up the wall.' She walked me into the building. 'I said, driving me up the wall, Harold!' she bellowed for his benefit.

When I was safely inside, she scanned me from behind her glasses then turned back to Harold, who had visibly slumped at her appearance, his eyes hidden behind his own foggy specs.

'I don't know what you're doing with that suitcase, Harold. Honestly! It's as if you can't wait for them to bulldoze the place.'

She turned back to me, raised her eyes to the heavens and whispered, 'Let me take Harry back to his room and I'll let you in. You sure you're OK, love?'

'Thanks, Nurse.'

'Just Olive, dear. Make yourself at home.' Then she steered Harold down the carpeted hall.

I smiled, trying to get my breath back, rubbing my arm where Harold had gripped me. "At home" was the last thing I felt here. The place hummed of perfume, old sheets, and onions. It was clean and quiet, but stale too, like a made bed that's never been slept in. Dried flowers bowed unhappily in a vase on a wooden table. Above them was a noticeboard advertising daily activities like bingo and a day trip to Manchester Museum. I remembered Dad telling us about the coach-loads of OAP's he used to see traipsing round the museum. *'Some of them were older than the exhibits, Est.'* I bit back a laugh as dry and unfunny as the flowers.

Gran was sitting rigid in an armchair, trussed up in a blue fluffy dressing gown. She stared at me with expectation when I sat in the only other chair. It was a look she offered pretty much everything recently. It was the look she gave her crosswords. It was the look, I imagined, that she woke up with every morning. Waiting for someone to tell her what to do, for some kind of clue.

Someone had brushed her hair and applied foundation and blusher to her cheeks. But I didn't understand why anyone would bother in a place like this.

She settled down with a sigh of resignation and pointed to a book sitting on her bedside cabinet. The same as always: *On a Soldier's Honour.* When I lifted the book, it sprang open at Chapter Six. Same chapter every time. Never forward, never back.

Gran creased her forehead, reached under her pillow and took out a folded one-pound note, which she fluttered at me. 'Read?' she croaked.

I waited, staring into her pale, grey-green eyes.

I pocketed the note and began to read. I knew the text almost by heart, not the exact words, but the rhythm of the sentences.

'But for the damned war,' I read in the rough Mancunian accent I imagined the young soldier might use to speak to his lover. 'This damned war…'

The story was set during the First World War. It was about a woman whose fiancé leaves for the trenches. She spends the rest of the book waiting for him. Fending off the attentions of other, less worthy men, until his eventual triumphant return. By Chapter Six, he'd not yet left; his departure hung in the balance.

There was still hope.

It didn't take a Psychologist to work out why she might want to keep re-reading that chapter. Mum once told me that mothers shouldn't outlive their sons. That was supposed to be another law of the universe.

I was still a bit on edge after my meeting with Harold but I read on automatically, hardly aware of what I was saying. After a few minutes I realised I wasn't actually reading at all. My mouth was moving, but I wasn't telling a story. Not the one in the book anyway.

I shook my head to clear it and re-focused on the words. They were smudged and a bit raggedy. I glanced at Gran, expecting her to look the same, but she was staring at me with piercing eyes. My head snapped backwards in shock. The room was suddenly freezing. The old woman's lips were moving.

'Gran?' I said, leaning forwards, trying to catch what she was saying.

She leaned forwards as well, so our heads almost touched. She smelled of toothpaste and perfume.

'What did you say, Esta?' she said, her voice cold as cracking ice.

Confused, I looked down at the book then back up at her. She had *never* called me by my name before.

She placed her hand over the page and stared into my eyes. 'Did you see him?' she whispered.

Shooting up, I dropped the book then scrambled behind the chair, putting it between us. 'Gran?'

The door burst open and Nurse Olive barged in. 'Everything OK, ducky?'

I turned back to Gran. Her eyes had closed, her chin had dropped to her chest. A string of saliva hung from her thin lips.

No one spoke.

Gran gave a loud snore, Olive tutted and smiled at me.

'I'd fall asleep too if you kept reading me that rubbish,' she said, bending down to pick the book up.

I offered the nurse a weak smile and hurried out of the room, the image of Gran clinging to my mind: sitting all by herself in that stale room, hair brushed, make-up done. Waiting for things to make sense.

My eyes were dry, but I wiped them anyway with a napkin from reception. I didn't know what had happened, but for a second Gran had woken up. For a second, she had reminded me of Dad.

9

THE GOBSTOPPER

I joined the main road and the usual traffic on its way to pick up children from school. The grind was made worse by the roadworks. Cones marked an area set for digging and a bored looking man twirled a lollipop STOP sign from time to time. Mum reckoned at the rate they were going they'd reach Green Gables by the May half term. Just a few weeks to pack all the fogies away, or, if Mum had her way, a few weeks to save them.

If I turned right, I'd be home by three o'clock. Way too early. Mum would still be home. I thought about the way she could eat a meal in silence, every click of cutlery an unspoken question. About half a mile down the road to the left was *Aslams:* a newsagent which never seemed to close. Mr Aslam never asked questions of his customers either; you know, like how old they were when buying cigarettes, or why they weren't in school during the day.

Gran's one pound note rustled between my fingers. Mum would leave for the Home by Five. Two hours to kill. I paused a second, then headed left.

I sauntered back from the shop in a daze, scuffing my shoes along the pavement and eating blind from a pick and mix bag. My thoughts drifted back to Gran. I'd not been reading the words from her book. So what had I said to get that reaction? Was it about Gatley House? Did she know something? I remembered the old man—Harold—the way he'd stared at the Orb. Those strangely familiar eyes: *Did you see?*

I picked a boiled sweet from the paper bag, my thoughts turning once more to the face of the mysterious figure I'd seen in Gatley House. I tried to form a clear image, but now all I could see were the crazy eyes of Harold staring at me.

A shout from across the road made me look up in alarm.

'Oy, Detesta! Giz a toffee!'

It was the kids from last night: Kev and the boy in the hoodie. They were threading their way between traffic. I groaned and stuffed the sweets in my blazer pocket.

'What you doin' owta school?' Kev called in his broad Mancunian accent. A car beeped its horn as it braked to avoid him.

'No!' Kev shouted at the driver. 'You look where *you're* goin'!'

I sped up, wondering if I could outpace them. From the corner of my eye, I saw the other boy—his face still hidden beneath his hood—make it across to my side. His scrawny legs, inside a pair of drainpipe jeans, stretched out as he matched my pace. There was no way I'd win a race with someone who'd borrowed his legs from a giraffe.

Kev must have made it across too because when he called me again, his voice was right behind me. 'You skivin' school, Detesta?'

I looked along the pavement ahead of me. There was a stone wall about head height to the left, with no break for a hundred metres. The worker holding the lollipop sign seemed a long way away. I looked behind me. The boys were just a few paces away and gaining. I was quick, but not that quick.

'Giz a toffee and we won't snitch that we saw yer,' Kev said with obvious glee.

I slowed down. They were on either side of me, trapping me between them. No point running now.

I pulled the bag from my blazer pocket.

'Nice one,' Kev said, a little out of breath. 'Got any Cola Cubes? I luv them.'

I shot a glance at the traffic crawling past, cars driven by parents on their way to pick up their kids. No help there. I could have done without questions about what I was doing out of school with a couple of tearaways. I was best playing along, hoping they'd get bored and leave me alone.

'That's all I've got,' I said, holding out the paper bag. There wasn't much more than a few chews, a gobstopper and a pile of sugar at the bottom of the bag. 'You can have them.'

Kev's mate scowled, but put his hand in the bag and grabbed the chews. I could see his face now, white, but punctured with fiery looking spots. 'What's that?' he said, pointing at my waist.

Quick as a flash Kev snatched the Orb from my pocket.

'Give it back!' I snapped, grabbing for it.

Kev's mate laughed.

'Metal work project?' Kev said, turning it in his hand. 'Where d'you get it?'

'I found it,' I said quietly, fear twitching inside my stomach. My fingers tightened around the gobstopper in the bag.

'What's it for?'

'I don't know. Give it back.'

If there had been a door, I would have slammed it in his face.

'You found it last night in that house,' Kev said, then handed it to his mate. 'What you fink, Spenner? Reckon we could sell it?'

I swiped at it, but the boy with the giraffe legs lifted it over his head. 'Don't be stupid mate, it's just junk,' Spenner laughed.

'Give it back,' I said through gritted teeth.

'What?' Kev said. 'Are you gonna get your dad—Ow!'

Everything happened in a blur. Without planning it, I flung the sugar at the bottom of my sweet bag into Kev's eyes. Then I stamped the heel of my shoe into Spenner's foot, making him bend double in pain. I wrenched the Orb from giraffe boy and, almost in the same movement, leapt at the wall. Somehow I found a foothold, and I'd scrambled over before the boys reacted, crashing through branches down a slope on the other side while the two boys swore at me and each other.

I crouched behind a bush trying to hold my breath, listening out for them following and wondering if kids my age could die from a heart attack.

After a couple of minutes it became obvious they weren't bothering to chase an annoying little girl into the shrubbery. I let out a huge breath, which led to a minor coughing fit. When I recovered, I looked down at my hands. In one was my Orb, in the other, the now empty bag.

Almost empty.

I pulled out the gobstopper I'd been gripping and popped it into my mouth.

Sugar never tasted so good.

The little wooded area opened up into a dead-end street of boarded-up houses. A rusty street sign read "Grover Close" and by the looks of it, Grover Close was ready and waiting for destruction. Simon had said something about the estate last night. This row of houses must have been what we could see from the upstairs window. I pictured the long building we'd seen in the empty field. I tilted my head; if you looked at it from the right angle, the houses *could* appear to be a single building. But they had been directly *opposite* Gatley House hadn't they? So why couldn't I see that from here?

I put the Orb in my pocket and went to explore.

Sixteen pebble-dashed terraced houses. Grimy, curtainless windows faced each other. Lawns with grass shin high, random stuff scattered along the pavement. At the bottom of the street was a gate leading to a wall of thick bushes and trees.

About halfway down the close, I picked up the discarded head of a Barbie doll. Its hair was in knots and someone had felt-tipped smudgy circles on its cheeks. I weighed it in my palm and pictured a family: kids playing on the front lawn, neighbours waving to each other over a buzzing mower. Dad spraying rainbows with a hosepipe…

Engines rumbled overhead; I cursed myself for looking up. When you live near an airport you quickly work out how many people in the world aren't your dad.

Anyway, something told me—don't ask me what—that if he was coming back, it wouldn't be by plane.

That's how ordinary people came home.

I hurled Barbie's head up at it. She landed on her nose and took a jagged bounce down the empty street towards the gate. I frowned and followed.

The gate led to a muddy track choked by rhododendrons and closely packed trees. To its left was a thick wall of holly bushes. To its right, through branches of a knotted plant, I could make out the machines I'd passed in Fletcher's Field last night. Except now they glowed yellow in the daylight.

I looked back at the gate. The gobstopper fell from my open mouth and rolled towards a wooden sign that was propped up against the bottom slat.

GATLEY HOUSE. KEEP OUT!

10

THE WEEPING WILLOW

I approached the house along the overgrown track, muddy despite a day of sun. It was still only four o'clock. There were three hours before sunset, but the further I walked, the colder and gloomier the track became. It went beneath a tunnel of swaying branches: towering oak and silver birch, choking out the light above.

After two minutes the trees finally opened up to be replaced by hedgerows twice my height. They hemmed me in like those blinkers they put over horse's eyes, focusing all my attention on the track ahead.

Eventually, the hedge to my right thinned. The machines digging up Fletcher's Field flickered into view between its branches. A few feet ahead, the hedge on my left made way for an old gate I recognised. The hedge kept on after that. A wall of green wrapping around the grounds of the house, like out of Sleeping Beauty.

I slowed before reaching the familiar gate. That feeling of being close to an unseen drop tugged at me again.

Gatley House was waiting for me. Standing alone, same as always. Nothing would have changed on the outside, but at the same time, *everything* had changed.

I'd been inside. I had seen its secrets. It was kind of like when you find something out about a person you thought you knew. They seem the same to everyone else but, to you, they've changed—and somehow, *they know it too*.

Footprints mashed up the track where it met the gate. Muddy echoes of everyone last night, I thought. I smiled at the memory of the commotion as Simon, Graham and I scrambled out of the basement window. The others bolting over the gate and in their rush to get away. And Hannah had the cheek to say *I* bottled it.

I leaned on the gate, keeping my forearms away from the barbed wire and watched the old place. Heavy curtains hung behind the second-floor window. I waited for them to twitch.

A movement in the garden caught my attention. The trailing branches of an enormous weeping willow parted. I ducked behind the gate and peered through the slats as a figure walked across the choked lawn. I recognised his loping step and stood up with a warm flush of relief.

'Graham?'

The boy ducked too, but straightened when he saw me. He wore a Luke Skywalker T-shirt and faded skinny jeans, which made him look even taller than he really was. His satchel was hung over one shoulder and he carried a large jar filled with what looked like muddy water.

'Have you been here all day?' I called.

He glanced left and right. 'Is there anyone with you?'

I shook my head.

He waved at me with his free hand. 'Come and see.'

I cast a nervous glance up at the house, then climbed over the gate.

'What's in the jar?' I asked.

He ignored the question, grabbed my arm and led me back across the squelchy lawn towards the weeping willow.

The damp seeped through my shoes and between my toes as I waited for him to lift the curtain of branches for me to stoop under.

'It's all true,' he said, letting the branches collapse behind us.

Darkness descended. An even darker square shadow leaned against the trunk of the tree.

'This,' breathed Graham, 'is the stone. I don't know why I've never thought to check here before.'

When the taste of my fear had dulled, I shuffled forwards. Graham lit a match. I knelt—the ground was drier here—and reached out to touch markings someone had scraped into the mossy slab. Lichen and the dancing shadows made it difficult to read. The match went out.

'Ouch!'

Graham sucked his finger, then reached into his satchel and pulled out a notebook. 'I made a rubbing.'

He'd used a pencil to trace the outline of the letters he had rubbed from the headstone. Now, more used to the light, I could make out some of the words:

> *Beloved Wife,*
> *…oline… in another life.*

The rest was too smudged to read.

I leaned against the trunk, my fear turned to sadness. This wasn't a ghost story we had walked in on, it was a sad and lonely one. Just like the house. It was old sighing rooms, creaking floorboards and shadows.

I thought of Gran in her makeup, with her novel stuck on repeat like a scratched record. Mum, fighting an impossible battle with the diggers, worrying about her unhinged daughter and radioactive rain. I pictured the hook in the ceiling. Then I thought about the last time I saw Dad's face. How pale it was. The sunken, bloodshot eyes, the uncombed shock of hair, the patches of stubble that scratched my face when he bent to kiss me.

I let Graham's notebook slip from my fingers. People spend their whole lives building something and then they lose it anyway. You hold on to those you love and then you find yourself hanging from a hook in an empty room.

'What's the point?' I muttered, staring at Gatley House through the branches of the old willow tree.

Graham stashed the book in his satchel and began rummaging

around for something else. 'I've been watching all day, plucking up the courage to go in again.'

But I suddenly wasn't interested. I slid down the trunk to sit on an exposed root. The pictures, the objects we'd found meant nothing. So what if that's what Dad was really searching for in the house? So what if it explained why he'd gone inside to find Charlie? My dad was still gone wasn't he?

'Simon didn't lock it up last night, you know?' Graham continued. 'I wanted to go in when it was still light this time,' he took an A4-sized brown envelope out, 'and get better photos than these.'

I looked him up and down. He was a couple of years older and half a foot taller than me when we were standing. His faded t-shirt, his uncombed hair and his nervous, wide eyes made him seem more my age though.

'Why d'you come here Graham?' I said, scratching a line in the damp soil.

He paused, midway through sliding a sheet of paper from an envelope. 'What?'

I shrugged. 'I've seen you lurking around.'

Graham's face changed, like a shadow passed over it. He lost his puppy dog eyes and suddenly looked every one of his eighteen years. He pulled what I now saw were large photos all the way out of the envelope. He crouched down, put the envelope on the earth and placed the photos on top of it.

'What's with the jar?' I asked. 'Is that why you come?'

'There's stuff living in the pond,' he said, jerking a thumb behind him. 'It's a hobby.'

I considered the grey sides of the jar. 'A hobby?'

'Kind of a Biology project, but that's not the only reason I come.' He stared at the photos that lay between us.

'You're hunting for ghosts?' I asked.

He shrugged. 'I know why you come.'

'Really?' I said, my voice dry as toast. I grabbed a handful of the earth I'd been drawing patterns in and squeezed until I could feel the damp trickling between my fingers. *Here it comes…*

'It was your dad who found Charlie,' Graham said. 'You think this place has got something to do with what happened to him, don't you?'

I got up and let the mud scatter at my feet. 'Whatever,' I said. 'Think what you like.' I stooped under the branches of the willow tree, letting them drop behind me. I straightened and stood on the boggy ground, trying to ward off the feeling that someone was watching me from the house. *Because that's what ghosts are, Dad: memories, hopes and dreams bound by shadows… and creaking floorboards.*

'You saw something, didn't you?' Graham said from behind the curtain of leaves.

The image of the old man's face appeared—the one from last night—as if it were floating right in front of me. I stared at it, unblinking, waiting for it to fade. When it didn't, I whispered, 'Just shadows,' and it dissolved.

I pulled the Orb from the pocket of my blazer. 'Shadows and bits of rusty junk.'

'You kept that?' Graham said, peering through the branches at me.

'It looked nicer at the time,' I sighed. The weak sunlight gave the thing that golden glow again. *Trick of the light.*

I thought about dropping it in the tall grass, letting the old lawn swallow it up. 'I should have picked up the bell instead. At least that *did* something.'

'What bell?'

'The thing Simon took.'

There was a momentary silence behind the leaves. 'A bell?'

'Yeah. You know, a thing you ring,' I said sarcastically.

'Seriously?'

'Yes.'

There was another pause. 'Come and have a look at these photos, will you?'

I sighed, dropped the Orb into my pocket and dipped my head back between the branches. 'Why?'

'Because from where I was standing,' he said slowly, 'Simon wasn't holding a bell.'

11

Photos Never Lie

'Just look at them. I don't know. You might see something I haven't.'

I was crouched back under the branches of the weeping willow, the pile of photos between us. My eyes were used to the dim light now. Even so, the photos were still all a bit gloomy. The first one was of the pond during the day, with Gatley House in the background; there was another blurry one of a blueish frog-thing in some weeds. I raised an eyebrow.

Graham gave an apologetic smile, 'Not that one. Biology project. Wait.' He rifled through a couple more photos. Then handed me an even murkier one.

'Is that the landing?' I asked, staring hard at it.

'Yeah. Your mate, Simon, told me to take it on our way out before you nearly flattened him. But it's just bare walls as far as I can see. I was in a rush, to be fair. The exposure's appalling and he wouldn't hold the torch still.'

'He's not my mate,' I murmured, taking another photo.

'This one's better. It's the room we went in.'

I squinted at it, looking for an old man standing in the shadows. Nothing obvious, but I did notice that the floor was carpeted in the photo. I remembered the sound of my hard steps against the landing as I ran along it. I was panicking; you miss things when you panic. I handed him the photo back. 'Show me the table.'

He placed another photo in my upturned palm, 'I'm sure we could get better ones during the day. A torch is no substitute for proper light, or a flash.'

The picture of the table was actually quite clear despite what Graham said. A layer of fuzz covered the objects in the photos. I frowned. It looked like dust. No sparkling goblets, daggers or necklaces either. From the looks of it, the table was just a dumping ground for rusty junk. My frown deepened. I searched for Simon's bell or the object I'd picked—'*chosen*' a little voice in my head reminded me—resting in my pocket. Neither of them were in the picture, just… junk.

'Here you go. Weird souvenirs, and…' Graham handed me the last photo with a finger pointing at something in Simon's hand, '… that's no kind of bell I've ever seen.'

This image was of Simon and me smiling by the gate. Simon held… what? Something knobbly and grey. Definitely not a bell.

In the image, I held up something flat and brownish. I peered more closely, looking for the glint of gold, the fancy symmetry. But there was just a rusty piece of metal.

'Well, that's weird,' I said.

'That's what I thought. The look on your faces, as if you'd found hidden treasure or something.'

My mind raced with thoughts about the object in my pocket, the feel of it. Had I really looked carefully at it? Was it just the light from the torch that had given it a golden glow? I remembered Spenner's comment: *It's just junk.*

'I have to go,' I stammered, getting back to my feet and bashing my head against one of the lower branches.

'Go?' Graham protested. 'You only just got here. What about the house? The photos?'

I could feel my face heating up; electricity balling up like a fist in my stomach. If the past was anything to go by, any second now my vision would darken and I'd do something stupid.

'You said you saw someone,' I heard Graham say through the rush in my ears.

'No,' I squeaked before making for the safety of the curtain of branches.

I'm a rubbish liar. Mum told me once that I wear lies on my face in bright red splodges.

I pushed through the leaves of the willow. 'Thanks for the photos, and…' and I say the dumbest things when I get flustered, '… the gravestone thing.'

'Wait!'

Out from under the tree, I let myself breathe. The rushing in my ears subsided. 'I better get back,' I said. 'I'm on last warnings and stuff. Mum'll be glued to the window and her watch.' That was true at least, and I felt the rising heat cool a little.

'You sure you're alright?' Graham asked.

'Course. I just didn't know the time's all.'

There was a pause as Graham made rustling sounds, collecting his things to join me. I decided to wait, now that my face had stopped being a flashing "I'm lying" beacon.

Graham emerged, satchel over his shoulder, jar in hand. 'I heard what you did to Bleakly by the way.'

It took a second to work out what he meant, 'You mean Mr Blakely? That was an accident.'

'I heard why, too.'

I started walking towards the gate, keeping my eyes on the muddy ground to avoid looking at the house. 'Well, don't make the same mistake then.'

Graham caught me up easily with his long strides. 'No. I understand.'

I didn't answer, but the anger retreated some more.

'Did Culter tear a strip off you?'

'Course. I told you, I have to keep my nose clean.'

Graham laughed, spilling water from his jar.

'What's so funny?'

'Oh,' he said, straightening his face, 'Was that not a joke? Nothing. Sorry. I'm imagining you slamming a door in to Bleakly's nose. Miserable git.'

'Thanks for your understanding,' I said flatly. We were a few paces from the gate, and now I was wondering how to shake him off. I needed a moment to check the Orb. I had to see if it was the same as the thing I held in the photo.

'Is that all though? Just, "Stay out of trouble"?'

'Not really. I have to do something positive for the community.'

'What's that supposed to mean?'

I placed a hand on the gate. 'I dunno. He wants me to present something in assembly.'

Graham shrugged, 'What's your problem? I bet if I'd smashed in a teacher's nose they'd have me cleaning bins for a week. And then kick me out anyway.'

I climbed over and landed in the muddy track. With the hedge blocking out the house, I felt myself immediately relax.

I looked across the gate at him. He wasn't leaving with me. He had placed the jar at his feet and was just watching me with wide eyes. The same way a dog might, waiting on the promise of a ball.

'The problem is,' I said, 'that I can't stand up on a stage in front of people who either hate me or think I'm some crazy person. No one likes me. They'd probably laugh, or throw things.'

'That's because you won't let anyone get to know you.'

I flung my arms in the air. 'I might as well be a frickin' exhibit in a museum so people can point at me.'

'You need to get out more. Speak to people. Relax.' He flashed a nervous smile at me, put his jar down and rummaged in his bag, drawing out the envelope with the photos in it.

I narrowed my eyes, 'What?'

'I know they aren't the best photos,' he said, 'but there *is* one upside.'

He showed me the picture of Simon and me holding our souvenirs. 'It doesn't matter what anyone else says. These are proof we completed the dare.' He waited for me to react, but I had no idea what he was getting at. I barely even remembered that there *was* a dare, let alone what it was for.

'It means you and I can go to Simon's party.' Graham grinned, then put the photo back in his bag, and picked up his jar of muddy water. 'His dad's away for the weekend on some court thing. He lives in this mansion. It'll be huge.'

I gave him my cynical/horrified look that was meant to say: *Are you out of your flipping mind?* But he didn't read it, or he did and he didn't care.

'I'll pick you up at seven on Friday.'

12

DAD'S BOX

'Not this one, Mum,' I pleaded.

Mum had brought down Dad's cardboard box from my room while I was grabbing breakfast before school on Thursday. 'It's mainly junk, hon,' she sighed.

'Why are you determined to get rid of everything?'

'Because,' she paused a second, 'it's time to let go of him, Esta, which means getting rid of everything but the most important stuff.'

I dropped my uneaten toast on the plate and followed her into the living room. 'You're getting rid of him,' I said. 'It's like you're rubbing him out.'

She sighed. 'No. I'm just trying to keep... the colouring inside the lines.'

I scuffed the sofa with the side of my foot. 'Why don't we get rid of that then? Is that outside the lines?'

She considered it for a moment, her head cocked to one side. 'I know... I should...'

'Let me keep the box.'

'Go through it after school,' she said, still contemplating the sofa. 'You can keep three things.' Then she shook her head like she was clearing it and considered Dad's box again before completely changing the subject. 'What are you doing with toast in the living room anyway? Crumbs.'

I backed in to the kitchen with a frown.

'I spoke to Aunty Marge,' Mum said. 'We can stay at hers until we find a place of our own.'

'I'm not going.'

'It's just in case. If Miss Nuttall and the governors decide to…' she left the words "expel you" unsaid. 'We'll have six weeks to find a new home and you a new school down in London.'

'And what about Gran?'

'Honey, if the court agrees with the Council, then she'll be kicked out too.'

'But,' I said desperately, 'the Home said they'd relocate her nearby. Same nurses and everything. They promised that.'

'It's not that. It's the upheaval and if we're ever going to move on, then now is as good a time as any. What that road will do to this town… Honestly, I'll be glad to leave.'

The ball of energy sparked into life inside me, the edges of my vision darkened, 'You just don't want to be in this house,' I snapped. 'You want to pretend he doesn't exist.'

Mum's face stiffened. 'I don't want to pretend anything Esta. Everything is… what it is and not something else. I can't live a life where your dad is alive and…' she stumbled over the word, 'gone… all at the same time.'

'Then don't,' I said trying to control my voice. 'Just believe he's alive.'

Mum looked back to the sofa. 'I've tried.' Muscles bunched in her jaw. 'But it's almost two years.'

'According to the law he's still alive until he's been missing for seven.'

'Oh Jesus, Esta. The law doesn't make him alive.'

'Yeah, well,' I almost shouted, 'you giving up on him doesn't make him dead either!'

Mum raised her hand towards me as if she was going to stroke my hair. I flinched away.

'Esta, your father was ill before he… You know that.'

'Then why didn't he go to a hospital?'

'You know I don't mean that kind of ill.'

'People don't just disappear, Mum. Something happened.' My face burnt. I felt the tears coming again. Should I tell her what I saw?

Should I tell her what I found in Gatley House? I thought about Graham's photos: *bare walls, rusty junk.*

I sniffed my tears away. 'He needs us to be here for him when he comes back. And if we're gone… then how will he know where to find us?'

'No,' she said firmly. 'Your dad. The man he used to be,' she raised her hands in a shrug that took in the whole room, the box, me, the sofa 'Even if he *is* still alive. He wouldn't want this. He's gone, Esta. He'd want us to move on. Start again.'

I wiped my eyes with the sleeve of my shirt, 'So… why are you trying to stop them knocking down Green Gables? Isn't Gran being kicked out your excuse to leave?'

Mum's forehead creased in anger, 'Because it's not fair!' she said, all of a sudden looking close to tears herself. 'Because it's not just about me, or her, or you… or him. You don't kick old people out of their homes. It's just not right.'

'Just out of the goodness of your heart?' I said dryly.

That comment must have pushed a button, because she raised her eyebrows at it. 'Why the hell not?' Her voice came out sharp and wild, like a broken shard of glass. 'You've just stopped caring about anyone else outside of your own little bubble. And anyway, I thought you wanted to stay! If you would *just* take an interest in other people, Esta. That's all Mr Culter wants you to do.'

The ball of energy in my stomach became cold. I took a bite out of my toast. It was cold and dry too. 'I've got a lot on my mind,' I mumbled.

Mum almost exploded. '*You've* got a lot on your mind?'

I considered telling her about my visit to Gran yesterday, but she stormed from the room, ranting away about protests, lawyers and placards, all talk of Dad seemingly forgotten.

I dropped the rest of my toast on the plate and took out the Orb, running my fingers along its rough edges. It was oddly relaxing to hold. Graham's photo had shown me holding a piece of rusty metal, but this thing was anything but junk. It was beautiful. I let it sit in the palm of my hand and considered it. *What are you? Were you like this yesterday? Did you change shape overnight?*

Mum's voice floated from the hall as she pulled an envelope from the letterbox. 'You know millions of people in America made a human chain the other week, spanning the whole country to stop homelessness and poverty. People who care about others can make a change, Esta, never doubt...'

I stopped listening. I didn't have Mum's optimism. I couldn't see how ordinary people could stop the bulldozer of progress. There would still be plenty of poor people in America, even after they'd all held hands.

After a while I realised Mum's lesson on civil action had fizzled to a halt mid-sentence. She'd become stony silent in fact. I looked up from the Orb to see her standing in the doorway, another open envelope in her hand.

'It's asking for a note of absence for yesterday afternoon,' she said.

I slipped the Orb back into my coat pocket and made for the door. 'I'm going to be late,' I said, pushing past her.

She stood and watched as I marched down the hall, 'Where the hell were you yesterday afternoon?' she called, but I slammed the door and dodged traffic to the other side of the road, just in case she followed me out.

I took the long way to school past Green Gables, thinking about old men standing in shadows, while tracing the edges of the Orb in my pocket. The protest banners Mum had erected yesterday flapped over the entrance to the nursing home. It stood on a slight rise so it was possible to make out the yellow of the bulldozers over the top of Grover Close. It wouldn't be long now. The airport road wasn't going to have wiggles. Although I remember Mum driving me to visit a friend of hers in Yorkshire once; the motorway over the Pennines split around a farmhouse. The farmer must have refused to budge when they wanted to tear down his home, so they just went ahead and built the road around him. That was the inevitability of progress. I didn't think it was the sort of solution Mum was after though. In my experience, once people latched on to an idea they tended to stick to it, whether it was saving your own home, plans for a road or something else entirely. It was difficult to change the course of your story once you'd started.

13

THE DUCK/RABBIT

Mum clearly *did* have a lot on her mind, because the absence note wasn't mentioned when I got home. She was glued to the six o'clock news, fingers locked together, watching a report about the power plant accident. There was an animation showing clouds of radiation spreading across Europe. A reassuring newsreader-y voice-over explained how there was almost no chance of it getting to Britain.

Mum sighed heavily and shook her head at the screen before switching it off. She checked the kitchen clock, apologetically dumped a can of soup and a packet of sliced bread on the table for my tea, then bundled herself out of the house for yet another 'important' meeting about Green Gables Nursing Home.

Graham called round for me at seven as he said he would. He wore black chinos and an ironed shirt with a grandad collar. He'd combed his hair into waves. I didn't say so, but I preferred his scruffy look.

My hair was up in a rushed ponytail; I wore an Adidas tracksuit top over a t-shirt and pale blue jeans. I did own a dress, but it was a black one my mum bought me, and I was still angry with her about the box. Anyway, it didn't have a pocket for the Orb and I wasn't the sort of girl who carried a bag.

'You combed,' I said as we walked.

'You did too.'

'Just my fingers and a rubber band,' I laughed. 'Graham, why are we going to this party? It's for the cool kids and, no offence, but I don't reckon that's either of us.'

He gave a '*maybe*' tilt of his head and stuffed his hands into the pockets of his chinos. 'You see the news?' he said, filling the awkward silence.

'Mum's obsessed by it.'

'Personally, I believe it's all just an over-reaction.'

'Really? You're not worried?'

Graham grinned. 'It's supposed to be a joke.'

'I don't get it.'

'Over-reaction. Like nuclear reaction?'

I screwed up my face. He was such a geek. 'Really? Graham? That's not funny at all.'

His shoulders sagged and he blew out a long breath. A deflating balloon.

'Have you been practising that?' I asked, trying to catch his eye.

He shook his head and sped up.

He was, no doubt, already regretting inviting me to the party. I *did* warn him.

'Graham?' I asked as I caught up.

'What?'

'Why are we really going?'

To my surprise, he slowed right down again, so I almost shot past him. He stared at his muddy leather boots, the one thing he'd not compromised on. I got an uneasy feeling that he wanted to "talk". I was hoping he wasn't about to say something embarrassing, like suggesting we arrive at the party as a couple for instance.

The streetlamps flickered carrot orange above us while the sun dipped towards a horizon of rooftops. We turned a corner, Graham stopped, his back to a fence and stared at me with pleading teddy-bear eyes. My toes curled inside my pumps.

'Esta?' he said.

'Yes?' I croaked.

'Alright, I wanted to go to this party.'

'Ooh Kaay,' I said, slowly dragging out the two syllables.

Graham on the other hand spoke in short bursts. 'She's called Lily. She works. She left school last year.'

I let out a breath, feeling tension leave my body.

Graham ran fingers through his hair, undoing the damage the comb had done. He spoke even more quickly. 'I met her a few weeks ago. She loves travelling. And I'm going with her to India. Well, when I finish my A-levels. I know that sounds a bit, you know, rash. But we were watching the Breakfast Club—'

My mind was racing to catch up with his machine gun delivery. Did he say he was going to India? With some girl?

'Graham, what on Earth are you talking about?'

'The Breakfast Club—have you seen it?'

Of course I'd seen it. Everyone had seen it. It was a movie about a bunch of kids 'finding themselves' during a Saturday detention. I'd even bought the soundtrack and played air guitar to the Simple Minds theme tune. The one with Jim Kerr belting out: *Hey, hey, hey, haay* at the start. But that's not what I wanted to know.

'You're going to India?'

'Yeah, with Lily. She's the one I was telling you about. She has the same colour hair as Molly Ringwald.'

'Who?'

'She's the one in the Breakfast Club. The posh one.'

'The ginger one?'

'No, not ginger.' Graham's cheeks kind of went ginger then. 'It's strawberry blonde.'

Oh. My. God. I hadn't figured Graham as a romantic. I tried to stop myself giggling. 'You know she ends up falling for a delinquent, don't you?'

'You're missing the point of the movie.'

'Which is?'

'The point is not to stereotype. Anyone can be anyone.'

'The geek didn't get the girl though, did he? That's the message I got from it. The sporty one and the criminal are cool. Nerds never win. And they make him write the letter at the end.'

'You're not helping, Esta. We had a connection, and she's

coming to this party. So that's why I'm going, OK?'

'What do you want me to do?'

'You're supposed to be boosting my confidence. You're doing a rubbish job of it by the way.'

'You think if she sees you with me you'll have a better chance with her? Have you read the news? No one talks to me. I'm the weirdo everyone avoids.'

'You're not one of them. That's the point and I couldn't go to a party full of beautiful people by myself.'

I gave him a mock-outraged look.

'I didn't mean it like that. You're different. That's a good thing by the way.'

I knew what he meant. Hannah Piranha was right, parties weren't my scene. Simon and his group were definitely not in my league. Breakfast Club be damned.

'Come on,' I said, 'before I abandon you for someone normal.'

We walked for five minutes, arguing about the film. Then Graham said something that made my thoughts leap elsewhere.

'Let's just agree to disagree. Everybody sees things differently.'

I remembered his photographs and the realisation that maybe he and I really *did* see things differently.

Graham nudged me. 'You've gone quiet. Does that mean I win?'

'Wait,' I said, pushing him against another fence. Graham looked petrified. 'Don't worry,' I said, 'I'm not going to kiss you.'

I pulled out the Orb and held it up to the orange light of the streetlamp. The Orb glinted like fire. It gave me that slightly cross-eyed feel again to look at, but I couldn't help being amazed at its beauty.

'What do you see?' I said.

Graham cocked his head, 'Are you going to tell me it's a bell?'

I held it closer to him. 'What? What is it?'

He took it from me and inspected it. 'It's…' he looked at me with one eyebrow raised, and handed it me back, 'It's a rusty hinge.'

I swore. 'Everyone's right. I've lost it.'

'What's up?'

'I don't see a hinge Graham. I see a… a… I don't know what it is, but it's golden and it's not rusty and it's definitely not a stupid hinge.'

He took it from me again and peered at it from an angle. Scratched his head. 'I don't see anything else. You're sure?'

I grabbed it back off him and stuffed it in my pocket; the thing was making me sick all of a sudden. 'The room was cold,' I said. 'The other night at Gatley House. There were images on the walls and there was ice, not dust. And… and I definitely saw someone.'

Graham remained quiet. He seemed calm, and I didn't think he was looking at me with suspicion, or ridicule.

I gulped. 'Mum said I'm caught up in my own bubble or something and Culter said people are concerned about my mental health and stuff, so… not sure I trust myself, you know?'

Another couple almost bumped into us as they turned the corner. They giggled and crossed over the road.

'I don't know,' he said finally. 'It's weird.'

'You think I'm crazy too, don't you?'

He paused, frowned, then looked at me with something like fascination. What he said next was a surprise coming from a science geek. 'No. No, weird doesn't have to mean crazy. And anyway, crazy doesn't mean it's not true. Plenty of weird stuff is true.' He smiled. 'Did you know Hippo milk is pink?'

'What? That's not the same thing at all.'

'And… You can't hum while holding your nose.'

'I'm talking about something that is…' I clenched my fists in frustration, '… impossible.'

Graham smiled at me. 'You should try it.' He went to hold his nose. I swiped his hand away.

'Graham? I'm being serious. It's your turn to boost my confidence.' I glanced around me. A steady stream of teenagers were making their way along the pavement now. I lowered my voice. 'I'm seeing things that other people don't see.'

He nodded at a couple who sidled past us, then stared up at the darkening sky while he waited for them to walk out of earshot.

I looked up too. Somewhere beyond the halo of orange lamplight, the stars would be popping out. Dr Harkness had said something about stars in today's lesson. About how far away they were. About how the light took so long to get from them that when you see them twinkling away, you were looking back in time. 'Some stars may have died hundreds of years ago,' he'd said, 'and yet their light has taken so long to arrive here that when we look up into the night sky, we still see them burning brightly as if they still live. And in a way, I suppose they do.'

'Earth calling Esta. Come in, Esta.'

I blinked. 'What?'

'You were drifting.' Graham lowered his voice an octave. 'I said, does Simon see that old door bolt differently too?'

'It was a door bolt? I told you, he picked up a bell. He, you know…' I twisted my fist like I was swinging a hand bell, '… dinged it.'

Graham arched an eyebrow. 'Did you talk with him about it?'

'I've tried to, but he won't talk to me. He's always surrounded by his groupies. I thought maybe—'

'You thought he'd speak with you tonight? I wouldn't put a bet on it.'

'I know,' I said gloomily, remembering my humiliation in the Geography classroom.

A group of girls rounded the corner and whistled at us.

Graham took a step away from me. 'Come on. It looks like we're fighting or snogging.'

'You worried in case Molly Ringwald comes by?'

The Taylor house was impressive. That's not to say it was

beautiful, it just made an impression. It was broad and white, reminding me of the White House in America. Fake marble lions sat guard on the gates, and even more fake-looking Greek pillars supported the front porch.

We paused by the lion on the right-hand gate post. It was in mid roar and reminded me of one of Dad's old Santana album covers.

Graham held my shoulders and stared straight at me. 'Look. I know one thing. There is something about Gatley House. I know that for sure. Trust me. I don't care what your mum or anyone else says, I don't think you're crazy.'

'Thanks,' I said, distracted. I was still picturing the album cover. It was of a roaring lion too, except when you looked more carefully it was really six different heads with a woman in the middle wearing a grass skirt.

'Optical illusion,' I said.

'What is?'

'It's like one of those eye puzzles, you know where it's a duck when you look at it one way or a rabbit if you look at it the other?'

Graham smiled. 'You see? Now you're thinking. Come on,' and he led the way down the immaculately laid drive. 'Why don't you draw it?' he said as we approached the porch.

'The duck rabbit?'

'No.' He pointed at my pocket. 'The thing you picked up. The golden thing. Draw what you see. Maybe I'll see it too.'

A boy, roughly the size and shape of a brick wall, thrust a sheet of paper towards us. He was as tall as Graham and as wide as the both of us put together.

We pointed to our names, the last two on the list of course, and the walking, talking oak tree ticked them. Graham peered at it as he did so. 'Is Lily here?'

The man/boy ran his finger down the sheet. 'Yep, mate. I remember her. She's the ginger. Brought a bottle of Thunderbird.'

'Strawberry blonde,' Graham said and slipped passed into the dimly lit hallway.

'What happened to me boosting your confidence?' I said.

'Tomorrow,' he said, turning back to me, as he disappeared behind a wall of unfamiliar faces.

The boy/tree checked me out with a distinct lack of enthusiasm and then stood aside to let me in.

Every room was loud and packed. There was nowhere to stop. Hannah was right, this wasn't a place for me. Cheesy pop music blasted from speakers in the living room. Most of the kids were a year above me. The boys wore pastel Pringle shirts, buttoned up to the top; most of the girls had back combed hair and heavy makeup. Their arms jangled with bangles and bracelets. Cigarettes perched between the garish fake nails of one hand, bottles of cheap wine or beer in the other. I couldn't believe Simon's parents would have allowed this. It was chaos. *No,* a voice that sounded horribly like Hannah Piranha's said in my head, *it's normal. This is what normal people do.*

I nudged my way through the various rooms, looking for Simon. Half hoping *not* to find him in case he had one of his fan girls wrapped around him, tongue rammed down his throat. The house was too packed, the music too loud, the air foggy with smoke. After twenty minutes, I gave up. I hadn't said a word to anyone else other than, "Excuse me" and no one had regarded me with anything other than pity or dim annoyance. Prickling claustrophobia danced up and down my body.

As much as I needed to see Simon, I couldn't stay here. The air was too warm, the perfume sickly.

The sixth former at the door had ticked off all his names and was busy swigging from a bottle of cider, his pen discarded on the floor. I pretended to drop an earring and picked the pen up, then headed to the upstairs toilet. I had to wait for a pale-faced boy to leave before ducking inside and locking the door behind me. I knelt on a clean patch of floor, trying to ignore the stench of puke from inside the bowl; I took out the Orb and balanced it on the toilet lid.

Graham wanted a drawing. I would give him a drawing.

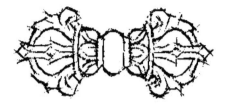

When finished I folded the paper and wrote Graham's name on it. This would have to do.

I found him talking to a pretty red-haired girl in the hallway, overcame an irrational pang of jealousy and handed him the tissue. 'Here,' I said.

Graham widened his eyes at me. 'Not now,' he hissed.

I stood on tiptoes and whispered into his ear, 'She's definitely ginger,' while stuffing the drawing in his shirt pocket. I flashed Lily a smile I'm sure fooled no one, then squeezed past her to the door.

A heavy weight lifted from me as I put distance between myself and the party. I'd not even caught a glimpse of Simon. I didn't belong there. Right then, I didn't know where I belonged.

Clouds had gathered, threatening rain; the night was cool, but not cold enough to force me back home, so I thrust my hands into my tracksuit pockets and walked in the direction of Gatley House.

This time, I was going alone. This time I wanted to see if it was a duck or a rabbit.

14

FORGETTING TO BREATHE

By the time I reached the track leading to the house, I had to wrap my arms around myself to stop from shivering. I climbed the gate and was about to hop over the other side when a figure stepped out of the bushes. My heart shrivelled up to the size of a sultana. I swallowed a yelp.

'Hello Esta.'

I landed in the mud. 'Jesus! Simon! Why d'you keep doing that?'

'What?'

'Appearing!'

He pulled my arm and dragged me further down the track, away from the street.

'What the hell are you doing here?' I hissed, 'You're hosting the party of the century, remember?'

He lowered his head and kicked a pebble. It was the sort of thing you see a seven-year-old doing.

'Turns out everyone just came to raid the drinks cabinet. I bet no one even knows I've left.'

'Won't your parents kill you? Sorry to say, but the place was a tip.'

He raised his eyebrows. 'You came?'

'Graham persuaded me,'

'You're a bit young for him, aren't you?'

I winced. 'No! Not like that. He was meeting a girl.'

The tree branches leaned over us as we walked, leaves dripping on to our heads.

'My dad doesn't care. He'll hire a cleaner, as long as nothing's smashed.'

'What about your mum?'

He shrugged, 'She'd never let me have a party in the first place.'

'So how—?'

'I don't live with her anymore.' He booted another stone which skipped along the track.

'Oh.' I didn't know what to say. This was Simon, the boy who every boy wanted to be, and every girl wanted to be with. We walked slowly in silence for a moment. 'I don't understand you,' I said finally. 'You're not what I expected at all.'

'It's not me,' he said, eyes still on the track. 'Everybody expects something. You know, the clothes, the music I listen to.'

'The parties you throw.'

He shrugged, looked up at last and gave me a sheepish grin, 'The parties.'

'When you're here on your own,' I said, 'you seem... I don't know, quiet.'

'And you're bossy.'

I laughed, the sound seeming out of place in this forgotten part of the world.

The moon slipped out from behind a cloud, highlighting the edges of a wide pool of standing water across our path. I stopped and considered my pumps. 'What happened with your mum?'

He paused, staring straight ahead. Above us, the rain clouds had already sped on. It was one of those spring nights when the weather is always in a hurry. Now fragments of moonlight filtered through the branches and made silver ripples on the surface of the water.

'Sorry. You don't have to answer that,' I said.

'No, it's OK. She left my dad after we came here from Brighton.'

'Is that normal? Staying with your dad?'

'We had a choice. I chose to stay with him, Charlene stayed with Mum.' He looked up at me. 'My dad's loaded. He lets me get away with anything.'

'Charlene?'

Simon rammed his fists into his pockets, 'My sister.'

'I didn't know. I've never seen her, is she…?'

'She doesn't go to school anymore.'

I frowned, trying to catch up. 'Wait. Charlene?'

Simon took one of his hands out of his pockets and pointed towards the puddle. 'You want me to carry you over?'

I raised an eyebrow at his white Hi-Tec trainers and pristine pale-blue drainpipes.

He laughed. 'Alright, follow me.'

We tiptoed along the edge of the puddle, guided by the moonlight. I stared at the back of Simon's head. *What was the deal with him? Missing his party to come to this rotten old house… Unless…* Cogs whirred in my brain. *Unless…*

'Charlie!' I said suddenly. He stopped. 'Charlie Bullock.' He turned slowly round, but his foot slipped and before I could see the expression on his face, he'd flung out his arms and disappeared from view with a yelp.

'Simon!'

I ran to where he'd fallen. He was clinging on to a dangling branch, but his knees were in the mud, and as he scrambled for footing, I could make out two round patches on his jeans like a pair of brown knee guards.

'Stop laughing and help me up,' he said.

I gripped his outstretched hand and almost fell on top of him, which made him laugh too. He got to his feet, held me around my waist and heaved me up so our faces were inches apart. The alcohol on his breath was sweet.

'Hello,' I mumbled.

'You want to go on my shoulders?'

'I think I'd squash you.'

'You're light as a feather,' he grinned.

I let go of him and turned away to hide one of my back-stabbing flushes.

A spark of light in the water caught my eye. I forgot my

embarrassment and peered at it. Something about the shape poking out from the surface was familiar. I knelt for a closer look. Metal. 'What's that? It's like...'

Simon pushed me aside and re-entered the puddle with a splash, lifting the object from the mud.

Moonlight caught the handle of the bell. He wiped it dry on his top and without looking at me, or waiting to explain, headed off along the track towards Gatley House.

All thoughts about Charlie were gone now. Simon had kept his object too. And it *was* a bell. By the laws of photography and from what Graham said, it should have been nothing more than a door bolt. No one holds on to a door bolt, just like no one holds on to a rusty hinge.

I called out his name again as I staggered along the track after him, the grass slippery beneath my stupid, gripless pumps. I almost ran into him just meters from the gate, just where the hedgerows were thickest on either side.

Simon had stopped dead. A pale glow cast a halo around him and tipped the leaves of the hedges in silver light. At first I thought he'd brought his wonky torch because he was looking down at something in his hands. I tapped his arm, but he hardly moved, just stood, staring down at whatever he was holding. I stepped around him to see. He wasn't holding a torch. The glow was coming from the bell.

Spider webs of white light skated over its surface as if it were bursting with electricity in some tacky sci-fi movie. My first reaction was to knock the thing out of his hands. But the look on his face stopped me. It was the same look he'd had when he first picked the thing up from the table. It was the look that had been bugging me ever since; the look of a boy who's found a real life light-sabre.

My second reaction was to reach cautiously for the Orb in my own pocket. Before I even got it out, I could see the glow through the fibres of my jeans.

It didn't burn to touch or anything. It wasn't even warm. The light that crackled across each spoke didn't hurt my eyes either. It was like staring up close at a cinema screen or something. As I watched, transfixed, the light became steadily more intense. So bright that it blotted everything else out around me; the muddy path, the hedges, the sky above, even Simon who was practically right next to me.

For a moment it might have just been me and the glowing Orb floating alone in space. No body, no thoughts, no memories, just a warm buzzy feeling. It was beautiful. Like the sensation of floating in warm water. I could have stayed like that forever.

But nothing lasts forever.

And soon the light began to wane, and the bleak, dull world started seeping back. Eventually the Orb faded to a molten ember in my palm and I felt someone shaking my shoulders.

I tore my gaze away from the Orb and looked up at Simon. 'Did you see?'

He didn't answer at first. His face was pale and he wasn't even looking at me. He was looking over my shoulder. And then he whispered.

'The house.'

I turned, following his gaze…

…and forgot to breathe.

PART THREE

Rigpa Gompa

15

HAIL

Gatley House was washed in a pale milky light, but there was nothing about this building that resembled the dirty, run-down house we'd broken into the other night. It was taller and wider for starters, more than double its original size in every direction. Its walls weren't crumbling and stained with graffiti. They were washed a brilliant white. Previously, its six boarded-up windows looked blindly out at its overgrown lawn, whereas now there were three rows of six windows, each outlined in red paint, with golden silk billowing around them.

For a moment another cloud covered the moon. I expected the illusion to fade—just like the Orb had done—for the old wreck to appear again, back to its ramshackle self.

When it didn't, I tried to blink the illusion away.

But those imposing walls remained.

That thing I said about how the universe was just a row of dominoes? Well, this building was like a brand new tile. And it was just standing there bold as anything at the head of its very own row.

I don't remember exactly what we did next, but we must have climbed over the gate—if the gate was even there—in a sort of daze, because we were suddenly standing at the base of five wooden steps which lead up to a porch held up by rickety wooden pillars. There was no board covering the door. No padlock either, and there was that drumming sound I'd heard the other night coming from inside.

Did I believe what I was seeing and hearing? I honestly don't know. If it hadn't been for the Orb that still spat tiny embers of white light along its central rod I probably would have just assumed I was going mad and backed off. But that, and the fact that Simon was there too, drew me on.

I don't remember being afraid. The only thing on my mind was to keep moving forward. Simon must have felt the same because he reached for my fingers and together we climbed towards the sound of the drums. Each step upwards as unreal as the next.

We reached the porch and stopped. *It's an illusion,* I told myself. *When you touch it, your fingers will go right through, just like they went through the old man the other night.*

So I did. I reached out to touch the beams holding up the porch, waiting for the vision to dissolve or something.

'Esta,' Simon said, holding his own hand out to stop me. 'Wait.'

I glanced at him. What was to fear? It was just a piece of wood.

I raised my eyebrows and touched it.

The wood was smooth and old.

I took a careful step toward the door. Would it open? It looked as broad and heavy as a barn door. Something stopped me from touching it. Sometimes doors should stay shut. I knew that much.

To the left of the door a shape was drawn on the wall. I leaned over for a better look. It was a painting of a fierce creature like the ones I'd seen on the walls inside—this one was surrounded by cartoonish flames and clouds. I inched closer. The image seemed to brighten. Two burning eyes glared out at me from the wall. A third eye flamed in the middle of its forehead. A fanged mouth bit down on the upper part of a large circle that was large enough to cover almost the rest of the thing's body. A set of claws gripped the edges of the circle.

I didn't like it. Staring at the thing's eye made me cringe. Like the visual equivalent of sucking on a raw lemon. But even so, it drew me in.

I leaned forwards, examining the circle beneath it. Dividing lines came out from its centre, like the spokes on a bike wheel, splitting the circle into six segments. Figures filled each one, but no matter how hard I stared, the details kept blurring. My head started to throb, and I got the feeling that if you looked into them too long, those fiery eyes would suck you in.

If this was what Dad had seen, no wonder he'd started behaving strangely.

A deep rumble echoed against the walls, vibrating the platform we stood on. I tore myself away from the painting. Simon was looking up at the sky. Beyond him was just a black expanse. No driveway, no hedge, no gate.

'I don't like any of this,' he said.

The rumbling noise dwindled to nothing, leaving an eerie silence in its place, just the *shushing* of a breeze whipping up dust at the base of the steps.

'You hear that?' he said.

'What?'

'The drumming noise,' he said under his breath. 'It's stopped.'

'D'you think that's a good or bad sign?'

'Probably bad. Let's go.'

A feather of warmth brushed against my neck and I had the same feeling I'd had before of being watched from one of the windows.

There was a creaking, scraping noise behind us. We both turned.

The front door was opening inwards.

Simon pulled me to the wall so our backs were against the painting of the monster.

Flickering light danced against the floor. The sound of voices and footsteps. Shadows extended out and over the lip of the top step.

I held my breath.

Two figures shuffled over the threshold on to the platform beside us. A tall one dressed in a white monk's robe and a smaller one in scarlet stood in the doorway scanning the grounds.

'What is it?' the small one whispered. 'It doesn't smell like Mamos.'

'No,' the other replied. 'You shouldn't have opened the door,

Thubten.'

'I'm scared, Rabjam,' said the boy. 'What if it's him?'

I glanced across at Simon. He had the sort of wide-eyed, wide-mouthed expression of someone who'd had an ice bucket emptied down his pants. Kind of scary, but sort of reassuring that I wasn't the only one seeing this.

The one called Rabjam put his arm around the younger boy, 'No. We'd know if it was Mara.'

'How?'

'Because we wouldn't be here talking about it, would we?'

A rush of wind and a shower of dust billowed out of the door. A third figure had joined the two boys—this one dressed in blue robes.

'What are you doing outside?' a girl's voice said. She sounded angry.

'I smelled something,' the young boy said.

'What did I tell you? You stay *in* when you smell something, Tub.'

'It's not the black ones. This smells different.'

The girl in blue robes walked to the edge of the platform and stared out into the emptiness. All she had to do was turn her head twenty degrees and she'd see us. We were hardly blending in against the backdrop of the monster with the wheel.

'Thieves,' the girl spoke into the darkness.

I instinctively pushed the Orb deeper into my jeans pocket.

'Karma Chodron?' Rabjam said, joining her at the top of the steps. 'You should go back and play.'

'What for?' the girl replied. 'If we've got more thieves, I can take them out before they know what's hit them. Anyway, Lama la and Sera are still inside.'

'That's not enough. It's not safe.'

'Sshh! Can't you smell that?' the boy, Thubten hissed.

The three children became still.

'Something's close,' he said.

I tensed, every knotted muscle ready to fight or fly. There was nowhere to run, and I was too bewildered to fight, so I tried to dissolve into the wall instead.

It didn't work.

The three children turned almost as one.

'Thieves,' the girl said, her voice bristling with anger.

The three children stood in a line facing us while we shivered against the wall. The boy in white called Rabjam was in the middle, his arms folded over his chest. The smaller boy he'd called Thubten clung to the older boys' robes. To Rabjam's right, the girl in blue glared at us, her hands clenched into fists by her sides. 'Thieves,' she spat again.

Normally, this was the sort of time my insides would start to burn and the world would turn red. But standing there in front of those strange children, it was ice that crawled through my veins.

I could feel Simon's body shaking next to me. His breathing shallow. In the great survival choice of fight or flight, it seems we had both chosen: 'Freeze'.

Rabjam, shook his head. 'Even if they hadn't chosen—'

'Stolen,' the girl corrected.

'That's not what Lama la told us,' the small boy said.

'I know what he said, Tub.' The girl snapped back. 'He said there are *no* coincidences.' She turned her fiery gaze to the others. 'Why do you think the Mamo are getting stronger? The Vajra and Ghanta were our protection, and these thieves took them.'

Took them? I felt the lump of the Orb in my pocket. Had we stolen something important the other night? Right then if I could have unlocked my limbs I'd have pulled the Orb out and thrown it back at them. I mean, what was the thing to me, right?

I glanced to my right for an escape route while the three children argued. But there were no trees, no bushes, no Sleeping-Beauty-hedgerow surrounding us. Just a pale, smooth expanse smudging into pitch-black. Just like Simon and I had seen from the window the other night… *edge of the world.*

'But Lama la said—' Rabjam was saying in calming tones.

'I agree with Lama la,' the girl snapped. 'No coincidences. Ever since *she* came, we've been like an open wound. You suppose chanting, drums and incense sticks will keep working against an army of Mamo? You think it'll protect us against Mara when he comes?'

They had seemingly lost interest in us for the time being, so caught up in their impenetrable debate.

I elbowed Simon. 'Is this making any sense to you?' I whispered.

He shook his head slowly. 'They can't be—' his sentence died in his throat. The boy in white had taken a step forward, staring right at us.

'These aren't like the last ones, Karma Chodron,' Rabjam said. 'These are different.'

'It doesn't matter,' she said. 'The door is wide open. Seems like anyone can come through now.'

Thubten, looking braver now that the older children had the upper hand, sidled away from behind Rabjam and shrugged. 'Lama la told us to wait.'

'Wait for what?' she snarled. 'For a couple of thieves? We should be out there trying to bring back the Kila, not—'

'What's the matter?' A deep voice called from inside. A voice I could only just hear above a sudden, violent gust of wind and the pattering of rain against the broken stone.

Karma Chodron's face immediately lost its angry creases. She placed her hands together as if in prayer and bowed slightly. The others did the same.

'The Mamo will attack again,' the voice said, louder now as if the figure inside were approaching the door. 'What are you three doing out here?'

Karma Chodron spoke without lifting her head. 'We found the thieves, Lama la.'

The rain suddenly became heavier; thudding against the roof of the porch and kicking up the gravel at the bottom of the steps. Mist hung across what used to be the drive and the rest of the garden. Black puddles grew, forming a choppy moat around the front door. It gave rise to an unpleasant stench, like the background smell of fumes I'd sensed on the way to Green Gables yesterday. But much stronger.

'Come!' the voice said. 'All of you! It's not safe out here.'

Obediently, Karma Chodron, and the two boys, Rabjam and Thubten went inside.

My muscles unbuckled, and I dropped to a crouch as the rain clattered against the flimsy porch. It was all so real. The steps, the door, the children. And yet none of it made a shred of sense. How did all these people get here? What had they been talking about? Us? Really?

I tried to slow my breathing, stop my head from spinning. I had to collect myself and get the hell out of here. But as I watched, the rain became a raging waterfall, heavy enough to rip holes in the porch ceiling. And then it got worse. The dull thud of rain became the sharp crack of hail. Ice snapped at the ground like bullets, sending water exploding from the expanding puddles.

A voice cut through the din. 'You too,'

Simon and I both shuffled back against the wall, arms shielding our heads.

The new figure now faced us. An old man standing where the children had a moment ago. He was holding an umbrella which sagged under the weight of the hail. Beneath it, intelligent, narrow eyes twinkled in a wizened, brass-coloured face. A face I had seen once before.

The old man held out an arm and said in a gentle, almost sing-song voice that somehow carried, even against the rat-a-tat-tat of ice, 'You'd better come inside.'

Neither Simon nor I moved.

'Come inside, or stay out in the storm,' the figure said.

Wood splintered above us as the porch began to sway in another swirling gust of wind.

The figure looked up and then back to us, 'You think this is bad? Wait till they start throwing rocks at you.'

16

THE GREAT HALL

The door slammed shut behind us, cutting off the sounds of the storm. The old man, wider and taller than the others and wearing maroon robes, shook his umbrella, closed it and left it dripping against the wall by the door. Without speaking or turning to us, he shuffled into a large, dimly lit hall. One hand making a beckoning gesture for us to follow.

I stood my ground, letting my eyes adjust to the light.

The place smelled sweet and dusty, like perfume and cigarette smoke. A single drum played somewhere deep in the building. Dust drifted down from a low slatted ceiling. To my right, candlelight played against the walls. Monstrous shapes seemed to leer and dance at me in the flickering shadows.

I glanced across at Simon, who was as still as me. 'Did you know it was like this inside?' I whispered.

He didn't answer for a moment. He was staring towards the far end of the hall. 'I don't think we're in Gatley House anymore.'

Behind a veil of drifting smoke, a statue dominated the far wall. It was sitting cross-legged on a platform, but it was so large, its head disappeared above the rafters twelve feet or so above. Small square flags hung from its arms like bunting.

The old man waved at us again.

'Don't move,' Simon whispered, backing away. 'Let's just go.'

But did I have a choice though? Turn back into that violent storm, or follow this funny old man. Retreat back into the world I knew; a world where Simon's party was in full swing, a world where Dad was gone for good. Or I could step forward into this one: a world I didn't fully believe, a world I didn't understand. *But a world with the possibility of an answer.*

There are moments in life where you feel like you're on the edge of something. You could flip a coin and go left or right and you know the choice you make will change everything.

Jump, or stay safe and shivering on the slippery rock.

Behind us, the door rattled on its hinges again.

I turned. Simon had stopped his retreat for the door.

Standing in front of it was the girl in blue robes: Karma Chodron. Her arms were folded, her face shrouded in shadow. 'Let's get something straight,' she said very, very quietly. 'When Lama la asks you to move, you move.'

We stopped by one of the pillars about ten feet away from the statue. A row of silver offering bowls were arranged on a table in front of it, containing fruit and flowers. To the left of them, a wooden throne stood on tall legs, so that its empty cushioned seat was almost at head height.

The old man faced the statue, placed his palms together and bowed at its feet. The drumming stopped as he mumbled something deep and foreign sounding.

On the floor to our left were the other children. Rabjam and Thubten were already seated cross-legged, facing the statue, their eyes closed, lips moving silently. There was another one I'd not seen at the door, a girl—although it was hard to tell at first because of the shaved head—dressed in yellow robes. She held a long stick up in the air, an inch away from a drum that hung on its side next to her.

We waited in silence, interrupted only by the crackling of lit candles. They must have been burning oil or butter because the smoke climbed to the ceiling in thin black pencil lines and the air smelled greasy.

Then, out of the blue, Simon made a sort of grunting noise. I looked at him in horror as his face creased up. He raised his arm to his face as if shielding it from something. Then, with a nerve-jangling suddenness he sneezed full and loud.

The echo bounced off the stone walls, loud as a clash of cymbals.

I cringed and shut my eyes. The hairs on my body stood on ballerina tiptoes. After several seconds, the echoes faded. I opened one eye to see what damage he'd done to the silent room. Simon was bent over, his arm still over his face as if hiding some hideously deformed nose.

'Sorry,' Simon said from behind his forearm, 'it's the dust.'

There was an uncomfortable silence.

I looked across at the children. They stared silently up at us. A few feet behind me, cutting off our path to the door, was the sour-faced Karma Chodron. She was leaning on the umbrella.

I looked back at the old man and took out the Orb for him to see. 'We didn't mean to steal them,' I said, I straightened my arm, offering it to him. 'Please take it back.'

The old man cocked his head to one side, his eyes flicking from the Orb to me and back again.

'We're sorry,' I said.

The old man nodded gravely. 'Come with me. We don't have much time.' He turned, dipped his head once again to the statue's feet and headed off towards an open doorway at the back of the room.

The three kids stood up as one. I exchanged a glance with Simon and lest we forget her, Karma Chodron jabbed me in the back with the tip of the old man's umbrella.

We followed the old man through the doorway and then along a narrow corridor, deeper into the building. Simon and I side by side, Karma Chodron behind us, occasionally tapping the umbrella against the wall.

There were more paintings on either side of us. These ones drawn on cloth and hanging off the walls: dancing figures with long black hair and ugly, snarling faces; pot-bellied men surrounded by flames.

'This is weird,' Simon whispered, but if he was trying to keep the comment between us, he failed; the corridor funnelled his voice into contorted sounds: *is weird, s'weird, swee,* until it was lost amongst the hissing of our echoing footsteps.

'How long do you think they've been here?' I said under my breath. 'You said the man who owned the place went mad, talking about people who lived here. Maybe these are the ones he meant,'

He shook his head. 'There's no way we're in Gatley House. This hall is way too long.'

'What if we're underground?'

'We went *up* steps to get here, Esta. Remember?'

'Your dad didn't mention anything about passageways?'

Simon shook his head irritably. 'He wouldn't tell me stuff like that.'

At the end of the corridor we stopped at a winding stone staircase—the narrow sort you get in castles. The old man held on to a rail that was screwed into the wall and hobbled up the steps.

The wall hangings flapped in a breeze. Behind us, the corridor disappeared into murky shadow. Karma Chodron tapped the umbrella *tuk, tuk* against the wall. She was trying to look relaxed, but she was casting glances behind her as well. She was nervous as hell about something.

'Move it!' she hissed. 'They're getting stronger.'

'Where's he taking us?' Simon asked.

'What are you frightened of?' Karma Chodron replied. 'He's just an old man... what can he do?'

'Lock us in a room and torture us?'

She pointed the point of the umbrella at us. 'You want to follow him, or do you want to stay here with me?'

17

REMEMBERING TO BREATHE

The old man led us up another set of steps to a hallway with low doors down either side. I ran my fingers along stripes of red and blue painted on the walls and stopped at a series of painted images on the walls. 'Remember these?' I said to Simon.

He nodded silently, then carried on after the old man.

Eventually we reached stairs going down. These were wider. Wooden. And I recognised them too. They were the ones—I recalled with a cold shiver—that ended at a door to a floorless room with a meat hook for a lampshade.

The old man hobbled past them without a glance.

I stopped and grabbed Simon. 'We're back in Gatley House? This is the staircase.'

He shook me off. 'How am I supposed to know?'

I counted fifteen steps from the top of the stairs to the door at the far end. Instead of a wooden door, a curtain hung from the frame. The old man lifted it and beckoned us inside.

The room glowed with candlelight. It was the same size as the one in—what I was fast beginning to think of as—'my version' of Gatley House; the same heavy curtains covered the windows, the same warped floorboards. But this room had three tables: A low one under the window with a large flask, three china cups and a bowl of ripe bananas; a smaller, squarer table to the left—some sort of shrine—with seven bowls placed in a row in front of a small golden statue; and a higher table to the right with rows of gleaming objects.

Two of the rows had a gap.

'Please sit,' the old man said.

I tore my gaze from the table. He was pointing at two cushions on the floor in front of the low table.

'Tea?' he asked and poured steaming brown liquid into the two cups.

Simon sat and took his in both hands. He looked like he'd sort of just accepted the weirdness of all of this.

The old man smiled at me, still holding out the other cup. He winked. 'You're doing pretty well so far,' he said.

I surveyed the room for some sort of clue. It *did* look exactly like the room in Gatley House. I glanced left. More painted figures hung from the wall.

'You're doing better than the others before you at least,' the old man said. He raised the cup a little higher. 'Drink. It'll help.'

I cautiously sat down and took the drink off him. The liquid was brown like tea, but little pools of grease floated on its surface. I sniffed. It smelt salty, like warm sea water. I lowered the cup to the floor next to the cushion without letting it touch my lips.

The old man took a noisy slurp from his own cup, never taking his eyes off me. He wiped his lips with the sleeve of his robe, then said: 'You call me Lama la.' He regarded my untouched tea. 'A friend used to tell me it tastes better if you pretend it's chicken soup. It keeps your belly warm.'

I eyed the drink, and glanced across at Simon, who was looking suspiciously into his own.

The floor shook, making the surface of the greasy-looking tea vibrate. Fine dust drifted from the ceiling causing the old man to raise his eyes, scowl and place a cloth doily over his cup.

'They'll be here again soon. I'm afraid there will be little time to catch up.' He coughed—a throaty mucousy cough, took a handkerchief from his robes, spat into it, then, disturbingly, opened it up and examined the contents.

'There are two of you,' he said, folding the piece of cloth away and rubbing his stubbly chin with forefinger and thumb. 'Do you know why you're here?'

'Because of the things we took?' I answered.

'We didn't have much choice,' Simon said, putting his cup down and looking behind him at Karma Chodron. She glared back from just inside the doorway.

'I'm not talking about tonight,' the old man replied. His voice was serious, but not angry. 'You *chose* to enter. You *chose* the objects on my table.'

There was a long pause while he inspected us. A guilty shiver travelled up my spine.

The old man leaned forward so his huge forearms rested on the low table. He fixed me with steady eyes. 'Do you know why you chose them?'

I looked across at Simon. He was staring at the old man, hands clenching and unclenching like he was squeezing invisible stress balls in each fist. 'They were just there,' he said. 'Bits of junk. How were we supposed…? You shouldn't even be here. This is my dad's place now.'

Something heavy knocked against the wall from outside, making the curtain vibrate with the force. More dust fell, coating the skin on my hands. Simon sneezed.

The old man glanced over his shoulder at the window behind him. 'I told you. We don't have much time. Karma Chodron?'

The girl bowed.

'There's no need to stay here. Go and join the others. They'll be needing you.'

Karma Chodron backed out of the curtain.

When she was gone, Lama la nodded towards the doorway. 'The children are talented, but these walls are weak. I have to know how much you remember.'

I had that horrible burning sensation in my stomach; the ugly feeling that usually turned into me pushing someone over or running out of a room in tears. I gritted my teeth. I wasn't going to fall apart tonight. I was done with falling apart for the time being.

'An hour ago,' I said, pointing to Simon, 'I was listening to Duran Duran, walking through his dad's house and trying to avoid people snogging all over the place. Now I'm sitting here with…' I held a hand out to the weird old man watching me silently from the other side of his table. 'You, who… I don't know, must have literally just moved into this place.' I took a breath and looked at Simon for help. Nothing doing. I carried on, '… and feeding us some sort of chicken-soup-tea thing. And *you're* asking what *we're* doing here?'

The old man didn't respond.

'So, I'd say the real question is,' I said, 'what the hell are *you* doing here?'

There was silence. The old man considered my question for a moment, but then smiled.

I held his gaze. He could stare at me all night if he wanted. I could do uncomfortable silences as well as anyone. I had Mum to thank for that training.

But he didn't have to wait. Because Simon snapped.

'She's looking for her dad,' he whispered. His words were quiet, but they spliced the air between us. They say words can't hurt. But those did. They stung like a wasp.

I opened my mouth to deny it. But nothing came.

'Is that true?' the old man asked.

I stammered something even I didn't understand, then shut my mouth.

The old man took another sip of his broth, while my brain clanked inside my skull.

I scowled at Simon. It's fair to say I could have strangled him then.

A door slammed downstairs—loud as a gunshot.

Other sounds multiplied and swelled from below. The drumming sped up. A muffled horn played a long, unpleasant note. Every instinct screamed at me to run. But of course, I didn't.

The man—without losing eye contact—dabbed at the corners

of his mouth. 'You don't remember anything?'

'Anything about what?' I said angrily.

'There'll be a moment before the next wave comes,' the old man said placing both of his hands on the table, pushing himself to his feet. 'Maybe this will jog your thoughts. Come. See.'

We both stood. My body tensed, ready to run or fight.

He held a finger up in the air. 'But be warned. When I open the curtain,' he said, 'try to breathe normally, OK?' He prodded the end of his finger into my shoulder, then Simon's arm. 'Breathe. OK?'

He was going to open the curtain? I glanced behind me in case Karma Chodron had sneaked back, ready to push us out of the window. But it was just us.

He reached for the curtain, looked at us. 'Are you ready? This can get a little intense,' he said, and pulled the material aside.

The clouds must have covered the moon again, because I could barely see anything at all. Just as before: no gate; no track; no garden. The overgrown lawn that should have been below us, the pond and everything else was shrouded in mist. I narrowed my eyes. "Intense" was hardly the word. The contours of the grounds faded in and out of view, as if they appeared behind a silk screen or something. I had the cross-eyed sensation again, as if at any moment my eyes would refocus and everything would come back again. I blinked a few times, but nothing changed. No gardens, no estate, no Fletcher's field, no diggers.

As we watched, a thin strip slanted out through a crack in the black sky like a theatre spotlight. Too bright to be the moon, too still to be the lights from a plane coming in to land.

The old man muttered something under his breath and touched the window with his forehead. The clouds shifted some more and gradually the strip of light widened in to a shaft of golden daylight.

Breath jammed in my throat.

Out there, just beyond a small courtyard and the outline of some kind of outbuilding, was what looked like a wall of emerald green.

As the sun expanded, the colours deepened and stretched away from me into a valley. A valley so deep it was impossible to see the bottom. Its slopes reaching so high they were coated in dazzling white snow. Clouds hid their peaks.

'Are you breathing?' The old man asked.

I shook my head slowly.

The vista outside warped and bent as I tried to take in the immensity of it all. It was like sitting at the front row at the movies. I had to move my head to take it all in.

Way down in the valley, waterfalls sprinkled tiny diamonds into its depths. Rainbows criss-crossed like bridges from one valley wall to the other.

'What happened to Gatley?' Simon asked weakly.

'Look up,' Lama la said.

Directly above, emerging from a cold blue patch of sky, was another rainbow stretching down towards us like some kind of gigantic multi-coloured slinky.

'And remember to breathe,' Lama la said.

The light grew so intense I had to shield my eyes from it. This wasn't like before with the Orb. This wasn't fuzzy and relaxing. This was downright terrifying.

The light engulfed us in a rush of icy wind.

And for a brief time, I went blind.

The old man's calm voice came as if out of nowhere: 'Welcome to Odiyana. Just remember to breathe.'

18

THE WHEEL OF LIFE

Dad used to take me to Bruntwood Park on our bikes. He'd lead the way, and I'd pedal as fast as I could to keep up with him. He'd wait for me at the top of School Hill, raise his arm and point straight ahead and bomb down the slope, yelling 'See you at the gate!'

There was a dip near the entrance and I had to bank right, change gear and stand up on my pedals to keep up my speed. I used to hold my breath and only let it out when I had made that little manoeuvre.

But one time… I don't know what happened. I turned a bit too sharply or must have changed gear too late or something, because when I pushed down, the pedal stuck, the chain jammed, the back wheel locked, slid underneath and I skidded into the grass verge. When Dad reached me, I was practically wearing the bike for a coat.

That's how I felt now. The cogs had jammed in my brain, and it had crunched to a shuddering halt. My body on the other hand was as light as a feather. And for a few moments it felt like I was drifting effortlessly in space.

My sight returned in a single, painful instant. Suddenly the mountains I'd seen from out of the window were sailing towards me. Their peaks now touched a bright coral blue sky.

I had to look away and made the mistake of looking down.

Way below me, the valley descended into black-green. As you know, I'm not one for heights and even though I seemed to be floating rather than falling, the gears in my brain clicked into panic mode.

I wildly searched for the other two, but there was no one beside me. And… for that matter, there was no one in my place either.

I mean nothing. No arms, no legs. Total 360-degree vision.

I waited for gravity to figure out what was happening. When I didn't fall, I tried to speak. 'Where the hell am I?' I croaked.

'Are you still breathing?' came a disembodied voice that sounded as if it were calling from way down in the valley and from right next to me at the same time.

I shook my invisible head, then remembered to breathe into my invisible lungs.

'Simon? Are you there?' I gasped.

'Yes,' came a mouse-like response.

'Are you seeing this?'

'Erm, I don't see my legs. I've lost my legs.'

'Don't worry,' said the calm voice of the old man, 'this is a mental projection. It's like a dream. Your body will take form shortly as your mind fills in the gaps.'

Right.

'So, what? We're still in Gatley House?' I said.

'You mean that place down there?' the old man replied.

Below, way beneath where my feet should have been, a square, white building the size of a matchbox sat huddled at the head of the valley, in the folds of another snow-peaked mountain.

'Not really, no,' I whimpered.

'Well. We're a little down there and a little up here. But don't worry, there's no danger while the skies are clear. Remember it's all—'

'In the mind. Yeah, I remember. It's not really helping though.'

'I told you it was a little intense.'

My invisible heart slowed a little then and my poor brain had finally figured out I wasn't actually falling, so it allowed me to take another tiny breath. I took another glance around.

A wall of dark thunder clouds gathered on the other side of the mountain peaks, threatening to break over and flood the valley in black.

And still we rose. Even higher than the mountains.

Soon the valley was just an emerald eye in the midst of a black, writhing ocean of cloud.

I took another gasp of air and tried to touch the place where my face should have been. I felt the faint brush of fingertips against my forehead. Then, like someone was drawing me in pencil, my whole body became a sketched outline, slowly becoming more substantial. Beside me, Simon was taking on a wobbly, indistinct shape too. I didn't know whether to be relieved or alarmed, because now, I could *see* us floating a couple of miles up in mid-air.

'Where is this place?' Simon said.

'Directly below us. That green diamond shape. That is Odiyana,' the old man replied. I could see him now, he was sitting cross-legged, just as he had been in the room, his purple robes rippling. 'An island in the storm; a training place for great beings; the doorway to the Pure Lands and the protector of the realm of humans.'

'OK,' I said without the least bit of enthusiasm in my voice. 'It's nice. Can we go down now?'

'Soon. First, let me show you the rest.'

Clouds separated and on either side of us, vast lands stretched out to the horizon. I'd not travelled around the country much, but there was no way we were looking down on Lancashire.

'You saw the picture on the outside wall of the palace?' Lama la said.

I remembered it—the picture of the monster biting down on a wheel and now as I focused on the scene stretching away in either direction I could make out divisions separating the landscape. *Just like the spokes of a wheel.* Borders created by rivers, mountains and other valleys, all meeting around the diamond shaped valley directly below us.

'It's moving,' Simon whispered.

'What is?' I asked.

He opened his arms up. 'Everything is moving.'

I looked again. It *was* moving. A vast turntable rotating, slow as a lunar eclipse, around the green valley we'd risen above.

'The Six Realms,' Lama la said. 'The Great Wheel of Life.'

I twisted round, trying to take in the enormity of it all.

Ahead, to the north, glistening and silvery in bright sunlight, was an enormous snow-peaked mountain. This one was far, far bigger than the ones we'd soared over to begin with. Foothills sloped away from it into fields and forests which in turn become steadily darker and more arid the farther they were from the mountain.

'Mount Meru. The center of the universe. Impressive, isn't it?' Lama la said.

I didn't answer.

The darker regions to the south came into view as the whole scene spun slowly beneath us. Here, the land was barren and scorched. Strangled rivers oozed through the bleak terrain. Even this high up, there was an unpleasant smell that rose from those streams.

And far below… it wasn't just the streams that moved.

'God, things are alive down there,' I said.

'I'm afraid so.'

'I think I'm going to be sick,' Simon said.

'What could live down there?' I said.

Lama la drifted across. His body radiant. His legs folded beneath him. 'Each realm is defined by the dominant emotion of its inhabitants.' He pointed behind him toward the green, flowing lands near the mountain. 'Those who are motivated by love, generosity and hope. And there are those whose lives are shaped by jealousy, greed, ignorance…' His hand gestured to the scorched earth directly below. '… and hatred.'

'I'd be dominated by hatred if I lived down there,' Simon grunted.

'The environment reflects the attitudes of its inhabitants, not the other way around,' Lama la responded.

Simon's face may have been a mental projection, but by the looks of it, he was planning to project something else. His eyes began to flutter.

'We should go back,' I said. 'It looks like they've got it bad enough down there without Simon puking on them from up here.'

'Very well,' Lama la said. 'Simon. Hold it in. You may feel a rushing sensation. It's all perfectly normal.'

Without warning, we plunged down at an impossible speed. Mountains reared up again and I think I'd have puked if I'd had the time… and an actual stomach.

We flew along the bottom of the dark green valley, past shining waterfalls, beneath soaring rainbow arcs.

At the head of the valley, nestled in the arms of one of the snow-mountains, was a small square courtyard and a white building with a curved golden roof.

The rushing in my ears stopped. I felt pressure against my feet and buttocks.

'Now both of you take a breath,' Lama la said.

I opened my eyes. We were sitting back in Lama la's room.

'And you'll want that tea now.'

19

BARDO

Outside, the clouds had closed in again, blacker and more menacing than before. Thunder shook the curtains, and jagged lightning momentarily lit up the room. The hangings on the wall ruffled and candle flames sputtered and died.

'Rigpa Gompa has been here for thousands of years,' the old man said, pulling the curtains together, 'and now a storm is coming.'

'Rigpa Gompa,' I repeated in a trance, my brain still reeling from the journey.

'Drink,' the old man said. 'It'll help you calm down.' He reached over and lifted the cup to my lips, just like Nurse Olive sometimes did with Gran. 'When you're calm, you'll relax. Then we can talk.'

I sipped. It was warm. He was right. It did taste like chicken soup. I tipped up the cup and downed it. When I finished, I held it out for more.

'So did we go somewhere or not?' Simon said, massaging his temples.

'You never left this room,' Lama la replied.

'So, it was in the mind?' I said with relief. 'It wasn't real?'

Lama la smiled. 'Just because it was in your mind, doesn't mean it wasn't real.'

'Who are you?' Simon said, wiping off a moustache of tea with the back of his hand. Despite his near-miss earlier, he sounded calmer than me.

The old man smiled and filled Simon's empty cup. 'I am the Teacher. But everyone calls me Lama la.' He looked at Simon and then me. 'And what are you calling yourselves now?'

Simon told him our names and the old man nodded seriously, then bent his head down and remained silent; as if he were contemplating the information.

Lightning flashed through a gap in the curtain, apparently waking up the old man, who leaned over and filled my cup again.

I blew on the surface of the tea. Little bubbles spun around, bumping against each other.

'Those people in the black lands,' I said. 'What were they?'

'Sick,' Lama la said. 'Sick with greed and hatred.'

'It looks like a cruel place,' Simon said. 'They were suffering.'

'A being chooses its reality by its actions. No one controls the system. It's just the mechanics of cause and effect. You've heard the phrase: "What goes around comes around"?'

'What you do… you get? Is that what you mean?' Simon said.

'Exactly. The law of Universal Justice.'

More thunder. And now a heavy flurry of rain hit the windows.

'And what's this place?' I said, raising my voice over the din of the storm. 'You said this place was different. An island in the storm.'

'That's right. Odiyana is a hidden valley,' he answered. 'In a time of great peril for beings, Odiyana will open and become a place of refuge for millions.'

The curtain moved behind him as he spoke. A gust of damp air made the candle flames stutter on their wicks.

'The nuclear accident in Russia,' I said under my breath, remembering Mum's radioactive clouds that were supposed to bring toxic rain. 'Is that now?' I asked. 'The great peril.'

Lama la twisted round and peeked through the curtains. 'Nope.'

'Then…' Simon said, '… why is it open then? I mean how come we can see it?'

The old man slid his palms over the top of his table as if cleaning it. 'That's the problem. It's opened too early,' he said, 'and in the wrong place.'

Fresh thunder shook the curtains.

The old man took another sip from his own cup, then pointed it towards me. 'He looked like you, you know?'

My eyes widened. I stared at the old man and finally found my voice. 'Sorry. What did you say?'

'Your father. You look a lot like him. He had nicer hair though; a little thicker than yours.'

The rain drummed harder. Inside, the floorboards creaked and the remaining candle flames wagged. But my heart, unheard by anyone else, was being played by a thousand drummers.

Sudden images of my dad tumbled freely like the rain outside. His beard tickling me when he rubbed it against my cheeks, his hair smelling of dust and wood and spices, the way he slid a palm over my face when I was in one of my tantrums: *Turn that frown upside down, Esta Brown',* dozing on his lap while he read a newspaper that was bigger than me, rustling it whenever he turned a page.

A new memory came then; or maybe it was a really old one.

The wind ruffled Dad's shoulder-length hair, sea spray plastered his beard to his face. In the distance, grey cliffs bounced at his back. He was steering a little motor boat. His pale green eyes stared out past me. Over my shoulder. Staring into the horizon. *Dad?*

A loud, inhuman screech pierced the air, shocking me back to the present. The curtain billowed inwards, clattering Lama la's cup to the floor.

'That's not good,' he said and got up to peer at the pool of spilt tea. 'We have to move. You can't stay here.'

'Wait,' I said. 'My dad?'

Simon was already on his feet though. He pulled at my arm, looking nervously at the window. 'Not now, Esta. I don't think whatever made that noise is friendly.'

The old man picked up some of the fruit, stuffed it in his robe and shuffled us away from the window. 'The bardo is stretching. We have less time than I thought.'

There was another howl, cold, hollow and as desperate and sad as an unanswered baby's cry.

'Where's my dad?' I asked as we moved. But even I couldn't hear my voice over that depressing wailing. I grabbed the old man's robes and shouted: 'Where is he?'

The old man glanced at the dancing curtains, then back at me. 'We really must go. That's not a normal storm. They get worse and worse each time.'

Another screech—this one an angry one—came with a blast of freezing air that shattered the window into dust. Hailstones followed it. Ice the size of pebbles smashed through the curtain.

'Go!' Lama la shouted, shoving us through the door curtain, out into the landing.

Simon ran to the stairs. Lama la made to follow, but I grabbed him, ignoring the squealing coming from the room. 'Please? Tell me how I find him.'

He placed a hand on my shoulder. His eyes were dark, and the lines in his face deep. 'I'm sorry. The bardo should have closed long ago, the connection is more disordered than ever before and Mara feeds on uncertainty.' With that, he headed for the stairs.

I stood and watched him hobble away, hailstones snapping at my ankles.

'None of that makes any sense!' I shouted. 'You know that, don't you?'

Lama la stopped mid-step, he tipped his head to one side. 'Which bit?' he shouted back.

'All of it! Everything that's happening. This house. Those worlds you showed us. That noise… All those… those words you just said?'

I held out my arms and gave him my *what-the-hell-are-you-talking-about?* look.

'Oh. I see.' He pointed down the staircase. 'Could we maybe talk about that elsewhere?'

A massive hailstone the size of my fist blasted through the doorway and smashed against the wall. I wasn't going to argue with that. So I ran.

It was quieter in the stairwell. The screams faded out as we descended. When we were half way down, the old man stopped.

'Tell me.' I said.

'What do you want me to say?'

'What has all this got to do with my dad?'

'Ah, yes. That.' Lama la said, scratching the nape of his neck. 'I will tell you, Esta. In time. There are things to know first before we come to that. Things you have to understand. Can you wait?'

There was a loud flapping sound above us. Lama la looked towards the landing. 'Let's walk and talk, shall we?' he turned and continued down the stairs. I joined him. 'What do I have to understand?'

'The valley is open. But it shouldn't be. It was opened too soon and now… it has created a bardo. A sort of middle state,' he said. 'Like a bridge that connects two worlds. Or,' he patted the bannister, 'like a staircase between two floors.'

We turned the corner. The sound of drumming increased.

'The space between two moments cannot last forever,' Lama la continued, his voice rising above the drums. He reached for the curtain, 'There is a beginning, a middle and an ending. The bardo is the middle. But it should *end*. The longer it stays open, the greater the connection between worlds. If the demons of the desire realm break through, then… then…' He bowed his head and sighed.

We reached the bottom of the staircase. Simon was rooted to the spot, facing another curtained doorway, his head cocked to one side. In Gatley House that doorway led to a room missing a floor, a razor-straight line of rope. A hook.

The ceiling rumbled like it was hungry.

Lama la reached for the curtain.

'Wait!' Simon grabbed the old man's arm. He looked at me with desperate eyes. 'This is where Charlie fell through the floor. How do we know same thing won't happen to us?'

Another pitiful howl wailed from above. It was closer now. Whatever it was, it was definitely *inside*.

Lama la pointed back the way we'd come with his free hand. 'You want to wait out here to see if they make it down the stairs?'

Simon didn't budge. 'Tell me what the *hell* is going on!' he shouted. 'In words I can understand. Or I'm not moving.'

'You as well? So many questions. Can we please get inside first? This is not the time or the place. Mara—'

'No!' Simon said firmly. He shook his head. A crazy, slightly unhinged grin spread across his face. 'What is Mara? Is that a person? A thing?'

Lama la blew out. I recognised the expression that flashed across his face. Mum did the same thing when she was trying not to shout at me when I was being particularly annoying.

'Mara,' he said, glancing back up the staircase, 'is the embodiment of hatred, confusion, and greed. He's a black cloud over the sun. Blinding and binding us.'

Thunder shook the walls as if agreeing with him.

'He's the storm?' Simon said in the sudden hush.

'Mara wears many faces,' Lama la replied. 'That's his best trick.'

'What does he want?'

The old man tried to side-step Simon, 'We really should be going through that door.'

Simon blocked him. 'No. Tell me.'

Lama la glanced behind us at the stairwell. Then bowed his head toward Simon and spoke slow and carefully, like he was telling a young child why they couldn't eat the *whole* cake. 'He wants to grind us into dust.' He took another deep breath, wiped his brow, pointed up the stairs with a shaking finger. 'Those noises you can hear are the Mamo. They used to be bound to protect us, but they've broken their vows. Mara has unbound them, and now they bring only pollution, disease and corruption. So stay out here and say "Hello" if you want…' he pulled his arm free from Simon's grip. 'But I'm going in here to get away from them.' He reached for the curtain again. Simon didn't stop him this time and the old man flung it aside.

This room had a floor.

And there was no hook. Instead there was a huge golden head. Fierce red-rimmed eyes and snarling lips glared at us from it.

The old man patted my arm. 'Nothing to fear,' he muttered. 'This is Padmakara. The Lotus-born. They won't come in here. Stay or come, whatever you want.'

Needless to say, neither Simon nor I wanted to be the welcoming committee for whatever a Mamo was.

20

THE GOLDEN PACKAGE

Lined up before the chin of the enormous golden face were seven large metal offering bowls. Garlands of flowers hung over its huge ears. Curls of painted black hair spilled over its shoulders from underneath some kind of crown. Clutched in its raised right hand was a giant-sized version of my Orb.

Lama la dropped the curtain behind us and went over to the statue. I looked at the material that separated us from whatever was making the noises and was not filled with confidence.

The drumming paused somewhere below us. A cymbal crashed. The horn answered in one long, clear note.

I sidled towards the row of bowls, testing each floorboard as I went. Just in case. I was mostly on board with this new world thing. But you can never be too careful when it comes to parallel realities, can you? That had become a new rule.

I peered down into the hall below. Sitting in front of the giant statue's lower body were the children—Karma Chodron included—in their different coloured robes. They were reading off thin oblong sheets of paper. The girl in yellow robes hit her drum. The others started chanting in time with it.

'Why are they still singing when we're being attacked?' Simon asked.

'They are trainee *Dharmapala*,' the old man said without looking round. He was tracing a finger along a strand of the statue's hair, like he was testing for dust. 'It's their job to help protect this place from Mara.'

The thunder rumbled on. The drums beat as if in competition

with it. The Dharmapalas kept up their rhythmic chanting. There was another thump against the ceiling. Simon and I looked at each other and then up.

'That's no hailstone,' I whispered.

Whatever it was scraped along the floor over our heads.

Simon scanned the room. 'There's no way out,' he said.

I peered over the offering bowls again. 'Unless we climb down the side of that statue.'

The hard floor was a good fifteen feet below. The sides of the statue were made of smooth metal—no secure footholds.

'We'd break our necks.'

We shared another look. I was sure we were thinking the same thing. *Is that what happened to Charlie?*

I stepped away from the drop, shaking my head. 'Lama la. Is there anything we can do?' I asked.

The old man held up a finger for silence. His face red with frustration. 'This is useless. It should be here.'

'What's wrong?'

He pinched the bridge of his nose, then paced to one side of the room. 'I've been banking on it being there,' he said, when he reached the far wall. He spun round and paced back. 'It's supposed to tell us what to do when…' he stopped when he reached me, tilted his head and squinted. 'In case of…' His eyes slowly widened. 'Of course!' He pulled me over to the statue's head. 'You should do the looking,' he said with enthusiasm, pushing my hand upwards.

'What for?'

'I don't know. Anything out of the ordinary!'

'But *everything's* out of the—'

'Just look for something. And you,' he let go of me and waved to Simon. 'Come over here. You look too. Search the walls.' The tone of his voice was so excited that we both started searching, for god knows what. The scraping, sliding noise above moved again. Something large had made it to the landing upstairs. Surely it was only a matter of moments before it reached the stairs.

'Lama la? Shouldn't we—'

'Keep looking!' he snapped, tipping up a bowl, spilling water over my shoes. Then another, this time scattering dried rice over the table.

I went back to running my hands over the hair of the statue. *What the hell were we doing?* I touched the smooth cheeks of the golden face while listening out for the horrible slithering, scraping sound of the thing that had come through the window. Simon was on his knees, patting the walls. 'Dream or not, if that thing makes it to the stairs, I'm out of here,' he mumbled.

'It has to be somewhere!' Lama la growled, swiping all the objects from the shrine table to the floor. The table wobbled, knocking my hip and unbalancing me. I almost dived right over the railing to the floor below. I flung out a hand, clinging on to an enormous earlobe to stop myself.

My fingers touched something soft inside the ear.

I recoiled in disgust,

Once I'd decided it wasn't a hibernating creature or some kind of statue version of ear wax, I tugged at it. A corner of gold material appeared. I gripped it with both hands and leaned back. A thin package about the length of my forearm slid out of the earlobe, and I fell backwards. The room exploded in a sparkle of white as my head hit the floor.

Everything stopped. The drums, the chanting, the rumbles of thunder.

I lay for a second, wondering if the fall had made me deaf.

Then the thing above us moved again. It made a slithering *FFFT* sound followed by a *THUD*. Whatever it was, it was heavy, and it was getting closer. On the bright side, at least I wasn't deaf. Every cloud has a silver lining, I guess.

'It's coming down the stairs,' Simon whispered. 'Can you move?'

'Get her up and out of here!' Lama la said.

'I thought we were safe in this room?' Simon said.

'Of course not! You think a cloth doorway and a statue would scare a hoard of Mamo?'

'But you said—'

'We needed to find the treasure. Now we have it, we have to get out of here. Go left. I'll meet you at the stairs.'

Simon hauled me to my feet and we were out of the shrine room before I took a breath.

A high-pitched scream tore like a freight train from above, funnelling down the stairwell.

'The stairs!' Lama la called pushing us along.

We reached a door at the end of the hallway. If the layout was anything like the other version of Gatley House, it would open up to the stone steps that led down to the basement. Lama la nudged past and wrenched the door open. The staircase descended into darkness.

The scream came again and the walls shook. Splinters of wood and stone scattered around us. The ceiling groaned and a road-map of hairline cracks appeared in the plaster.

'They've never been this bad,' Lama la muttered, backing away from the stairs and pushing me aside. 'You two go ahead before the whole thing falls in.'

Simon didn't hesitate. I did. I wished I hadn't. Shadows slithered along the walls towards us like the fingers of a giant hand.

The old man pulled a string of beads over his head and gripped them tightly. 'Don't worry. I'll deal with them. You go down.'

'But—'

The old man raised a finger. 'I need to concentrate.' Then he prodded me in the shoulder, sending me down the first few steps.

I saw Lama la turn to face the advancing shadows. There was a flash of red.

Then the door slammed shut.

21

THE VAJRA AND BELL

I avoided breaking my neck by dropping the golden package and grabbing on to Simon instead, and then we were down into the darkness. At the bottom, we turned and stared up at the door.

Red and orange light flashed through the gaps in the frame as if there was a raging fire on the other side.

The drumming was louder down here. It shook the ground beneath us, and the walls shuddered with it. The door rattled madly on its hinges and we staggered backwards against the wall.

The bright orange light intensified, creating a molten outline of the door. Just as it looked like it might be consumed in lava, it slammed open and a howling wind blew hot dust into our faces.

Burning red flames filled the doorway.

Simon whimpered.

I pushed myself further into the wall. The flames roared, then subsided into grey.

The deafening noise of the drums stopped.

Standing in the spot where the flames had been was the silhouette of a figure. It brushed itself down. Then it coughed, bent down and picked something up.

'We're safe for now,' Lama la's voice said as he replaced the string of beads back over his head. He hobbled down the stairs, holding the wall for balance. 'All this running around is making my knees ache,' he said. When he reached the bottom, he handed me the golden package. 'Here. You dropped this.'

I kept my distance from the old man as he joined us. Sure, he had dodgy knees and a hacking cough… but he had also just stepped out of a wall of fire unharmed, so… due caution and everything.

The old man pulled a blue plastic lighter from inside his robes and lit a tall candle. To be honest, by then, I was half expecting him to light it with his fingertip. We watched quietly together in the newly hushed room as the candle flame reached tall and straight. Even though my heart was still using my ribs as a punching bag, something about the stillness and quietness of the light calmed me.

I took a slow breath.

The cold, stale air smelled familiar. It smelled like… like the basement in Gatley House.

Were we still somehow *in* that old place? Even now, I can't tell you. But if we could travel miles up in the sky and never leave the room, then *couldn't* we still somehow be in Gatley House as well?

I looked around at the dingy room. The geography of the building was mostly identical: the landing, the stairs, the size and location of each room. But the large hall with its statue? That wasn't even close. And then there was the passageway through to the back of the building. *Not completely the same… not completely different either, though.*

'What,' Simon said, after a minute of contemplating that strangely hypnotic flame. 'The bloody hell.' He spat grit from his mouth. 'Was that?'

Lama la lit another candle, obviously over his little panic from upstairs. 'Everything passes,' he sighed, as if that might answer Simon's question. 'Do you remember anything yet?'

'Are they gone? Are we safe?'

The old man placed a finger to his lips. 'How many cycles has it been, I wonder?' he asked himself. 'The connections are strong… but there have been many lives lived in between.' He fixed me with a steady eye, 'You don't remember. But you aren't like the others.

You *see,* like they did. But you two both passed the test.'

'What test?' I said. 'Did my dad see? Did he—'

Lama la shushed me. 'Please. We'll get to your father. First—'

'Yeah, yeah,' I said impatiently, 'Stuff to know first. I remember.'

He nodded, then turned pointed to Simon. 'You chose the Ghanta: the bell,' he moved his finger to me, 'and you: the Vajra.'

I felt the thing I called the Orb against my thigh.

Simon took out the hand-bell from his pocket and held it up to the candlelight. His hand was still shaking.

'What do you know of it?' Lama la asked.

Simon shrugged. 'The girl outside said we stole them. She said that's why whatever that thing up there was, is attacking. She said we did something by separating them. Is that true?'

'A bit true. She's right about not separating them for too long. Your objects belong together or they won't work properly.'

I slipped the golden package inside my jacket and took out the Orb. 'What won't work properly?' I asked, looking at my object again with renewed interest. *So it did something?*

'The Vajra and Ghanta are like the wings of a bird,' Lama la replied. 'A bird can't fly with only one wing. Each object has limited power by itself. But together… Very powerful.'

'So, they're weapons?'

'They can be. But… Give them to me for a second.' He took my Orb in his right hand and, reluctantly I noticed, Simon handed him the bell.

Lama la held them both to his chest. 'They belong together. This,' he lifted the Orb, 'represents compassionate action. It is the thunderbolt of the Gods. And this,' he held up the bell, 'represents the wisdom that sees the true nature of reality itself.' He handed them back to us. 'Wisdom and compassion. Mind and body. Tea and cake. Now. Where is that handle? They won't stay away for long.'

I stared at the Orb before pocketing it again. *Compassionate action? What kind of weapon is that?*

'What was she wrong about?' Simon asked.

'What?' Lama la asked.

'You said that girl was only partly right.'

'Oh yes, of course. She's wrong about you stealing them,' he said.

'But we *did* take them,' I said.

He picked up a shard of plaster and held it between forefinger and thumb. 'I don't believe in coincidences. I believe in cause…' he dropped the shard of plaster to the floor where it shattered into fine dust, '… and effect.'

'You mean we were *supposed* to take them?'

Lama la wiped his palms against his robes. 'How can you steal something you already own?'

'No,' Simon said, shaking his head. 'I definitely never saw this before.'

'Me either.'

Lama la shrugged. 'Oh. OK. Then maybe Karma Chodron was right after all.' He held out his hands. 'Give them back and we'll forget the whole thing.'

I closed my fingers protectively around the Orb, I noticed Simon drawing the bell in towards himself.

The old man smiled and lowered his hands. 'I'm not surprised you don't remember. So many things have happened in between. You've both changed so much, it's impossible to know who is who.'

I turned the object in my hands, feeling the carved ridges, the smooth edges, and the weight. Maybe there *was* something familiar about it. I remembered the way it gleamed on the table like it was signalling to me. I remembered the deliberate way Simon chose his bell, that look on his face that had bugged me so much.

'How?' I said. 'I mean…'

He sighed again. 'You came back. You both came back after so long. I knew you would come. The signs have been good.'

'But,' Simon said, 'it's only been three days.'

'No, no. You don't understand me fully. You see, when a master dies they return to a new life to continue their training. We call these beings: Tulku.'

I searched the old man's face. 'New life?'

Lama la barely moved. Just raised his eyebrows a touch.

'What are you saying?' Simon said.

'You're saying we've been alive before?' I asked.

'And now,' the old man replied simply. 'You've come back.'

Neither Simon nor I responded to that. We just stood still and gawped at him in stunned silence. He, meanwhile, turned his attention to the far wall and started patting at it. 'I know, I know. It's a lot to take in.'

I thought about saying something, asking another question. But really? What do you say to that? If he'd been some bloke off the street, I'd have brushed it off as ridiculous, but after everything we'd just seen, I wasn't that confident about anything anymore.

'Ah ha!' Lama la exclaimed, yanking on an iron ring in the wall. He pulled open a door that had been concealed in the shadows. A violent gust of wind burst through the opening, slamming the door out of his grip and against the wall. A flurry of snow filled the room.

Lama la stood still, even though the gale ripped at his robes. He lowered his head, raised his joined palms and spoke something into the storm. The wind snatched away the words, but within moments, the snow drifted obediently to the floor and the wind became a whisper. The old man straightened up, staring out of the opening at the snow-blasted courtyard beyond. 'Come on,' he said. 'It's time to talk about your father.'

We emerged at the base of high white walls. It was cold, but the sun reached through the mists, revealing the slopes of the valley. The mountains on either side soared up into the swirling black clouds. I stood for a moment trying to take it all in. Everything was vivid, crystal sharp and *real*. And then there was the smell. Cold, fresh and earthy: the smell of ice, rock and trees.

I followed Simon into the courtyard, turned round and stared up at the old house. Except it wasn't Gatley House now, was it? It was *Rigpa Gompa*.

Lama la joined us. 'When you return to your own world, this will all become a foggy memory.'

'Everything's so clear though,' I said. 'How can anything so alive and real become hazy?'

'It's difficult to hold two worlds simultaneously in one mind. Only the great masters can do that. It will be hard for you to come back here. But both of you must try if…' he tailed off.

'If what?' Simon asked.

'You will find it difficult to remember everything. So I've left the most essential things to the end. Cling on to these if you can. Try to remember.'

'Remember what?'

He looked at us. One after the other. His eyes searching ours. Then he headed off across the snow towards the corner of the building. We followed.

'These two worlds have become entwined. And as I've said, that's not good. So it is imperative that we sever the connection between our worlds until the time is right. Do you understand?'

'You said you'd talk about my dad,' I said.

Lama la glanced across at me. 'We must undo the accident.'

I stopped dead. 'My dad had an accident?'

'Not that kind of accident,' Lama la said, not breaking his stride. 'More like a mistake.'

I watched the two of them walk towards the front of the building. 'Mistake?' I said under my breath. A cold breeze clawed up the back of my neck, and I moved again.

'You mean a mistake, like a coincidence,' Simon said. 'I thought you didn't believe in coincidences?'

'Oh. I don't. There are wheels turning within wheels. The accident brought you both here after all.'

I quickened my pace to catch up. '*What,*' I said, hissing between my teeth, 'has this got to do with my—'

This time it was Lama la who came to a halt. 'I believe *you* came here,' he said, 'to return the object *your* father took from us.'

22

THE KILA

'The Kila is a powerful ritual dagger,' Lama la said.

We were seated on the steps leading up to the porch at the front of the building. 'An implement that can be used to bind worlds. It's like a peg pinning two sheets of paper together. Your world and this one are like those two sheets.'

'Why's that bad?' Simon asked.

'I told you. It's the wrong time. The wrong place. And the longer we stay connected, the stronger Mara becomes. It's like a wound in reality, and he is like the bacteria trying to infect it. We have to fight him off every day while the wound is open.

To put it another way, this place, Rigpa Gompa, is a doorway between Odiyana and the other six realms. And Mara is knocking louder every day.'

'What happens if he gets in?' I asked, thinking about those shadows that had slithered along the walls of the landing.

'Rigpa Gompa is the difference between order and chaos. If we fall, then Odiyana falls.

'The connection between our worlds right now is disordered. The Kila kept the connection neat and tidy at least. Now your world is bleeding into ours, and ours bleeds into yours. And Mara feeds on the confusion.

'If Mara overcomes Odiyana, he'll be able to open the doors between *all* realms thereby disrupting the law of cause and effect and undermining Universal Justice itself.

'He'll mess with cause and effect?'

'If Mara wins, the wicked will prosper, the good will suffer.'

I thought of Mr Taylor's mansion with his roaring lions and fake pillars. 'That doesn't sound much different from how it already is,' I said.

'Whatever injustice there is in your world will be nothing compared to what Mara will fabricate.'

'Why don't you just… shut the door?' Simon asked.

'To do that, I need the Kila back.'

'Wait, wait, wait,' I said. Something had clicked, not something I fully grasped yet though. I stepped away. 'You've lost this peg?'

'Kila,' Lama la corrected. 'And, yes. It's lost.'

'Someone took it, didn't they?' I had an image of the distant expression in Dad's eyes the last few times I saw him. He'd been eaten up by something. Obsessed by it.

'So…' Simon said hesitantly. 'Someone stole a dagger from you and now the world is falling apart?'

'That makes it sound a little simple, but yes, that's about it. But we should never have been connected in the first place. This was always bound to happen ever since we were tied together.'

'My dad,' I said with absolute certainty. It was the only thing that made sense. Well, you know, *relatively* made sense. 'He stole it, didn't he?'

'He didn't know.' Lama la looked up at the sky. 'He couldn't have known what he'd done… He kept coming back, *searching* for something, like a thirsty man drinking salty water. But his sight wasn't as clear as yours.'

So that was it. I felt a dull weight sink in my stomach. After two years of wondering, here was my answer. My dad had seen all this. He'd been here. It explained everything. I should have been happy, or relieved at least, to have finally got my answer. But I didn't feel like celebrating at all.

'He took it,' I said.

'He couldn't have known its significance.'

'Where is he now?' I asked, not really wanting to know the answer. It's funny. It's all I'd wanted to know since he left, but just at the moment when I could almost touch it... it was the last thing I wanted to hear.

The one positive thing about uncertainty is that there's always hope.

Lama la looked over my shoulder towards the valley. 'He's still searching.'

'For the Kila?'

He returned his gaze to me. 'And he will never find it.'

There was a rumble of thunder down in the valley. The storm clouds gathered and swirled, like muddy water draining down a plug hole. I thought about the sound of screeching barrelling down the hall, shadows creeping along the walls. What chance did my dad have in a world like this?

'Why don't you help him?' I asked.

Lama la shook his head. 'I can't leave the Gompa. If I leave, the forces of Mara will attack and we'll be defenceless.'

'And the kids?' Simon said. 'I mean, the dharma whatsits?'

'The Dharmapalas? They're only children in training.'

'So, you've just been waiting?'

'Waiting... training. Defending ourselves from Mara's armies. Waiting for someone who can bridge worlds. Someone to bring us back the Kila.'

I turned away from the darkening valley. 'If my dad can't find it, how are *we* supposed to?'

'He's looking everywhere for it, but sometimes the treasure you seek is right beneath your feet. And anyway, he can't see like you two can.'

'Where would we even start?'

'I have no idea, but...' he pointed to the golden package poking out from the inside of my jacket, 'I don't believe in coincidences. It's time we took a look at what you found.'

I rummaged in my jacket for the package. 'This tells us? And you let it sit here all this time?'

'There's no time like the present.'

I began tugging at a corner of the package. 'You could have opened it. You could have helped him.'

Lama la patted the golden fabric. 'Only one person could find this. Don't you see? Only you could find this, Esta.'

I looked up, confused. 'Why me?'

'Because it is my belief that it was you who wrote and hid it.'

We sat down on the steps by the front door. I unwrapped the cloth with shaking hands, the old man's words echoing around my head. Inside was a single, oblong sheet of paper filled with spidery black writing. I squinted, trying to make sense of the scratchy marks. It looked less like writing and more like a lizard had dipped its claws in ink and scuttled across the page. I turned to Lama la, who was peering at it over my shoulder.

'Read it,' he said.

'What does it say?'

'You have to work it out. If I'm right, you wrote it many life-times ago, you hid it there and now you have found it again. You and only you can read it. That's how it works.'

I frowned, laughed and looked up at Simon so we could share in the ridiculousness of the moment, but Simon's eyes were on the sheet. His arms were folded. He was biting his lip. 'Read it,' he said when he realised I was looking at him.

I sighed and skimmed the page again, searching for anything recognisable. This time the ink marks *did* seem a little less chaotic. Maybe there were patterns with spaces between them. I tilted my head for a different angle. 'It's no good,' I said. 'I still can't make it out.'

'Listen to each word,' Lama la said. 'Let them come to you. Pacify your thoughts, let the meaning in.'

I almost laughed again. *Pacify my thoughts? This guy's hilarious.* My shoulders were in knots. My fingers were gripping the page so hard I thought I might rip it.

'Take a breath,' he said. 'Focus on your body. Let the muscles relax. Feel the sensations of the breeze against your hair. It's OK. Quiet your mind. Trust your ability. This place is powerful. Concentration is easy.'

I let out a breath, blinked and focused on the writing again. This time—maybe it was the sun breaking through the clouds—but the symbols actually seemed to glisten.

'Open your thoughts, the meaning will come,' Lama la continued. But his voice was distant now. The message on the page was suddenly clear. Except it wasn't just a message. It wasn't an instruction. It was a story. And it went like this:

23

THE STORY OF THE JEWEL ISLAND

'A long time ago,' I read. Each word moved and curled a little on the page, 'there was a young merchant called Me… Met…'

'Metok?' Lama la suggested.

It might have been. The words weren't English, but each one *suggested* something. A sound formed in my lips and it was only when I heard myself say it that I knew what I was reading. I carried on. 'Metok spent his life searching for wealth. One day he came upon a map which would lead him to an island made of jewels. If he could find a ship, he would have all the silver, gold, diamonds and jade he could want.'

I looked up. 'What is this?'

'Read it,' Lama la said.

'It's just a fairytale.'

'Whatever it is, it's for you. You wrote it. You found it. And now…' He considered the menacing clouds. 'You hurry up and read the damn thing.'

'OK, OK.' I found my place again, the letters arranging themselves like little soldiers in a line. 'Metok travelled to India to find a ship, and he gave the map to its captain, with the promise of wealth beyond measure.'

'They set off across the ocean. After many weeks of sailing, they spotted land in the distance.'

I frowned. There *was* something about the story. If it was meant for me… Well, it had to mean something.

A drop of rain landed in the centre of the page, smudging some of the words.

'Hurry, Esta,' Lama la urged.

I continued, more confidently now. 'The boat couldn't anchor. So Metok swam to shore. The captain agreed to pick him up the next day. Metok scrambled on to rocks made of diamond. His bare feet sank into a beach of gold dust. After months of travelling by sea, the young merchant was so relieved to be on dry land that he lay on the beach to rest. But when he woke, the sun had already sunk behind the horizon and thick, dark clouds threatened rain. The ship returned, and the captain waved to him from the deck, shouting, "The tide is turning. The wind is rising. We must find shelter."'

The writing stopped and lost the sparkle. I looked up at the others.

'Turn it over,' Simon suggested.

I flipped the sheet over. The same black scratches covered this side of the page too. I read on.

'With a glance at the surrounding island, Metok returned to the boat. The captain and the crew pulled him from the water before raising their sail.

"Was there gold?" they asked. "Were there diamonds?"

"There was gold and diamonds," Metok replied. "I saw them and touched them."

"Show us the jewels you saw and touched," they cried with excitement.

The merchant hung his head. "I ran my hands over the diamond rocks and felt the gold dust between my toes, but I did not bring any back with me. But don't worry, I will collect many sacks tomorrow."

But that evening the wind ripped the map from Metok's hands and the storm blew the ship far into the ocean. Although they searched for many more months, they never found the island again.'

I finished reading, and the letters became nothing more than dull scratches again.

24

CATCHING BATS

'What's it supposed to mean?' Simon asked.

'My dad,' I said, pointing at the page. 'This is where he is.' I turned to Lama la. 'You said he was looking for the dagger. This is where he was looking for it. This story is about him.'

The old man tipped his head from side to side—it wasn't a nod, or a shake. 'Sometimes the things we want are not the things we need and the real treasure is—'

'Buried beneath my blah blah. I know.' I stood up, impatient. 'He's lost.' I held the golden material, which rippled and unfolded in the strengthening breeze. 'Is there a map?'

Simon stood too, 'Esta, what are you doing?'

'He's alive,' I said, feeling heat rising within me. 'I have to find this island. That's where the Kila is and that's where he'll be.'

Above us, the clouds boiled and swirled. Simon shook his head. 'You don't know what it means. The old guy said you wrote it lifetimes ago…'

'No, Simon. If that's true, then clearly I'm the only one who *would* understand it. Don't ask me how. It's obvious. I need to find this Jewel Island. Lama la?' I held out the sheet of paper. 'How do I find this?'

Lama la took the sheet, stared at it and rubbed his eyes. 'I don't know. It may be that Simon is right. Maybe you're asking the wrong question.'

'I only *have* one question,' I pleaded. 'You said I wrote this story. That it's just for me. What's the point, if it isn't some kind of clue? You want the Kila, I want my dad. Don't ask me how I know, but they're both there,' I said, jabbing a finger at the paper.

'But Esta,' Lama la said, 'The Kila is somewhere out there in *your* world.' He walked down the steps into the courtyard. I hurried after him, snow whipping against my face as the storm grew. Lightning crackled, and the sun became a pale coin behind shifting mists. A bat swooped past my cheek.

'Tell me how to find this island. Then I promise I'll find the dagger. But if my dad is somewhere out there...'

The old man pursed his lips and made a squeaking, kissing sound. He withdrew one of the old, brown bananas that he'd brought from his room, unpeeled it and held it aloft. A breeze ruffled my hair. A dark shadow fluttered and landed on his hand; a small bat, munching on the soft fruit. Lama la stroked its head. 'Bring the Kila to me and your father will return.'

When the bat had finished, it clicked a few times then disappeared in a flash of wings up into the oncoming storm.

'I don't even know what one looks like.'

Lama la broke up the rest of the banana and flung the chunks into the courtyard. 'The Kila has a carved head and three sides that join at a point, like this.' He joined his index, middle and ring fingers together. 'I don't know much about your world, but there are flashes. Mara is not bound by the same rules as us. He has an advantage. As long as the connection between our worlds lasts, Mara will be able to operate between them. I believe he's already searching for the Kila in both our worlds *simultaneously*. If he finds it, he'll make sure it's protected in some way.'

'What does he want with it? To destroy it?' Simon said.

'He'll use it to widen the bardo. But even if he doesn't have it, it serves him to keep it out of my reach. It can't be far away though. At the moment...' Lama la curled his two forefingers together and pulled. '... the Kila acts like a hook pulling on a thread, distorting time and space. If it were too far away, it would rip a hole right through reality. No one wants that. Not even Mara. He wants to manipulate the connection between cause and effect, not destroy it completely.' The old man rubbed his scalp like he was trying to warm up his brain. 'He can't destroy the Kila and he can't take it away either, so he'll want to keep things as they are.'

'Which is?' Simon asked.

'Uncertain,' he replied. 'His greatest skill is uncertainty. Deception. He likes to keep us guessing. Likes to tease us. Give us hope. It's hope that cuts the worst.'

The clouds spilled over the mountains, rolling down the valley walls like volcanic ash.

Lama la pushed Simon and me towards the courtyard wall. 'If I can get the Kila back, I can close the door for good. Mara wants to keep us in this bardo. It's uncertainty that he wants.'

Mum's voice echoed inside my head: *It's the not knowing that kills me.* I reckoned I knew all about the bardo already. I'd been living in one for the past year and more.

'OK. But where do we look?' I asked.

'If he has it, my guess is he will hide it in plain sight. It'll be staring right at you. That's how he operates. But be careful; you won't be able to just lift it without some sort of sacrifice. Trust your feelings. You will know how to retrieve it when the time is right. Be brave. You are stronger than you know.'

Freezing rain spat against my cheeks, making me blink.

Lama la laid a hand on both our shoulders. 'You understand? The danger is from inside and the outside. Mara attacks us with demons here. He'll use other means in your world.' He steered us on to what now looked more like the drive of Gatley House. Simon pulled away and stopped halfway down it. Beyond him was the faint outline of the hedgerow and the old gate.

'Remember,' Lama la said. 'When you're back home, it will not be easy to recall everything that happened here. You will doubt your memories. You will doubt that two places can exist in a single location. You will doubt everything you have heard. But you must have confidence and faith that the impossible can be possible. You have each other and you have the Vajra and the Ghanta. They will remind you. When in doubt, rely on them and remember.'

Trees swayed above us and there was the distant swish of cars as they drove along the main road.

'Can you see this?' Simon asked, pointing to the overgrown lawn.

Lama la waggled his head. 'A little. Grass, trees?'

'So, what happens here... does it happen with you as well? What's the connection?'

Lama la looked up at the skies and drew his robes around him more tightly. 'Every realm lies on the next. Each one influences the other. Like when you draw on a stack of paper and it leaves an impression on the sheets underneath. That's how Mara influences your world.

Now go before they come back.'

When we didn't move, he shooed us with both hands. I backed away.

'Seek help,' he said, though his voice was muffled behind a wall of hail. A mist rose from the ground, swirling around him, almost rubbing him out of sight.

'Where from?' I shouted as the ice hissed and snapped at my feet.

'There are others who see.'

'What?' I shouted. I stepped forwards, but the hail battered the ground and spat shards up at me. 'You tell me this *now*?'

A voice drifted out from behind the hailstorm. 'I forgot. There was a lot to cover...' His voice was snuffed out by the rumble of thunder and the sound of Simon landing in mud on the other side of the gate.

Then the hail suddenly stopped. There was silence. A wind ruffled the rising mist like a hand swishing bubbles in a bath.

'Lama la? Old guy? Seriously?'

But, when the mist lifted, I was shouting at the empty, broken drive and Gatley House's boarded windows gazed back at me blindly from the end of it.

By the time we reached the estate, the moon had appeared again and flecks of rain sparkled on the ground as we picked our way through the mud. Neither of us spoke until we were through the row of boarded-up houses along Grover Close.

'Did that just happen?' I asked eventually.

Simon didn't reply. His expression was set, and he walked so fast I had to jog every few steps to keep up.

'Simon?'

'I don't know,' he said angrily, speeding up even more. 'I have to get back.'

My damp pumps slapped in the newly formed puddles. I was ready to grab him by the time we reached his street. Force him to say *something* at least. But when I caught up to him, his face was distorted into a look of pain.

'Oh no,' he croaked.

Blue lights flashed against the lions perched on the gates leading to Simon's house. Neighbours peered from their bedroom windows. One man stood at the end of his drive in his dressing gown, holding an umbrella and speaking with a police officer. He pointed at Simon, who groaned again. 'You should go,' he whispered, thumbing behind him.

The policeman adjusted his hat and crossed the street towards us.

'I'll call you tomorrow,' I said and backed off.

The policeman gave me no more than a glance before turning his attention to Simon. 'This your dad's house? It's alright, son, we've sent everyone packing and called your father. He's on his way now.'

I waited for a moment, watching Simon walk alongside the policeman, his head bowed.

By the time I reached home, my memories of the evening were as slippery as the greasy paving stones leading to the front door. We'd been inside a house, but it hadn't been Gatley House. There had been an old man who'd spoken to us. But I couldn't remember much of what he'd said. *He told me to seek help… others who see? See what?*

There was a pale light in the living room. I peeped inside. Mum was asleep on the sofa. The TV displayed a screen of silent, white noise that reminded me of snow storms.

Upstairs, I dried my damp hair with a towel. *What the hell happened?*

I pulled the Orb from my pocket and placed it on my bedside table. I squinted at it. It had a name. It had a purpose, but what? When nothing came, I stared through the gap in my curtains. Something had happened. I gulped. I'd learned something about Dad. A jigsaw piece had fit into place, but I had no idea which one.

The sound of footsteps on the stairs sent me under my covers. I lay still and quiet. After a minute, the footsteps padded away and Mum's door clicked shut.

I stared at the shadowy space where Dad's box of junk lay. *Tomorrow.* I'd sort through it tomorrow. I sat up and gazed out of the window. The rain had passed, clearing the air, so that stars now glittered down at me. I had scattered images of dark halls, angry faces and mountaintops. But they became vague impressions of shadow and light, and then nothing in particular. After a while, a solid thought emerged. Something I'd remembered from so long ago it felt like a whole lifetime away. That thing my Physics teacher said about the starlight. About how it takes thousands of years to reach Earth and how, by the time we see their light, they might have already died. *'So, I suppose it's all a matter of perspective'* he'd gone on to say. *'Depending on where you're standing, they both exist and don't exist at the same time…'*

I watched the stars track across the sky before they faded into the milky dawn.

PART FOUR

THE KILA

25

MINDFULNESS

'Keep your eyes closed, you're supposed to concentrate.'

It was Saturday morning. Mum had arranged two cushions in the centre of the living room. We sat facing each other, me cross-legged in my pyjamas, Mum kneeling.

'It feels weird,' I said. 'Like you're watching me when I close my eyes.'

'I'm doing it too, honey.'

'Well then, how do you know I had my eyes open?'

'I guessed.'

'I'm not feeling calm, Mum.'

'Esta. Shut up and be patient. Breathe and concentrate on the outflow of your breath.'

'Are you going to talk all the way through this?'

'In… and out… Breathe.'

'You are, aren't you?'

'Inhale…'

'I know how to breathe,' I grumbled.

This was beyond uncomfortable. I had barely slept last night, and I had a banging headache. Mum didn't look much better to be honest.

'Exhale…'

'I even do it while I'm sleeping.'

Her eyes snapped open. 'Esta!'

'This is pointless,' I moaned.

'I thought you wanted to stay in school?'

'I do.'

'Then you have to control your anger. That's what Mr Culter wanted you to—'

'Or other people can stop winding me up.'

'Meditation has been proven to calm and focus the mind.'

'Who by?'

'By… I don't know. India…'

'That's a country.'

'… and The Beatles.'

'Right. And you're an expert because you listened to Dad's Sergeant Pepper album?'

'I took a class.'

'You went to yoga for two weeks.'

'It's not rocket science, Esta! You sit. You count your breaths. And then you relax, for God's sake!'

I opened my eyes and uncurled my legs. 'Well, it's not working.'

'Sit down!' Mum pointed at the floor. 'You're doing this! We are sitting down and bloody-well meditating, Esta Louise Brown!'

'Oh. It's a middle name command, is it?'

'You're damn right it's a middle name command. You and I are meditating whether you like it or not, or I will *never* feed you *ever* again.'

'You don't mean that.'

'Of course I don't mean it!' she yelled.

I crossed my legs.

It took a few moments for Mum to get her breath back and for the blood to retreat from her face. Then we both shuffled uncomfortably through twenty breaths without any success. Mum got up, leafed through Dad's record albums and pulled out one with some long-haired hippy bloke on the front cover. She put the record on, dropped the stylus and adjusted the volume to low. 'OK. So forget the breath counting. Let's listen to *Tubular Bells* instead.'

I focused on the first few minutes of soft chiming and fluting, squinting through my lids from time to time. Then a strange thing happened. The muscles in my neck loosened, the knot in my stomach relaxed, my breathing slowed and the music faded to nothing. Images rose through the centre of my body like party balloons. Patterns, shapes and half-memories:

The party; meeting Simon on the track to Gatley House; a moon-white mansion; mountains and valleys filled with rainbows, shadows slithering along a wall.

My dad sailing on a boat looking for something across the sea.

I frowned. I had a vivid memory of the Cornish cliffs. I was young—five years old maybe—sitting at the prow of a little motor boat, tasting salt as sea spray streaked through my windswept hair. Mum was staring back to land, her face hidden. Dad, hands on the wheel, was staring out to the horizon. I smiled at him. He pointed into the distance, his eyes fixed: 'A storm is coming!' he shouted into the wind. I turned to see a bank of black clouds, like a range of mountains in the distance. When I turned back Dad was staring right at me with the wrinkled gaze of an old man. *'Seek help. There are others who see.'*

'Dad?' I whispered, opening my eyes.

The music had stopped. Mum sat with her head hanging low against her chest, her back resting against the sofa—she was snoring.

26

THE GARDEN SPADE

Simon made no contact over the weekend and he wasn't at school on Monday either. I had no one to talk to about what had happened on Friday night, so my thoughts became gossip chatting away in my head.

As usual, I sat on a table by myself at lunchtime, lifting and dropping strips of greasy meat on to my plate. I did the same with my thoughts about Friday night: *Why wouldn't Simon speak to me afterwards?* If only we had shared one brief word about it, then I could be sure at least *something* happened. But he'd not said anything. Was I sure he'd even been there at all?

The Orb dug into my thigh as it sat in my pocket. I took it out. It still gleamed. Gleamed just like a rusty hinge *doesn't*. That meant something, didn't it? I was sure it meant something.

I had this sense that Dad had been near, but I'd had those sorts of feelings before and learned to ignore them. Those moments where you think you recognise a stranger's face in a crowd, the sound of his laugh coming from a radio show in the background, his smell. He used to wear an aftershave with some Greek name: *Kouros,* I think. He'd splash it on in the mornings like they do in TV adverts. At bedtime I could still detect it on the collar of his shirt when he bent down to kiss me goodnight, or when he wrapped his arms around me after I woke from a nightmare. I'd rest my head on his shoulder and the scent would say: *Dad's here. Don't worry. Dad's here.*

After school, I walked—as I often did—to Gatley House. That undercurrent of diesel or sulphur increased the closer I got to

Fletcher's Field. The builders had erected a barbed wire fence around it and the place was full of machines that belched smoke into the sky. I walked around the perimeter of the field trying to catch a glimpse of roof or wall, anything to reassure me that it was still there. Still the same old run down thing. But eventually the road veered away and before I knew it, I was on the main road and heading for Green Gables.

The driveway was full of cars, including Mum's. The place was buzzing with people. Some were packing boxes, getting ready to leave. Everyone else was using it as headquarters for whatever name Mum was calling her campaign now. 'Ban the Bypass' or 'Put the Bulldozers to bed,' or most cringe-worthy of all: 'S.T.O.P'—Save The Old People.

Mum looked like she'd seen a ghost when I walked through the door.

'Esta?'

'I thought I'd say hello,' I said, trying to avoid eye contact with the nurses.

Mum's face broke into a nervous smile, and we almost hugged. 'Come see Gran, she's looking so much better.'

Gran was standing up when we entered her room. I hadn't seen her do that for weeks. She still seemed a little lost, but she was moving around, taking ornaments from the shelves and replacing them carefully. When she recognised me, she hobbled back to the bed and rummaged under the mattress for a one-pound note. Habit, I guessed. Mum placed a hand on Gran's, whispered something to her and lowered the old lady to the bed. Mum nudged me to the door, 'She's improving, honestly. You'd be amazed.'

I hung around for a bit, while volunteers shared out wads of S.T.O.P leaflets. I took a few, too embarrassed to refuse.

As I left, I caught a glimpse of Harold—the old man who'd accosted me at the front door—standing in the doorway of his room staring at the volunteers with a cold eye. Under that mop of white hair his face was dark and creased in what could have been rage, or maybe fear. A tear clung to one eye and when he saw me looking at him, he wiped it away and slammed his door.

Mum came out of Gran's room and clocked I was holding a pile of her leaflets. She grinned and gave me a double thumbs up.

I don't know exactly what made me do it. I could have waited, but my thoughts about Friday night were like a maddening itch I couldn't scratch. I had to know. I had to know what Simon had seen.

The stone lions stood in their frozen pounces on the gate posts. A blood red Jaguar—the car variety—was in the drive. Mr Taylor liked his big cats.

Lights shone through gaps in the curtains. Simon might not want to answer the phone, but maybe a knock on the door would work.

I paused at the gate, gripping the leaflets with tightening fists. I stuffed them into the open jaw of the nearest lion and made my way up Mr Taylor's drive for the second time, my feet leaving prints in the pristine stone-chip. External lights illuminated the walls. It was eerie, familiar somehow. I stood at the porch, closed my eyes and imagined Dad's face urging me on. *Feel the fear.*

I knocked and waited.

After thirty long seconds I bent and peered through the letter box. People were talking somewhere, but no one came to answer. I waited another minute before giving up.

Halfway back down the drive, a crunching sound made me stop.

I turned, expecting to see Simon. But it was a girl in a wheelchair. She had blonde hair like Simon's, but hers was shorter; her thin arms hung either side of her, resting against the chair's wheels. Her legs were covered by a tartan patterned blanket.

'I'm looking for Simon,' I said. But a voice was screaming someone else's name in my head.

The girl continued to stare. There was a sheet of paper on her lap, a couple of pencil crayons lying on it.

'My name's Esta,' I said.

The girl pushed the wheels, so she backed away. Her mouth moved as if trying to form sounds, otherwise her face displayed no other emotion.

'What?' I said trying to read her lips.

'Watching,' she croaked.

I took a step towards her and peered at the paper on her knees, 'What are you drawing?'

The girl let go of one of the wheels and picked up her picture, holding it vertical so I could see it more clearly.

A bolt of electricity shot up my spine.

A bloodshot eye surrounded by curling orange flames stared at me from the paper.

'Watching,' the girl whispered.

'Charlie?' barked a voice from the side of the house.

A large bald man was standing at the entrance to a side-passage. His shirt sleeves were rolled up to his elbows, his forearms were caked in mud. A garden spade dangled from his right fist, the sharp edge of it tapping gently against the wall of the house.

'Get back here, princess,' the man said. His accent was hard. The kind of accent I'd only ever heard in EastEnders, or films depicting London gangsters.

Charlie dropped the picture onto her lap, but didn't move. She kept her eyes on me and whispered something else: 'Did you see?'

Metal scraped on stone. My eyes darted back to the large man. He'd raised the spade and was holding it in both hands now. 'Who are you? Whaddya want?'

I backed away, my palms raised.

The man stepped on to the gravel. 'Speak up!'

'You're Mr Taylor... I was looking for...'

He raised the spade higher while he approached, pointing the edge at me. 'I know who you are,' he whispered. Reaching Charlie, he glanced down at her and pointed the spade back at the house. 'Go to your mother.'

'I'm sorry,' I said, trying to sound polite. 'I knocked. No one answered. I was just leaving.'

'You're his daughter, aren't you?' he said, small, black eyes burning out of his round face. 'I seen you hanging around that house.'

Something hard prodded my back. I glanced behind me at the lion I'd backed into, Mum's leaflets hanging from its mouth. When I looked back, Mr Taylor was even closer. He towered above me, not much more than a spade's swing away.

'Your father knew she was lyin' there all that time. And he did nothing!' The word came out as *'naffin'*.

'I don't know…' I sidled away from the lion. Mr Taylor had a wild gleam in his eye and his fists had tightened around the handle of the spade. A couple more steps and I'd be off the drive and could run. The guy looked like he could flatten me with one swing, but I bet he wouldn't get much past a jog if it came to a race.

'He brought his madness into my house,' he said through gritted teeth. 'He infected my princess wiv it.' Spittle flew out from his mouth as he spat the words.

'Dad!'

A shadow passed over Mr Taylor's face as Simon called from the front door.

'It's alright. I'll get rid of her,' Simon said, pulling a coat on as he jogged up the drive.

The man lowered his spade, so he was holding it in his right hand like a sword. He pointed it at me. 'Don't you come back here. Don't you infect my boy.'

Simon walked around his dad and reached for the crumpled leaflets I'd shoved into the mouth of the lion. 'Give me a minute,' he said, grabbing my arm and frog-marching me down the road.

'Get back 'ere, son!' shouted the man. 'Get rid of her and get back!'

27

DAMAGED

Simon stopped at the corner of the street, right where we'd been met by the copper on the night of the party. He swivelled round, holding up a fistful of leaflets. 'What were you thinking?'

I could hear the London in his accent even more clearly than ever: *Finkin.*

He flung the leaflets into the road, and ploughed on, forcing me to run to catch him.

'So,' I said, panting, 'do you mind telling me what the hell that was?'

'He gets angry.'

'Angry? He was going to flatten me with a spade!'

'Don't be stupid. He just gets emotional, protecting his turf.'

'That was Charlie Bullock.'

Simon stopped and raised his face to the sky. 'Please don't tell anyone, alright? She's not supposed to come round the front. When she's here she's supposed to stay round the back. I don't know what made her—'

I was dumbfounded. 'But how?'

'No one else knows, alright. Mum and Dad split before they came up here. Bullock is Mum's surname. She's not even my proper sister.'

'I always thought it was supposed to be a boy,' I whispered. 'What happened?'

Simon checked around us and sat down on a low wall. It was quiet off the main road and apart from a bloke raking fallen leaves off his lawn there was no one else around. Simon stared across the road for a minute without speaking. I waited, watching the wind picking up the gardener's leaves and making them dance down the street.

Eventually Simon sighed again and started talking.

'She had started working for Dad. She used to do sketches for him. Floor plans and stuff for his properties. But… I don't know. She started drawing funny things.'

'What sort of things?'

'Like that eye you saw. She was drawing stuff on the walls that wasn't there. Except…' he tailed off.

I pictured the monsters we'd seen that first time inside the house. I wondered if Simon was too because they were most *definitely* there.

'Dad told her to re-do her sketches. Made her draw out all the floor plans from scratch. So, a couple of days later, she took his key. Went in by herself…'

'Like you did.'

He shot a look at me. 'Why d'you think I needed someone to go in with me?'

The gardener dumped another pile of leaves into his black bin. He stared at us for a second, scratched his balding head, then went back to get more.

'Your dad must have known she'd taken the key. Didn't he tell the police?'

'Dad told 'em to search there when he found it was gone.'

'They didn't find her?'

'They went in the same night she went missing. They didn't find anyone, and there wasn't any sign of her anywhere else.'

'So…'

'So when your Dad found her in that house a couple of days later with her back all… you know.'

There was a long pause. Simon stared at the ground.

'*You* don't think my dad did anything to her do you?'

Simon raised his head and scowled at me. 'No. Course not. It's just that… Well, why didn't they find her when they first looked?

And how come your dad was poking around?'

'And what do you think?'

'My dad's convinced he knew all along.'

I almost exploded. 'That's ridiculous! He didn't even know her!'

'The police did tests,' Simon continued. 'Charlie hadn't moved since she fell through the floor. She was there the whole time. When she came back, she could barely talk. Never looked anyone in the eye. But... she wasn't hungry or anything. She should have been dehydrated after two days.' He sighed. 'I don't know. There were no other footprints. Just your dad's.'

I pictured Dad—not for the first time—finding Charlie. He never talked about it afterwards. Never explained why he'd been there.

A car crawled past. Yet another plane soared overhead. The gardener dumped more leaves in his bin, grumbling to himself the whole time. What *was* it with all the leaves?

'I'm sorry,' I said finally, turning back to Simon.

He shrugged. 'I wanted to see what she saw before Dad pulled it all down.'

'He bought Gatley House just so he could *destroy* it?'

'He doesn't own it yet. Some legal thing. He was going to do it up to begin with. But he says it reminds him of Charlie every time he drives past. Just looking at the treetops. Says it's evil. Soon as he owns it outright, he wants to flatten the whole site.'

I let my head drop. I noticed Simon's Hitecs had a line of mud an inch above the soles.

'Simon?'

'What?'

'Do you remember what happened on Friday night?'

'What I remember is the police. You should've seen the house, it was a right state.'

'Something happened. You know it did.'

'Between us? Don't kid yourself.'

'No.' My thoughts began to race. 'Something in Gatley House. I

162

can't put my finger on it though. I remember meeting you on the track. You fell in the mud. I remember... it started to rain. Then I remember the police at your house. Other than that, it's just flashes.'

Simon watched me silently for a moment, chewing on his lip, then stood up and shoved his hands in his pockets. 'The track was muddy. We came straight back.'

'No. I thought we went to the house again. Don't you remember?'

Simon closed his eyes and shook his head, then started off towards the corner of his road. 'You're not making sense. I have to get back. You heard Dad.'

'Why do things always have to make sense?' I called, getting up to follow him.

'Don't be stupid. Because they do.'

'You sound like your dad.'

'You don't know my dad.'

'I know he likes threatening girls with spades.'

Simon stopped. For a second I thought he would shout at me, but he just rubbed the nape of his neck and said, 'I have to go back. Dad'll have calmed down by now. If he thinks I'm out with you though he'll still kill me.'

'Wait.' I held his arm. 'I've been having these flashes all weekend. Something happened. You were there with me. You must remember *something*.'

He shrugged me off with a look of contempt. 'Hannah's right about you.'

'Hannah?' *As in Piranha?* I thought, anger blocking up my throat.

'Says you're...'

'I'm what?' A muscle in my eyelid twitched.

He stared at his toes. 'Damaged.'

My face went numb apart from the twitch in my eye. Heat welled up inside me, burning like acid, making me want to spit it out.

Simon scrunched up his face, then walked away, leaving me alone on the pavement. I squeezed the Orb in my pocket until I thought my fingers might bleed. 'Have you still got the bell?' I shouted.

He slowed. I thought he might stop.

'I'm going back,' I called.

But Simon kept walking.

28

THE GREASY SPOON

At the end of the school day on Tuesday, I slipped through the crowds of homebound students, lost in my thoughts. I was debating whether to go to Gran's or go back to Gatley House when a hand grabbed my arm, and a girl's voice said my name.

I stared at her for a moment as other kids streamed around us. She was the girl from the hallway at Simon's party; almost as tall as Graham with long, ginger—definitely not strawberry-blonde—hair in a ponytail. She wore a bright green grocer's apron over a white shirt and a pair of dungarees. On anyone else the work clothes might have been ridiculous, but somehow everything fitted and she carried it off with confidence. I could see why Graham was besotted. Despite myself, I already trusted her.

'Come on,' Lily said, leading me through the crowd. 'Graham's got something for you. He's in the Greasy Spoon.'

The Greasy Spoon—real name: 'The Teaspoon' served tea, coffee, all-day English breakfasts and not much else, and so probably deserved its nickname. It was on the main road opposite the grocers where Lily told me she worked. It was usually filled with older boys eating toast while discussing girls or football. Today, it was full of workmen in yellow vests. I'd never been inside. It wasn't a place you visited if you were a girl on your own.

Graham stood as Lily and I entered. He was in yet another ironed shirt although, thankfully, his hair was tousled and he wore a scruffy pair of cords. His satchel hung across the back of the chair and a large book lay on the table in front of him.

He'd already bought me a tea in a dark blue mug. I peered into it before sitting. A sliver of memory rose like a greasy bubble in my mind: *Salty tea?*

Lily sat next to Graham and touched his shoulder. I shot a look at him and gave him an appreciative smile which was supposed to mean: *Way to go, nerd boy.*

Graham gave a curt nod in acknowledgement and spread out the scrap of toilet paper I'd given him at the party. He looked different, more serious somehow. 'This is your object?' he said and shared a glance with Lily.

'Graham showed me the picture you drew,' she said. 'We had some time in the library and we reckon we might have found something.' She nudged him. *Proper little double act.* 'Show her.'

He opened the encyclopaedia to a page he'd bookmarked with a paper napkin, and placed his finger next to a picture, his eyes tinged with triumph. 'That's it, isn't it?'

My heartbeat quickened; it was a colour image of my Orb. I pulled the real one out of my blazer pocket and placed it carefully on the table. It wasn't exactly the same, but it was close enough. Next to it was a picture of the ornate bell Simon had picked up.

'It's called a Dorjay,' Lily said, picking up and examining my object with interest.

My brow creased. That name didn't sound familiar, but there was something, a vague memory.

'It says it's a symbolic ceremonial object from India,' Graham said, moving his finger to the text below the image.

'He called it something else,' I said distractedly, not fully aware of who "He" was, nor what "He" had called the object. I was attracted to another photo: a whitewashed series of shoebox-shaped buildings set into a cliff face, window frames painted red. Underneath was the label: *Tiksay Gompa, Ladakh, India.* I gasped as chaotic images paraded through my mind like a flipbook of cartoon drawings. A great hall, white walls, those mountains, rainbows…

'What is it?'

I pointed to the picture of the building. 'I saw that. Not that one. Something like that. And I think I… I think went inside and…'

'Steady on,' Graham said, leaning towards me. 'You're not making any sense. What are you talking about?'

What *was* I talking about? Simon and I had been on the track. His bell had started to glow and… the images rifling through my mind were nonsensical.

I let out a long breath.

Graham was staring at me with concern. 'It's OK,' he said. 'Say whatever you need.' He glanced at Lily. 'Don't worry. We'll listen.'

I sat back and ran fingers through my hair. How was I supposed to talk about all this stuff racing around inside my skull? I opened my mouth to speak, but then stopped. I remembered Simon's parting gift to me: *Damaged*.

Lily and Graham had found a picture of my object, but they called it by a strange name that didn't ring any bells and looking at it again, maybe it wasn't all that similar after all.

Lily was studying my Orb, comparing it with the image in the encyclopaedia. I tilted my head, blinked, crossed, then uncrossed my eyes and stared hard at it. But whichever way I looked, I just couldn't see it as the rusty hinge I'd seen in Graham's photo.

'Esta?' Graham asked.

I sighed. 'It's nothing.'

Lily interrupted me. 'Oh. Wait, it's got another name.' She pointed at some writing. 'Vaja?'

I sprang to attention. 'What?'

'Varja? It's the Sanskrit name for the object you drew.'

'Vajra!' I said, feeling warmth flow through me now. Yet more memories leapt from some dark place. 'That's what Lama la called it! Vajra!'

'Who the hell is Lamala?'

I don't think I could have contained it any longer. It must have been filling up like water in a dam, and it practically burst out of me. More crazy images from Friday night: The hail storm, the children in coloured robes, the old man, the valley, the bats. Gobbets of memory spilled out of me. I don't remember what order I told them or whether I'd remembered everything and I doubt I made much sense, but Graham and Lily never stopped me, and even though it must have come out as garbled gibberish, there was no eye rolling or smirking.

When I finished, sweaty and out of breath, neither of them spoke for a minute. They exchanged looks, stared down at the encyclopaedia, then back to me. I fixed my eyes on the table top, feeling like I'd just confessed to something unpleasant, like eating my bogies.

I picked up my tea. It was cold. I drank it anyway.

'OK,' Graham said finally, leaning back in his chair.

'Do you believe me?'

'Well,' he said, 'are you telling us the truth?'

'I have no idea. But if it's true, then my dad might still be…'

Graham and Lily exchanged another one of their looks, which made me not want to finish the sentence. 'I'm not just making it up though,' I said in a rush. 'It feels too real for that. It feels like it all somehow actually happened.'

Graham put a hand on mine, 'I believe you experienced something. What about Simon? Did he see the same thing?'

'I don't know,' I lied. 'Maybe?'

'What do you mean?'

'He said "No", but I don't believe him.'

'You believe he saw what you saw?' Lily asked.

'Yes.' I replied like I meant it.

'What do you think, Lil?' Graham said.

That comment briefly changed the direction of my thoughts. She was "Lil" already?

Her eyes were wide and bright, her face rosy, 'It's like a fairy tale.'

'Thanks,' I said glumly.

'No. I mean, I believe you saw what you saw, but a completely different world? Some demon who wants to…'

'Mess with cause and effect, right Esta?' Graham filled in for her.

'Yeah,' she said. 'Well, it's kind of hard to take in.'

'How do you explain the thing she drew?' Graham said, pointing at the picture of the Vajra.

'I'm not saying she isn't seeing what she says, it's whether what she's seeing is true, you know? Objectively. People see stuff that isn't really there all the time. I mean, your dad…' she exchanged yet another look with Graham, 'Your dad worked for the museum for a bit, didn't he? Maybe he showed you some of this stuff before. Maybe in one of his books?'

'But I imagined whole buildings. A valley, mountains…' I tailed off, a significant part of me knowing she was probably right. I swilled the remains of the tea in my cup, 'What about the tea that tastes like chicken soup? How do you make stuff up like that?'

'And it wasn't just her,' Graham added. 'Simon was there too. Two people can't have the same delusion, can they?'

My nose developed a sudden itch which I rubbed with the palm of my hand. If Simon was witness for the defence, I didn't fancy my chances. *But if he still has his bell that would be proof, wouldn't it?* I told myself. *Even if he denies it. If he sees a bell and not a door-bolt, then it's not just me.* And it was that thought that kept me from just shutting down and dismissing everything.

'You remember I mentioned…' Graham waved me out of my thoughts. 'Esta. Hello?'

'What? Sorry. Miles away.'

'I told you, we study this German philosopher at school called Immanuel Kant,' Graham said. He flicked to the K's in his encyclopaedia and showed us the image of a girlish looking man with one of those wigs people wore a few centuries ago. 'He talked about two worlds existing in the same place. The world of the senses—the world you can touch and see,' he lifted the Vajra and placed it next to Kant's face. 'And then there's what he called the *Noumenal World:* The world that exists beyond our senses. The world as it really is. But one you can't ever fully know or prove.'

I checked the picture of Kant again. *A world beyond the senses?* He didn't mean the world I'd been in though. I'd seen it, heard it, smelled it, and—I recalled the salty globules of grease sliding down my throat from the tea—*tasted it*.

Lily handed me back the Orb. 'I have to go back to work, but I want to be clear. We're saying you and Simon had a vision of some kind of mansion which is linked with Gatley House and your dad, right?'

I nodded. Hearing it out in the open like that made it sound ridiculous.

'You know what I reckon? There are three possibilities.' She tapped the tips of her fingers, counting them off. 'One: You're flat-out lying.'

'I don't think she's lying, Lil. You can tell.'

She slapped Graham's hand playfully, 'Wait. I'm considering the possibilities. This is logic, Gray. You of all people should appreciate that.' She tapped her middle finger, 'Two: You and Simon had your drinks spiked in that party and had a collective hallucination or whatever, or Three,' tapping her ring finger, 'Kant-boy over here is right. There are two worlds. There's a falling down house in one and a… a magical mystery monastery in the other.'

I smiled and nodded, but there was a fourth possibility she'd not mentioned: maybe it was just me. No alcohol required. Maybe Simon had not seen anything. Maybe it was just me being damaged.

'So, if we assume you're telling the truth,' Lily continued.

'Which she is.'

'Graham. Let me speak! Then we have to consider something odd is happening.'

'In which case, we'll need evidence,' Graham said, ever the scientist.

'Wait, I thought Kant said you couldn't prove the luminous

world?'

'Noumenal,' he corrected. 'And I didn't say he was right. Personally, I like facts, even if they are weird ones.'

I held up the Vajra: 'Exhibit one?'

'No,' Lily said, getting to her feet. 'Something provable. Something we can measure. Mull it over you two. I have to go to work.' With that, Lily kissed Graham on the forehead, turning him a vibrant shade of beetroot, then she breezed from the cafe.

Graham watched her through the window as she crossed the street to work.

'Hey. Thanks,' I said after she'd disappeared into the grocers.

He blinked at me, 'Huh?'

'For believing me. You know, not immediately jumping on the loony band wagon.'

He sat back on his chair and rubbed his face before peering over his fingers. His gaze was distant for a second, then it hardened. He grabbed the encyclopaedia and his satchel and pushed back his chair with an unpleasant screech. 'You better not be lying, Esta.'

When he'd left, I sat with my hands around the cold cup of tea and stared into the oddly bent reflection of myself on its milky surface. *I better not be lying.*

29

THE SECRET SPARKS

When I got home from school on Thursday, Mum was standing at the door waiting for me with an inane grin and a bunch of papers in her hand. I waited for her to tell me about the new home she'd found for us in London or something, but that wasn't it at all.

'Someone from the Council came!' she said, almost bouncing up and down on the spot, waving the papers at me.

I took them off her, leafed through one officially headed sheet after another, while Mum watched over my shoulder.

'That one!' she said excitedly when I unfolded some kind of complicated map.

'I don't get it,' I said. 'This is a map of—'

'The construction company have submitted alternative plans for the road!' she said, tearing the sheets from my hand again before I could take it all in. 'Something about fixing "land rights issues". Whatever. Come on.' She pushed me out of the door and fished in her handbag for her purse. 'Fish and Chip tea. The papers are coming round in an hour for an interview.'

Mum couldn't wipe the smile from her face as we ate our fish and chips out of greasy paper. When a bloke came from the local news, she could still barely contain herself.

'It just came out of the blue,' she said. 'The council have thrown years of planning down the drain they're so desperate to get this road built.'

'Will you continue demonstrating, Mrs Brown?'

'Of course.'

'Aren't you concerned about the jobs the scheme brings to the town?'

'But it's destroying the countryside.'

'But stopping a road already under construction would destroy the local economy.'

Mum looked a little unsure at that point, like she was being backed into a corner. She offered the journalist a cup of tea from one of the chipped mugs and soon after, the interview was over.

On Friday, cameramen came to the Home and Mum made new banners for the occasion; celebration ones this time. She persuaded school to let me out for the morning to help. It would "show a willingness to get involved with the community" she'd argued, and Mr Culter was all about community, so he let me go.

'What did I tell you?' Mum said. 'People joining hands can change the world.'

I smiled at her and picked up a plastic cup full of pale urine-coloured orange squash. I watched the old folks balancing plates of sandwiches on their blanketed laps. 'Well done, Mum. I'm proud of you.'

'Do you believe me now?' she said, nudging me.

My smile was as weak as my drink. To be honest, I didn't think Mum's posters had really made any difference. I doubted that even Mr Taylor could just click his fingers and alter the route of a new road. But who cares about facts? I preferred the idea that it was Mum's victory, so I wasn't lying. I *was* proud of her.

'Apparently it was never in the original plan to come this way,' she said. 'The Council are relieved. Mr Taylor is coming over to tell us in person later on. It's good of him, I suppose. But, I mean, it's terrible really. All these people upset over some stupid legal quagmire. Here, have a custard cream.'

Gran sidled across the room and palmed a pink French Fancy from a bowl on the table. She winked at me. It was amazing. The atmosphere of doom had lifted and not only Gran, but everyone—well, almost everyone—seemed to have lost ten years.

'There'd been a Protection Order on a property filed by its owner which prevented them from going through a Brownfield Site,' Mum was saying.

I finished my squash and nodded, not really listening. I didn't know what a Brownfield Site was, and anyway I'd noticed Harold. He was in his coat, facing the front door, the old leather suitcase in his right hand again.

'I didn't even know it still had an owner,' Mum said.

The old man leaned forward like a tree in a strong wind, reaching out for the door handle. It looked like he might topple over.

'Hold on, Mum,' I said, moving toward him.

Mum carried on anyway. 'Imagine. They were going to tear through here when they could have taken the slightest diversion through that old wreck of a property.'

Harold reached for the handle and was about to press down on it when he paused, shuffled round and stared right at me.

I lowered my biscuit.

Those eyes.

His mouth worked as if he were chewing on something. I cocked my head. No. He was trying to speak.

The old man craned his neck towards me and whispered. I must have been more than six feet away from him, but I heard him perfectly: 'Can't you smell it?'

I stared at him dumbly. We *were* in an old people's home. I could smell all *kinds* of things.

When he spoke again, it was louder. Spit flew from his lips: 'Can't you see what's happening?'

I looked to either side of me to see if anyone else was listening. They weren't.

'What's happening?' I whispered back, edging closer.

'He's already here.'

I frowned and took another step. 'Who?'

174

His face creased up in to a fierce scowl. 'The storm is coming.' Then, without warning, he swivelled round, swung open the door, stepped on to the porch and arched his head right up towards the heavens.

Nurse Olive bustled past me. 'Mr Sparks!' she said. 'What on earth are you doing? Close that door. You'll catch your death.'

Harold Sparks dropped his suitcase on the floor beside him.

I dropped my cup on the carpet.

'I saw your grandad,' I said, watching Graham over the coffee Lily had bought from the counter at the *Greasy Spoon*. It was early afternoon and quiet. It was a bit too late for the workmen with their mugs of dark tea and a bit too early for schoolboys and their endless rounds of toast.

Graham licked his lips and cleared his throat. He said nothing.

'Harold Sparks?' I said. 'He owned Gatley House, didn't he? He was the one who tried to put a protection order on it.'

Graham ran fingers through his hair and gazed into his cup.

Lily reached out to his hand, and he raised his head as if her touch had switched him on.

'How is he?'

I thought of the old man scowling at me. 'Angry, or scared... of... erm, the weather?'

'Why don't you visit him?' Lily asked.

'Because,' he said slowly. 'I'm not *supposed* to go.'

'He was the one who put the hook in the ceiling didn't he?' I said. 'And the gravestone under the willow?'

No answer.

Lily put an arm around him. 'When was the last time anyone visited him?'

Graham stared into space, his voice a quiet rattle, 'It's not what everyone thinks. People say he went crazy and killed her, but that's just gossip.'

We sat in silence. I held the cup of tea in both hands, feeling the warmth between my fingers. The pop song finished. I caught snippets of the normally enthusiastic DJ talking seriously about winds blowing a storm in from the east. *'The government is playing down reports of high levels of radiation detected in Northern Europe...'* The radio crackled, the signal weakening. *'High-altitude winds... contaminated rain...'* The owner grunted, reached over and switched the channel.

'That's what your grandad was scared of,' I said, jabbing a thumb at the radio. 'He said a storm was coming.'

Graham nodded. 'Though my dad *says* the winds are blowing the radiation south. *Says* we're safe here.'

'You don't sound like you believe him.'

'Est,' Lily said. 'Trust me. Don't get him started on his dad.'

'He's a soldier. He just believes whatever he's told to believe,' Graham said.

'Gray's got this radiation measuring thing—' Lily said.

'It's a Geiger counter.'

'Right. Well, he's been waving it about for the last two days.'

'There're a lot of things Dad says I don't believe,' Graham said.

Lily raised her eyebrows at me in a: *See what I mean?* look.

'Is that why you went to the house?' I asked. 'Because you didn't believe the stories about your grandad?'

'Not at first,' Graham said. 'But, when Simon showed me that key... I wanted to know what happened. I needed to see it for myself before they tore it down.'

'See what?'

'Inside the house. It all happened before I was born. I thought I'd learn something about what made him and Grandma...' He tailed off.

I swallowed a lump in my throat. *Him and Grandma, what exactly?*

Graham wiped his face and took a deep breath. After a moment, he continued, 'He must have put the memorial stone under that tree for her. Even after she disappeared, Dad told me he kept trying to go back to the place. That he'd never sell up, even when it started falling apart.'

'Wait,' Lily said. 'She disappeared too?'

'She's not buried in the garden, Est. Grandad just put the stone there to remember her.'

'Hold on,' Lily said. 'Your gran, Esta's dad, Charlie Bullock? All of them missing.'

We sat in silence. Water glugged from something behind the counter; the owner hummed to a pop song on the new channel he'd found while he lined up a row of toast. A knife slipped and clanged to the floor—a metallic ringing in the quiet.

'Oh God!' I blurted, suddenly remembering Mr Taylor's tapping spade. 'I saw Charlie!'

'You saw Charlie Bullock?' Graham said, straightening up. 'Where is she?'

'She's…' I thought about Simon's plea for me not to tell anyone. Then I thought about how he'd called me "Damaged". 'She's in a wheelchair.'

Graham's face was back to full colour now, his voice full of urgent interest. 'Did you talk to her?'

'No. Not really. But she had this drawing of an eye surrounded by flames, which was… weird.'

'Weird?'

'Like I'd seen it before.'

'She might know something about the house,' Lily said. 'We could go talk to her.'

I pictured Mr Taylor holding his spade like a sword, 'She's kind of well protected and I don't think talking is exactly her… thing anymore.'

'Well. I don't know about you two, but Gatley House is definitely at the centre of *something*,' Lily said. 'Three people disappeared and only Charlie came back?'

A bit of Charlie came back, I thought. I pictured Dad's unshaven face in the days before he disappeared: bloodshot, staring eyes, fidgeting fingers. I looked down; the surface of the tea was vibrating in my shaky grip. I set it down.

'Why did your grandad sell the house to Taylor?' I asked Graham. 'After all this time. Why sell up?'

'It wasn't his to sell. He's...' Graham raised two fingers up like quote marks. '..."incapable of understanding what's in his best interests." So the deeds went to Dad, and he's been trying to get rid of it ever since. Says it's a family shame.'

I pressed a finger against the rigid edges of the Orb—*the Vajra*— in my pocket. It was still solid; I imagined it gleaming gold against my skin.

'Why don't we go see him?' I asked. 'Maybe *he* could help.'

Graham shook his head, 'I don't think he's all there.'

'You should go see him anyway,' said Lily. 'Listen to his story.'

Another spark of memory flashed in my head. 'Story!'

Graham and Lily jumped.

'I can't have made that up,' I said, squeezing my eyes shut, trying to hold on to it.

'What is it?' Lily asked.

'I remember something else.' A nest of golden cloth; black scratches glistening on a single sheet of paper. 'Something I read.'

'There's an island of jewels?' Graham asked after I'd told them the story.

'Lama la said my dad was searching for an object. A weapon of some sort. He said if I found it, it would bring him home.'

'And you reckon the weapon is on this jewel island?'

'Why else would he show—' I stopped. *He didn't show it to me.* And it wasn't just something I'd read either. Lama la had said *I'd* written it. A more disturbing memory now crawled inside my head to make its home:

Tulku.

I didn't say anything about that to the others. A different, parallel world was one thing, but past lives? Even after everything, I didn't even swallow that one.

'That's all he told you?' Graham said. 'That there's some kind of weapon you're supposed to find? Sounds dodgy. And, you know, highly unspecific. Did it have a name? Do you know what it looks like at least?'

I pushed my new thought to one side. 'I can't remember the name, but he said it'd be hidden in plain sight. And it's…' I attempted to close my three middle fingers together. '… sort of peg shaped?'

'I dunno about this, Est. It seems really vague.'

'The last thing he said was that there was someone who could help me. Someone who could see.'

I looked at Graham, then at Lily.

Lily raised an eyebrow. 'That's settled then,' she said, almost to herself.

'What's settled?' Graham said.

Lily leaned forwards and whispered. 'We go and find the person most likely to help.'

He raised an eyebrow. 'And that is?'

'We go and see Charlie.'

30

CHARLIE BULLOCK

'You sure Simon's not here?' Graham said as we approached the Taylor house.

'He's at football practice. Every Monday after school.'

'And Mr Taylor?'

'He's supposed to be at Mum's meeting, and anyway,' I nodded at the driveway. Mr Taylor's Jaguar wasn't in it. But there *was* a silver Ford Escort in its place. 'That's got to be Mrs Tay — Mrs Bullock. I doubt Simon's dad would be seen dead driving that.'

'We just have to hope Charlie's in, then,' Lily said.

Graham raised an eyebrow. 'What's the plan then, Miss Pink Panther?'

'Est, you said she draws pictures in the back garden didn't you?'

'Yes,'

'There's a side passage, right? I remember it from the party. So, you go round the side, just to see.'

'She won't be on her own though will she?' Graham said. 'Her mum'll be with her.'

'There's three of us.'

'What?' Graham snorted. 'Me and you pin Charlie's mum down while Esta helps her choose the colour of her crayons?'

'Don't be silly. I'll ring the bell and talk to her, while you two go round the back.'

'And say what?'

She held up one of Mum's leaflets. 'I'll say I'm here to ask her questions about the bypass.'

Graham looked doubtful. I, on the other hand, thought she'd

probably keep the woman talking for an hour if necessary.

'Alright clever clogs,' he said. 'How will we know when you're finished talking? She might come back while we're there. We'd be trespassing. She'd call the police.'

Lily grinned and fished in the front pocket of her overalls. She handed me one end of green twine. 'There's about forty feet of it. I'll tug it when I'm done. Then you come running.'

Graham and I waited by the corner of the house. The exact spot where I'd first seen Mr Taylor and his spade. Lily rang the doorbell. There was a pause. The sound of the door opening. Lily smiled and started talking.

Graham tapped me and we tiptoed along the side of the property towards a gate that was as tall as Graham. He tried the handle. It wouldn't budge.

'We doing this, then?' he whispered nervously.

I looked at the twine between my fingers. It was slack. I gave him a nod. He linked his fingers and bent his knees, then looked up at the top of the gate. 'Unbolt it when you get over.'

Graham left the gate ajar as we crept to the edge of the house and peered into the garden.

It was a huge flat lawn with freshly dug borders and a spade leaning against a fence to the right. I preferred it there, rather than in the hand of Mr Taylor.

Charlie was on the patio near what I guessed was the kitchen window. She was sitting in her wheelchair, hunched over a large open book in her lap.

'Jesus!' Graham hissed. 'You're right. It *is* her.'

'You came all this way even though you didn't believe me?'

Graham shrugged. 'I like to see things for myself before I believe them.'

'Right.'

'And I still owe you one for escorting me to the party. Without you I'd have never met Lily.'

'You're welcome. So, now what?'

Graham made a flicking gesture with his hand. 'Ask her what you need to ask her and then we leg it. Get a wriggle on.'

I leant round the corner feeling like the stupidest-burglar-in-the-world and wondering exactly what I was going to ask her. *Excuse me. Can you tell me where to find my Dad?* I coughed as quietly as I could. It wouldn't have startled a sparrow. Charlie kept on drawing, her tongue poking out in concentration.

Graham nudged me in the back. 'Quit stalling.'

'I don't know what to say,' I whispered.

Graham bent, picked up a small pebble. 'You're not asking her out on a date.' He flung the pebble under arm so it skidded along the patio. 'Tell her what you told us.'

Charlie raised her head. She didn't seem at all surprised to see me standing in her back garden. Although, I'm not sure she'd have shown it even if she were. I smiled, but didn't move. Right here by the wall was just fine. I wanted to keep my escape route close. After a second or two, I did what I do when I'm nervous. I gave her a finger-wave. She looked back down at the book on her lap, then back at me, mumbled something, flipped over a fresh page and started scribbling again.

'Has she seen you? What's she doing?' Graham said from the safety of the passageway.

'Nothing. She's just drawing.'

'Drawing what?'

'I can't see.'

'Then you have to go to her. Or we leave. Now.'

I looked at the piece of string in my hand. Slack. I reckoned Lily could talk the back legs off a donkey, but for how long? How long had we been? Two minutes? That was a long time to talk to someone about their ex-husband. Or… I don't know, maybe not.

Charlie glanced up at me again, her hand still working furiously.

OK, Dad, I said to myself, rolled the twine between my fingertips then crouched so I was beneath the sill of the living room window and walked on all-fours, feeling tiny daggers of guilt, fear and embarrassment pricking me all over.

The girl finally stopped scribbling when I got to her. She peered down at me with watery eyes and pointed to the page.

It was some sort of landscape: hastily scribbled trees in the foreground, a suggestion of mountains in the background. Two stick figures stood next to each other beside a boulder. Or maybe a building—she hadn't finished that bit. One of the figures was taller than the other. I rose to get a better angle. It could have been a father and child. The smaller one had long hair. Charlie scribbled something else in the bottom corner: another figure next to a tree.

'Are you trying to show me something?' I guessed.

Without looking up from her drawing, she pointed the end of her pencil over my shoulder.

'I don't understand,' I whispered.

She put her pencil to paper again. At the bottom, in the centre, she drew another figure leaning over a couple of circles, a square on top of them. Some sort of contraption with… with wheels.

'Wait. Is that supposed to be us? That's you in the chair, isn't it?'

Charlie jabbed at the figures by the boulder and began to shade in some details. She dropped one pencil, selected a different one from the pile in her lap and started colouring in the hair of the shorter figure. Red.

'Lily?' I hissed, pointing to the house. 'Is that supposed to be Lily?'

Charlie swapped back to the darker pencil, she made the taller figure wider, thickened its arms and rounded off its head.

Lily's talking with Mr Taylor? Is that what she means?

I glanced at the spade leaning by the wall. If Lily pulled the string now, I didn't want to be anywhere near that. I looked through the kitchen window; you couldn't see the front door from here… so… how the hell did Charlie know there was a girl at the door?

'Wait,' I said, forgetting about the spade for a second and

pointing at the scene she'd drawn: the trees, the mountains. 'What is this? What are you drawing?'

Charlie's lips moved. She was saying something. I leaned in closer. She was repeating something, but there was no sound.

She blinked. Flipped the page on her pad to the previous drawing.

Charlie had seen, hadn't she? She knew something. What was she trying to show me? 'Is this the Jewel Island?' I asked excitedly.

Charlie lifted the drawing up, but as she did, the twine bit hard into my fingers, jerking my hand downwards. My breath caught in my throat. A door slammed inside the house. I backed off, almost tripping over my own feet to get away.

Mr Taylor shouted Charlie's name. Another door slammed.

My eyes flicked back to the spade, then back to the girl in the wheelchair.

Charlie's lips moved, whispering something too quietly to hear. 'What?'

The twine tugged painfully at my hand again. I dropped it, letting it scuttle back to the wall.

Charlie opened her mouth again. A dry rattling hiss came out: '*Hee...*'

I refocussed on what she was holding up in her lap. Another sketch.

'*Toookit…*' hissed the girl.

Mr Taylor's voice boomed from inside the house. 'Charlie?'

My body wanted to run, but my eyes were pinned to the drawing.

If it hadn't been for Graham hauling me away, I might have stayed rooted to the spot until Mr Taylor had flattened me with his spade.

Etched in deep lines in the centre of the page was an image of an ornate three-bladed dagger.

31

VENUS FLYTRAP

'I thought you said he was out?' Lily gasped between breaths as we rounded the corner at the end of Simon's road. 'I thought he was going to strangle me when I showed him the leaflets.'

I was too shocked to speak. The image of the drawing was still stamped into my mind.

'He had this vein that throbbed in his temple,' she was saying. 'I couldn't keep my eyes off it.'

'What did she say?' Graham said, slowing down to a fast walk.

'He was just ranting on and on—' Lily said.

'No. Charlie. Esta spoke to her. What did she say?'

I stopped walking altogether. Bent down. Hands on my knees, gasping for air, my head filled with Charlie's drawings. 'She drew stuff,' I panted. 'She drew Lily talking with her dad. She drew you standing behind the...' *Tree?*

'How could she have known who was at the door?' Lily said. 'I tried peering over Taylor's head while he was ranting. There's no way she could have seen me.'

'She didn't draw you standing by a door. You were by some sort of cliff, or a rock or something I think... I think she was drawing us all as if we were somewhere else.' I closed my eyes and recalled the scene: mountains, trees. 'She was drawing us as if we were there,' I said.

'Where's there?' Graham said. 'Are you talking about the island?'

'The valley. It's like we were all standing where we were, but...' I shook my head. 'Somewhere else at the same time.'

'What was the thing she was holding up when I came to get you?'

Graham said. 'It looked like a dagger. Is that the weapon you're supposed to find?'

I stood up. Charlie's rasping words echoing in my head: *heee tookit...*

I wiped sweat off my face, then nodded. I was sure of it.

'What did you see?' Lily asked.

'It was some kind of knife. A bizarre-shaped handle, with a face carved on it,' Graham replied, looking at me for confirmation.

I nodded again.

'You have to go back,' Lily said. 'You have to talk to her. She might know where it is.'

He took it. That's what she'd been trying to say.

Graham ran his fingers through his hair. 'We can't. We left the gate in the side passageway unbolted and there's that green string of yours Esta dropped on the drive. Taylor will know someone's tried to break in. He'll know you were in on it, Lil. He'll bloody kill us if we go back.'

I thought about Charlie sitting in her wheelchair, jabbing at her drawings. 'I don't know if Charlie'd tell us much anyway.'

I didn't tell them what she'd whispered to me though.

'So what do we do now?' Lily said.

I looked at Graham. I didn't know how he'd take this, but... We had to speak to the only other person who might know something.

'We have to go and see Harry Sparks.'

'Hello Esta,' Nurse Olive said brightly as she held the door of Green Gables Nursing home for us. 'Come in; your Gran's sleeping, but you can wait if you like.'

'Actually, we're here to see Mr Sparks.'

The nurse lifted a pair of half-moon glasses to her forehead and peered at Graham. 'Mr Sparks,' she said. 'You're Harold's grandson, are you?' There was a slight barb in her voice.

Graham cleared his throat and nodded.

She lowered her glasses. 'Well it's about time.' She tapped his shoulder, then smoothed her outfit at her hips. 'You wait here. I'll tell him you've come. He's probably still in his underpants. That's something you don't want to see, I can assure you.' She smiled at me and disappeared round the corner.

Graham put his hands in his pockets and stared up at a painting of a horse, while Lily peered at leaflets on a bureau.

'I never want to end up in a place like this,' Graham whispered at the horse.

'Oh, I don't know. There's lots to do.' Lily held up one of the leaflets, reading something printed on the back. 'Bingo, crochet classes. There's a trip to an exhibition at the museum next week.'

'I'd rather go out in a blaze of glory than playing Bingo, Lil,' he said.

She grinned, 'That can be arranged. But in case you change your mind...' She put the leaflet in the back pocket of her jeans, stood on her tiptoes and kissed him on his cheek.

I looked away.

A local newspaper folded on a wooden chair grabbed my attention. I picked it up. The front page was more headlines about the accident in Russia. I flipped over the page.

VICTORY!

Underneath it was a picture of the nurses and a crowd of old folk standing in front of Green Gables. Faces beaming. All of them waving pieces of paper in the air.

I searched the faces. Mum was at the edge of the photo with her eyes closed. She always did that for a photo. Even in the ones of her and Dad when she was young. Big grin. Eyes closed. She blinked a lot, I guess.

I recognised most of the nurses and some of the old men and women. Gran was concentrating on something in her hand, a cake or a biscuit most likely. But no Harold. He hadn't come out for the photo shoot. I bet he knew what victory meant for him. If the road wasn't going through Green Gables, it meant it was going through Gatley House instead. Harold Sparks had lost whatever battle he'd been fighting to keep his old place standing.

But what did he know about Rigpa Gompa? Had he seen it too? Is that what drove him mad? Is it why he had tried to hold on to it all this time?

'Your grandfather is ready,' Nurse Olive said after five or so minutes. She stood at the corner of the hall, beckoning us. 'He's tired, but he's wearing trousers now at least.'

Harold Sparks sat in a high-backed chair, his skinny hands resting against its arms. One finger curled back and forth, stroking the material, like he was stroking a cat. His long white hair had a yellow tinge at the roots. He'd shaved since the last time I saw him. The skin of his face was almost transparent, so you could see fine blue veins criss-crossing along his nose and cheeks. His crystal blue eyes were a paler version of Graham's. They creased a little at the corners and his tongue flicked out like he was concentrating on threading a needle.

He pointed at the three chairs Nurse Olive had placed in a horseshoe shape around him.

He licked his lips.

'Grandad?' Graham said.

The old man coughed, wiped his mouth, 'Sit,' he said in a voice as brittle as his skin.

We sat: Graham in the middle, me on his left, Lily to his right.

I glanced around the room. Newspapers with apocalyptic headlines about nuclear fallout were scattered across his bed. There were three shelves of books along one wall. One shelf filled with wooden statues, spoons and stuff. A weird looking potted plant stood on a shelf beneath the window.

'You're my grandson, I'm told,' Harold said.

'How are you?' Graham asked.

'What do you want? Make it snappy, I have errands.'

Graham shuffled in his seat; he glanced at Lily and me. 'We came about the house.'

His face changed immediately. His eyes widened. 'Have they found Carol?'

Graham shook his head. 'Nanna's still gone, Grandad.'

The old man silently closed his hand into a fist like he was slowly squeezing something to death.

'What happened?' I asked.

He looked straight at me, recognition lighting up his eyes. 'You…' He licked his lips again, unfurled his fingers and waggled one of them towards the window. 'Bring it over here,' he croaked.

Graham raised his eyebrows at me, shrugged, then nodded at the window.

Outside, the lawn was neat—like a bed with its sheets tucked in. What was I supposed to do? I turned back to check.

The old man's arm was still up, pointing at me. His finger wagged up and down as if he were pressing a button. 'Bring it,' he said.

I looked down at the window shelf. The only thing on it was the plant. It was a funny looking thing: small and green. Spiky half-moon leaves that looked like mini eyelids with fluttery lashes. Or, less amusingly, mouths with teeth.

I lifted it up. 'This?'

Harold gave a single tip of the head and curled his fingers back toward himself in a beckoning gesture.

I walked back with the plant and handed it to him. He hunched over it, turning the thing around on his lap, inspecting its leaves. 'See,' he whispered, holding it up again.

One of the leaves had closed. I looked more carefully. Inside was a black shape.

It twitched.

I lurched away. Hand over my mouth.

'It's a Venus Flytrap,' Graham said, standing up and taking it from his grandad. 'The leaves snap shut like a spring hinge as soon as something touches it. That's how it feeds.'

Harold watched me. He licked his lips. 'Did you see?'

I looked back at the little twitching leg. Then back to the old man. 'I don't know,' I said.

'Tell me,' the old man whispered. 'You saw something. That's why you're here.'

I gulped. 'I saw a… some kind of mansion,' I said uncertainly. 'An old man. Children in coloured robes. A valley. Mountains.'

'Is it true?' he hissed.

The room seemed to contract around us.

The fly's leg stopped moving.

'It felt true,' I said.

'Shadows,' he said. He ran fingers through his hair, just like Graham did. 'They close around you. Consume you.' His lips began to wobble, his eyes filled with tears. 'Nothing lasts. You can't hold on to shadows.'

Graham crouched by his grandfather, then looked at Lily and me with anguish in his eyes. 'I told you. We should go,' he mouthed.

'No,' Lily said under her breath. 'Esta, ask him about the jewel island. Ask him about this weapon you're supposed to find.'

'But he's not…' Graham let out a despairing sigh as Harold's head dipped.

Lily rose from her seat. 'We have to ask him now, or it'll be too late.'

I winced and looked at Graham. His face had lost any colour.

'One question,' he said. 'Then we leave him alone.'

Lily rested her hand against Harold's arm. 'Mr Sparks? Can Esta ask you a question?'

The old man raised his head. His eyes were misty but hopeful behind the tears.

I blew out a breath, calmed myself.

One question to find my dad.

'Mr Sparks?' I said, words inching out of my mouth like treacle. 'Do you know anything about an island of jewels?'

The old man stared at me, his eyes searching my face. Then his gaze dropped back to his lap.

Graham grimaced and shook his head at me.

'Esta,' Lily hissed, 'ask about the knife.'

Graham patted his grandfather's hand. I felt a window of opportunity shutting.

'There's a knife,' I tried. 'A three bladed knife that's... that's missing. Do you know what I'm talking about?'

Harold peered at Graham's hand on his and then up at his grandson.

Graham withdrew his hand and took a step back, head still shaking. 'No more,' he muttered. 'No more.'

I looked for inspiration on the shelves. Something that might trigger an idea. I was *supposed* to know what to do. I was supposed to *know*. A metal bowl; miniature wooden dancing figures; a random collection of pebbles.

'I'm sorry, Grandad,' Graham said, heading for the door, grabbing at me as he walked past. 'I'll come back to visit. Promise.'

It was hopeless. Harold Sparks was as broken as Charlie. Charlie could barely speak and whatever Harry knew about Rigpa Gompa was hidden behind a fog of age.

I thought of Dad when I last saw him, the wild hair, and the faraway look in his eye. *Was he already lost then?*

We filed out of the door, past Nurse Olive, standing like a guard outside.

Graham's face was white. He looked devastated.

'Did you see him?' he said. 'I should never have come. My dad was right.'

'I'm sorry,' Lily whispered as she led him to reception.

The door to Harold's room opened.

'Esta?' Nurse Olive snapped. 'What did you say to him?'

'Sorry?' I said, exchanging a worried glance with Lily and Graham.

'I've never seen him so worked up.' She shook her head in despair. 'The thing he said.'

I shook my head. 'I just asked…'

Lily let go of Graham's hand. 'Nurse. What did he say?'

'I can barely repeat it. You must have said something… It's too terrible.'

'Nurse. Exactly what did he say?'

Nurse Olive took a second, flashed a look at me, then back at Harry's door. She lowered her voice. 'He said he wanted to kill you,' she leaned back. 'I've never heard the like.'

Lily held the woman's arm. 'Nurse Olive. What *exactly* did he say?'

The nurse sniffed. Looked at me again, then held out a crumpled leaflet and spoke in a voice I could only just hear, 'He showed me this and said: "Kill her".'

The leaflet opened up like a concertina. I bent my head sideways to look at the image in the centre of the page. 'Oh my God…'

'I'm sorry, love. He gets so confused.'

I grabbed the leaflet off her and opened it fully.

It was the advert for the exhibition at the museum.

'SHAMBHALA—SYMBOLS FROM THE HIDDEN KINGDOM.'

Slap bang in the middle of the page was a line drawing of an ornate dagger. Almost exactly the same as the one Charlie had drawn.

32

ON THE NO. 42

'I don't get it,' Lily said as she took her seat near the back of the bus. Graham sat next to her and rummaged in his satchel for something.

It was late afternoon, and it was already getting dark. Rain tipped down outside. It had started while we waited in the bus shelter and, although none of us said anything about radiation or fallout, we each kept our toes clear of the expanding puddles. Now threads of water were snaking along the windows as the bus made its stop/start journey into the centre of town.

'I thought this Kila thing was on the desert island in the story,' Graham said. 'What's it doing in a museum?'

I sat in front of Lily and Graham and leant back against the cold window, my legs stretched across the double seat. 'Maybe that's why my dad's still looking. Maybe he's been looking in the wrong place. Lama la said it would be in plain sight. This exhibition was what my dad was working on before...' I stuttered to a halt.

Graham held up the leaflet with the image of the Kila. 'You believe this will bring him back?'

'How am I supposed to know?' I said, irritated. How *was* I supposed to know? What was he, a homing pigeon?

'This is kind of mad, isn't it?' Lily said, not concealing the excitement in her voice. 'I mean, what do we do when we get there?'

'Buy an umbrella.'

'No, Graham. When we find the object?'

He tapped his satchel. 'Take a photo.'

'What good's a photo?' I said. 'I'm supposed to bring it back.'

'That's what you're supposed to do?' Lily said. 'Get this Kila thing and bring it to the Lama man?'

Graham leaned forwards and whispered, 'You can't be serious? We can't steal something from a museum. It'll be behind a glass case, they have security. What makes you think you'd get away with that?'

'Lama la told me I'd know what to do,' I said simply. 'This is what I have to do.'

'This could all be a wild goose chase,' Graham hissed. 'We go. We take a look. We decide what to do. No point talking about it until we get there.'

Lily smiled at me, 'He's so commanding when he's angry, isn't he?'

'For a geek,' I replied.

Lily laughed.

Graham flicked my arm with the back of his hand. 'Don't forget, apart from Lily, I'm the only person in the entire world who doesn't think you're off your rocker.'

I looked across the aisle. The rain streamed across the window opposite and I smiled at the reflection of the three of us in the glass.

Passengers got up as the bus slowed down. We sat in silence until they got off and the bus pulled away again into the rush-hour traffic.

Lily leaned in again and spoke under her breath. 'So, let's rewind. What do we know? Esta, we know your dad found Charlie in Gatley House. We know they both started acting strangely afterwards and then your dad disappeared, right?'

I nodded. It was the first time anyone except Mum had ever spoken so matter-of-factly about what happened to my dad. It was strange. I wasn't sure I really liked it. It felt like brushing your teeth after eating cake. You know it has to happen, but maybe not so soon.

'Gray,' she said, 'we also know, before that, your grandad lived in Gatley House until your grandma went missing. So what else do we know? What did he do? What was his job? He was a soldier, right?'

'Grandad Harry? Yeah, he was in the army. Everyone ends up in the army in my family.'

'Second World War?'

'He fought with the Gurkhas in Burma.'

'Gurkhas?' I asked. 'What's that?'

'Who,' Graham replied. 'They're soldiers. Regiments made up from the Nepalese. They've fought with the British army for ages.'

'Nepalese?'

Graham squinted at me. 'Don't you do geography?'

'Nepalese sounds like a type of illness.'

'From Nepal. It's between India and Tibet.'

I gave him a clenched smile. My geography was as good as my history: ropey.

'You heard of Mount Everest?'

'Yeah.'

'It's in Nepal.'

'Mountains and valleys then?' I asked.

'Lots.'

'Like I saw at the house. Did Harry ever go there?'

'After the war. He was a cartographer. That's where he met my grandma.'

'A carto fa what?'

Graham gave me a disgusted look, 'You really need to spend more time at school. He used to map out the borders between India, Nepal and Tibet.'

'Shambhala is supposed to be a hidden valley in Tibet,' Lily said, pointing to the leaflet. 'Maybe your grandad found it?'

Graham frowned at her. 'It's mythological; it's not supposed to be a true, physical place.'

Lily laughed.

'What?'

'You don't believe that!'

'What's that supposed to mean?'

'Gray, we're on a bus looking for a sacred object because we were told—'

'Esta *says* she was told,' he corrected.

'Told to by an old man who lives in a place that is *literally* hidden from everyone except a few people.' She beamed at us both. 'It's the very definition of a hidden valley.'

'Yeah, well,' Graham grumbled, unimpressed, 'It's *supposed* to be in Tibet, Lily, not Northern England.'

The brakes squeaked, the bus slowed, the walls of a large Victorian building filled the window behind Lily's head. I swung my legs from the seat and pulled myself up. 'This is our stop.'

Graham placed his bag on top of his head.

'What are you doing?' I asked.

'Keeping the rain off. I suggest you do the same.'

33

THE EXHIBITION

Huge oak doors led to the museum reception. A large poster hung on wires from a high ceiling displaying the image of the Kila. Beneath it stood a serious-looking usher checking her watch.

'First floor. Through Egypt,' she said, pointing to a broad wooden staircase. 'But we're closing in a few minutes,' she called after us as we headed for it.

A stuffed polar bear in a glass cabinet stood guard at the base of the staircase. It reminded me of Mr Taylor's lions: claws out, teeth bared. Graham took the steps two at a time. Lily and I followed more slowly, our clothes dripping from the rain we'd failed to avoid.

'Graham said you were travelling to India?' I asked.

'Eventually. That's why I'm working at the grocers. I'm saving up. It's only a couple of hundred quid for a flight. I'm staying with a family.'

'Why? I mean, why are you going?'

'I'm volunteering at a school for a few months. Then I'm planning on travelling to the Himalayas,' she gave me a smile. 'Maybe go searching for hidden valleys.'

'Won't you miss home?'

Her smile dropped for a second. 'Not really.'

'That bad?'

'Some people travel the world to find new things. Some do it to escape old things...'

Graham reached the top of the stairs, pointed to the left, then headed towards a golden-faced mummy.

'And what about him?' I whispered.

197

'He's joining me after his exams.'

'You're both actually going then?' I said with a little more desperation in my voice than I'd intended. I'd not remotely believed Graham was actually going to go through with his plan. 'I only… I mean, you only just met.'

She shrugged. 'He was going to join up with his dad in India anyway. I guess it's what brought us together. Knowing there'll be a friend in that big faraway country.'

Rainwater trickled down the back of my neck and the cold locked my jaw shut. I forced a smile. The only two people who actually talked to me were going to travel halfway across the world. What was it with people I liked? Why did they all want to escape?

We walked through a room filled with mummified corpses, hieroglyphs, and masks of gods with faces like animals. Their eyes seemed to follow me as we passed.

'D'you reckon these guys really existed?' I said, briefly inspecting the statue of a man with the head of a dog. "Anubis", the label read.

'Don't be naïve,' Graham said.

'How do you know?'

He pointed to a sign stuck to the wall above my dog-headed god. It read: EGYPTIAN SYMBOLOGY. 'Symbols stand for something. They're not *real*, Esta. Just like…' he tailed off.

'You think Rigpa Gompa is symbolic?'

He tilted his head to one side in reply.

'What's that supposed to mean?'

'It means,' he whispered, pausing at the end of the Egyptian room, 'let's not make any assumptions about what we're doing here, alright?' He left that hanging in the air between us for a moment.

'You don't believe me, do you? After everything you said in the cafe.'

'It's not that I don't believe you. I'm here aren't I? But, weren't you listening to my grandad? It's easy to get sucked into things. Charlie, Grandad, your dad? I'm just trying to keep a clear head.

Let's not do anything stupid.'

The room behind the arch was dark, except for glass cabinets around its walls that were illuminated from the inside. They gave off a ghostly glow as if they were floating in the darkness. There were no visitors here, just a security guard dressed in dark blue so you could only tell he was there when he moved.

It wasn't cold, but something about the place made me shiver.

Graham went to the cabinets on the right side, Lily and I went to the left.

In the first display case was an array of objects laid out in neat rows. 'That's like the table we saw with Graham,' I said, my voice echoing around the room. The guard pushed himself away from the wall he'd been leaning on, looked at us, checked his watch and folded his arms.

'He told me,' Lily replied. 'Said it was all rusty junk.'

I traced my finger along the glass cabinet. Golden bowls, silver spoons, porcelain cups, some ordinary looking cutlery, a pair of old, round-rimmed glasses.

Lily read from the sheet stuck to the inside of the glass: '*In Shambhala, before a Tulku is formally recognised, the candidate must pass a series of tests.*'

'Tests?' I murmured, 'He mentioned that.'

'What's a Tulku?' Lily whispered.

I felt a twang of electricity at the word.

'It says that one of the tests is: *"checking whether the child can recognise the possessions used by the previous master. This display of objects is an example. The candidate must choose"*—' She broke off. 'You think this is what you and Simon took?'

'I don't know,' I said as flatly as I could and turned my reddening face quickly away, as if searching for Graham. He was on the other side of the room, bending over another display case. The guard had wandered across and was watching him too.

'Check this out,' Lily pointed at one of the objects in the next cabinet. 'That's like the picture you drew of the Vajra.' She looked at me. 'Esta, your dad was collecting this stuff. You must have seen it all before…' She didn't complete her sentence, but I knew what she was thinking. It wouldn't have been hard for me to make all this stuff up. Maybe I'd seen all this stuff before, maybe, but… I let my fingers rest on the Orb in my pocket. *Not a hinge.*

I swallowed, broke eye contact and looked down at the cabinet again. Next to the Vajra was a hand-bell, almost identical to the one Simon had picked up. There were several similar objects lined up and numbered under the glass case. None of them the Kila, though.

We moved to the next cabinet. This one was tall and fixed to the wall. I backed away like you might from a stray dog in a dark alleyway. A painted image about eight feet tall hung down. A monster with swollen eyes held a wheel in its fangs and clawed hands.

'The Wheel of Life,' Lily read. '*To the inhabitants of Shambhala, existence is said to be a cycle of life, death, rebirth and suffering that they seek to escape altogether. The Wheel is divided into six realms, or states, into which a soul can be reborn. It is held by the demon, Yama.*'

I sensed her looking at me again. I had my hand up, covering my mouth, staring at the wheel; at the flaming eyes of the demon holding it, the same eyes Charlie had drawn on her sheet of paper.

'Do you recognise this?' she said.

I gulped, my throat dry, and walked towards the painting. Did I recognise it? I'd *been* there. I'd soared above it.

In the image there were little figures in each segment of the wheel. At the top, they were dressed like princesses. At the bottom, they were naked and misshapen, climbing out of flaming cauldrons. In the centre were three animals chasing each other: a cockerel, a pig and a snake.

Lily traced her finger along the explanation. '*It's divided into six co-existing realms. Each realm is defined by the dominant emotion of its inhabitants: Pride, Jealousy, Greed, Ignorance, Hatred, and Love.*'

She pointed to the top segment. 'So those king and queen types at the top represent pride. These guys...' she pointed out some figures with enormous stomachs and flames shooting out of their mouths, '...are greed. Then these...' her finger moved along more images around the edge of the wheel. 'It says: *all realms are sustained by Karma. The law of*—'

'The laws of Universal Justice,' I said breathlessly. Almost exactly the words I remembered the old man had said.

'It says cause and effect here...'

'Same thing,' I mumbled, but my attention was fixed on something else. Something I'd not seen on the wall of Rigpa Gompa or floating in space....

I pointed at the middle, not wanting to get close enough to read it myself. 'What does it say about those things?'

'It's a pig, a snake and a... some kind of chicken.' She returned to the text. '*Representing greed, hatred and ignorance. They make the whole wheel turn around.*

'So, Rigpa Gompa is somewhere in one of these realms?'

'Maybe.' I recalled the little emerald jewel in the centre of the dark massing clouds. But that wasn't on this image. I leaned in closer. There was something at the bottom of the picture, beneath the feet of the demon, underneath the wheel. A green pyramid shape surrounded by blue; three coloured pebbles in the centre of it. 'What do those look like?' I said pointing to it.

Lily leaned in with me. 'A sea or a lake?'

'No, what's in the centre of it?'

She paused, then whispered, 'You think that's the island of jewels?'

We both straightened, Lily looked at me with arched eyebrows.

'You two,' Graham whispered from across the room. 'I've found it.'

34

THE THIEF

The Kila was no more than half a foot long from handle to tip. It gleamed gold behind a single rope fence and cast shadows against a velvet background. Its handle sparkled, the edges of the blade shone a polished black. I took the Orb out of my pocket to compare them.

'So, what's it do?' Lily whispered. 'It looks vicious when you see it for real.'

Graham read:

The Tantrikas use the Kila to cure disease, kill demons, and change the weather. The blade of the Kila is used for the destruction of demonic powers. The top end of the Kila is used for gathering blessings.'

'So not a butter knife then,' Lily said.

Graham took his camera out from his satchel. This apparently woke up the guard again, who cleared his throat and wagged a finger.

'No photos!' snapped the guard, swaggering towards us.

'Sorry,' Graham said with a grin. 'Didn't hear you.'

The guard stopped a few feet away, his eyes hidden by the peak of a cap. He held out his wrist and tapped his watch twice, then pointed to the door.

'We're going,' Lily said, pulling at my arm. Graham was already on his way. I glanced at the Kila. Was this what Dad was looking for? Was this really the reason he'd walked out on Mum and me? It was no more than six feet away. Four paces and I'd be able to touch it. But the guard was in between. It might as well have been in another room. *Another realm.* Graham was right. I couldn't just *take* it. The photo would have to suffice. I could bring that to Lama la, then he could figure out what to do.

I turned to go.

'Wait,' the guard said, staring at me. 'What's that?'

I dropped the Orb into my pocket. 'Excuse me?'

'What have you got?' His voice had changed. It was gruff and slow now.

'Come on, Esta.' Lily said, tugging at me harder now. 'It's almost closing time. There's a bus back at ten past. If we run, we'll get it.'

'No,' growled the guard. He was close now; close enough for me to smell him. He smelled of gravy, sort of sweaty, sort of meaty. His hair was thick, black and greasy, poking out from under his cap. A ponytail slithered from behind, resting like the tail of a dog on his shoulder. I closed my hand around the Orb and backed away.

The guard held out his own hand, balled it into a fist and then opened his palm. 'Show me,' he said, so quietly I was sure only I could hear him.

'Come on, Esta,' Lily said. But her voice was slow and distant. All my attention was fixed on the guard who stood between the Kila and me. Very still and suddenly very large.

My gaze moved up to his face. I could only see the lower part. The cap covered the rest. He was grinning. It reminded me of Kev: teeth yellow and uneven. Humourless.

He raised his head, his eyes emerging from behind the peak of his cap. Irises, black as coal and flecked with fine spots of gold.

'*Show me,*' he whispered.

Except his lips didn't move.

Heat boiled up inside my belly. Smoke spiralled inwards from the edge of my sight, a dark whirlpool with a nasty, grinning face in the centre of it. A pointed, bright red tongue flicked out, licking his thin lips, '*Stole it,*' he said.

A wiry arm reached out to me. The guard, or whatever he'd become, wasn't *wearing* black anymore. His *skin* was tar-black and smooth. Winding veins bulged under it. Bony fingers stretched out, each fingernail long and curved like the beak of a crow. I tried to step backwards but my feet were stuck. I tried to turn away, but my gaze was pinned on the ugly thing that was transforming before my unblinking eyes. I tried to call out, but I could only manage a wheeze.

The guard's dank hair, somehow free from the cap, hung to his shoulders. His eyes had widened into dark globes surrounded by rings of fire, burning in the centre of his face. Any hint of humanity was gone. His nose was flat to his face, two slits for nostrils; his flicking forked tongue searched the air. He stank of sewers. The fumes coming off him crawled up my nostrils and nestled there, like a smelly dog settles in its bed.

'*Thief.*' This time the word crackled like sparklers inside my head.

The burning acid in my stomach sizzled upwards in a straight line—a flaming arrow from my stomach to my throat.

Jagged fingernails scraped against my wrist. They slithered in to the pocket of my blazer, clawing at my fingers, searching for the Orb.

He bent low, hissing and sniffing. Behind him, I could see the Kila. The thing that would bring my dad home. *Just a few paces away.* It hung there like heavy fruit in the glow from the three spotlights—clear and sharp.

Dispels Demons, I thought desperately.

Fingers closed over my fist, pins prickling my flesh. The tendons in my fingers slackened, my grip around the Orb loosened.

But the Kila was so close. It was all I could see. Five steps and a stretch. That's all. If I could just pull away from this stinking, moving oil slick.

My fingers opened slowly, the Orb slipping from them.

'*Take it,*' the guard hissed.

My vision tightened into a single point. I focused on the Kila.

For a brief moment, the darkness lifted. I saw Dad. Clear as anything. He was surrounded by others, but their faces were blurry. His green eyes were sharp, bright and full of life. He was young. No scraggly beard. His lips moved silently like he was shouting something, clapping his hands…

I looked down at a pair of shiny white trainers. Mum had bought them just for the race. And they were chewing up the grass. I could feel my lungs burning up, my chin jutting out, my head wobbling from side to side with the effort... *just don't be last. Not while he's here. Please don't be...*

I stopped struggling.

Dad's face, the school field, everything disappeared. And the next second there was a blinding, burning light. It was like sitting at the front of a rollercoaster as it bombs to the ground. The heat gathering at my throat exploded upwards into my skull. It blasted the fog in my brain away with sparkling Disney Land fireworks. A freezing wind rushed through me, blowing the heat from my veins, and suddenly...

... And suddenly, the pain in my hand had gone, the foul stink, the oily face was gone too. My feet were moving. The floor was hard. Fingers gripped my hand. But they were soft. I was staggering, out of breath.

A polar bear reared up at me.

I looked down, disoriented and confused. Lily's hand held mine. There was a heavy wooden door. Cool rain hit my face, and there was a glare of headlights.

'What just happened?' I said between breaths.

'I don't know,' Lily said, panic in her voice, 'but we need to get out of this bloody rain and catch that bus.'

'What happened?' I asked again when we were huddled together on the back seat of the bus.

Graham was angry. He was rummaging in his satchel, 'That guard was a flippin' jobsworth, that's what happened!' he grumbled.

'What do you mean?'

'I mean, who did he think he was?'

The faint stench of sewage still clung to my nostrils. I stared at the marks on my fingers, where... where *whatever it had been* had attacked me.

'He could've busted my camera!' Graham spat, pulling the thing out of his bag and inspecting it. 'I swear to God I'm going to write a strongly worded letter to the museum!'

Lily laughed, 'You're such a dweeb, Gray. You sound like my dad.'

'He wanted the Vajra,' I said under my breath, lowering my hand into my pocket for it.

'How would he know?' Lily said, 'I mean it's only a rusty old—'

'No. He saw it. He was trying to get it.' I reached inside my pocket. My heart was doing disco beats again. The Vajra was still there, but... I closed my fingers around something else and pulled it out.

'Jesus, Esta!' Graham said, almost shouting. He jumped back in his seat away from my hand as if I'd pulled out a viper.

Lily gawped with wide, unbelieving eyes.

I stared at the Kila, *how...?*

I looked up at my two friends, 'So. We *are* all seeing the same thing, right?'

'Esta?' Lily whispered.

I ran a finger along it, inspecting the carved design in its handle... *Dispels Demons*... The dagger Dad was after. The object that would bring him back.

'How did you get that?' Lily asked.

I frowned, trying to recall what had happened with the guard. I remembered his foul breath, the oily feel of his fingers, the burning eyes. I remembered focussing on the Kila, the memory of sports day... the molten rod of light that shot through the centre of my body, then running outside with Lily. I shook my head. 'I don't know. But you can definitely both see it, right?'

'Let me have a gander,' Graham said, stretching out a hand for it. I paused, thinking about the creature in the museum. But this was Graham. He was no demon. I handed it over and he held it to his eye, staring down the edge of its blade.

'So, what does this mean?' Lily said to both of us.

I shrugged, 'That I'm not making it all up?'

'Not necessarily,' Graham muttered.

'What? Why not? The Kila was there, just like I was told.'

'That picture was advertised in your Gran's Home for weeks. Your dad probably talked about it. Maybe you saw it already. Subconscious.'

'I thought you believed me?' I said, suddenly regretting letting him have the Kila.

'What's got into you, Gray?' Lily said. 'Imagine she didn't make it up. Just for a second. Stop being such a grump.'

To my relief he handed me the Kila back, folded his arms and stared out of the window at the rain.

'So,' Lily said, shuffling an inch or two away from Graham. 'What's it supposed to be for?'

'It's got something to do with keeping the two worlds knitted together.'

'So…?'

'I guess there must be a way to *unhook* them.'

'So, if they knock down Gatley House…'

'Rigpa Gompa will be safe.'

'So what happens in our world happens in the other world?' Lily suggested. 'Or is it like the Wheel of Life picture? You know, each world side by side?'

I thought about that thing in the museum again. The others hadn't seen it, so why could I? Was the demon and the guard the same thing? I remembered Charlie's drawing of Lily and Mr Taylor standing in a whole other place, as if she were seeing both worlds at the same time. 'I don't think so,' I said. 'I think it's more like tracing paper.' I placed one palm over the other. 'Like one world is layered on top of another.

'So…' Lily poked the top of my hand. 'If something powerful enough happens in one place it leaves an impression on the other?'

'Or breaks through entirely,' I added.

Graham, still glaring out of the window, said, 'What about your dad? If we're pretending it's all true and you manage to separate the two worlds, how's he supposed to come back?'

I placed the Kila in my pocket. 'I told you,' I said hesitantly, trying to bring back that image of him encouraging me at the side of the track. Why had I had that memory then? It was so vivid. Was dad communicating with me from some other place? What if all the worlds were laid out on top of each other like a stack of cards? 'It's what he's been looking for,' I said eventually. 'When he sees I've found it, he'll come back.'

Graham looked at me, 'How can you be sure?'

When I didn't answer, he slumped back into his seat, and ran his fingers through his hair, muttering to himself, 'I can't believe you actually stole it.'

We sat in silence for the rest of the journey.

This time when I looked out of the window, I only saw my own pale reflection. Outside, the burning globes of car brake lights blinked at me like the eyes of a pack of wolves.

The bus pulled into a stop near the church, not far from the Greasy Spoon. We got out. It was dark and cold after the rain. Graham took the lead again, his long legs striding away from Lily and me.

'I hate this rain,' Lily said, carefully stepping over a puddle.

'You're as bad as my mum,' I replied, irritated. 'What are we *supposed* to do about it? You can't stop the rain?'

'And the trees,' she said. 'Have you seen? It's spring and they're already shedding leaves. It's all wrong.'

'Cause and effect,' I said. 'It's all breaking down. Just like he said it would.'

Lily sighed. 'Maybe. The world's so big. There are so many things we can't control… Sometimes I just want to be ten again and hide under the bed covers, you know?'

We walked on. I thought about my torch and dad's poetry book.

I knew exactly what she meant.

'I have to tell Simon about the Kila,' I said eventually.

'I thought he was being an idiot?'

'Yeah, but he's got the bell. Lama la said we shouldn't keep the Vajra and bell apart for long. I think he has to come with me. I've never seen Rigpa Gompa without him being there.'

'From what I hear, Simon's more worried about his hair than helping nerd girls—no offence—save imaginary worlds from his dad's bulldozers.'

'But if I can just show him the Kila,' I said with more confidence in my voice than I felt. 'It'll trigger something for him. He'll remember. He has to.'

We reached the turning for my road. I stopped. Graham kept walking on, avoiding the newly formed puddles. Lily held both of my hands. 'If you're sure about Simon.' She glanced down the street after Graham. 'I'll speak with Gray. He'll be alright. This rain and seeing his grandad spooked him.' She gave me an encouraging smile. 'I'm going to make him come over to Gatley House tomorrow after lunch to poke around, OK? Meet us there after school. With or without Simon. Then let's save everyone in your invisible world with that weird little tent peg.'

'Thanks Lil.'

She smiled once more. 'It's better than hiding under a blanket.' Then she turned and jogged over to Graham, leaving me alone with the Vajra in one pocket and the "weird little tent peg" in the other.

I didn't know about saving invisible worlds. I thought about Graham's earlier question. How would Dad know I'd found the treasure he'd been searching for all this time?

And even if he found out, would he really come back? *Could* he?

PART FIVE

The Burning House

35

Dropping my Bag

'How can you stand there?' I shouted, my voice echoing off silent, goggle-eyed faces.

It was Thursday lunchtime. I was in the middle of the geography room where Simon was surrounded by his classroom cronies. I hadn't meant this to be so public, but every time I tried to get him alone, he'd pull away or make some excuse. So I'd walked into the lion's den. His popularity control centre.

He'd stood at my appearance and, for some odd reason, buttoned his blazer at the sight of me. He looked flustered. All I'd wanted was to chat. A chance to speak. To show him the Kila. But he'd just stared at me and played dumb.

'Your dad's knocking it down and you do nothing? After everything…' I could hardly form any words, my mouth was dry, my tongue had expanded to fill it. The weight of the room bore down on me. I stood and simmered.

Something was up. The atmosphere was different in here. The atmosphere was *wrong*.

'Calm down,' a voice purred behind me.

Hannah Piranha.

At *every single* opportunity she had to twist the knife. Every time I screwed up or lost it. There she was. Hannah Piranha with her snide remarks and her crocodile smile. I wheeled round to glare at her. She'd changed. Her hair was different, her clothes too. More expensive. She might have even gained another inch since the last time I'd seen her as well. Standing next to her, his arm around her waist, was none other than buckle-toothed Kev. In school uniform, no less.

'I told you he was out of your league,' Hannah said, indicating Simon with an arch of a plucked eyebrow. 'Anyway, this is our room now, Depresta Brown.'

I gave her and Kev both a swift, poisonous stare. 'What's *he* doing back in school?'

Kev smiled. His teeth were straight and white, and for some reason they scared me even more than the demon in the museum.

I turned back to Simon with pleading eyes. 'You won't even come and talk?'

His expression was like someone had stood on his toe and he was trying to hold in a scream. I waited, certain that even now he would come. But I guess the pull of his cronies was too strong. He was frozen by panic, caught between talking to me and his precious popularity.

'You can't.' I snapped. 'You can't be seen with me, can you?' I reached into my pocket for the Kila. 'You want to do this right here?' I squeezed the dagger. 'Your dad is going to knock it down. You know. You *know* what this means.'

How could he *not*? And yet, here he was, hiding behind his stupid, plastic friends. At that moment I knew how Harry Sparks must have felt as he stood in the doorway of Green Gables while everyone else celebrated.

Except I'm not going to drop my bags, Harry.

'I'm going to stop it,' I said.

Simon cocked his head. I noticed with a sense of moral victory his cheeks had taken on a rosy glow. Shame, anger, embarrassment? I didn't know or care, at least it was a reaction.

I pulled the Kila out and raised it, my eyebrows raised too: *ignore me now you spoilt brat.*

For an acre of time nothing happened.

Then all hell broke loose.

Hannah shouted, 'She's got a knife!'

I frowned and glanced up. To be fair, I really *was* waving a dagger in the air, no matter how ceremonial. I pocketed it in a hurry and tried to catch Simon's eye. Surely he'd seen it, surely he'd remember?

But there were just faces, horrified, scandalised faces. My lip quivered, my eyes stung. I bit hard on the inside of my mouth. The burning sensation began in my stomach—a hot poker in my solar plexus. My vision darkened. This was not going as well as I'd hoped.

Hannah Piranha—the only clear thing in my field of vision—slid from her place on the table towards me. She was a white face surrounded by a storm of dark red. I heard whispers over the rush of blood in my head.

'Crazy cow,' 'Who does she think she is?' and, 'She should be kicked out.'

Hannah backed up toward the door. 'Can't you see no one wants you in here? If I were you, I'd run away again. Because when Culter hears about what his precious little *project* has been up to in his school, I'm sure he'll think twice about letting you stay here.'

The heat became a furnace inside me. I breathed through clenched teeth. She needed to *stop* talking.

Hannah's face was everything. Like the thing in the museum. Her mocking face glared at me from the centre of a whirlpool of black. Her laughter warbled like I was hearing her underwater. 'You reckon you can get away with anything,' she sneered as she reached the door.

I knew this classroom like the back of my hand. I closed my eyes and pictured it: the worn carpet, the rows of desks, the way the chairs didn't quite fit under them. I could see it all clear and sharp. And there was Hannah Piranha, fifteen or more feet away, with all her makeup and her hair and her gaudy nails closing around the door handle. Her red lips still moving. Making ugly sounds.

'Just because your daddy—'

The pain in my belly sliced through me like a knife. When I opened my eyes again, Hannah's nose bloomed red against the heel of my palm. I bent my knees ready for her to hit back, but she stood quite still, her hand cupped under her chin, spitting blood into it.

Her eyes were wide and full of tears.

I straightened up and wiped my bloody wrist against my blazer. I glared round at the open-mouthed faces of the other students. Simon had emerged from behind them, looking as shocked as the rest.

'Cause and effect!' I shouted at him, swung open the door and stormed out of the room to total silence.

Turns out I did drop my bag. I slammed it into the corridor wall. Exercise books spewed from it, scattering across the floor. *Cause-and-bloody-well-effect.* I stomped past Culter's stuttering secretary in the entrance hall and kicked the doors wide open.

The burning sensation ebbed away as I marched off. Someone calling my name made me stop at the school gates. I turned, still expecting to see Simon rushing after me.

It wasn't. It was Mr Blakely—the teacher whose face I'd flattened. He stood about twenty feet away in the centre of the school drive. A strip of plaster was stuck over the bridge of his nose, bruises beneath each eye.

'Come back, Esta,' he said. 'You're angry. Out of control. You want to leave, I don't blame you, but if you stay, I might be able…' he left the last part hanging. I guessed he couldn't promise anything. I also reckoned he didn't know about the dagger waving incident yet—I glanced at my hand—nor the fact that Hannah's blood was splattered against the cuff of my shirt.

'I can't help you if you run away,' he said, walking slowly towards me.

I took a step back.

'We can call your mother, take time to calm down, it'll be OK.'

I looked around me. Oily clouds drifted overhead, fallen leaves lay scattered on the ground. I shook my head. 'I don't think so, Sir,' I said. 'I think things are a long way from OK.'

'Est, things are never so bad that they can't be—'

A loud beeping behind me interrupted him. I backed a few more paces through the gates and on to the pavement. 'I'm sorry about your nose,' I said.

'Esta?' Mr Blakely said, but I was focussing on the beeping noise now. It was the noise of a truck reversing, or something else. Something big.

I turned, scanning up and down the road. There was definitely something moving on the other side of the houses. I focused on the junction at the end of the road. The row of houses came to an end. I'd be able to see whatever was making the sound from there.

'Esta?'

Mr Blakely's voice came again, but this time more distant, like how Lily's voice had faded out in the museum. He was suddenly very far away, standing at the school gates, his head twisting left and right as if looking for me. As if I had simply vanished from view.

I watched him from the junction, amazed I wasn't out of breath. Come to think of it, exactly *how* was I at the junction already? I didn't even remember running there. I stared at my bloody hand and wondered how I had managed to reach Hannah so easily through a crowd of students. I didn't remember running through them either. Before I could follow that thought though, I was round the corner and could finally see what was making the noise.

Crawling along the main road, book-ended by two police cars, was a tall yellow crane. Huddled on a platform at its base, held in place by chains, was an enormous steel ball.

The kind you smash into walls.

36

JUST LOOKING

Fletcher's Field was quiet. The bulldozers were still, but their claws rested in the torn earth like threatening gestures. The crane and its convoy would take a while to snake around the town. That was one good thing about the increasing unpredictability of everything. The roads were clogged up more than ever. It was chaos, but it was a slow chaos at least.

Mr Taylor's men had put up impressive warning signs and fortified the gate at the end of Grover Close. I raised an eyebrow at it but climbed over anyway. In a short walk, I'd be able to see through the thick hedge to Gatley House. I paused. What did I want to see? A broken, empty house that everyone else saw, ready for demolition? Or a pristine, towering palace, full of life, mystery and possibilities? I rubbed my hand where it had connected with Hannah's nose. I thought of Mr Blakely and his trailing sentences. Reassurances he couldn't give me. They would kick me out for sure now, but so what? If I was right about Rigpa Gompa, then they could do whatever they wanted to me. Small price to pay for fixing the world and finding Dad, right? And if I was wrong? If it was nothing more than an old creaky house? Well then... who cared? I mean: no Rigpa Gompa, no Dad. No point sticking around.

An out-of-breath voice from behind shook me from my thoughts.

'Esta?'

For a second, I thought it was Blakely again, and I got ready to sprint through the mud. But it was Lily who jumped over the fence.

Graham was right behind her. She was in jeans and walking boots and had been running, her hair as messy as Graham's usually was. He had one of his over-sized jam jars—empty this time—in one hand and the ever-present satchel over his shoulder. He wore a green t-shirt and green, knee-high wellingtons. He could have been the man on a street 'walk' sign.

'Wait,' Lily said, squelching over to me. 'What happened? Why aren't you at school?'

I didn't answer, instead I slid the blazer sleeve over my bloody shirt cuff.

Graham splashed into a puddle I'd had to jump over. 'Good grief, Esta! Are you *trying* to get expelled?'

'They're going to do it soon, Graham,' I said. 'I saw them bringing the crane and a wrecking ball.'

'We saw it too,' Lily said, then she turned to Graham. 'How are the levels here?'

Graham lifted a box out of his satchel. Not a camera this time. A bright yellow rectangle shape, smaller than a shoe box, with a handle and a big white circular dial on top. He flicked a button and waved a wand shaped thing down at the track, then along the hedge. The box made a scratching sound.

'It's the same,' he whispered.

'That's the radiation measuring thing?' I asked. 'Is it bad?'

'Not yet. But it's getting higher…' Graham checked the sky. 'Let's hope my dad's right and the winds keep blowing south.'

The dark clouds curled above us like the disturbed surface of a muddy pool. Maybe it was the proximity to the bulldozers, or maybe there was something rotting along the track, but the air had taken on a sickly sweet smell like overripe bananas. It was sour on my tongue.

'Are you going in again?' Lily asked. 'I thought you said Simon—'

'You were right, Simon's pathetic.'

I picked up a pebble, feeling the weight of it in my hand, then threw it high into the field. It landed well short of the nearest machine. 'I'm such an idiot.'

'Have you still got it?'

I lifted the dagger from my pocket.

'Well. What are we waiting for?' she said. She held out her hand for mine. 'Sod Simon.'

We picked our way along the track. Me on the grass verge avoiding puddles, Graham and Lily tiptoeing through the centre in their boots.

'You see anything?' Lily said when we reached the gate.

I sighed, letting my shoulders drop. The boards were back up over the windows. The door too. The walls were streaked grey after last night's rain.

Lily climbed over. I followed. Graham hesitated, his jar in his hand. It reminded me of the last time we faced each other across this gate, except we were now on opposite sides.

'Gray?' Lily said. 'We're going to look. Nothing else.'

He glanced at the diggers through the branches behind him, to the house, then back to us. He shook his head, then handed Lily his jar and climbed over. 'The moment they start moving, we're out of here,' he said.

As we picked our way between puddles and pot holes on the drive, I tried to remember the night Simon and I had done the same. The moon had been out then, the windows had reflected its light, there had been steps and a front door. I remembered the image of what I now knew was the wheel of life on one of the walls—the same image I'd seen in the museum. I tried to recollect the outside of the palace as I'm sure I'd seen it from the courtyard. Shining white walls, rows of square windows, wooden pillars by the doors. But all that came was the jarring image of Mr Taylor's mansion, with its fake columns and roaring lions. *God. Please don't let me have imagined it.*

'You see anything yet?' Lily asked.

I shook my head again, rubbing the Kila with the tip of my finger as if that might magic up the palace.

Graham had done his usual thing of going on ahead. He was already at the front door, running his hands along the edges of the wooden board that covered it.

'It's locked,' he said when we reached him. 'Someone's definitely been inside though. Did Simon have the key to this as well?'

I racked my brain. 'We walked up to it… but there wasn't even a board over the door. Then it opened. Someone else opened it.'

Graham pulled on the wood, rattling it. 'Well it's secure now. We aren't getting in that way.'

'What about the window?' Lily asked. 'Didn't you go through a side window the first time?'

That was bolted too. I kicked the board.

'Maybe it only works at night,' Lily suggested, a little desperately.

But I was picturing Hannah's bloody nose. Blakely's bruised face, pleading with me to return. What the hell was I doing at this old crumbling house?

'Guys,' Graham said, pointing to black smoke curling over the top of the hedge, 'something's coming. We should go.'

I booted the boarded window again. 'Damn it!' My toe curled in pain as I stubbed it against the wood. But I kicked out again and again anyway, shouting, 'Open up!' until tears blurred my vision and Lily put an arm around me.

'Est,' she said, 'something isn't right. We can come back later this evening when the workmen have gone. Here, you dropped your hinge thing.'

I wiped my face and looked down. The Orb had fallen from my pocket and lay in the dirt. Fat lot of good it was being. I half-thought about leaving it there. *Out of sight, out of mind.* But Lily picked it up and handed it over. As she did, the rod that ran down the centre of it began to crackle and sparkle.

'Can you see that?' I asked.

'No,' she said slowly, 'why?'

I stared at the glowing metal. 'Something's happening.'

'Stop!' Graham hissed. 'Someone's coming!'

I wrenched my gaze from the Orb. Someone was standing on the other side of the gate watching us.

37

THE CHARRED BOX

Simon landed on the drive, his Hitecs splashing in the mud. He bent double, catching his breath. 'Jesus,' he gasped when I was close enough, 'what the hell was that with Hannah?'

I had nothing to say to him. If he planned to drag me away, he'd find his posh little backside in a radioactive puddle. So I waited in silence with folded arms until he was able to stand up. Cheeks red as cherry drops.

'Esta?' he said.

Him using my name seared through me like a poker. How *dare* he come here after blanking me?

'What?' I said through gritted teeth.

'I'm sorry.'

'So am I!' I made to barge past him to get to the gate, but he grabbed my arm.

'No. Esta. Listen. I'm sorry.'

I shrugged him off and put a foot on the first slat.

'I'm sorry I didn't say anything, it's just—'

'This isn't about me,' I snapped, sounding like Mum.

He touched my arm. 'Even so.'

'Don't you get it?' I swivelled to look at him. His uniform was mud-splattered, his tie loose around his neck, hair a mess, nothing trendy about him at all. His raggedy appearance kind of rained on my fire. I peered into his grey eyes. Opened my mouth to say something, but unwelcome tears threatened, so I shut it again.

An engine behind the hedge roared into life, filling the silence.

Graham put his arms around us and leaned in. 'Come on. I'm

glad you're being friends and everything, but we have to go.' He pointed at the yellow crane now peeping over the hedge. It was already at the edge of the field.

Simon didn't break eye contact with me, 'No,' he said.

'Go back to school, Esta,' Graham pleaded. 'Whatever you've done… if you go back now, you might be able to—'

I cut him off. 'What do you care? You and Lily will be off to India before the summer's over. All this is just a game to you.'

He grimaced. 'What if you're wrong? What if it's just an old house? Two places can't…'

I exhaled a sudden blast of air, which I'd been holding. It almost became a laugh. *Exist in the same space… Yeah, I know.* 'So, we're ignoring Kant and his two worlds now are we?'

Graham scratched his head, 'He wasn't on about haunted houses and fairy tales, Est.'

I looked to Simon. 'Well?' I said, not really knowing what I was expecting him to say. I just wanted the ball to be in his court.

Simon considered our muddy feet.

Graham said, 'It's still lunchtime, you haven't missed any lessons yet. I'll bring you back, say I'd asked you to do something for me.'

I kept my eyes on Simon. He glanced at me and pulled the bell from his blazer pocket.

The handle glowed just like mine.

'If it's only a house,' he said slowly, eyes not moving from mine, 'then we'll come back with you. No harm done,' he glanced at the blood stain on my wrist and winced. 'Almost no harm.'

Lily slapped Graham on the back. 'Two minutes,' she said. 'Then we leave.'

The four of us stared down at the side window again.

Simon took out the key he'd used the first time we'd entered. He looked at me sheepishly—he must have made a copy and been keeping hold of it all this time—then opened the padlock.

'You good?' he asked me, swinging the board aside then sliding in. I still wanted to hit him for hanging me out to dry in front of Hannah, but the Orb was warm in my hand. Things were changing. And it seemed I was right. We only saw this place when we were together. I crouched down, ready to follow him.

Simon winked at me. 'See you inside,' and then jumped.

'I'll be right behind you,' Lily said to me as I wiggled through.

I landed in darkness. Way darker than it should have been.

'Are you there?' I hissed.

'I can't see anything,' Simon replied to my relief. I reached back to help Lily down, but there was no window.

'Lily?' My hand was touching cold, damp brick. 'Graham?'

No answer.

I raised the glowing Orb to the wall. The window was gone. In its place was a low door with a ring in the centre.

'Simon?' I whispered, holding the Orb to the door so he could see. 'I think we're in.'

The glow from the Orb and bell were enough to pick out the stairs leading upwards to the first-floor landing. The ceiling sagged heavily above us, reminding me of the violence of the attacks when we were last here.

Now everything was eerily quiet.

'So, you remembered everything, then?' I whispered spikily as we walked along the hallway.

'I told you, I'm sorry.'

'Did you always remember?'

'I don't know. I had weird dreams. How was I supposed to know?'

'Did you speak to Charlie?'

He was silent for a second. 'She doesn't talk much.'

I knew that. But...

'Sometimes she's with us. Sometimes she says stuff. But when she draws her pictures, they're of…'

'The valley? Mountains?'

'How did you know?'

I stayed silent. Now was not the time to tell Simon about my little visit yesterday.

'It's like she's seeing the valley,' he said. 'Constantly flipping between here and there.'

I remembered Charlie's feverish scribblings. Did she see Odiyana *all* the time? Like seeing it through the tracing paper? Or maybe that's how she was seeing *us*. Did she know where Dad was?

We reached the curtained doorway that led to the giant statue in one world and a floorless room with a hook in the ceiling in another. If we really *had* shifted to Rigpa Gompa—a fact I was still only seventy five percent sure of—this would be the test.

'You ready?' I said.

'Moment of truth.'

I flipped the curtain aside. It was dark. No flickering candlelight. I held out the glowing Orb into the room.

Two giant eyes glinted back at us. I sighed with relief. 'Yep. You wanna go in first?'

Simon nudged past me and slid his foot along the floor in front of him like he was testing the thickness of ice on a newly frozen pond. When he was confident, he crossed to the table of offerings and leaned over, 'So, what do we do?' he asked. 'The hall's empty. No candles down there either. The place is dead.'

I took out the Kila, which, unlike the Orb and bell, remained unchanged. 'We take this to Lama la.'

'Then what? What's it supposed to do?' as he spoke, he reached up to touch the Vajra held by the statue of Padmakara. The thing was about the size of a small sofa,

'It's supposed to pin the two worlds together.'

'So then, it can separate them too, right?'

'Yeah. Which means when your dad knocks down Gatley House,

this place won't be touched.'

'It's different to yours,' Simon said under his breath, still staring up at the enormous Vajra. 'The bits at the end don't meet up.'

'Come on,' I said, pocketing the Kila again, and headed through the curtain for the stairs opposite.

'Wait, what's this?' Simon said.

'What's what?'

He came out of the room holding a thin, oblong box. It was roughly the same size and shape as the golden package I'd found last time. Except this was charcoal black.

'It was inside the massive Vajra,' he said. 'I must have pressed something, and it appeared. What do I do? Open it?'

I held the Orb up for a better look. The box was made of roughly cut wood and looked as if it had been scorched in a fire. There was no apparent way inside. 'Maybe it *doesn't* open,' I suggested.

Simon shook it. It rattled. 'Interesting,' he said, raising his eyebrows at me. He tried to prize it apart with his fingers. 'There's no join.'

He banged it against the step. The noise ricocheted around the stairwell. Something hissed in the dark. I swung the Orb round, making shadows slide and grow around us.

Simon slammed the box against the wall to more clattering echoes.

'Stop it!' I whispered.

'What?'

'Just stop banging around. I heard something.'

He cocked his head. A low rumbling, so low you could feel it as much as hear it.

'The diggers?' he suggested.

'If we're lucky.' I didn't feel the need to remind him about the last time we were in this hallway. 'Let's find Lama la, then get the hell out. I don't like this one bit.'

We climbed the stairs, alive to every creak, every shifting shadow. At the switch-back Simon—a couple of steps behind me—

whispered for me to stop. I turned. I could just about look down on him.

'What if this Kila works? What happens to us?'

'What do you mean?'

'I don't know. If it separates worlds, then… which one do *we* end up in?'

'I'm trying not to think about that.'

'But what if—'

'All I know,' I hissed, 'is that my Dad was trying to find it. This is the key to bringing him back and stopping Mara. So now we both know the same, OK?'

I turned and climbed more swiftly to the first floor. There was nothing about what we were doing that I liked at that moment.

The landing creaked.

I held the Orb at arm's length, illuminating a hallway of low doors to the left. Murals on the walls. I turned to the right.

A ghostly light spilled from under the curtain covering Lama la's doorway. A faint sound of murmuring came from behind it. I took out the Kila, held it tightly, then walked the fifteen steps down the hallway. The light flickered against my muddy school shoes as I stood before the curtain. I waited, letting my heart settle. Questions jostled about in my head: Would Dad know I'd found it? Would he really come? What would he look like after all this time? Would I recognise him?

I raised my free hand to knock, then stopped. If he was there would he recognise *me*? Would he be pleased to see me?

'What's up?' Simon whispered.

'Are you supposed to knock on a curtain?'

'What?'

'It won't make any noise if I knock against the curtain will it?'

'Just open it.'

'What if Dad—'

'Bulldozers. Remember?' Simon said, pushing me aside and lifting the curtain.

38

THE DISCO BALL

The room was so bright with colour I had to shield my eyes.

Floating in the middle of the room was a huge ball of light. It was silent. Spinning and throwing rainbows against the walls like an over-sized disco ball.

I scanned the room for Dad.

Sitting on the floor around the globe of light were the four Dharmapalas. Each dressed in robes: blue, white, yellow, red. They were rocking back and forward, eyes closed, murmuring spells or whatever. At the back of the room, behind his low table, was old Lama la himself.

I stepped inside, feeling like a cardboard cut-out. Flimsy; not fully there at all.

The place was bathed in light, but it was a cold and empty light.

I'm not sure how I knew. But somehow, the farther in I went, the more certain I was that Dad wasn't there.

'You brought it,' a voice said, drifting inside my head like a breeze from nowhere.

I inched closer to the edge of the disco ball, holding the Kila up as if it were the Olympic torch. 'Where is he?' I asked, trying not to stare into the light.

Lama la's silhouette rose slowly from the other side of the ball. He stepped over his table. 'You know he's not here,' he said, his head passing through the spinning globe as if that weren't there either.

I breathed out. *Of course he isn't.*

It was almost ... almost a relief.

When Lama la's face emerged from the light, it was even more lined and aged than I remembered.

'Why didn't he come?' I asked. Although, I knew the answer already.

Lama la looked me in the eye and shook his head about a millimetre, then clicked a finger.

The sphere suddenly stopped spinning behind him. It sharpened up like when you focus a camera. I recognised it straight away. Six separate segments, like slices of pie.

'The Wheel of Life,' I said.

Lama la nodded.

I remembered what Lily had read in the museum: *existence is said to be a cycle of life, death*. Blood seemed to drip through me like water from a leaky tap. Drip, dripping. Filling me with a tightening cold.

'Why are you showing me this?' I said, letting him have the Kila.

The old man placed the edge of it in his teeth, biting down on it like you see people testing gold coins in the movies. Then he squinted down its length, same as Graham had done on the bus.

'Your father is a wanderer,' he said. 'A hungry spirit, thirsting for something he cannot have.'

Drip drip, through my veins. I felt my throat tightening.

'The more he desires it, the further away it becomes.'

'But...' I croaked. The cold was painful, it made it hard to speak. '... you said he'd come back if I brought you the Kila.'

Lama la tilted his head, looked at me grimly and then handed the dagger back. I stared at it dumbly, then up at the wrinkled old man. His expression made my insides shiver; made me think of standing on a rock in my swimsuit staring down at a grey sea...

A soft and low sigh escaped from Lama la's lips, 'But you brought me the wrong Kila, Esta.'

I let out my own breath. It felt like the last bit of warmth escaping my body, leaving me empty and hollow. I stared in frozen horror at the dagger in my palm; its blade reflecting rainbows from its polished surface. 'It... it can't be. You said it would be hidden in plain sight. That Mara would have a demon protecting it.' I thought of the guard—*the demon*. 'How?' I tried to say something more, but it wouldn't come. The ice running through my veins was making me thick and slow.

'I told you, Mara is the great deceiver. Do you remember how you got it?'

'One minute this... ugly black thing was attacking me and the next...'

'The next minute you had it in your pocket and the demon had disappeared?'

'You mean, the *demon* gave it to me?'

Lama la, his face pale, nodded once. 'This is how he wins. Deception and trickery. Soon he will attack again and this time we won't be able to stop him.' He swept an arm in the direction of the four children. 'The Dharmapalas have power. But their minds are young and unformed.' He tutted and limped back to his seat, ducking under the still image of the wheel of life. 'We're not ready.'

'Wait!' I said, following him, suddenly remembering what Charlie had said to me in the garden. Something she'd mouthed to me: *He took it.*

'What if Dad knew?' I said. 'What if he's got the real one already? If you tell me where he is, I can find him and bring it back.'

The old man eased himself back down on to his cushion and pointed up towards the pulsating globe. 'Consider the image, Esta.'

The wheel shifted again. This time it crawled round, like the second-hand of a clock. There were moving figures in it: people, animals, gods, demons. Each of them occupying a different segment. *A different realm.* I stepped closer, trying to focus. Looking for... what? For Dad?

'Where is he?' I said raising a hand up to the luminous image. 'Is he here?'

'Where else would he be?' replied Lama la.

'How can I find out which realm?' I asked, side-stepping and examining each segment in turn. *Gods, Animals, Ghosts.*

The old man sighed, 'You're looking at it all wrong.'

I tried to recall the picture in the museum. The island. There had been an island at the base of the wheel. 'Where's the Jewel Island?' I asked, searching the ball of light for the green pyramid I'd seen. I stood on my tiptoes, I crouched. 'It's just the wheel. So where is it?' My fingers curled into a clutching fist, the blood in my veins suddenly running warm again. I dropped the fake Kila and grasped at the wheel, but the mirage slipped through my fingers like a reflection on the surface of water.

Lama la clicked his fingers again, and the image began to spin faster. 'You have to let him go, Esta,' he said quietly.

The globe moved quicker and quicker. So fast that all the separate worlds began merging into one.

'The wheel turns,' said the old man.

I strained to focus on anything now. It was a blur of light. Tears burned at my eyes. 'Stop it!' I shouted, swinging an arm at it. I lost balance and stumbled forwards, plunging inside the spinning globe. Colours flashed in front, above and around me. One realm of life followed by another. The soft golden warmth of pride, followed by the hollow grey of greed, then the burning red of anger. Hunger, comfort, pain, confusion. Fear. Rage. One life to the next. Rushing through me.

'Make it stop!' I sobbed, falling to my knees.

'To live is to change,' Lama la said, his voice back inside my head. 'Even if it frightens us.'

'Please, stop!' I cried.

'It is stopping that freezes us,' he whispered. 'You have to feel the fear, feel the anger and the pain and the loss and then...' He clicked his fingers, and the wheel froze. 'Then you have to let it all go.'

The lights began to fade above me like a cloud in the summer sky. I lay on my back sucking in air as if it had been me spinning and not the magic ball of light.

'Rigpa Gompa will fall soon,' he said, 'and Mara will reach out into every single realm, twisting cause and effect to his own ends.'

I pushed myself to my knees, wiped the tears from my eyes.

The remains of the wheel dissolved into individual spots of light, small as grains of sand, until all that was left of it were sparkling pin pricks hanging in the air.

Lama la swept dust from his table. 'A river is supposed to flow. Everything is supposed to change. People move on from life to life.' His voice broke. 'But if Mara wins, then there will be no punishment for the wicked, no reward for the kind.'

My breath slowed. The room was silent. A *swish* of dust skated across the floorboards. Little grains chasing each other in a mad gallop.

'Tell me what to do,' I whispered.

'Without the Kila we are all dust. The true Kila was our only hope. Your father may once have possessed it. But it slipped through his fingers. He cannot help us now.'

I looked around me. The four children sat motionless, their eyes open, gazing at me.

'There must be something we can do,' I said. 'You said what happens here, happens in my world too. So if Mara destroys Rigpa Gompa, then Gatley House will fall, right?'

The old man nodded.

I got to my feet. The wide, silent eyes of the Dharmapalas followed me. 'You said the worlds influence each other. So can't we turn that round? There are bulldozers…' I tailed off, looking around for Simon. But the room was dark now beyond the circle of faces. Full of shadows.

'There are machines,' I continued, my mind wheeling. 'Metal machines in my world that are coming to tear down Gatley House. What if… What if I can stop the machines, wouldn't that stop Mara too?'

The ground rumbled, plaster showered upon my head. Lama la looked old. Really old. He slowly scanned the room, then shook his head and brushed some specks from his prayer book. 'Even now I can feel him reaching through the walls.'

There was silence. Then more rumbling.

An attack was coming.

Hanging from a wall was a painting of one of the demons. *A black grinning face, slick, oily limbs.* She swayed, raised a bony leg, and opened her mouth, revealing a row of yellow fangs and a crimson forked tongue. I shut my eyes and listened to what I hoped was nothing more than a fresh scattering of hail against the windows, or the rumbling of machines taking up positions around the house.

'The diggers are out there,' I said. 'They're real and they're coming. And I could stop them, Lama la.'

My brain pulsed as if someone had their fingers inside my skull and were kneading it like bread dough. I stared at the upturned faces of the Dharmapalas, the image of the demoness on the wall, and the thought occurred to me that this paper-thin reality might rip apart at any moment. And what if I found myself sitting inside a dusty room in an empty, condemned house, waiting for a steel ball to rip *me* apart?

Harry Sparks had lived with these shadows for decades. Maybe he *had* gone mad after all. I remembered the fly-trap plant. He'd seen delusions too. *Shadows*, he'd said. *Closing round you. Consuming you.* He'd put a hook in the ceiling of his living room and taken out the floor, for god's sake!

The paintings on the walls, the little shrine, the crumbling ceilings, the children. Everything shifted as if it were all part of a wrinkled picture. Whispers started chattering in my head. A half-remembered voice: *It's impossible for two places to exist in a single location.* The voices… not in my head. Outside. They were calling my name. *Lily and Graham.*

I squeezed my eyes shut. It was too much. What was I doing here? I almost wanted to laugh. I would wake up. I would wake up.

It was the middle of the day. I'd broken into an old building. There was the sound of engines outside.

I'd broken into a building they were about to knock down.

I opened my eyes a crack. Glanced at the Kila lying where I'd dropped it. *False hope.*

I wondered about the Orb in my pocket. Was that fake too? Was everything fake?

I took it out. To my dismay, it no longer glowed, in fact it had lost its golden colour altogether. It was flatter, somehow less fancy, like it was fading from view.

My head dropped. *The Orb was fading.*

It was Simon's voice that pulled me out of my sudden gloom.

'I did it!'

My head sprang back up.

Simon emerged out of the shadows. *His* bell still glowed at least. It illuminated him like a ghost.

'It opened,' he whispered.

Simon handed me a single sheet of black paper, the same shape as the one I'd read from. On it, picked out by the glow from his bell, were glistening rows of golden symbols.

'The letters,' he said, 'they were all scrambled. I was trying to read them, but then they jumped out at me.'

Lama la looked up from his tea. He beckoned Simon forward, 'Show me.'

We sat by the low table once more, while the room continued to rumble. The vibrations underneath me did nothing to dispel my growing feeling of unease about this place. About how fragile and loose it suddenly felt, like the skin of a bubble ready to burst at the slightest touch.

Lama la lit a candle and skimmed the page, holding it up close so it almost touched the tip of his nose, then he closed his eyes, murmured something under his breath and handed it back to Simon. 'If you found it, it must be for you.'

Then Lama la winked at me. 'If it's not the end,' he said. 'Then there is still hope.'

39

THE BURNING HOUSE

Simon cleared his throat and began to read, his voice thin and stuttering at first. 'One day, a fire broke out in the house of a wealthy man who had many children. The wealthy man shouted for his children inside the burning house to flee.'

He looked up at us both, then read on, this time with more confidence. 'But as flames consumed the house, the children were so absorbed in their games they did not heed his warning—'

Simon stopped as the walls rumbled around us again. Several silver bowls clattered to the floor from the shrine. Fluttering shapes exploded from behind it. Bats circled around the room, before escaping through a gap in the door curtain.

Lama la took a sip from his tea and licked his lips. 'Keep reading,' he said.

Simon placed a finger on the page. 'The wealthy man devised a practical way to lure the children from the burning house. Knowing that they were fond of interesting playthings, he called out to them, "Listen! Outside the gate are the carts you have always wanted."' Simon looked up at Lama la. 'Carts?'

'Like toy carts. Go on.'

Simon shrugged. '"Carts pulled by goats, carts pulled by deer, and carts pulled by oxen. Why don't you come out and play with them?" The wealthy man knew these things would be irresistible to his children.

The children, eager to play with these new toys, rushed out of the house. But, instead of the carts he had promised, they found just the arms of their happy father.'

Simon stopped reading. 'I don't get it. Is this something to do with Esta's dad?'

Lama la took another sip of tea, gave a low grunt and one of his throaty coughs. He wiped his lips and held out his hand for the page. 'So?' he said, inspecting the golden symbols, 'what is your opinion? Did the man lie to his children?'

Simon stared at him with wide eyes, his mouth ajar just like Gran used to look at me when she was still waiting for some kind of clue.

My heart was cold. I ran a finger along the straight edge of the Orb in my pocket—except I knew it wasn't the Orb or Vajra or whatever Lama la called it—anymore. It had become something far, far less interesting. And the story Simon had just read only reinforced my doubt.

'It's a lie, isn't it?' I said, pushing myself up. 'It's all a lie.'

And almost as if by saying the word, the room changed. It wobbled, like seeing something through a heat haze. A heavy mist crawled through the windows and crept along the floor. The room reeked of oil and burning rubber. At the same time a buzzing sound like a thousand angry bees filled the air.

An overpowering weariness dragged at me. 'It's a lie,' I murmured.

The floor lurched, making me stumble. Like the Orb before it, the room became old and grey and flat.

In the distance, a voice called out my name.

I leant against a wall, trying to balance myself.

The voice called out again, more urgently this time. Lily's voice. *Thank God.*

'Simon,' I said, making for the door. 'We have to go.'

But he didn't move. He was still gaping at the bare walls. Mouthing silent words at them.

I pulled the Orb from my pocket to light my way. But the thing was dull and cold. The metal was square, rough and flat. I shoved it back in my pocket. I couldn't look at it. I stopped at the door and shouted for Simon again.

He stood in the centre of an empty room, gripping his hair with his fists, ignoring the violent noises coming from outside. 'Don't you see?' he said turning to me, his voice crackling with static, 'Don't you see?'

I heard Lily calling my name.

I blinked. Bare floorboards. Bare walls. A dusty table.

Something yanked at my blazer. My shoulder burned. The room strobed on and off. Light and dark. Black and white. My body jerked sideways.

'Esta!'

I tried to breathe but choked on dust. I stumbled down a flight of steps. A rush of wind slapped my face; a bright light hurt my eyes.

And then there was Lily's desperate voice calling me again:

'They're coming!'

Lily dragged me from the small side window. My whole body throbbed with a freezing ache. My face stung, my ears rang. I slumped into her arms. She almost fell backwards, 'I've got you,' she said, heaving me upright on to wobbly legs.

'What the hell were you doing? We have to move,' Lily grunted, heaving me across the drive towards the lawn.

A scuffle broke out to my left. Graham had his arms around Simon's chest, dragging him away from the house too. Simon was reaching out for the crumbling walls, yelling something at it.

Clarity returned in a rush. I shrugged Lily off. It was daytime. We were crouching in the long grass of the overgrown garden. My feet were semi-submerged in the boggy soil and the weeping willow swished its branches behind us.

Gatley House stood as it always did, but more lonely and fragile than ever before. To its right loomed the crane. Bulldozers had flattened the hedgerow separating us from Fletcher's Field. Four men in hi-vis jackets and safety hats bustled around the track, clearing branches out of the way. Some had already begun pulling the gate apart. Two men in suits picked their way across the track, glancing up at the old house.

'What were you doing?' Lily repeated, looking into my eyes.

I shook my head, perplexed. 'What happened to us? Did you see anything?'

Lily put a palm to my cheek and tilted her head with a sad look in her eye.

I gazed at the Orb still clutched in my hand, but its sides remained flat and rough. My stomach twisted.

Graham hissed, 'Get down! They'll see you.' He'd lost grip on Simon, who tripped to the muddy grass.

'Wait!' I said, holding what was now nothing more than a rusty old hinge in the air.

Simon turned, his hair standing out in crazy directions, his forehead caked in mud, electric blue eyes staring out at me. 'We have to stop them,' he rasped.

I stared at the hinge, then to Simon, who smiled back at me from a grimy face. He held something up in his own hand. My heart dropped like a stone.

He was waving a rusty door bolt.

I clenched my fist, trying to recall something, anything that made sense of all of this. But memories slipped through my grasp like water. I wanted to believe we'd seen something, to share the conviction I saw in Simon's eyes. But the look Lily had given me, the feel of the hinge and the sight of the bolt robbed me of hope. *It was all a lie.*

Emotions flickered across Simon's bewildered face like clouds skating across the sky. Anger, frustration, hope, confusion.

He took a step towards me, his eyes wild, his free hand reaching out to me. 'If we stop the demons, the bulldozers will stop,' he whispered.

I swallowed. A part of me wanted to take his hand, to run with him in to Gatley House. But the old place loomed behind him, bleak, hollow, and dead, surrounded by workmen and fallen trees. And nothing had ever seemed so horribly real to me as that miserable sight.

His face collapsed, as if every muscle gave up at once. I think he realised the same thing I had.

We were strangers to each other.

'The burning house?' he rasped. His arms stretched out, the door-bolt clacking pathetically in one hand. Pleading with me. 'Remember the burning house.'

I knew it meant something. Knew I'd heard the phrase before, but I couldn't hold on to it, couldn't pin it down. My brain was a fog, and my memories were disappearing into it.

There was a crunching of wood as the workmen lifted the gate from its hinges—the gate I used to stand behind while I watched the old house sleeping. It fell apart before hitting the ground, ravaged by rot and disease. They had broken through the final barrier to the property and now they saw us.

Simon stood tall and stared at me, the faintest glimmer of mad hope in his eyes. 'You said it. We have to stop both. Demons here. Bulldozers there. Promise me? We have to stop both.'

I didn't know what to do or say. I just nodded, tears spilling from my eyes.

Simon nodded back stiffly, then turned and without warning sprinted to the house.

Before anyone could respond, he dived through the basement window. The last I saw of him were the mud-caked soles of his precious Hitecs.

Graham, Lily and I stood in frozen silence, watching the house and the advancing workmen angrily waving us away.

We waited until the closest man was within a few feet before running; pushing through spiny branches, spurred on by the shouts and threats being hurled at us; only stopping when we tumbled out on to the estate, clothes muddy and torn, breathing heavily and pale-faced.

Lily said something, but I was deaf to her. A phrase rolled

through my mind, rolled and returned like waves against the rocks:

The burning house.

PART SIX

THE TRUTH

40

MISS NUTTAL

That night I thought of Simon with growing dread. I tiptoed downstairs to call his home number, but the possibility of speaking to his dad stopped me before I'd even lifted the receiver.

I'd wanted to go back to Gatley House, but the place was crawling with workmen. They'd already stuck up fences around Fletcher's Field. They'd fixed even more barbed wire to the gate at the end of the close too.

On our way home Graham had told me to calm down. 'They won't knock it down until they've capped the water and gas pipes and other stuff,' he'd said. He and Lily led me to my front door. 'We have time.'

I didn't believe him. That place had been ready to go for years and—although my mind was foggy about everything—I got the sense that somewhere down the line, rows of dominoes were busy knocking each other over.

'Simon won't stay there all night,' he'd said. 'Don't worry. He'll have been found already. He'll be home being howled at by his dad.'

I didn't believe that either.

I couldn't sleep for ages. Whenever I closed my eyes, there was Simon. He was sitting in a hall surrounded by people in robes, mouthing strange words. His eyes were closed and his face was ghost white. I shook the image from my mind and peered out of the window in the direction of Gatley House. *Demons there. Bulldozers here. We have to stop both.*

I must have fallen asleep, because I opened my eyes to the morning sun streaming through my curtains. I dressed without thinking. Dirty shoes, torn shirt and all.

Mum barely noticed. Instead she waved yet another letter in front of me, her mouth moving like Simon's had done in my dream. I blocked out whatever she was saying. Probably a report about poor little Hannah's nose. Or my very public flight from school yesterday.

It was a surprise to see her smiling though. She was obviously distracted by something. A happy thing that stopped her from seeing what a mess I was.

I tuned in.

'... success. So lovely of him to want to recognise all the hard work.'

I smiled back, confused. *Who?*

Mum strode across the kitchen, and with no warning hugged me tight. She buried her face in my hair and said something that came out all muffled.

When she drew away, there were tears in her eyes which she blotted with a knuckle. She sniffed twice and held my cheek—just like Lily had done last night—searching my eyes. Her own eyes flickered uncertainly; she took a step back and finally saw the state I was in. 'You look like you've been dragged through a hedge backwards.'

I winced in reply. That was kind of true. She touched the tip of my nose clumsily; this whole showing affection thing was alien to her.

'Don't worry,' she said with what she probably thought was a reassuring smile. She flapped the letter at me again, 'Mr Culter will understand. We'll make him understand. You're going to be fine.'

The name of the headmaster clanged in my muddled brain. Mum kissed my forehead with busy optimism. She jangled her keys and strode to the front door with more purpose than I'd seen from her since... since Dad left.

'Mum?' I said as she stood in the doorway.

'Yes?'

For a second I considered telling her about Simon. Tell her what though? I didn't even know myself.

'Honey?' Mum said.

'I… I don't want them to knock down the old house.'

'What?'

'I want to stop the road.'

'Altogether?' She shook her head. 'Esta, protest is about fighting the things we can change and accepting the things we can't. Green Gables could be saved…' she let that trail away. 'But no one's ever stopped a road just by protesting, Honey.'

I cocked my head. She'd changed her tune all of a sudden.

'This is something good happening to us!' she exclaimed.

My expression must have been a forlorn one because she rushed over and kissed me again. 'We won one battle,' she looked at me meaningfully, 'and today you and me are going to win another one. We're going to show them the real you. Make them understand. Give you a chance. And at worst, they'll give you a good reference.'

She wore heels, I realised. I'd not seen her in heels for two years. They *click, clicked* back to the door.

'The box is still here, darling,' she called, as she stepped outside. 'Have you made your mind up about what you're keeping?' She said it as if I was choosing something for a bring-and-buy sale.

I shook my head, even though she couldn't see. For some reason I couldn't quite put my finger on, I never wanted to look in that box again.

I called after her.

'Yes, Honey?'

'You said about everyone holding hands across America. You said if we made enough noise.'

She smiled and raised a victory fist. 'I'll see you at school.' She blew me a kiss and closed the door. Her heels clicking on down the garden path.

See me at school?

Hannah had obviously not stayed quiet about our little 'coming together' yesterday. Although no one said anything to me, I felt eyes trailing me wherever I went. In class, the teachers avoided eye contact with me and I noticed them hovering by their doors as if blocking off my escape route should I decide to leg it.

I didn't share any classes with Simon, so I had no idea if he was in school or not. I drifted through the morning trying to get a grip on what to do. During lessons, every time a door opened, I had two thoughts. The first one was that—improbably—it would be Simon. When it wasn't, my second thought was about how far I'd get if I just made a dash for it.

I didn't utter a single word to anyone, not even to Dr Harkness when he asked me about something called 'Red Shift', in Physics, even though I knew what it was.

It's the universe telling us that everything is flying away from everything else.

At lunch, I raced to the one place I knew he would be. The Geography classroom. But it was empty. Just a couple of boys chatting in the corner. Not even one of the brutal card games.

That was it, then. Simon wasn't in school. What if he was another Charlie Bullock, lying hurt in the old house? What if he had fallen through the rotting floorboards?

I would have to report what had happened, or at least say something to somebody.

Instead, I tried to slip away across the fields. If I could just get inside…

But I barely made it halfway to the hedge before I was collared by Mr Culter's out-of-breath secretary who practically frog-marched me to his office.

Mum was already inside. There was another lady who joined us this time. A large-breasted middle-aged woman in a badly fitting flowery dress sitting beside Mr Culter. She had cropped peroxide blonde hair and a cut-and-paste smile which would have suited a politician. She flashed it at me as I entered. Her teeth were the colour of margarine.

The headmaster pointed me to a chair.

'Mr Culter was saying how happy he is about Green Gables,' Mum said, all in a rush. 'I was telling him what an important role you played. How you helped out with the leaflets.'

I bit my lip, picturing the crumpled pile Simon had pulled out of the jaw of his dad's lion. I rubbed the heel of my hand, recalling the feel of Hannah's nose against it. There was still blood on my shirt sleeve.

Mr Culter didn't seem impressed. 'Esta, we have also been talking about the sort of support we can offer to help with your emotional issues.'

I saw Mum's face redden. 'Mr Culter, this isn't what we—'

He stopped her with a raised hand, which he then angled towards the woman in the flowery skirt. 'I want you to meet Miss Nuttal. The Chair of governors.'

Mum tried to speak, interrupting Culter's flow, but he barged on anyway. 'Her behaviour is no reflection on you, Mrs Brown. You have tried your best in difficult circumstances.'

'But you said, if she could change—'

He cut her off again, just like he did with the students, 'If only for Esta's benefit...' Once Culter was on a roll, he was like a talking bulldozer. '... her educational and—'

'She can change!' Mum said, looking at me. The tip of her nose was crimson, there were dark crescents beneath her eyes where she had dabbed away her make-up. 'She's confused. You should be offering her support, not—'

Culter talked over as if she wasn't still speaking, '—and emotional needs might best be served with a brand-new slate.'

'Please,' Mum whispered.

Miss Nuttal obviously felt it was her time to speak. When she did it was in soft, calm tones. Even softer than Culter's best sponge-cake.

'Mrs Brown. Perhaps you aren't aware…' She paused as she checked with the headmaster. 'I have been informed that Esta was caught fighting yesterday. Not only that, but she absconded from school yet again.' Her lips smiled. Her eyes didn't. She raised a cup of tea to her lips. Her fingernails were varnished a shiny red, clashing with her dress. The woman sipped her tea, then continued. 'The school has been very clear about its expectations.'

'But you said this was a last resort,' Mum replied.

I looked at her. She dipped her head as if she were searching for something in the bag on her lap. I placed a hand on hers. She glanced at me, then at Mr Culter. 'She's getting better. She can change.' Her confident tone had disappeared.

She was pleading for me, I realised. The thought made my face go hot.

I loved Dad.

But he wasn't here.

Mum was.

'We've been through this, Mrs Brown,' the lady said in calming tones, 'I'm afraid words and promises are not enough. Neither Mr Culter, nor I, have seen any evidence of progress. Frankly, her violent outburst yesterday was frightening for all those who witnessed it. It may be that Esta is beyond any help we…' She slurped from her tea again, raised her eyebrows, '… or you, are able to provide.'

Mum almost exploded. 'What are you saying?'

Miss Nuttall placed the teacup very slowly and deliberately on Mr Culter's desk. 'I'm saying, Mrs Brown, that your daughter is displaying consistently disturbing behaviour that is damaging not only to her own well-being, but to others—'

Mum slammed her palm on the desk. 'My daughter is not crazy! She needs encouragement. She just needs...' Her voice broke.

I felt a rock lodge in my throat.

The headmaster gave me one of his beady looks. He leant back, studied both Mum and me again in silence, then nodded at Miss Nuttal. The lady took another sip from her tea—this time using her left hand I noticed—then cleared her throat and addressed Mum: 'Mrs Brown, we're not ogres. I understand how confusing this must be for her,' she sighed. 'And we only have her best interests at heart.'

I stopped listening. My attention was suddenly on the woman's hand holding the cup. The nails were painted blue. I cocked my head. She was twirling the pen with her right hand. Red nails. *Who paints their nails different colours on each hand?*

'Esta?'

My attention shot back to Mr Culter, who was leaning over to catch my eye. 'Esta,' he said, 'you had better go back to your lessons while we discuss this with your mother. I'm sorry to have dragged you away from your studies. We'll be in touch when we have come to… a better understanding.'

Mum smiled at me. 'Come straight home after school,' she whispered. 'I'll be in.'

I paused at the door.

'Yes, Esta?' Mr Culter asked.

I should have said something. I should have told Mr Culter about Simon. But what? I just had snippets of memory and none of them made much sense right then.

'Nothing,' I mumbled.

He smiled. 'Don't worry about Simon,' he said, as if reading my mind. 'He's done this before… Going missing. He'll turn up at his mother's house.'

I seethed over that comment until the afternoon bell.

I stormed home, not caring if they wanted to kick me out or keep me. As soon as I got in, I was going to call Simon's dad until he answered. If not, I'd call the police and tell them everything.

Not *everything,* of course, just the *real* things.

I needn't have worried with such a plan though.

It was the police who came to me.

The car engine was still ticking over when I nudged past it to get to the garden path. I pushed open the door, glancing at Dad's cardboard box at the end of the hall.

There were voices coming from the kitchen.

At last it was time to talk.

I clenched my jaw and walked in.

41

THE TRUTH...

We sat around the dining table. Mum to my right, nervously sipping milky coffee, a police officer opposite stirring a third spoonful of sugar into his tea.

'So, you saw Simon Taylor yesterday?' the officer asked.

'Yes, sir.'

The policeman swapped his tea for a notepad and wrote something down. I'd not been this close to a proper policeman since Dad left. This one was called 'Bennett', a shiny badge by his left shoulder said so. Everything about his face was streamlined, thin and sleek. His greying hair was neatly trimmed; his hands were smooth and his sharpened pencil looked at home between his fingers. He wrote his notes without hurry.

'At Gatley House, you say?'

I nodded, chewing on my lip and fiddling with the rough and depressingly flat hinge I still kept in my pocket.

'What were you doing there?'

'What does it matter?' Mum said. 'She was there. She saw him run inside. Have you searched the place?'

Bennett flicked a glance at her and repeated his question.

'We were curious about the demolition,' I said.

'During school hours?'

Mum thumped her mug on the table, 'Oh, for goodness' sake! Are you looking for this boy or giving her a detention?'

The officer paused, licked the tip of his pencil. 'Was it just you and he at the location?'

I developed a number of itches on my scalp and the nape of my neck. 'No. Graham Sparks and a girl called Lily. I don't know her second name. She works at the greengrocers.'

The officer raised his eyebrows and wrote down the names.

'Is there anything else?' Mum asked.

'Mr Taylor, Simon's father,' Bennett said to me, 'suggested I came to see you. He says Simon has been acting oddly ever since you and he became friends. Can you shed any light on that, Esta?'

I remembered seeing Mr Taylor with the spade in the air. 'I don't think he likes me,' I mumbled. 'That's why he sent you round, I suppose.'

'Mr Taylor?' Mum exclaimed. 'The developer?'

The officer frowned at her interruption.

I gave her a weak smile and picked up the officer's discarded teaspoon, giving my nervous fingers something to do.

Bennett continued, 'For example, would this have been the first time you and he had visited Gatley House together?'

'No,' I said.

'And what did you do when you were there?'

'You don't have to answer that, Esta.'

'Mrs Brown, please, these details may be important.' He turned to me, staring down his nose. 'Esta, I need you to tell me the truth. You understand that Simon is missing and that you and your friends may have been the last people to see him. Whatever you tell me now could save his life.'

The thoughts flooding my mind threatened to escape right there on the table in a luminous, radioactive splat. *Tell him the truth?* I'd spent so long wondering what that was myself, the very idea of it made my head spin.

I opened my mouth to speak. He was right, every detail might be vital. I stared at the table top. *What was the truth?*

A pair of kind, crinkled eyes blinked up at me from the polished surface of the table. A quiet voice said: *"Did the man lie to his children?"*

'Esta?' said the officer. 'It's important we know everything as soon as possible.'

I spoke and let the words leaving my mouth guide me. 'It started with a dare,' I began.

By the end of my story, the policeman had stopped taking notes. He exchanged a glance with Mum, who gave him an apologetic smile.

I regretted opening my mouth. These two weren't Graham and Lily. Adults don't listen. They don't see between the lines.

'So you're saying Simon is trying to stop the bulldozers because...' Bennett paused and checked his pad, '... he believes people are living there. Kind of a commune?'

Mum offered another pained smile, 'She has an overactive imagination.'

Bingo! Thanks Mum! Did you tell Miss Nuttal that as well?

'Squatters?' said Bennett, his pencil poised.

'Maybe.'

'And you've seen them too?'

And I don't know what happened then. The world tilted. It was as if I was suddenly seeing everything from a different angle even though my head was still bowed towards the table top. I stared at my fingers; they'd bent the teaspoon out of shape. I dropped it.

'Maybe it's like the duck and the rabbit illusion?' I suggested desperately, 'You know, when you look at it one way it's a duck...' I closed my hands into fists. This was not going well. Adults aren't easy to talk to. Their grasp on reality is all black and white. Everything is all duck, or all rabbit to them.

The policeman leaned forwards over the table, his breath sweet, his voice low, less probing. It reminded me of Mr Culter.

'Esta, it's all right. You aren't in any trouble. We only want to find your friend.' He gave Mum a glance. 'So if you could be more... specific?' He rose to his feet and unhooked his radio. 'Either you saw someone, or you didn't. This is very important.' He beckoned Mum to stand as well. 'We'll give you a moment to collect your thoughts.'

Mum smiled at me encouragingly and they both walked to the kitchen door, Mum nursing her coffee, the officer raising the radio to speak. It crackled and whatever he said into it was muffled by the closing door.

42

GIVING UP THE BOX

When I exhaled, it felt like the first time I'd breathed since sitting down. My hands shook. I inspected them. My nails were short and jagged from nervous nibbling. A swarm of tiny black dots swam at the edge of my vision and my ears hissed. I pulled the hinge from my pocket and placed it on the table.

Vajra or hinge? I blinked, rubbed my eyes, closed one, then the other. *How come the other day I couldn't even see the stupid flipping hinge?* I lowered my head to the surface of the table. Tiny particles of rust had dropped from it, which I touched with my forefinger. I stroked the metal, feeling for a hidden edge, or the suggestion of a pattern.

I trawled through everything that had happened: *Duck or rabbit?*

The drums and clashing cymbals we'd heard on that first night: *Rats? Settling foundations?*

The face of the old man: *Fear? Squatter?*

The Vajra and bell. I glanced at the hinge: *ancient, rusty bits of junk?*

Hot tears dropped to the table. I sniffed and wiped my cheeks.

But I'd seen Gatley House transform. The faces of the children in different coloured robes; the smell of incense; the salty butter tea; pictures of demons hanging from the walls; the chanting in the hall. It was too much. Like nothing I'd ever experienced. How could my imagination conjure that level of detail out of mouldy bricks and empty rooms?

And Simon. What had Simon seen?

Was this all in my head? I recalled Graham's German philosopher. The one who thought there were two worlds. Simon's wild eyes flashed before me. He had seen something, hadn't he? The very moment I had begun to doubt, he had finally been convinced.

Birds sang in the early evening outside the kitchen window. The front door creaked open. The adults needed me to say something. The adults needed *facts*.

Mum's face appeared through the crack. 'We're coming in. Are you ready?'

'Give me one more minute,' I said, squeezing a fist against my temples to dull the throbbing pain, trying to squash my confusion into something I could understand. Something I could put into words.

Maybe the illusion was neither duck nor rabbit, I thought. After all, the picture was merely lines on a page, wasn't it? The observer made them into the ducks or rabbits. Both existed in the mind, not in the lines.

The shock of that realisation made me sit up straight. I stared blankly at Mum and Officer Bennett as they re-entered the room, hardly registering them. I glanced out of the kitchen window. Unseen birds twittered in the back garden; a trail of silver was scratched across the sky; a distant roar of engines faded into nothing. My brain clenched in concentration. Could something be true in two different ways? Could Rigpa Gompa be imaginary and yet still somehow real? It was the sort of question that changed everything, and nothing at the same time. I can't fully explain what it meant to me then, or how it changed anything. I wasn't sure the insight was true or even made any sense, but it unlocked something in my mind.

'Esta?' Bennett said, sitting down. 'I've spoken to Mr Taylor. His men have searched the house from top to bottom and inside out. He's not there.' He let this information settle. 'Tell me the truth, Esta. What happened?'

I lowered my eyes. The dull metal thing stared back at me from the table and the feeling of breaking through to some sort of realisation shut off. *A hinge is a hinge.*

The man in the black and white uniform said my name. He waited. He said Simon's name. He waited some more. Finally he said: 'The truth.'

I hesitated a moment, then looked him dead in the eye and told him the truth he was after. The only truth he would be able to accept.

'I saw nothing,' I said.

Mum's face softened.

I shrugged. 'It was just a game. We imagined everything.'

The policeman nodded.

'Simon just got caught up in it,' I continued. 'I tried to stop him, but he was too fast. The last thing I saw was him running into the house. I've not seen him since.'

Mum smiled and reached out over the table, a rescuing hand ready to grasp mine and pull me back from a precipice.

'I didn't know what to do,' I said, with tears in my eyes. Genuine ones.

Mum nodded more vigorously than the policeman and squeezed my fingers. The officer scribbled in his notepad. He lifted the delicate china cup to his lips and finished his tea. He thanked us and left without any more questions. Mum walked down the hall to see him out, asking him what the police were doing about the radiation cloud, leaving me alone, staring at the bent spoon.

I went to the window and watched another plane make its approach. Millions of people took off and landed every day. Each one with their own stories, their own dreams and plans.

I gulped.

A thought came that pricked my scalp.

Dad was not one of them.

He never was.

He never would be.

The growl of the engine faded away. The birdsong came again. Maybe they were hurling abuse at each other. But it was still beautiful.

Dad had left Mum and me. But he wasn't waiting to return, was he? Wherever he was, he wasn't coming home.

I glanced towards his box, filled with his bits and bobs, filled with stuff.

The front door clicked shut. Mum padded back along the hall in her socks. Before she entered the kitchen, I spoke two words to the fading plane trail and the birds. Because when you finally say it out loud, it becomes a kind-of real. I whispered the words, my breath forming a misty cloud against the cold glass that disappeared almost as soon as it formed:

'Dad's gone.'

I slipped out later that evening, carefully placing Dad's cardboard box at the end of the drive for the bin men like I'd seen Mum do before.

43

POETRY

It was nearly nine and the evening sun was a rusty echo in the gas-flame-blue sky. There were no more planes coming in to land, although a few had left geometric patterns in chalk-white high up in the night. There was no twilight birdsong as I approached the torn up field lying between Gatley House and me. Frightened off by the machinery and harsh electric lights maybe, or—I remembered Graham's yellow radiation box—something worse. Whatever. The silence was disconcerting.

As I walked, my mind became quiet too. Thoughts rose but dissolved before they took form. I'd not eaten, and hunger made me feel hollow inside. I drifted, ghostlike along the street towards the security lights, which hung over the earthworks near Gatley House.

Eventually one thought took shape. A thought so heavy its gravity threatened to pull me down into the earth itself.

Dad's gone.

I was drawn out of my thoughts by stumbling into the fence leading to Fletcher's Field.

I'm not sure why I was making for Gatley House. I didn't know if there was anything to find, but I had to do something. The officer was right; I was the last one to see Simon. I didn't doubt that the workers and the police had searched the place from top to bottom, just like they'd done with Charlie Bullock. But if Simon wasn't there, where was he?

I jumped the fence, trying to glimpse the house through the remaining trees. But security had been stepped up since last time.

They'd erected barbed wire fencing along the perimeter of the new road. "No Trespassing" signs were nailed to posts at regular intervals. It wasn't exactly Alcatraz, but it was definitely a statement of intent. I skirted the fence, trying to judge the distance it would take to run across the open field.

A dog's aggressive bark tore the darkness between the trees and me. A man's voice joined in. Two jacketed figures emerged from the trees. Torch beams waved across the ground, swinging along the line of fence. The barking strangled, became a yelp, and then ceased. The torch beam swung past and off to another part of the fence.

I didn't fancy my chances against dogs and I couldn't face going home, so I went to Green Gables instead. Even if, at this hour, it was only to watch Gran's window from the outside.

The entrance porch of the Home was aglow with light and bunting still flapped above the door. Although it was way past visiting hours, when Nurse Olive saw it was me, she grinned and let me right in.

'She's awake,' she said, leading me to Gran's room. 'Everyone is excited for Friday. It'll be a lovely day out.' She flashed white teeth at me and selected a key from a large ring. 'But none of them can get to sleep! They're like kids on Christmas Eve. Here we are.'

'Excuse me?' I said, perplexed.

'The school's Community Prize? At the assembly on Friday. I know how pleased your mother is. We're all so proud of her.'

The assembly! The interview with Officer Bennett had pushed that little fact right out of my mind. I tried to hide my horror. In the whirl of Simon's disappearance, Mum and I hadn't spoken about the meeting with Culter and Nuttall. I didn't know if they were kicking me out of school or not, but surely they wouldn't make me go through with the assembly now? It was a stupid idea.

The nurse made to knock on Gran's door. She paused and

lowered her head. 'Though it's disturbing about the Taylor boy. I do hope he's OK. I hear it's not the first time he's run back to his mother. It would be a terrible shame to cancel the thing. The old boys and girls are so looking forward to it.' She gave me a sad smile, then squared her shoulders and knocked lightly on the door.

Gran looked up when I entered. She had her book flat against her lap. Fresh tears marked her cheeks. She smiled at me through glistening eyes before blowing her nose with a handkerchief.

'Are you all right?' the nurse said.

Gran let out a silent laugh. She patted the book on her knee. 'He's gone,' she said, now dabbing her eyes with a clean corner of her handkerchief. Her words sent a shiver down my spine. *He's gone?*

The nurse smiled and let me in. 'I'll come back in fifteen. She's a tonne better, but don't overdo it, love.' Then she shut the door.

I stood still, facing Gran. Astounded. Her whole face was transformed. She wasn't wearing makeup now and her hair was a mess, but to me, she'd never looked better. There was colour in her cheeks that hadn't been painted on. There was a glint in her eye like she'd finally found the answer to one of her puzzles. She was crying, but I'd never seen her so… happy.

'You've nearly finished your book,' I said, nodding at it resting on her knees.

Gran dropped her handkerchief to the mattress and held out her hand. I took it and she drew me closer. I sat next to her on the bed.

'You're a good girl. I remember how you come to visit me, you know.'

'Why are you crying?' I asked tentatively, replaying her words in my head: *He's gone.*

Gran took a deep breath, 'He died.'

I gulped. A tear rolled a cool track down to my chin.

Gran picked up her handkerchief and touched my cheek with it. 'He was a hero,' she breathed. 'He died to save her.'

My other eye welled up. All the crying I had done in my mind about Dad was ready to burst out of me. I had no words, only raging bulls stampeding in my brain and I was helpless against them. My body rocked and I let out a noise I had never made, never even heard before. A moaning, high-pitched noise that didn't sound like me, or anything human. My head dropped with the weight of something that had been lying within—maybe hanging off a rope—for almost two years.

Gran placed a hand on the nape of my neck and patted it. 'Something can be sad, but wonderful as well, Esta. It's strange when two different feelings exist at the same time, but I expect you know all about that, don't you?'

I sniffed and almost laughed.

When the heat of my tears faded, I lifted my head. Gran was watching me with a distant look and the faintest of smiles, like she was recalling a memory. I wiped my face with the sleeve of my blazer and straightened up. The pressure in my head was gone. It was like the feeling of relief after vomiting up something poisonous.

She picked up her book and handed it to me. 'I waited for you to help me finish this. You read so beautifully.'

I took it off her. The pages were crisp and white. She'd read on past the usual yellowed, over-thumbed pages, almost to the end.

The paper smelled of almonds. The pages were old, but flat and crisp. They were old, but they were also new. It's funny how sometimes words don't describe the world like you need them to.

I read the last chapter of Gran's book, while she listened, holding her handkerchief up to her face in readiness for more tears.

It was the corporal who had died, not Dad. I realised Gran had been talking about the book earlier. But she'd been talking about Dad on some level as well though, hadn't she?

In the story, the woman married an officer who survived the war. The last chapter ended with her watching the kids she'd had with her new man. She wept happily as she watched her children playing in the garden where she'd met her corporal so many years ago.

I laid down the completed book, confused.

Gran gave a satisfied sigh, then answered a question I hadn't asked: 'The corporal lives,' she whispered with a wink. 'In the children and in the tears she sheds for them.' She smiled and patted me again. I nodded like I understood what she meant.

We sat in silence for a while until the clock chimed ten o'clock. For some reason the sound made me remember Simon. Thinking of him brought back images of Rigpa Gompa and a thought occurred to me. 'Gran? Do you believe in ghosts?'

Her expression didn't change, 'Depends what sort of ghost,' she said, matter-of-factly.

'I don't know—like seeing someone who isn't there. Looking into a different world. But the same one at the same time?'

'Seeing something that no one else sees?'

'Maybe.'

'A lot of us do that in here. See things, hear things. People call it senility.'

'What do you think?'

Gran shifted herself to face me more directly

'I think, as your body grows weak, your mind sees the cracks in the pavement. They were always there. You were just too young and busy living that you didn't pay attention.'

'What if I've seen something like that? Does that make me mad?'

Gran scowled, then paused, letting her eyes wander upwards. 'One day,' she said at last, 'you'll fall in love and the universe will flip over. You'll see a stumble as the first step in a dance. You'll see beauty in everything.' She smiled. 'Then, maybe just as suddenly, it'll all end.' She licked her lips. 'And every single thing becomes dark and unfriendly. You see the skeleton beneath the skin.'

Gran examined me with milky eyes and put a hand against my shoulder. 'You think the universe really changes because you fell in and out of love?'

I stared at her, considering her question. I didn't know if she was making sense or not. For an instant a tired, defeated expression flashed across her face. For that moment she looked like she had done before the Home was saved.

'It's all just poetry, dear,' she said with a brief smile.

'Poetry?'

'Everything is poetry, didn't your father ever tell you that?'

I thought of his book of poems lying by my bed. 'Not exactly.' But somehow, by leaving his book, maybe he did.

'Gran?' I said after a few silent moments. 'How well do you know Mr Sparks?'

'Harry? He's down the hall.'

'He owns Gatley House. The house they are—'

Gran interrupted me. There was a barb to her voice, 'Used to own.'

'Have you ever talked with him about what happened?'

She stung me with a piercing eye. Her gaze had a youthful ferocity like the one she'd once given me the day after my first visit to Gatley House. For the briefest of moments she was like the final pages of her book: old and new at the same time.

'Of course we talked, Esta. I helped him erect the memorial stone for his wife.'

44

THE ISLAND OF JEWELS

When the shock had died down, my thoughts began to race with possibilities. 'You know about Gatley House?' I whispered, a spark of hope igniting. Was *Gran* the one who had seen? Was *she* the 'other' that would help me? I remembered the day I'd read to her—my mind on Gatley House—and she'd stopped me: *Did you see him?*

'I know what Harry told me,' she said.

'Did *you* see?' I asked, repeating the question she had once asked me.

She smiled bashfully and shook her head, 'Only shadows.'

'Did you believe what he told you?'

'Of course I did. The place took almost everything from him.'

'And Dad?'

Gran lifted a tissue to her nose and sniffed. There were fine cobwebs of red in her eyes. 'Dickie's lost, Esta,' She sniffed again, cleared her throat. 'Harry escaped with his life, but not Carol and not Dickie. The place gobbles you up if you let it.'

'I know what he was looking for.'

She placed a hand against my cheek. 'It's hard to let go. Trust me, I know. A mother shouldn't outlive her son.'

'No. Listen. He was searching for something. He was trying to find an island. Lama la…' I paused, looking at Gran to see if she knew who I meant. She nodded me on and I was too excited to be surprised.

'I found something in the house. A piece of parchment meant just for me. There was a story and I'm sure it's about what happened to Dad.' And then I told her the story of the Jewel Island; about how the merchant had left it empty-handed, never to return.

'What do you think?' I asked when I'd finished.

Gran seemed surprised by my question. But she answered immediately. 'Do you know what a metaphor is?'

'You're saying the story means something else?'

'Of course it does.'

'But…'

'Whatever Dickie was looking for, it wasn't an island of jewels.'

'But Lama la told me—'

'Life isn't precious,' she said, one finger in the air as if she were telling me off. 'Only a meaningful life is precious.' She stood up and tottered over to her bookshelf. 'Now, I think we need a new book.'

'The story isn't about an island?' I asked, perplexed.

Gran ran a finger along the shelf. 'Non-fiction this time,' she muttered.

'Wait. Gran. What do you mean: A meaningful life?'

She turned and smiled at me. It was an energetic smile. 'The story isn't about your father, Esta.'

'Where's the jewel island then?'

Her eyes lit up and she laughed. Her laugh became a cough, and I had to get her another tissue. She placed a hand on her chest when she had recovered and looked at me. 'And the story isn't about gold or diamonds either,' she said. 'The story,' she touched my face. 'Is about *you,* Esta Brown.'

I must have looked confused because Gran patted my arm and smiled. 'Carol told it to me many years ago before she left. The island is a symbol for this life, right now. The jewels stand for all the things that are valuable to us.

You see, it's not enough to have the *opportunity* for happiness, Esta. You have to grab it. Make use of it. Do something with it. Or, one day, the winds come, your ship blows away and you never find it again.'

I had that weird rollercoaster feeling again and my thoughts turned back to Simon, maybe still alone in Gatley House; then to Mum with her banners and the thumbs-up gesture; then to the way Graham had looked at Lily in the Greasy Spoon.

The fire in Gran's eyes dimmed. She gazed at the bare wall for a moment like she was counting her own treasures, then she returned to the bookshelf as if nothing had passed between us. 'Natural History. Something your father was always interested in. Here.' She handed me another book. 'This was one of his.'

It was a hardback with a glossy black cover and stark white writing.

'You want me to read this to you?' I asked.

She went back to her bed, empty-handed, still not meeting my eyes. 'No, dear. That one is for you. It's the least I can do.' She lay down. 'Now, I'm tired and you're going to need your strength.'

I watched as she settled herself into bed.

'Stop the chaos, Esta. Save the house,' she whispered.

'I don't know how,' I whispered.

She rolled on to her side to face me. 'Yes you do.'

'I was supposed to find something to help. But I found the wrong thing.'

'Then you must find the right one, dear.'

'I wouldn't know where to look. I don't even know if any of this is real. What if none of this is real?'

'Maybe *everything* is poetry, Esta,' she murmured, closing her eye. 'Did you consider that?'

The feeling I'd had earlier that the world had tipped suddenly returned. Gran had said something that was like the corner piece in a jigsaw. This realisation came as a flash. My thoughts had to catch up with it: *Everything is poetry?*

Everything I see, hear and smell. Everything I say and do can be true in different ways at the same time.

Does that make sense? It made complete sense to me at the time. Ever since I'd seen the old man's face at Gatley House, I'd been trying to get my head around the other world I'd stepped into. Was it real? Hannah had told Simon I was damaged. But what if I was simply using the wrong words? Maybe poetry was the language I needed: Symbols, similes and metaphors. Maybe there were other forms of language too. Ways of speaking that made sense of the worlds I saw on top of one another.

I thought about the policeman with his notepad and pen: *Tell me the truth, Esta.*

But the world that existed for me at that moment wasn't black and white. It wasn't full of true and false. Not at all. For me, right there, in that room with Gran, everything I thought I knew stood for something else. That's what a metaphor is, right?

I waited for more, listening to the beating of my heart and her breath as they both slowed to a constant rhythm.

The clock chimed for 10.30.

I pulled a sheet over her, kissed her forehead and left the room, clutching the heavy book she'd given me.

It's all poetry, I said to myself. *Poetry.*

Before I went to sleep that night I replayed the visit to Gran in my mind.

He still lives in the tears she sheds.

I smiled at the incredible change in her condition, and that led to a surge of pride for Mum who snored lightly in the next room.

You did that, Mum. Just by caring about her. Even if they were never going to tear down Green Gables, I think you saved her anyway.

I took the hinge out and inspected it, willing it to stop being a *stupid* hinge, willing it to turn back into the golden orb.

'Everything is poetry,' I whispered as if it were some sort of magic spell. But the hinge stayed stubbornly rusty and flat.

I sighed and opened the book Gran had given me. It was about the Natural History of Britain. Not exactly a page turner. I was flicking through it, considering whether to give it to Graham—it was more his kind of reading material—when a sheet slipped from the central pages. It was full of tables and dates and tiny writing. *Facts,* I thought, folding it away. *What use are facts when everything is poetry?*

45

CARTS

In the morning the sun rose as a fuzzy orange ball before being consumed by thick smog. It was like dawn on Mars.

The breakfast weather report on the radio made no mention of anything unusual, but I'd never seen a sunrise like it.

When I walked to school that gloomy morning, the air was cut through with the smell of diesel and an unusually warm wind picked up fallen leaves, swirling them high like a flock of starlings.

But there was no birdsong.

'We have to do something,' I said, sliding onto a bench in the Greasy Spoon. It had been another tense day at school; a day when no one mentioned Simon, even though his name screamed at me from every empty chair.

Lily peered at me over the rim of her mug. Her skin was pale, and she had beads of sweat pricking her brow. 'We had no deliveries at the grocers today,' she said. 'No one could get through. The roads are clogged up because of the construction. I mean, they're so intent on knocking the thing down.' She coughed and took a sip of tea.

I considered her while she drank. She was pretty and almost as tall as Graham. Today she'd tied her bronze-coloured (OK, I admit, not really ginger) hair in plaits. I thought she looked like Mum might have done twenty years ago and I suddenly couldn't imagine being in this situation with anyone else. She couldn't see what I did, but I got the feeling she *wanted* to.

'Have you seen the road?' she said. 'They've never worked so quickly since they started. It's like they're obsessed. Graham reckons we should raise it with the Council. The police too.'

'What,' I said tentatively, 'if it has to be *me* that looks for Simon?'

Lily's face was unreadable. 'You still reckon he's in there?'

Graham returned with a mug, a plate of toast and a troubled scowl. 'I knew it!' he hissed. 'I told you Lil. There's something wrong about that place. Grandad knew it. I felt it the other night. It's sucking us all in. It's madness. You saw the look in Simon's eyes.'

'We have to *do* something though, don't we?' Lily protested, repeating my words.

Graham sat down heavily. He looked as tired as Lily. 'Well, it scares me. It's all getting out of control and we have bigger things to worry about. Real things.'

There was silence for a moment. Graham looked from Lily to me and leaned in. 'Grandad's right to be scared of the storm. Did you see the sunrise this morning? That isn't normal,' he whispered.

'The news said—'

'Lily, the news is wrong. Radiation levels are rising. We should forget about Gatley House and get as far away from this stinking town as quick as we can.'

'But...' Lily started. Graham shushed her and indicated the other customers. She lowered her voice. 'But what if there's a link? Remember what Simon said before he ran off? Something about demons there and bulldozers here. What if the storm is linked to what's happening at Gatley House?'

Graham rolled his eyes.

'I saw my Gran last night,' I said. 'She told me some things.'

'Your Gran?' Graham said. 'I thought she was... batty?'

'Not since they saved the Home. It's like she's woken up from a trance or something. She knows Harry...' I looked steadily at him. 'She knows about the house. She told me I had to save it.'

Graham didn't look persuaded.

'You know,' Lily said eventually, 'It doesn't matter. We all saw Simon go into Gatley House.'

'The police have searched the place,' Graham said.

'They searched it for Charlie too,' I said. 'But when my dad found her, she'd *never* moved.'

'So, we *have* to try to look for him, Gray,' Lily added.

'No,' I said. '*I* have to.'

Graham closed his eyes and raised his head toward the ceiling. 'Even if you're right, we can't get inside. We tried already over the field.'

'I know,' I said. 'Dogs.'

'They're down the track too.'

'If we can't get Esta inside,' Lily said, 'then we have to find a way to stop the bulldozers in case Simon is really there.'

Graham sighed. 'The only way we can realistically and...' he looked at me for the briefest of moments, '... rationally do that is to get the council, or the police involved.'

'Yes!' Lily said triumphantly. 'I knew you'd help Gray.'

Graham took a bite of his toast, 'No!' he said, crumbs scattering on to the table. 'They won't listen to us, Lil. Look what Esta's mum had to do to stop them bulldozing a nursing home for god's sake. And that was full of people everyone can actually *see*.'

'Whatever we do,' she said, doing her best to ignore his little outburst. 'It needs to be public.'

Graham shook his head. 'They've spent too much money. They have a wrecking ball. Those things cost a fortune to hire, I bet. They aren't going to stop—'

'Quit being a downer, Gray! There has to be something we can do!'

There was silence for a bit. Graham washed his toast down with a slurp of tea. Lily stared at her fingers spread on the table top, muttering to herself: 'Something public.'

'The Community Celebration assembly,' I mumbled.

'What's that?' Lily asked, looking up at me sharply.

'Every year,' Graham said, 'we celebrate community achievements at school. It's the Headmaster's Big Thing. He started it a couple of years ago. But I don't see what—'

I interrupted him, 'Mum's been invited and everyone from Green Gables. I was supposed to be doing a speech before they decided to kick me out. Mum was going to do it instead.'

'So *you* do it,' Lily suggested.

'You want her to hijack the assembly?' Graham said, wiping butter from the side of his mouth with a napkin.

Lily slapped the table top, 'Of course!'

I shook my head, 'I can't talk. I mean, what would I say? No one would take me seriously. They all think I'm a nutcase after Blakely's nose and the Hannah thing.'

Graham's eyes were wide, staring over my shoulder like he was doing long multiplication. 'She's right. You're *both* losing it. Don't you see? This is what Grandad said would happen. It's one thing talking about it between us, but in an assembly? In front of everyone?'

Lily ignored him, 'You're sure Simon's inside, Esta?'

'Stop,' Graham said. He placed his hands on the table like he was a newsreader about to make an important announcement. 'The real problem is that storm headed our way.'

'We can't stop a storm, Graham!' Lily hissed. 'But we can try to stop them flattening Gatley House.'

He shook his head at her. 'Grandad, Grandma, Charlie.' He glared at me. 'Your dad... and now Simon. Nothing good comes out of that house. Everyone who gets involved with it suffers. Look at us? What are we contemplating? We're going to tie ourselves to a tree to save it?' He looked at us both with wild eyes, his cheeks glowing with a rosy blush. 'Esta,' he lowered his tone to a whisper, 'you stole an artefact from the museum, then we nearly got busted at the house yesterday. And what real evidence have we got that any of... of your stories are true?'

'They're not just *my* stories, Graham,' I said, trying to keep my voice down to a whisper. 'Your grandad knows it, my gran, Simon, Charlie...'

'But I mean tangible evidence—'

Lily shot to her feet, scraping the chair against the floor. 'Oh, what does it matter if it's true?'

The rest of the café went silent. Graham stared up at Lily open mouthed. But her outburst cleared the fog in my brain. I stood up too.

Lily stared at me expectantly, 'What is it?'

A clear memory burst through... The last time I'd been with Simon inside Gatley House. The story he read from a piece of parchment.

'You're right. If we really have to do this,' I said, grabbing my coat and my school bag, 'then we can't tell people the truth. No one will believe it.'

'So?'

'So,' I said, rushing towards the door. 'I need to tell them about the carts.'

'The what?' Lily called.

But I was already gone.

When I got home, I scoured the table of facts that had fallen out of Gran's Natural History book. I read one small paragraph. I smiled. Then I re-read it just to make sure.

That night I dreamed of Simon, alive and well, sitting cross-legged in a gloomy hall. I dreamed of colourful gods and goddesses dancing in circles, surrounded by rings of flame. I dreamed of an old man sipping tea and winking at me, repeating the same phrase Gran had said the previous night again and again: *It's all poetry.*

46

PIPISTRELLE

Mum had reacted with surprise and relief when I told her I still wanted to speak for her at the assembly.

'I can do it, Mum. This is what Culter wanted in the first place.'

Mum's face did a sort of twisted grimace. I'm not sure what you'd call it, the corners of her mouth turned down, her eyebrows arched up. She struggled to get her words out.

'You sure?' she sniffed. 'This isn't exactly your thing.'

But she handed me her notes quickly enough, so I guessed she'd been dreading doing it herself. *Like mother like daughter,* I thought with a smile.

I leafed through them without properly looking and gave her a smile-shrug. 'I know it's too late now, but, I wanted to show them… you know, who I really am.'

Mum touched my face, opened her mouth to say something, sniffed instead, then cleared her throat and said, 'I was going to read what's in the notes. You do the same and you'll be fine.' She glanced at her watch, tapped it. 'Nothing's working! The radio's all white noise, the TV's on the blink, and now this. Who *knows* what time it is? I've got to pick up Gran. You sure you don't want a lift?'

'No.' I held up her notes. 'I'll learn these on the walk.'

Mum leaned to peer out of the window at the dark skies. 'Have you seen the weather? They say it's going to tip it down. I know they say it's safe, but you can't be too careful.'

'It's alright, I'll use Dad's old umbrella.'

She kissed the top of my head and headed for the door. 'You'll be brilliant.'

I could have gone with her, but the truth was I wanted to walk past Fletcher's Field. I wanted to see how far the diggers were from Gatley House. Not only that, but I thought maybe Graham and Lily would meet me there. Just in case.

Before I left, I put the slip of paper from Gran's book in my bag, then noticed the hinge on my bedside table. I traced its rusty edges with a finger. *Poetry?* I gave it a half-smile and left it sitting there. It was a long shot, but if my plan worked, I wouldn't even need to go back to Gatley House.

I had to close my eyes on the way out of the front door. Just in case Dad's box was still there. I didn't need to see that right now.

No more ghosts.

It was gloomy under the slate-grey sky. It didn't rain, but I used the umbrella anyway as a kind of protection from the clouds that bore down on the town. I leaned against the fence and watched workmen arriving. They had already laid some of the tarmac. It was a shiny black scar cutting through Fletcher's Field. The top of the crane's high arm disappeared in the mist that hung between the remaining trees. Somewhere, resting at the end of a cable would be the heavy steel ball they would use to smash through Gatley House.

As I stared at the unstoppable metal army collecting before the old house, I thought of Simon and then I remembered the little farmyard standing in the centre of the motorway heading to Leeds. *An island in the flood of progress.* Not all islands need to be surrounded by water, do they?

After a while it became obvious that Lily and Graham weren't coming. I wasn't surprised. I'd known last night this was something I needed to do myself. I had nothing to lose anymore after all.

I briefly checked Mum's notes, then folded them up into my bag and made my way to school where I was planning to stand up in front of an audience of people who all thought I was damaged.

Shivers crawled along my arm as I climbed the steps up to the stage. The hall was filled with students and parents. Miss Nuttal was there in a bright Paisley dress. Mr Culter stood next to her, stroking his chin. At the back, Mum, anxious fingers at her mouth, stood with the old folk and the nurses from Green Gables. Mr Taylor was there too, talking angrily to the tall, stiff Officer Bennett. I felt a pang of pity for the man who had—temporarily, I hoped—lost a second child to Gatley House.

I faced them all. The audience faced me. Some wore blank, bored expressions, some smirked or whispered to each other. Hannah Piranha glared at me on the third row from behind a swollen nose, Mr Blakely smiled at me from behind his.

My socks itched my ankles. A curl of hair tickled my forehead.

Mr Taylor's conversation with Officer Bennett became louder. He jabbed a finger at the officer, then jabbed it in my direction. It didn't take a genius to figure out what, or rather who, his problem was.

I tensed, glanced across the faces of the crowd, took a deep breath and said, 'Good Morning.'

To absolutely no effect.

The argument continued at the back. A student on the front row shouted, 'Speak up!' A few girls hid giggles behind their hands.

I cleared my throat, and almost shouted, 'My name is Esta Brown.'

It had the desired effect. Simon's dad stopped in mid-rant and turned his head towards the stage, index finger frozen in mid-air.

A chill flowed through me. I resisted the urge to run. 'Today…' I cleared my throat. '… we are celebrating the Community Award.' I was making this up as I went. To be honest, beyond the fact that Mr Taylor had finally got the paperwork allowing him to bulldoze Gatley House rather than Gran's Home, I didn't really know what we were celebrating. I should probably have read Mum's notes more carefully.

'We saved Green Gables,' I said, my voice a little stronger now at least. That was the story we all wanted, wasn't it? There was a polite round of applause. I waited for it to end before carrying on.

I took a breath. 'But I want us to save something else. Something quiet, peaceful, something secret and hidden.'

I lowered my tone and fixed my eyes on Mr Taylor. 'Something no one else knows about. Something only Simon and I have seen.'

The man's forehead creased as if he were inspecting a bug. People were listening now. Not something I was used to, I can tell you.

Rabbit in headlights territory.

But whatever else was happening—the community award, the toxic storm overhead and my inevitable expulsion from school — I knew with a sudden and absolute certainty that I had to stop Gatley House from being destroyed. And I knew it had to be today.

'I believe that if you put a stop to the destruction of Gatley House…' *You will restore the link between cause and effect and save the world and…* 'Simon will come home.'

The man's face turned a vivid shade of watermelon red. I could almost feel the daggers of his glare against my crawling skin. I waited for him to explode. If he did, I didn't plan on hanging around. He looked more than ready to throttle me where I stood. He sputtered something to Officer Bennet, spit flying from his lips.

It had to be now. I opened up the sheet that had fallen out of the book Gran had given me and I cleared my throat. *Now or never.*

'The Pipi… pipistrelle,' I stuttered, stumbling over the word.

Blank stares met me. I cleared my throat again, '… or in other words, the Common Bat…' The stares became confused frowns. '… has been protected since 1981.'

I glanced to my side. The secretary looked cross. I think she realised I might be—as Graham had put it — hijacking the assembly. Mr Culter placed a calming hand against her arm. Miss Nuttal stared at me, one eyebrow arched. I decided to take that as encouragement to carry on.

I held up the sheet. 'This is a copy of the Countryside Act. In England and Wales it is an offence under the Wildlife and Countryside Act 1981,' I heaved in another breath, 'to intentionally or recklessly disturb a bat at a roost.'

The audience's frowns seemed to deepen all at once.

'I'm not standing for this!' shouted Mr Taylor from the back.

My heart quickened. So did my voice. I didn't have much time.

'Mr Taylor. Your son is in Gatley House, protesting against its destruction.'

Mr Taylor growled something I couldn't make out. He flung a disgusted wave in my direction.

'This is our community,' I said, glancing at Mr Culter. "Community" was his buzzword after all. He still looked nervous, but he was listening at least. Miss Nuttal had her eyes down; she had taken a pad from her handbag and was busy jotting notes in it.

'What you are doing, Mr Taylor, is illegal,' I said to the confused faces of the audience. 'You have no right to disturb the natural habitat of this endangered species.'

'Where is my son?' Mr Taylor barked.

Whispers filled the hall. Heads turned from Mr Taylor and back to me. What little confidence I'd started with shrank back into its hole. I'd never found it easy to maintain my cool, but having Mr Taylor yelling at me was not a morale booster.

I glanced back at Miss Nuttall, who was now whispering something to Mr Culter. *How am I doing?* I wanted to ask. I turned back to the audience and continued, willing my voice to stay steady and calm. It didn't. It wobbled all over the place. 'Bat numbers have...' I wiped my itching forehead. What had seemed like a stroke of genius last night and a long shot this morning now felt like more of a moon-shot. I raised my voice, '... numbers have declined by fifty percent in the last ten years because of the destruction of our countryside.'

I was exaggerating. I didn't have any statistics. I couldn't prove whether Mr Taylor's company had ever disturbed a single bat, but hey, why let the truth get in the way of a good story, right?

Simon's dad rose to the bait. Officer Bennett held an arm out, blocking him from taking matters into his own substantial hands.

I swept an increasingly desperate look across the rest of the audience. Mum's posture hadn't changed; maybe her eyes had widened a little. The headmaster folded his arms; the secretary had placed a clip board on the chair beside her. Miss Nuttal's furrowed brow was now concentrated towards Mr Taylor.

'How dare you treat my son's disappearance as a game!'

Faces turned to the back of the hall where Mr Taylor had freed himself. He was glaring at me with rage, his forefinger jabbing at me. 'There's not one flying rat in that place. If my son had been so worried, he'd have told me. Now.' The vein in his neck strained against his tight collar. 'You tell me where he is, or I'll...' he glanced at the officer beside him, and deflated a little '...press charges.'

An ember of worry sparked in my stomach. I wasn't sure exactly where to go with this. I'd lost my train of thought and stood nervously, holding out the Countryside Act like a shield. Looking for all the world like the mad little girl everyone thought I was.

Murmurs rippled through the hall, heads were shaking. Wide, scandalised eyes turned to me. I took a step backwards. Maybe this hadn't been such a good idea. I wondered whether Gran would come and read to me when they locked me up.

A shape came at me from below, a figure climbing up to the stage. I dropped the sheet and stepped away, ready to run for the safety of the fire escape.

A commanding voice I knew stopped me, though.

'You stay where you are.'

47

BIOLOGY PROJECT

Graham grabbed my blazer before I could get any further off stage and offered me a reassuring *"I've got this"* smile.

The murmuring increased. Mr Taylor froze, trying to recalculate the situation. Mr Culter stood on the balls of his feet, his jaw tensed.

Graham gave a thumbs-up to a small window in the back wall—the lighting booth for stage productions. I glimpsed a curl of Lily's hair. She must have pressed a switch because a slide projector whirred into life, blinding me for a second with rainbow light. I ducked and turned to the screen.

'This,' Graham proclaimed after the image had sharpened, 'is the Blue-Crested Newt. One of only fifty pairs left in the wild.' He paused. 'And the pond at Gatley House is a crucial habitat.'

I remembered him in the garden at Gatley House, the jar of grey water swinging in his hand. *Kind of a Biology Project,* he'd said.

He raised his voice, commanding the room. 'This means Gatley House needs to be preserved—not just the house, but its grounds as well—as a site of special scientific interest.'

There was a ripple of laughter. Mr Culter spoke with his secretary, who slipped from the room looking flustered. Simon's dad stood beside his police escort, staring hard at the image behind me.

A warm spring of confidence welled up, washing away my nerves. It wasn't exactly as I'd intended, but between my bats and Graham's newts, we had definitely got people's attention.

It was time to push. Graham's little speech had injected a surge of what-the-hell into my veins and anyway, it was all poetry, wasn't it? Or, it occurred to me, a song. And in my mind I heard the opening call from that Simple Minds track at the end of "The Breakfast Club". *Hey, hey, hey!*

I turned to Mr Culter. 'Sir,' I said, with a rock guitar riff running through my head. 'A couple of weeks ago, you asked me to change.' He acknowledged me with a tip of the head. It was probably the smallest ever nod. But it was a nod.

I carried on, my voice breaking, 'Today, I know we have other things to celebrate.' I tipped my own head at Mum, who could have been smiling behind her knuckles, or I suppose it could have been an expression of utter horror. 'And I know I can sometimes get a bit carried away,' I flashed a grimace at Mr Blakely. 'Be a bit selfish.' My eyes focused on Mum again, who was definitely grinning now. To her left was Gran. She stood by Mum's side, smiling at me with tears trickling down her cheeks. 'Well, with everything that's happened recently, I've learnt that life is precious.' I took a breath. 'But only if it's meaningful. So I want to do something meaningful. What with news of nuclear disasters and toxic rain and developers threatening to flatten a Nursing Home for a bloody... bloody road. I wanted to do something. I wanted them to stop the illegal destruction of our incredible wildlife and our local heritage.'

No one was laughing now. For the first time since Dad disappeared, everyone was looking at me and—I was certain—no one pitied me, or sneered, or judged me. And they didn't even know the half of it. There were bats, and now apparently newts, at Gatley House. That was true. They might not be the real reason I wanted to save the place, but it *wasn't* a lie. I meant every last word.

I focused on Simon's dad, who was still staring at the huge image of the blue newt.

'Mr Taylor, I understand you're upset. And I understand why you're determined to do this, but you have to stop this awful destruction. Believe me, whatever happens, wherever Simon is hiding, if you stop the destruction, Simon will love you for it.'

I turned to the headmaster. He was watching me with the concentration of a hawk. 'Mr Culter? First of all, sorry for the little swear word back then, secondly, I want to thank you for giving me the opportunity to see beyond myself.' I received another blink-and-you-missed-it nod.

'Mum? You saved Green Gables,' my voice broke and Graham held my hand. 'You actually did it. You taught me to stand up to those things we can change. But Mum, I've been thinking. Maybe we should stand up to those things we can't change too. Maybe we should especially stand up to those things.'

I cast my eyes at the front few rows of faces. Faces I recognised from class, some from the Geography room at lunch, some from Simon's party.

'One way or another I'm going to stop them destroying a place of natural beauty. And if you have any respect for our incredible world, you'll all come along too. Because if enough of us hold hands,' I winked at Mum, 'we can do anything.'

I took a breath. Bang. There. Did it. Probably over did it actually, but I didn't run away, did I?

Mum pulled her fingers from her mouth. She closed them into a fist and then, just like Judd Nelson at the end of The Breakfast Club, raised it in the air in silent salute.

The rest of the hall was silent too.

But I had Simple Minds blasting loud and clear in my head.

48

THE BINS

The back stage led to a fire escape. Graham pushed the release bar, and we ran across the school field, ignoring a deep rumble of thunder overhead. Lily caught us up at the smoker's hedge.

'Wait,' she rasped, out of breath.

It was only then, catching my own breath that I stopped. Our audience had spilled out of the hall onto the car park between it and the field. I scanned the crowd for Mum and Gran, but I was drawn to Mr Culter instead. He had one foot on the field, hands on his hips, staring in our direction. Beside him was the patterned dress of Miss Nuttal, her notebook flapping.

The large frame of Mr Taylor elbowed his way through the crowd towards his car. He was shouting into something he held in his podgy hand.

'So? What happened?' I asked Graham. 'What changed your mind?'

Lily beamed at me and kissed his cheek. 'He just needed some encouragement!'

Graham smiled back, 'She said she wouldn't tell me the address of her school in India if I didn't get on board.'

'Graham. There was more than that,' Lily said. 'Tell her.'

'I went to see my Grandad again… It's his house after all. He told me to stop them as well and…'

'Gray?'

He took my hand. 'There's nothing we can do about the storm… but I *do* believe in you, Esta and if you say we need to save the house, then that's what we'll do.'

I grinned back, but I wasn't sure I deserved the loyalty. Poetry might be enough for me, but trying to stop a wrecking ball with metaphors and similes was almost definitely madness.

Graham knew that too. But he was here anyway.

I broke eye contact and gave the crowd milling outside the hall a final scan. Still no Mum or Gran. Mr Culter on the other hand, was front and centre, pointing in a variety of directions and asserting his authority. It would be school as usual for everyone else. Meanwhile, glancing at Nuttall—who was scribbling something down now—I had a feeling this would be my last day here. To be fair, if I'd been in charge, I'd have kicked me out months ago.

'Now what?' I said, wiping strands of hair from my face.

'We stall while we wait for the council to open their mail,' said Graham.

'What?'

Lily smiled at Graham and then at me. 'He sent that photo of the newt to the council last night.'

'And the police. And the newspapers,' Graham said.

'And Downing Street probably,' added Lily.

I laughed. 'The Blue-Crested Newt?'

'It's a thing.'

'Is it?'

'It is now. And hopefully they'll spend months checking it out before they can sign off the demolition.'

We turned at the sound of furious and continuous beeping.

'We better go. If he knocks it down before he's officially notified, he'll probably get away with it. He'll plead ignorance.'

We ran through the gap in the hedge and onto the dark and empty streets. Our footsteps echoed against low garden walls. A drop of freezing rain touched my face.

I thought of Crawley Rock and then had an image of Dad tapping an imaginary bravery badge on my blazer lapel.

'Stop!' Lily shouted out of nowhere and grabbed me. I lurched back away from the road. A bin lorry rattled past, missing me by inches, blowing its angry horn.

'If we're going to kill ourselves,' she said, half laughing, 'we should at least do it trying to save Simon!'

To my surprise, Graham led us straight towards Green Gables. I didn't know whether this was part of an unspoken plan, or if he was making it up as he went along.

Lily and I stopped on the pavement as he made for the front of the Home.

'Graham?' Lily shouted.

He ignored her and walked to the large front bay window.

'Everyone's at school,' Lily called after him.

Not everyone.

Staring out at us was the familiar face of Harold Sparks.

Graham placed a hand on the glass.

Harold raised his hand as if to mirror Graham. Then he disappeared from view and within seconds the front door swung open and the old man was waving us under the porch.

It was a relief to get out of the spitting, freezing drizzle. It pattered noisily over our heads as we stood, shivering in the porch,

'He's here,' Harold said. His voice stronger than last time; his eyes alive, flitting between us. 'What are you planning?'

'We're going to stop them knocking down the house,' Graham said.

'No,' Harold said. His eyes settling on me. 'What is *she* planning?'

I placed one hand against my pocket, feeling for the Orb. But of course it wasn't there. What *was* I planning? The old man's piercing gaze was insisting on an answer.

'I'm going inside to save my friend,' I said hesitantly. I almost added "and my dad," but the words stuck in my throat.

'No, Est,' Lily said. 'Even I think that's too dangerous. We stop the bulldozers first and then we find Simon.'

'It's not enough though, is it?' Harold said, looking up out at the rain. 'To stop the bulldozers is not enough. You have to stop the devils too.'

Demons here, bulldozers there.

I pictured the hinge on my bedside table.

'You found the Kila, didn't you?' he said. 'But you're still fighting the devils.' He pointed skywards. 'And Mara is bringing the storm to poison the earth.'

I remembered with sudden clarity the disappointed look on Lama la's face as he handed me back the dagger. The odd feeling that something wasn't right in the museum.

'It wasn't the Kila,' I said. 'It wasn't the right one.'

'What do you mean?' Lily asked.

'I knew something wasn't right,' I said. 'Lily, Graham, you never saw the Orb. It was always some rusty thing, wasn't it?'

They both nodded.

'You didn't see the bell Simon picked up either, but you saw the Kila from the museum.'

'So?'

'So.' *Poetry…* I thought, *everything is poetry.* 'So, the real Kila won't *look* like one. It'll be like the hinge, or the door-bolt, it'll look old, worthless. Something you'd throw away.'

'But that could be anything, Est,' Lily said.

Harold reached out and placed his palm on my hand, 'Did your father leave anything in plain sight? Anything old and worthless… hmm?'

'Oh God!' I exclaimed, turning round and staring down the road. 'We have to go. Now!'

Lily and Graham looked at me, confused.

'The bins!'

49

PLAN B

I ran back home through the rain, cursing myself with every splashing step. Sitting in front of me for two years… I must have brushed against it every time I reached inside his box for the book of poetry.

'What are we looking for?' Graham said as we reached the end of my road.

'A box,' I said through heavy breaths. 'By the gate.'

'You put it out for the bin men?'

'I was… I was letting him go,' I panted. I hurtled round the corner of my road and skidded to a stop.

The garbage truck was idling a hundred yards away. Three men in orange jackets stood alongside it, empty-handed. Other than the truck, the road, like every other road we'd run down that morning, was empty of traffic.

'Which one's your house?' Lily asked as she caught up.

'It's too late.'

Graham ran ahead as a fourth orange jacketed man joined them and emptied his load into the jaws of the truck.

'Est?' Lily said. 'I only saw them carrying black bins. Maybe they left the box.'

'It's not there,' I said pointing to my gate, panic making my voice go higher. 'It was right there on the pavement.'

'It might be in the truck. They don't crush everything straight away. We could ask them to—'

But her words were drowned out by the hissing of hydraulics as the packer blade crushed the garbage inside. The men boarded the truck, and it pulled out into the empty street just before Graham got within a couple of yards. He tripped on a paving stone and almost face-planted. I smiled, watching him slap his thigh in frustration. Then, I leant against the wall and slid to the pavement.

My smile dried. 'I had it all the time.'

Lily sat down next to me and put an arm around my shoulders. I pushed it off and wiped a tear from my cheek. 'All this time. He was searching for something that was already his,' I said in a broken, croaky voice. 'It was there under his feet *in plain sight* and he couldn't see it.'

'We could go to the tip,' Lily suggested.

'No point.' Graham said, returning from his failed chase. 'By the time we find it, Gatley House'll be moon dust.' He held out his hand to me, 'So. Back to plan A?'

'Plan A was the bats,' I grunted as I rose.

'I meant *my* plan A.'

'Which is?'

'I'll tell you when we get there.'

I sighed, exhausted. I'd found and lost everything within minutes. I wasn't sure I had it in me to care anymore.

Graham shrugged. 'Maybe you were wrong about the box. Who's to say?'

I forced a smile. But I'd never been more sure of anything in my life. Dad had found the Kila. It had been sitting there in that box, along with his poems. And I'd let it slip between my fingers.

Lily put a hand on my arm. 'Fifteen minutes ago we didn't have the thing you were looking for. Didn't even know it existed. So nothing's changed. You said it in the assembly: sometimes you have to stand up to those things you can't change. We carry on. Right, Gray?'

'I don't know,' Graham said quietly. 'If there's a chance Simon's in there...'

The mention of Simon's name stirred me at last. I thought of my dream last night. Him sitting in a dim and dusty hall. I remembered his desperate eyes the last time I saw him, waving his rusty piece of junk at me: *Demons there, Bulldozers here. We have to stop both.* And that settled it. He was doing his bit, stopping the demons. I would do mine.

'Wait,' I said, pulling away from Lily's comforting hand. 'I have to get something.'

The hinge lay flat and old on my bedside table. I closed my eyes. *Please...* and I imagined it transforming into something golden, something gleaming. But when I looked, nothing had changed. It was still old and flat. I stuck my tongue out at its stubborn refusal to transform into a magical golden thunderbolt. Juvenile, I know, but that's all I had. I dropped it into my blazer pocket anyway. *Where it belongs,* I thought.

Graham shouted from downstairs. 'Esta?'

I took a glance around my room. The room where Dad used to come and tell me stories. The room of a child. I thought about opening the wardrobe door one more time ... just to check.

'Coming,' I said, pushing the door shut. There were no monsters hiding in there now.

'I thought you said you put the box out?' he called

I frowned, 'I did. Why?'

Graham and Lily were standing in the kitchen. Lily was smiling. Graham held a pair of scissors out to me.

There, on the table, still sealed with tape, was Dad's cardboard box.

I cut the tape with the scissors and flipped the box open. I rummaged through the junk until my fingers touched something hard and thin. 'Bingo,' I said, pulling out the letter knife. I held it up for Graham and Lily to see.

Graham nodded, 'Yep. It's a letter knife.'

'Do you see anything?' Lily asked me.

'No. But that's the point... I think,' I said with a wince.

Graham clapped his hands. 'OK, loving the weirdness and

everything, but… can we go and do something really, really stupid now?'

Lily grinned, 'You mean like stopping a wrecking ball with our frail little bodies?'

I slammed the door behind me and we ran across the eerily quiet street. Thunder growled overhead.

'Remind me why we're doing this again?' Graham said, trying unsuccessfully to cover his head with his heavy-looking satchel as we splashed towards Grover Close.

'We find Simon,' Lily replied, 'and maybe stop a bunch of demons from breaking the law of cause and effect.'

And, I thought, gripping the letter knife tightly, *bring back Dad.*

50

THE PINKY PROMISE

'One good thing about chaos,' Graham said as we jogged. 'Is the appalling traffic.'

Whereas the roads near my house were all empty, the roads near Gatley House were at a snail's pace. We spotted Taylor's bright red Jag nudging forwards half a mile away as we ducked into the abandoned estate. We probably had three or four minutes.

They'd reinforced the gate with rolls of barbed wire. Climbing it was out of the question.

'The hedge?' I suggested.

'Wait.' Graham pulled a pair of wire cutters from his bag. 'No point it just being us. We need to open this.' He closed the cutters around the chain securing the gate. 'We need the council, the police and the journalists to join us.'

'Handy, isn't he?' Lily said with an admiring smile as we watched him struggle.

Dogs barked in the distance, but they were getting closer. Graham groaned, tendons straining in his neck.

'It's no good,' he winced. 'The chains are too thick.'

The barking got louder, along with the crackle of a walkie-talkie. The engine of a car grunted from behind us.

'Taylor,' Graham said, out of breath.

We dived for the holly bushes and waited.

Mr Taylor's Jag skidded around the corner at the head of the estate in a spray of mud and grit, then sped between the boarded-up houses towards us.

'Why didn't we just wait for the council?' I whispered as the car screeched to a stop inches from the gate.

'That was the plan,' Graham hissed. 'But you kind of went public before I could stop you.'

'Next time we do this, we should probably talk it through first,' I suggested.

A large man holding two ferocious Dobermans appeared from the shadows of the track. He wrestled with the dogs as he unlocked and swung open the gate. The car slid through, windows sliding down, revealing Mr Taylor's face. It was screwed into a snarl worse than I'd seen when he threatened me with the spade. Even from behind the bush I recognised the poisonous glare he gave the large man with the dogs, Taylor's eyes were like black marbles. I bet that if I'd been a bit closer, I'd see a flicker of gold around their edges.

'Derek,' he growled. 'We go. Go now and fast. Call the rest of the guys. Tell them we're flattening it while we still can.'

'But what about—?'

'Just do it!' shouted Mr Taylor.

The wheels of the Jaguar spun, sending mud and pebbles up in an arc. Then there was the metal clang of the gate being locked again, followed by radio crackle and Derek's gruff voice relaying the message.

Graham swore under his breath, 'Why's he so desperate to knock it down?'

'It's like the guard in the museum,' I whispered. 'The same eyes. I don't think Mr Taylor's all there.'

'Right,' he said. 'Demonic possession. Brilliant.' Then he lifted a branch and ducked under it. 'Guess it's just us and the demons then.'

Lily and I followed, scrambling through the damp, strangling bushes. Thorns tore at my arms, thick brambles tangled at my feet, the stench of gasoline stung my nostrils. As we scrambled into the unwelcoming jungle, the sound of growling engines and angry, snapping dogs got louder.

We huddled within the shelter of the weeping willow. The leaves had thinned and turned autumnal brown since last time, but we were still just about hidden from outside.

I'd wondered what I would see as I struggled through the hedges: Gatley House or Rigpa Gompa? Or maybe both at the same time? Part of me still hoped that all of this was some stupid lie, some game; that nothing happening here really mattered in the great scheme of things. It was the north of England. We got bad weather a lot and old buildings get flattened every day after all. But my heart sank when I saw the crumbling bricks; rundown and miserable. Just as it had been when I'd last seen Simon.

For a moment I considered turning back. A precious life is a meaningful one, Gran had said. Well, I'd risk my life to find Dad, save Simon and the others, but not to save a meaningless old house.

Lily must have seen my disappointment. 'How confident are you, Est?' she asked.

I put my hand in my pocket for the Vajra/Orb/hinge. Still flat. Still featureless. Still just a hinge.

I nodded anyway. It *had* to be true. Just because I couldn't see it *yet* didn't mean it wasn't there. If it was true that I needed to be with Simon in order to see it, then maybe I just had to get closer to him.

'Est,' Lily said. 'This is your last chance. I don't want to do this if I don't have to.' She held out her little finger. I looked at it with a raised eyebrow.

'Do you pinky promise?' she said, waggling it, her expression deadly serious.

'Really? We're not a bit old for this?'

She didn't budge. 'The world might be uncertain and upside down. But not here. Not under this tree.' She waggled her finger again. 'I don't see what you see… but I do trust you, Esta Brown.'

I let go of the hinge and hooked my own little finger around hers, 'Pinky promise.'

Graham looked impatient. 'Nice one. But we have a wrecking ball to stop. One swing of that thing and the whole building might collapse.'

I stared through the branches at the enormous steel ball hanging from the crane. The cable was as high as the remaining trees, almost disappearing into the sagging clouds. Dogs were sniffing the bright yellow cabin, cocking their legs against the caterpillar tracks.

Lily cleared her throat, 'One of us will have to stand in front of it. A human shield.'

I turned from the dogs to stare at her with my *"even-I'm-not-that-crazy,"* expression. 'Don't be stupid, they'd just drag you away. Can't we jam it, or wreck the motor?'

Lily exchanged one of those infuriating, knowing glances with Graham. 'We've got an idea.'

Graham grinned as he pulled a pair of pink fluffy handcuffs from his bag and held them aloft. 'We're going to lock ourselves to one of the iron drainpipes.'

'You what?'

'Protestors do it all the time,' Lily said.

'Are they even real handcuffs?'

'Real enough.'

'They'd just cut through them,' I said.

'Maybe,' Graham said. 'I never said it was permanent. We just need time for the Council or the police to get here.' He checked his watch. 'Offices opened at 9. It's 10 now. Accounting for traffic…'

'You're not serious? What makes you think they'll just drop everything and come over?'

There was a distant whimper followed by a growl from near the house. Two of the dogs were straining on their leashes, noses pointed towards us. 'And what about them?' I whispered. 'They'll tear you apart.'

'Lily?' Graham said. 'Did you pack them?'

Lily rummaged in his bag and took out two large square cans, 'Spam. My cousin's dogs go mad for this.' She started twisting the metal key to reveal the meat.

'For god's sake!' I said, placing a hand on hers. 'I've seen dogs eat more than that in one gulp.'

Lily tilted her head, 'They're family sized.' She looked at Graham, who raised his hands up in defeat. 'We'll just have to hope they keep the dogs on a leash.'

The dogs started barking.

'Well, whatever happens, I'm going inside,' I said.

'No,' Graham said. 'We wait for the—'

'We haven't got time to argue. There's no way you can be sure the Council will come before that ball-thing starts up. And if Simon's there when they do…' I didn't need to finish the sentence.

A spluttering, coughing noise came from near the house. We peered through the branches. Grey smoke plumed from the cabin of the crane. Mr Taylor, or whatever demonic influence was currently possessing him, was screaming orders. The noise distracted the dogs, but not for long.

'It has to be now,' I said. 'Just give me ten minutes.' I held up Dad's letter knife. 'Let me get this to Lama la. It might be the only way. If I don't see anyone, if I don't find Simon, I'll get out. I promise.'

Lily raised her eyebrows. 'Five.'

The barking had become snarling. A voice shouted, 'Whatchoo found, fella?'

'Lily,' I said, 'hand me the Spam. Circle the house. I'll catch you up!'

Lily and Graham slipped under the arches of the willow branches while I hurled the first can of meat into the wall of holly. It had the desired effect. The dogs turned towards the sound, their noses twitching in the direction of the Spam. The other dog barked so loudly it drowned out the noise of the wrecker as its caterpillar tracks trundled closer to the building.

I finished jabbing holes into the second can with Dad's letter knife, then dropped the Spam by the headstone. 'Sorry, Carol,' I whispered, pocketed the knife, then followed the others.

'Did it work?' breathed Graham when I joined them. I shrugged. I doubted it. But the only noise was the smattering of rain, the engine of the wrecker and the ominous squeaking of metal as the ball was being raised on its chain. The dogs were silent, hopefully trying to reach the meat through the holes in the tin cans. They wouldn't be interested for long, but it gave us a few seconds.

I stared up at the walls as we ran around the back of the house: graffiti, old brick and moss, boarded-up windows; broken shards of glass crunched beneath our feet; the smell of rotting things and urine. *Where the hell is Rigpa Gompa?* I re-checked the smooth edge of the hinge and felt sick to my stomach. *Come on. Change, for god's sake. Where are you, Simon?*

Graham stopped us at the corner by an iron drain pipe. He took out the cuffs. 'We'll make as much noise as we can. That should give you time to jump through the basement window, OK?'

'No,' I said. 'It has to be the door. If he's there, he's in the hall.'

'But that's right in front of everyone. They'll notice you.'

'I'm not sure of the way to the hall from the basement. It's kind of complicated inside.'

He clipped one of the cuffs around Lily's wrists. 'OK. Do what you have to do. Just do it quickly.'

I nodded, hoping to God this was worth it. At the same time hoping it was one big mistake, because if everything I believed was true and we failed… they'd destroy Gatley House, the Gompa, and God knew *what* would come streaming out of the rubble.

There was a rumble of thunder. Fine, blue lightning webbed across the black belly of cloud.

I took a deep breath.

'Promise you'll be five minutes,' Lily said.

'OK.'

She gripped my blazer with her free hand. 'This isn't a game, Esta. You've seen that wrecking ball.'

'All right,' I said. 'Five minutes. I pinky promise.'

PART SEVEN

JEWEL ISLAND

51

TWO WINGS

The board from the door had been ripped away, so slipping inside was easy. Graham and Lily—locked to the iron drainpipe—distracted the workmen by singing "*Somewhere over the Rainbow*" at the top of their voices.

I picked my way over fallen bricks and lumps of wood, waving away the veil of dust and smoke. Simon had to be here. He *had* to be.

The singing—*there's a land that I dreamed of once in a lullaby*—thunder and rumbling of the engines became fainter the farther inside I went.

As the chaos outside faded, my worries about the wrecking ball did too. All I cared about now was finding Simon and getting this flimsy old knife to Lama la.

The hall was smaller than I remembered, its walls were just bare plaster, no pictures, no rows of pillars either. There were two doors at the far wall, and between them—just where the enormous statue would be in Rigpa Gompa—was a grand, straight staircase leading up to the first floor.

'Where are you?' I asked the empty room.

There was no staircase in the hall of Rigpa Gompa. If Simon was here, I doubted he'd be upstairs. If my dreams were anything to go by, he'd be sitting with the Dharmapalas at the feet of the giant statue.

Any second now the workers would have dealt with Graham and Lily and would be after me. I just hoped I could get near to Simon before they found me—near enough for the Orb to light up again. I took the door to the right.

'Simon?' I whispered as I entered the dark room.

A high-pitched whine began outside. A grinding sound like at the dentists. That was probably the handcuffs coming off. I doubted I had more than a minute before someone dragged me out.

I took a breath. I needed to stop being such a wimp.

'Simon?' I shouted into the shadows.

My voice rebounded off the walls.

'Where are you?'

I stopped in the middle of the room, my breath heavy, dust clogging my throat. Now that my eyes were getting used to the darkness, I could make out marks on the wall. Words, images maybe. Some sort of message? I couldn't be sure.

I ran over and wiped my hand across it, clearing dust and cobwebs away.

Blue graffiti, as unreadable as the engraving on Carol's headstone. The sort of graffiti you might find in a urine-stinking subway.

I coughed, spitting out the dust coating my tongue. I listened for the sound of heavy-duty work boots coming for me. Nothing yet.

An unpleasant idea surfaced. If I could only see Rigpa Gompa when I was with Simon… what if Mr Culter was right? What if Simon really *was* at his mum's while I was here, waiting for them to flatten Gatley House?

I shook the thought from my mind. There had been another door on the left of the stairs. I might make it before a workman found me. It might be just another empty room, but I had to try. I made for the door.

A noise made me freeze.

Chhoo.

It wasn't a loud noise. It could have been the sound of falling masonry or a steel capped boot scuffing against stone.

I cocked my head to listen. There it was again. Louder this time and nearby. It sounded like a…

'Atchoo!'

It came from behind the wall. It came from somewhere *beneath* the staircase.

'Simon?' I whispered.

I tapped on the wall. It made a hollow sound. There was a space behind it.

'Simon?' I called. My hands searched for a crack, a hidden hatch or doorway. Anything.

I took a step back and scanned the wall for a clue. No hidden door.

But the graffiti glowed: luminous lizard tracks etched along the wall.

A muffled voice growled from outside. 'Oy! You little brat. Where are ya?'

I tried to block everything else out. Focus on the graffiti. My jaw tightened. I'd done this before. Words that looked like random symbols. I'd read words like these before. *What were you supposed to do? Think, Esta.* I had to focus. Concentrate.

The footsteps got louder.

And I was so *close*. I just needed to remember how to read these damn symbols. I was certain of it. Simon was nearby, and somehow the glowing graffiti was the key.

I waited for the door to swing open, for a man in a hard hat to barge in and drag me out.

But the door didn't open. The footsteps thudded up the stairs along with a string of swear words.

I exhaled.

It wasn't exactly the lilting tones of Tubular Bells lulling me into meditative concentration, but it would have to do.

What would you do, Dad? I thought, trying to picture his face.

But he didn't answer.

Instead it was Mum's voice that whispered back: *Relax. Focus your mind, Esta.*

A floorboard creaked above me. More shouting. More swearing. *How am I supposed to focus with all this going on?*

Mum's voice whispered to me again: *It's not rocket science, Esta. You sit. You count your breath. And then you relax, for God's sake.*

'OK' I said, and this time I obeyed; I let out my breath and stared at the wall.

The graffiti was still an unreadable scrawl.

'Come on!' I hissed, willing the scratches to patter around in to something ... anything.

The clomping, swearing man was done with his brief search upstairs and now he was on his way back down.

I squeezed my eyes shut, trying to remember Mum's words:

'Be patient. Breathe and concentrate on the outflow of your breath. Count...'... One breath.

The workman made it to the bottom of the stairs. 'I'll find you, you little vandal...'

My chest rose and fell. My breath skittered:

Two.

The boots crunched across the hall floor.

I inhaled and let the breath drift from my nose. Warm air rushed past the hairs in my nostrils:

Three.

An image of Mr Taylor's angry black eyes came to mind. I tensed, ready to run. I clenched my teeth and squeezed my eyes shut. This was hopeless. *What number am I on?* I couldn't even focus on three breaths.

I uncurled my legs. I suddenly didn't want to be here in this dingy room waiting for an angry workman. I glanced at my watch. More than eight minutes since I'd left Graham and Lily. So much for a pinky promise.

Then I heard Mum's voice one more time. *Sit down! You're doing this! You are sitting bloody well down and meditating Esta Louise Brown!*

I took the hinge out to check. It was still a hinge, but... *was it my imagination, or was it glowing?*

The muscles in my neck and shoulders relaxed. *Yeah.* I smiled. *Maybe it is.* The crease on my forehead softened. My jaw unclenched. I let out another breath:

Four.

The door to the room on the other side of the staircase banged shut. The boots crossed the hall to my side.

Cool, clean air filled my lungs.

I opened my eyes.

The graffiti was clear. Clear as anything. I didn't understand it, but I could read it:

EM AH HO

Crash.

This time it was my door that swung wide open. A large workman's boot appeared.

I spoke the words.

And white light flooded the room, dissolving the walls, the floor and the ceiling, washing everything around me in a sparkling, diamond glow. A deep thrumming made my teeth chatter and the hairs on my arms stand straight. I looked towards the door. It was gone—along with the workman—hidden behind a wall of white.

I hadn't moved. But I was now sitting inside a tent of light which crackled like tumbling sparks from a Roman Candle. I watched wide-eyed as light rose from the centre of the room like a glowing fountain.

Sitting at the base of it was Simon. The bell—the source of the light—held at his chest.

I got to my feet, my mouth hanging open in shock. Simon's eyes were shut tight. His limp blonde hair hung down either side of his face. His lips, grey in the strange glow, moved constantly. He swung the bell in his right hand, its high-pitched ring making the air vibrate.

I placed a palm against his cheek: it was cold and clammy, the bone of his jaw flexing beneath tight skin.

'Simon,' I whispered.

He kept on as if I weren't there.

I brought my right hand to his other cheek and said his name again.

This time his eyes shot open. Crystal blue and cold like glacier ice. His bell became still. The delicate strands of light coming from it drifted to the floor like cut threads.

The room dimmed.

'Esta,' he whispered hoarsely. His head dropped, exhausted. 'He's too strong. I don't think I can keep it up.'

The tent of light was thin now. Dark shapes slithered on the other side. There was a stench of sewage.

He looked up. 'You have to get out, Esta.'

I grabbed his arm. 'Graham and Lily are buying us time, but your dad is ready to knock through. If you could just—'

'You don't understand,' he said, shrugging me off. 'Charlie was right. This place is real. Everything is real. The Dharmapalas, Lama la, the valley. All of it. We have to save them.' He switched his gaze beyond me, out at whatever lay behind the fading shield of light. 'I'm staying.'

'You'll die if you stay here. You can't save the world if you're dead.'

He shook his head. 'This is my fault.'

'Don't be stupid. We have to go.'

He looked at me with eyes that reflected the dying light. 'What goes around comes around,' he said. 'I told Charlie to come in here you know? It was me that gave her the idea. That's why she came. If she'd never come here, she'd never have fallen and Dad wouldn't be trying to destroy it now. Your dad wouldn't be lost either. Cause and effect.'

Dad. The sound of it made me shiver. *Was he here? Right now, at the end?* I gritted my teeth and pictured the crane outside.

'Who cares? All that matters is that you walk out there and let your dad see you. He'll stop when he sees you. I swear. If we stop the bulldozers, we'll stop the demons too. Remember?'

His eyes widened. 'You don't get it,' he whispered. 'He's everywhere.'

I stared at him for a second, not understanding. 'Who's everywhere?'

'It's not really my dad,' he said, his voice fading in and out. 'Mara's already infecting the world with greed and anger.'

I knew he was right. His dad, the storm, that thing in the museum. The two worlds were already bleeding into each other.

'We have to stop him here *and* there,' Simon said 'I have to do it from here.'

'But, why?'

He held up his bell.

'But why you?'

'It doesn't work for anyone else.'

'But...' Tears of frustration came suddenly. I didn't try to stop them. I tugged on his blazer. 'This is doesn't make any sense!'

The floor shook as something crashed into the side of the house.

'It makes perfect sense,' he whispered, pushing the fringe from my eyes. 'Your story about the jewel island wasn't about treasure was it?' he said.

I pushed myself up. Black tendrils, like vines were curling along the floor towards us. A silver tear cleared a path down Simon's cheek. He was searching my eyes. 'The island is right here, Esta. That story you read was about us. About what we do with our lives. I can't leave.'

My teeth chattered as the floor shook again.

'It has to be now, Esta,' he said.

I returned his gaze. He was nothing like the cool boy who used to sit in the Geography classroom with an army of friends around him. His eyes were steady, but scared and maybe a bit mad too. It reminded me of Charlie on the driveway of her dad's house.

'And you have to try to stop my dad, Esta. Because without the Kila...'

Dad's letter knife! I pulled it out and held it up for him. 'I have it—' I cringed at the pathetic looking blade, still smeared with bits of Spam.

Simon's eyes widened. 'You found it?'

I nodded.

'You sure that's going to do the trick? It looks kind of flimsy.'

I grinned with tears in my eyes. 'I don't know.'

'You have to find Lama la. But be quick. The shadows are getting thicker.'

The shield had almost faded to nothing. Contorted black shapes reached out, their spiny claws pulling at the threads of light.

Simon muttered under his breath and rang his bell. But this time the metal clanged dully. No light came from it.

A sleek black limb slid through the faint glow that still surrounded us.

Simon gritted his teeth. 'It's not working.' He swung it again.

More limbs punched through the gaps in the shield. Spindly fingers clenching and unclenching.

I leant over and kissed Simon's forehead, tasting the salt of his sweat. I lowered a finger to his chest and pressed an imaginary bravery badge to it. I took the hinge from my pocket: the thing I had once called The Orb; the object that had made me believe any of this was actually happening—and handed it to him. 'Play your bell again.'

Simon frowned.

'You need both. It's what Lama la said. A bird needs two wings to fly. Take it.'

He held it level with his heart, just above the bell. Then closed his eyes and began to chant; rocking the bell back and forth in his left hand. The hinge glowed.

White light forked through it, transforming it into the ornate Orb it had once been. *It had always been.*

Light crackled through its centre and collected at the prongs. Delicate silvery fibres radiated from it into a halo around us. Simon winked open an eye. 'I'll deal with the demons. You get that dagger to Lama la.'

He began to chant again. The halo became licking tongues of flame. The fingers recoiled, the limbs shrivelled and dissolved behind an expanding shield of roaring diamond-white fire.

As it grew, colour and shape bled back into the room. The blood-red pillars supporting the hall of Rigpa Gompa emerged. Behind us, the statue of Padmakara, and sitting in a row, chanting and playing their instruments, were the four Dharmapalas.

52

The Wrecking Ball

I stepped away from Simon as the silver shield grew around him. Drums and cymbals clattered noisily as the Dharmapalas chanted in low, rhythmic tones.

'I've never seen that before,' said a voice beside me. I turned to see Rabjam, the tall boy dressed in white robes. He was staring at Simon.

I poked his arm.

'Ouch,' he said, rubbing it.

'You can see me?' I asked.

'Yes. And feel you.'

'What's happening?' I said, pointing at the dazzling light display.

'Lama la taught your friend the protection ritual,' Rabjam said. 'He's performed it without stopping for two days. But the stuff coming out of his bell only started today.'

Simon was still visible, surrounded by gushing lights. Different colours now: rainbow arcs swirling and stretching to the ceiling. He was mumbling unrecognisable, whispering words. Beside him the other Dharmapalas were singing and playing their own instruments. Together they made a noise as loud as a football chant.

A deep thunder rumbled through the room, joining in with them.

There was a rattling at the far end of the hall. The double doors shook violently.

'Mara is coming,' Rabjam said. 'We need to make the protection shield stronger. Can you help?'

'Help? How?'

The two girls, one in yellow and one in blue, swung long curved sticks against heavy drums hanging by their sides. Thubten sat in a row behind. Next to him was what appeared to be an identical twin. They both held an instrument. One played a pair of what looked like tiny cymbals, the other, a small hand drum, and each clattered away in their own personal rhythm.

'I don't know how,' I shouted, glancing up at the empty throne. 'Where's Lama la?'

'In his study.'

'Why isn't he here? Why isn't he helping?'

Rabjam shrugged, 'What can he do? If there is nothing to be done then why worry, if there's—'

'I need to get him this.' I held up Dad's letter knife. Except it was no flimsy thing anymore. It was an older, heavier version of the one I'd taken from the museum, its blade shimmering electric blue. I smiled. *Yes.*

Rabjam stared at it wide-eyed, 'You found it? Where did you get it? How did you get it?'

Something heavy thudded against the doors, drowning out his questions and making the cross-beam wobble.

The drums and cymbals stopped. For a moment there was an eerie peace, only disturbed by Simon's quiet chanting and the tinkling of his bell.

I let out a breath into a deathly hush. Incense smoke settled in layers around the others; a high-pitched ringing chimed in my ears.

Rabjam took a step backward. The floor darkened where it met the doors. Shadows seeped between the cracks in the hinges, snaking over the cross-beam and then to the floor.

I moved forward, placing myself between Simon and the slithering shadows.

A crash shattered the silence. The main doors rocked on their hinges and the heavy wooden beam that held them shut clattered to the ground. A cloud of black smoke billowed through the widening crack.

'Mara,' Rabjam whispered.

Karma Chodron dropped her drumstick and rose to her feet. 'I'll hold him off,' she said, then bowed, put her palms together and vanished in a rush of air. Almost instantly she reappeared by the door, lifting the beam back across its centre. But before she could secure it, the door buckled again with a blow that sent her sprawling.

'Sera,' Rabjam said to the other girl, 'you need to help.'

'I need to play the instruments,' Sera complained, worry etched across her face.

'She's your sister!' shouted one of the Thubten twins. To my surprise, a third one appeared by her side. He pulled the drumstick out of her reluctant fist. 'Do what Rabjam says. I can play for you.'

The door shook once more. Karma Chodron had scrambled to her feet, but oily limbs were circling around her ankles.

'Sera. Help her!' Rabjam shouted.

The girl rolled her eyes and flung her arms in the air. 'OK, OK.' She loosened her yellow robes and strode towards the door.

I blinked. Normally when people walk away from you they seem to get smaller. Sera was the opposite. The further away she went, the *taller and wider* she grew. By the time she reached the door, she was twice her original size and filled the space from top to bottom.

Karma Chodron—no more than waist high to her sister now—stepped aside. Sera leant her shoulder against the buckling wood. The doors creaked. Sera's feet skidded backwards, but the door held.

I exchanged a look with Rabjam. 'Did she—'

One of the Thubten brothers blew a horn, drowning out my question. The other two crashed their cymbals and drums. Rabjam nodded and smiled.

My eyes returned to the now giant girl holding the door. Grinning, I spun around to the others. The brothers grinned back. The one on the left shouted: 'The Chodron sisters!'

'One's really fast,' the middle one said.

'And the other one's really fat!' said the third and newest member of the group.

The first brother paused his playing, reached over and thwacked the third one on the head with a drumstick. 'Don't be rude Thubten!' But they were all grins. Backs straight, shoulders square, they raised their voices, pummelled drums, crashed cymbals.

I shook my head in disbelief and turned back to watch as Sera, holding back an army of demons, gave a triumphant roar.

I slapped Rabjam on the shoulder. 'She's like the yellow Hulk!' I shouted.

Maybe we *would* hold them all back. Mara, the bulldozers, even the storm itself. We had a *giant* on our side!

Rabjam tilted his head and smiled weakly, 'We all have powers. She changes her size.'

'And you make terrible tea!' one of the increasing number of Thubten brothers shouted. 'Now help me hit drums! More noise!'

Rabjam grabbed a couple of drumsticks, handed one to me and pointed to one of the dangling drums. I hit it without really knowing why. Rhythm was never a strong suit of mine. But, you know, anything to help the cause.

'We're winning. We're winning!' one of the brothers sang over the racket.

Rabjam shook his head. 'Don't underestimate Mara. We might be holding the demons back here…' he gave me a meaningful look. '… but not the machines in your world.'

My smile dropped. I had an image of the wrecking ball swinging towards us. Even Sera wouldn't be able to hold a tonne of steel back.

'You know we can't do this alone,' Rabjam shouted over the noise.

But,' I said hopefully, 'we're winning.'

'You're not the only one who can move from one reality to the other, you know. Our two worlds are so close here, Mara can operate in both. If we stop his demons here, he'll just concentrate all his efforts on the machines.'

I stopped drumming. 'I can't go out there. They have dogs. I'd be ripped apart. We have to try from here.'

'You must! If the machines aren't stopped, Mara will get stronger. It doesn't matter *how* he destroys us.'

'Keep drumming. Keep in time!' Thubten shouted.

A familiar metallic taste coated my tongue. I swallowed it down. I knew he was right. The stench of the demon in the museum, the dark gleam in Mr Taylor's eyes, the storm. Mara wasn't just *influencing* my world. He was already in it.

Another blow from outside threw Sera's huge frame aside. Simon's protection shield flickered.

Darkness suddenly dropped like a blanket.

I let go of the drumstick.

The other drums and cymbals shuddered out of time, then stopped. Simon's bell chimed once and then even that became silent.

The door creaked open.

For a gut wrenching moment, the room folded in on itself. It was like someone had turned a page in a book and in an instant the hall was gone and I was surrounded by broken bits of wood, crumbling walls and the crawling stench of disinfectant. The front door was wide open. There was a glint of yellow. Men shouted, dogs barked, rain fell in thick grey rods. Someone screamed my name.

I blinked.

The room flipped back.

Now it was the black limbs of some enormous creature that reached through the doors of the glowing hall. Clawed fingers, each one the size of my arm, gouging at the floor.

I squeezed my eyes shut again. But my head was filled with the sounds of screaming and scraping; the smells of garbage, gasoline, grease ... *poison*.

I clapped my hands over my ears, trying to block it all out. It felt like I was on a tightrope wobbling between two worlds. Two realities, folding in and out of each other.

A rush of air brushed against me, and I opened my eyes.

Karma Chodron appeared in a flash of blue, her face black with grimy sweat. She ignored me and bent over Simon. 'Play,' she shouted. 'Or we're all dead.'

He gazed blankly at the girl. Karma Chodron grabbed his hand and shook it. 'The bell. Ring the bell.'

Thubten began to beat the drums. The others chanted, their voices loud and shrill. Simon woke from his trance and swung the bell again, the ringing as chaotic as the drumming.

'Focus!' Karma Chodron screamed at him.

Simon closed his eyes. His lips moved, and the bell rocked at his chest smoothly, the sound becoming steadier. The energy seeped from the Orb, filling the hall with light again.

Rabjam leant to yell in my ear. 'Find the Lama. Give him the Kila. He'll tell you what to do.'

'But the Kila keeps our worlds tied together.'

'If we can't stop the machines, then it's the only way.'

'But what will happen to me? To Simon, to my dad?'

'I don't know.'

'We'll be stuck in your world, won't we?'

'But it won't matter, because if you don't do it, Mara will have won! When you're shot with an arrow, you stop asking questions and pull the thing out. Now do it!'

I barely remembered the way. I ran along twisting corridors, then up the winding staircase to the first floor. Panicking, I headed down a hallway I didn't recognise, until, with relief, I reached the curtained doorway that either led to the statue's head or the floorless room with a hook in its ceiling. I took the steps opposite, two at a time, bursting onto the landing just as another impact jolted me to the floor.

In another world, the storm would surely be raging now. Bulldozers would be tearing down the walls of Gatley House. Graham and Lily probably screaming at them to stop. The wrecking ball would be swinging; a deadly pendulum punching holes through a forgotten building standing in the way of progress.

Fifteen steps to Lama la's room.

I remembered how cold the hall had been the first time I'd walked along it; the weathered face of the old man glowing in the beam of Simon's torch. What I would have done to see that face now?

More sounds from outside. Not the bells and cymbals from the ritual in the hall though. There was the growl of thunder, electronic beeping, the shouting of men. The smell of incense no longer lingered. Instead, the smell of concrete, diesel and rotting wood.

I reached out to pull the curtain aside, but I knew something was wrong even before my fingers touched wood. I pressed.

No movement. I closed my hand around the cool metal of a handle, turned it and pushed the door inwards.

It creaked open into a disused, dusty room: warped floorboards, a thick curtain hanging slightly askew opposite; the low, broken table empty now even of rusty junk. No pictures on the walls, no shrine. My breath was shallow as I entered. 'Lama la?' I choked, even though I knew he wouldn't answer. 'Lama la?'

I walked across the room, my hands shaking as they reached for the curtain.

Lama la had once opened these curtains to a vast land of valleys and mountains. Would they still be there now? Would Mara be standing in the courtyard with an army of demons?

I prized them an inch apart and peered between them.

Down below lay the overgrown lawn of Gatley House. There was the outline of the clogged up pond, the workmen staring upwards shielding their faces from the rain which fell from the dark sky. There was the wall of holly bushes lining the pitted track. And behind the curtain of rain would be Grover Close and the rest of my home town.

Standing in the middle of it all—glinting in a single shaft of sun that momentarily penetrated the storm—was the tall metal crane of the wrecker.

More thunder accompanied branches of blue lightning overhead. Machines rattled below. Men yelled instructions at each other. There was a jaw-clenching screech of iron as a cable stretched taut. Something dark hung from it, lifting into the sky. A ball the size of a car, rain streaming down its sides

I stopped breathing. Images flooded my mind. Mum raising her fist in the school hall; Gran's smile; a silver tear travelling down Simon's cheek; my dad's green eyes flashing up at me from a cold, grey sea.

The wrecking ball seemed to widen, as if it were merely inflating.

It was a dirty, beaten grey, and it sucked whatever light remained from the morning until it blocked out everything else.

Before it hit, I could just make out the bowing leaves of the weeping willow down in the garden. And for the briefest of instants, I thought I saw the shape of a dog pressing its nose against a tiny square metal can.

53

WORLDS WITHIN WORLDS

The steel ball tore through brick, plaster, glass and wood with an ear-splitting roar, hurling me flat on to my belly at the edge of a gaping hole that stretched down into the room below.

Another room without a floor.

Two stories below—where Simon should have been sitting— was a pile of broken furniture, brick and plaster.

The floorboards shuddered as the ball worked itself free.

I felt for the Kila. That was the key. It was the only hope. If I could just see it, maybe I could see Rigpa Gompa again. Maybe Lama la was in this very room. Maybe Simon would be visible through the collapsed floor.

My fingers touched metal. I lifted it to see if it glowed. But in my hand was nothing more than Dad's crappy letter knife, dull and blunt. I stared at it until my eyes hurt. 'Poetry,' I whispered to it, willing it... no begging it to transform. 'It's all poetry.'

But it didn't change. It was just a flimsy metal blade.

The deafening screech of the steel ball pulling away made me want to curl up into a ball of my own. Another hit and I would probably join the mess two stories below. *Just like Charlie Bullock.*

I looked to the side. The rest of the floorboards in that direction had collapsed. Only a supporting beam running along the centre propped up my section. The opposite wall had been torn apart, revealing the landing and the staircase, but there was no way to it.

No way out.

I closed my eyes. Even if I got to the curtains, gravity had already killed me. Once in motion, nothing on earth would stop the wrecking ball coming back to devour me.

I glanced down over the edge of the broken floor and thought of Mum again. I cursed myself. Miss Nuttal, Hannah, Mr Culter and everyone else was right. I lived in a dream world to protect myself from what had happened to Dad, pretending he hadn't gone for good; that he was off on some magical adventure.

But that lie was crashing around me now.

Mum would never recover. Dad broke her heart by leaving and now, just when she had almost fixed it again, I was going to take a wrecking ball to it.

I could do nothing more. Soon the wrecking ball would come tearing right through this floor again.

'I'm sorry,' I said to the broken bits of floorboard and the dusty floor below.

A screeching of metal resounded outside. A flash of lightning blinded me. The floor shuddered as the steel ball connected with the roof, sending fragments of wood and tile crashing around me. Rain poured down through the newly formed hole. I turned on to my side. Above me, the storm clouds boiled. I flung an arm over my face as the ball pulled away again with the sound of rolling thunder. And when it was free, the sound faded into what could have been faint drumming.

I felt a tear rolling down my cheek. I wasn't sad. I was angry. I had so *wanted* it to be true. I had *needed* it to be true. I thought about Gran going on about poetry but lying here, surrounded by the broken shards of wood and glass, it felt nothing more than wishful thinking now. I slammed a fist against the floor. How *could* two worlds exist in the same space? *Why* couldn't they?

I rubbed my eyes with a grimy fist. Rain spattered down on to my face—it tasted of vinegar. A dim solitary shaft of sun light filtered through a cloud of dust, making each mote glitter like wandering stars.

Starlight… What was it Dr Harkness had said about the stars? Something about it being a matter of perspective? His droning voice came back to me. *'Depending on where you're standing, they both exist and don't exist at the same time…'*

And maybe that was it. Maybe it wasn't the *house* that shifted from world to world. Maybe it was all just a matter of *perspective.*

I swivelled fully onto my back and screamed for Lama la, holding the letter knife up, as if it were a baton in a relay, hoping, praying he would be standing above me ready to pluck it from my hands and magic all the badness away.

But above me there was nothing. Nothing but a broken ceiling and the thunderous sky beyond it.

I lay there panting, sweat trickling painfully into my unblinking eyes.

But something *had* changed. The storm clouds directly above me were sagging unnaturally. As I watched, they seemed to shift and move and twist.

I tried to push myself up as the thick black clouds swirled downwards from above. Then they separated into a mass of blue-black shadows, tongues of flame dancing around them, bright red eyes seeming to blink from within, falling like tumbling, burning coals.

I squeezed my eyes shut. Because, to be honest, given the choice, I'd have rather taken my chances with the toxic rain and a wrecking ball than an army of demons. If that was what was happening.

I heard my name.

My eyes snapped wide. 'Lama la?'

Suddenly, the rain had stopped. The air was filled with curling smoke. It stank of disease.

'I've got the Kila!' I yelled into the darkness.

My ears strained for the slightest noise. The faintest reply.

I waited.

A voice from the other side of the room whispered my name again. It was the most beautiful sound I think I'd ever heard. Between laughing and coughing, I managed to shout. 'Lama la. I have it!'

The smoke cleared. The room resolved around me. There were the pictures on the wall; there was the small shrine. It had been upturned, bowls and fruit lay scattered across the floor.

'Lama la. I have it!' I said again, relief flooding through me. I attempted to stand. I had to get the knife to the old man, so he could end this thing.

'Don't move, Esta,' Lama la said abruptly. His voice was calm, but it carried across the room now as if he were speaking right beside me. 'The realms are unstable. Stay where you are.'

'What's happening?'

'You are slipping between worlds. Do *not* move.'

A great clap of thunder made the floor shudder. I dropped to my knees, almost letting go of the knife.

There was a flash of blinding white and when I opened my eyes again, the dust and rain had returned and the wrecking ball was tearing and screeching through another section of wall.

'Lama la?' I called in desperation. I didn't know if the old man could hear me. Were we both slipping through realms?

'How do we defeat him?' I shouted.

The rain was like a hail of bullets against the roof, the iron chain screeched somewhere out there in the storm. In the distance I could faintly hear what sounded like a car horn beeping incessantly.

I needed to get back to Rigpa Gompa. What good was I here on my own? I had to get back to Lama la, or everything would be lost.

The steel ball pulled itself free. Thunder rumbled again.

I waited for the lightning. Either that or the steel ball.

I waited as seconds passed. Rain trickled down my back.

Then there was the flash.

I blinked.

And I was right back in Rigpa Gompa, which was definitely a bad news/good news thing: I was slap bang in the middle of a room full of shifting, stinking shapes with red eyes... But there was no wrecking ball and Lama la was here.

I could see him clearly now. He was seated in his usual position—cross-legged behind his low table—while slick-limbed demons—*Mamo* like the one from the museum—circled slowly around us, *clicking their teeth.*

I held up the Kila, 'This is the one!' I shouted triumphantly.

Lama la didn't respond. There was something wrong. He was supposed to take it off me and do his ritual thing. Sever the connection between worlds, save everyone from this nightmare. But the old man just sat there with his eyes closed, a cup of tea with a doily draped over it sitting on the table in front of him.

Around us, twenty or more of the Mamo watched us hungrily. Waiting.

'I'm frightened,' I croaked.

'Fear is just a feeling,' the old man said. 'It's just your heart beating a little faster. Breathe and watch.'

'How do we fight him?'

'It's too late, Esta,' he said. 'We can't fight him. We can't win. The realms are open.'

'You're wrong,' I said, brandishing the Kila at him. 'We have this.'

I stared at the letter knife in my outstretched hand. I *had* to believe this was the real one.

'What does it do?' I asked, turning the thing in my hands now. What had Graham read in the museum? *The destruction of demonic powers'*

'It is just a knife,' came the reply.

'We have to use it!' I shouted, feeling the familiar heat rising inside me.

'But, Esta,' he replied in a resigned tone. 'You know you cannot defeat Mara with hate.'

My hand dropped an inch.

There was something familiar about those words.

Lama la continued. 'For his hatred is too great.'

I almost dropped the knife. Not just familiar. I *knew* them.

'We cannot defeat him with desire…'

I'd *read* them almost every night.

'… Desire fuels…'

The devils fire…

Dad's poem, I thought with elation. I could almost *see it* in front of me. Almost touch it. There was an answer here. It meant something, and all I had to do was remember how the damn thing ended.

Another voice spoke. It began as a gentle murmur at the edge of my hearing and, like an approaching plane, it grew and grew until it blotted out every other noise, blotted out my own thoughts, even.

A beautiful face emerged from the drifting smoke, as wide as the room itself. Eyes glinted with golden sunlight, bathing me in warmth.

It was Mum's smiling face. The way she used to look at me before Dad left. No. It was Lily's. She was laughing at something I'd said. It was… It was… Now it was some impossibly beautiful goddess, like the one painted on the wall of Gatley House…

I pointed the knife at the face and whispered: 'Defeats demons!'

I was too exhausted to be fooled by Mara's tricks anymore.

The beautiful lips opened and a lilting, calming sound emerged from them: *'But I am no demon, Esta,'* it said. *'I am in you. I am part of you and you are in me. Every tear of anger, every scream of rage. Your hopes and dreams and every yearning desire.'*

The face smiled so radiantly that I found it difficult to speak. I tore my gaze away and grunted Lama la's name, searching for him across the broken room.

He was still seated on pretty much the only remaining bit of floor. He smiled at me sadly: 'You cannot deceive his devilish eyes… Let go, Esta,' he said.

'Yes,' came the other voice.

I refused to look at the broad, smiling face of Mara, but the words slithered into my mind anyway. '*Let it all go and let your friend's actions go to waste. Your boyfriend down below fighting off the Mamo with every fibre of his being. Your friends in the human realm standing before the machines.*'

'He's not my boyfriend,' I breathed through gritted teeth.

The voice laughed. And I couldn't resist glancing. God, but now it was the face of Miss Nuttal. She was holding out her massive hands. Fingernails, gleaming red on one hand, blue on the other.

'Lama la?' I pleaded, my grip on reality loosening.

How could he *not* help me? How could he not at least *try* to fight? With so much at stake. Why was he *doing nothing?*

'Esta. You don't *want* to win,' the old man said as if hearing my thoughts. His voice sterner now.

'What the hell is that supposed to mean?'

A horrible idea occurred to me then. What if *he* was Mara?

What did it matter? Let him play his games. I knew what I needed to do. I needed to remember the end of the damn poem.

Something exploded to the side of me. A beam of wood splintered, bricks fell like a shower of Lego.

Miss Nuttal was reaching out for me, her face contorted into a grimacing, leering grin. Her painted nails had become sharp and hooked talons. The foul creatures surrounding her chattered in voices that reminded me of Hannah and her friends. Nattering voices: '*Detesta Brown,*' they mocked. Nasty and vindictive voices: '*Give us the Kila. Let in the fires of hate. Let the fire burn it all away.*'

A crack of thunder. A flash of jagged lightning.

I was jolted back inside another room.

I didn't recognise it. Brown walls. Hot wind. A sandstorm.

My head spun. I protected my eyes from a burning wind, and yet at the same time I could hear the screeching of iron, the nattering voices of the Mamo.

Three separate realities swam before me. Each one folding in and out of the other.

In this third world, it was a dry wind that roared in my ears. And over that, yet another voice spoke to me. It was a soft male voice. A voice I hadn't heard for two years. It said: 'All the gold and emeralds, Esta. If he had stayed on the island,' it continued, 'what good would the treasure have done him?'

Another flash of light.

Drops of something warm splashed against my face. It could have been rain, or blood...

In some other place, through a faint membrane, black bodies swarmed through the gap in the roof.

Then the soft voice came again, a whisper this time, almost conversational. 'He swam to the boat, or he'd have been lost forever. His real mistake was that he kept trying to find the island after he sailed away wasn't it?'

'Dad?' I called into the swirling smoke, dust and limbs. 'Is that you?'

But any reply was drowned out by the screaming, swinging chains of the wrecking ball blending with the wails of the circling Mamo, and I was blinded by the soaking rain mixing with the oily fingers of Mara's demons.

I fell to my knees. 'Dad?' I cried again. My tears hitting the broken floorboards. He was here. Another realm. Another layer of reality touching mine. He was close. I could hear him and maybe if I shouted loud enough he could hear *me*.

'Let go, Esta Brown,' the voice whispered. I raised my head in alarm. Was this another one of Mara's deceptions? 'No. Not you, Dad,' I moaned. 'Please not you as well.'

'Let it go. Give it up.'

'No,' I sobbed. 'I'll *never* give up!'

'A treasure only has value if you *give it* value.'

I looked down at the knife shaking in my hand. 'What d'you mean?'

'On a desert island, jewels...' said the voice. So faint I could barely hear it. '... are a distraction.'

A glimmer caught my eye. Several feet ahead and just below.

Something metal was screwed into the beam that held up the floor beneath me.

The hook.

Hanging from it was the frayed rope, trailing off into the gloom.

I stared down into the darkness. A cloud of dust shifted and swayed below me, like the rolling grey of the sea. And somehow Dad was down there, treading water, staring up at me. *'Come on, Est,'* he called.

Pale light danced on the surface of the waves.

I blinked. *Mara is the master of disguise,* I thought. *Focus on the rope. Nothing else. It's all tricks.*

I placed the Kila, still nothing more than a letter knife again, into the waist band of my skirt and pulled myself along the floorboards towards the edge of the drop closest to the rope. If I hung over a little, I might be able to reach it. But the floor was such a long way down. So far down it appeared to wobble and bulge.

Dad's face looked up at me. He was smiling, calling me to him.

The metallic taste of fear rose hot from my gut, like molten silver.

'I can't,' I sighed. 'It's too far. I won't make it.'

'Yes,' he said, his face breaking into a huge grin. *'Yes you can. The fear is just a feeling, Esta. You can't be brave without it though.'*

The broken edge of the floorboard dug into my chest. It creaked under my weight.

'How do I know it's really you?' I whispered.

'Find me…' the voice faded out. A hot wind made my skin crawl. The sand swirled in the gloom beneath.

'Don't leave,' I murmured. 'Daddy, don't leave me.'

Then, what was left of the day became blackest night.

A storm of broken glass and splinters of wood clawed at my back and neck. The remains of the floor cracked and tipped, pushing me over the edge. I shut my eyes, visualised the rope, breathed, reached out both hands…

54

LETTING GO

… and felt the burn as the fibres slid between my fingers.

I held on even though my arms wanted to pop from their sockets; wrapped a leg around the rope as falling masonry and glass rained down on me. A chunk of ceiling plaster hurtled past, bouncing once against a wall then crashing into the floor below in a cloud of billowing white. The rope bit at my palms as I slid downwards into a haze of dust. At the same time, black shapes rose, scattering past my ears towards the gaping hole of the smashed roof.

I gripped harder to stop myself slipping and craned my head upwards to avoid choking in the cloud.

I hung there, swinging in an eerie hush, waiting for all three worlds to collapse around me.

Time stretched.

My gaze settled on the hook directly above.

Except, now I looked at it, it wasn't a hook. It was more like a ring. I frowned. In a daze, my thoughts rolled over themselves. *A pulley? Who hangs themselves on a pulley?* In that weird, elongated moment, I realised the story about the hook wasn't true at all. Harry hadn't put it up there to hang himself. Of course he hadn't. He hadn't tried to kill himself out of grief. He'd made a memorial stone for his wife. He'd battled to preserve his old house—a living memory of something. A dry laugh caught in my throat.

Reality tilted again. It was as if someone had turned a page in a picture book.

Now, two giant eyes the size of beach balls glared at me from the gash in the floor above. Mara had finally dropped all pretence. I could feel the force of hatred peeling off them, the anger and malice casting everything in a flaming golden glow. Mamo emerged either side of those eyes, sliding over the jagged edge of the floorboards, slithering down the rope towards me.

I wrapped myself more tightly round the rope and reached for the knife, pointing it upwards. The shapes slowed.

I smiled behind gritted teeth. At last, the true form of the Kila shined in the light from Mara's burning gaze.

'Destroys demons!' I screamed.

Mara roared. The walls shook. A powerful wind tore at me, almost whipping the Kila from my grip. I hung on, but the effort was too much. Mara was too strong. All he had to do was reach down and take the dagger from me now.

My grip loosened.

The world jolted. The glow from Mara's eyes was momentarily replaced by the forked lightning of the storm reaching in through the broken roof. It sent claw-like patterns of light across the surface of the wrecking ball that was hauling itself away for another swing.

There was a single moment of calm between the lightning and the sound of thunder.

In that moment the last lines from Dad's poem finally came to me. The poem he had underlined. The one I read almost every night, while I hid under my sheets:

Whether a bishop or merely a priest,
There's only one way to tackle the beast…

Gravity pulled at me. Gatley House breathed me in, away from the destruction, away from the poisonous sky. I was powerless.

The rope swung as the wrecking ball finally freed itself.

'I'm coming Dad,' I whispered.

I closed my eyes, imagining a cold grey sea.
Then let go.

55

BINDING THE MAMO

I lay unmoving in the middle of a pile of split wood and cracked plaster. A loud whine rang in my ears. To my relief, I still held the Kila in my closed fist.

Someone whispered my name. I tried to raise myself.

Beside me, something rustled. I froze.

A movement dislodged a pile of dust. Smooth limbs. A creature pulling itself from the wreckage with long, bony fingers. Its body gleamed black in a pale light, sinewy muscles rippled under its tight skin. It drew back its lips, revealing a row of rotten, uneven fangs that reminded me of Kev's old teeth. A blood red tongue slithered around them. When it hissed, the stench of pollution came off it in waves.

I gripped the Kila more tightly and raised it high.

The thing blinked. The room flashed again.

For the briefest of moments I was on the floor of Rigpa Gompa. A distant ringing. Six figures around me, staring down. Four children in different coloured robes. Two larger figures. One in robes, the other... in black school trousers and a pair of muddy Hitecs.

And then—as if the pages of reality had been flipped again— just one figure. A tall man, long hair covering his ears.

He spoke. Softly. Whispering.

"There's only one way to tackle the beast..."

The dagger was suddenly heavy in my hands. Almost too heavy to lift. I gritted my teeth. 'He's gone!' I shouted. Trying to blot out the voice.

But it continued. Insistent. The final lines of Dad's poem spoken quickly, without a breath, like water rolling over a dry bed of stones:

'Pity his cries, pity his rage, pity the talons, pity the claws, pity the monster that is pained by its scars, that hasn't a care, but is tortured by kindness and bitten by sweetness and bound after all…'

Flash. I was back on the floor of Gatley House.

Beside me, the delicate limbs of a small, trembling animal not much bigger than my hand. Tiny, black eyes gleamed at me as it shuffled from under a splintered window-frame. Skin, black and smooth around its chest; arms bony and limp.

I let out a long breath, whispering the final line of Dad's poem:

'… and bound after all… by love.'

The creature shivered and blinked again.

I let go. The letter knife clattered to the floor.

'It's all right,' I croaked, darkness and exhaustion finally overwhelming me. I collapsed next to the animal. 'There's nothing to fear now.'

The black face stared at me, lost and in pain.

'He's gone,' I said, 'But everything's going to be OK.'

I felt myself slipping from consciousness. The house around me came to a complete hush. The pattering of rubble from the ceiling, the complaining creak of buckled walls, even the whistling in my ears faded.

Before complete blankness came, I could have sworn I heard the ringing of a bell. Out of the corner of my eye, the little black creature stretched, spread out a set of wings and disappeared up towards a jagged strip of sky way, way above.

56

FALLING PLASTER

Frozen pinpricks on my eyelids woke me. It was quiet. No screeching metal chains, no exploding brick walls, no wild drumming.

Something cold and wet landed on my cheek. I blinked. My vision was fuzzy. Dark blots filled the still air. *Snow.*

I put my hands on the floor to push myself up. My shoulders ached, my palms stung. I dropped back down with a sigh. But this time there was something soft propping me up.

An arm.

It was—as they often are—attached to a shoulder, and that, eventually, to a face. Hair flat against its forehead, cheeks black as soot.

I groaned. 'Dad?' Blinked again. The face smiled. *Not Dad.* Dad's eyes were green. Just like mine. These were blue.

'You did it,' Simon said, helping me up.

We were sitting on the lower steps of the wide staircase surrounded by rubble. I raised my eyebrows and grunted something that was supposed to be a question about what had just happened, but came out more like a 'Hnng?'

Simon seemed to understand, though. 'Everything went black,' he said. 'Then you dropped down from the ceiling. Right in the middle of the fight. There was one of those demons next to you. I thought it was going to attack. But you said something to it…'

I remembered the tiny black creature. The bat with its sad little eyes.

'… and it just melted away.' A whisper of a frown crossed his face. 'And so did everything else. Mara, the Mamo, they just melted away. What did you say?'

I rubbed a lump on the back of my head, 'Nothing. I fell.'

I coughed. It hurt my ribs and brought tears to my eyes. The room blurred into different colours, giving me a headache. I placed the heel of my palms against my eyes.

'Are you OK?'

'I saw the ceiling collapse. Mara was… the wrecking ball...' I remembered the voice reciting the words of the poem. 'And Dad?' I twisted round, searching the hall. 'He was here.'

The room was dark though. A thick layer of dust hung in the air. Water trickled on to us from above. But sunlight streamed down through the tear in the ceiling.

Simon followed my gaze upwards. 'The ceiling's not safe. Can you stand? I can lift you.'

I grabbed his offered hand. 'I'd flatten you,' I said with a smile that was half a grimace too.

I let him haul me up until I stood with our faces almost touching.

'You're light as a feather,' he whispered.

I think the layer of grime caking my face did a great job of hiding a treacherous blush.

'We better get out from under the massive hole,' I said eventually, pulling away and walking down the last couple of steps.

As we descended, a shadow flicked and darted around us before disappearing through the gap in the ceiling. A sudden thought made me stop and turn. 'The Kila?'

But the staircase was empty. Not even a rusty letter knife.

'Have you still got the Vajra and bell?' I asked.

He shook his head. 'I dropped them when I saw you fall.'

'We have to—'

A chunk of plaster smashed against the stairs where we'd been sitting. Simon held my arm. He shook his head. 'Let it go, Est.' and he led me towards the buckled front door. 'Let's go home.'

When we reached the door, we both turned to face the hall. Neither of us said anything. It wasn't planned or anything. It just felt right. Simon placed his palms together. I did the same. We bowed in the direction of the staircase.

Then Simon and I held hands and stepped out of Gatley House into the soft, late morning light.

PART EIGHT

SNOWFALL

57

LAST RESPECTS

We stood for a moment watching everything. The courtyard, the valley and the mountains were gone. In their place was the scene I'd viewed from the second-floor window, except the clouds had parted now and a patch of blue gleamed above us.

The crane glistened in the centre of the torn-up driveway and, thankfully, the wrecking ball was at rest by its muddy feet like a sleeping dog.

In front of it was a crowd of people.

Simon looked confused. 'Esta. What's going on?'

I grinned. 'Long story.'

We walked towards them, wet gravel crunching beneath our feet. Me in my school shoes, Simon in his—now distinctly worn—Hi-Tec's.

No one noticed us at first. They were focused on a noisy argument in the centre of the crowd.

Mr Culter's voice boomed out. Through the gaps in the bodies, I could see him shouting at a pale-looking Mr Taylor. The Headmaster was pointing a finger with one hand and holding—to the obvious terror of Simon's dad—a pair of chain cutters in the other. Beside them the school bus was parked at an angle in front of a bulldozer, as if it had skidded to a halt there.

'Esta?'

'I may have invited the school over,' I whispered out of the corner of my mouth. 'And Graham may have invited the police and the newspapers.'

'What for?'

'Bats and erm, Newts?'

'Newts?'

'Yeah.'

'Is this how you saved the house?'

'It's all good, Simon. Just roll with it, OK?'

A man in a suit, a hard hat and a serious face was one of the only ones not watching the argument. He was staring up towards the semi-collapsed roof of Gatley House, jotting things onto a clipboard. Three journalists clicked away with professional-looking cameras, one pointed at the house, the other two snapping away at everything else: Simon's dad and the headmaster; at the school bus; at the pupils standing in an arc around the argument; at their hastily felt-tipped posters with slogans like *'Gatley Needs its Newts'* and *'Batty for Bats.'*

One by one, faces turned to us. The arguing subsided until I could only hear the grumbling of an engine and a chorus of camera shutters. In the hush, Mr Culter's final words—which he shouted at Mr Taylor without a hint of his normal sponge cake—rang out: '... Your own son, for God's sake!'

Then there was silence. The crowd parted.

Simon gripped my hand and took a step forwards. Mr Taylor's arms hung loosely by his sides. I was relieved to see that his eyes had lost the darkness from before. Now, both they and his mouth were gaping wide.

We took another step into the uncanny quiet. I scanned the crowd for Graham and Lily and saw my mum instead. She had the wide-eyed look of someone about to hurtle down the biggest drop on a roller coaster. That made me remember my own drop through the floorboards.

'Si!' screeched a voice. The crowd parted.

Hannah Pritchard appeared.

My heart sank. For a moment, just for a moment, I thought we'd done it. I thought we'd fixed the world. But here was the Piranha herself to prove me wrong.

Tears smudged the mascara down her cheeks so you couldn't tell what was bruise and what was makeup. Not a great look. But there she was. We'd defeated the demons, the bulldozers, the storm, even Mara himself, but not Hannah Piranha.

Behind her, Kev appeared too. He was clinging on to her blazer, trying to hold her back. But she was having none of it. 'You're alive!' she squealed, freeing herself from Kev's desperate clutch.

I glanced at Simon, dreading what I'd see in his eyes. Could he still be fooled by this poisonous girl? His eyes were wide, taking in the scene. In all honesty, he looked more frightened now than when he'd been fighting off Mamos.

'Hannah?' Kev shouted. I turned back just in time to see him lurching after her. I watched open-mouthed as his foot caught a brick. He fell, arms flailing into the back of Hannah's heels, sending them both head first into the muddy gravel.

There was a stunned silence.

When Hannah rolled over and aimed a kick at Kev, catching him full in the face, I had to bite down on the inside of my cheek to stop from laughing.

Before the whole thing became utterly slapstick, another voice sang out, cutting through the rising sound of laughter.

'Son!'

Colour had returned to Mr Taylor's cheeks as he broke into a shuffling run, arms out wide, splashing past Hannah and Kev. I let go of Simon's hand and backed away. His dad had the look of one of his bulldozers and I didn't want to get caught between them.

Good job too, Mr Taylor was wide, and I guessed he packed some muscle because when he reached his son, he swept Simon off his feet and hugged him tightly. 'I don't know what came over me,' he sobbed, smothering his face in his son's chest. 'I had no idea, no idea.'

I don't think the journalists quite knew where to point their cameras. But eventually, they ignored the couple in the mud and clicked at the reunion of father and son in approval. Everyone else was too dumbfounded to react.

I caught a glimpse of Simon's face over his father's shoulders.

Tears rolled down his grubby cheeks, combining with a stream of snot, but he was grinning through it all. I gulped down a lump in my throat, looked over at Hannah, who was now pulling mud from her hair... and smiled.

Maybe we *had* fixed things.

As I stood and watched the scene, a breeze caught my hair and touched my cheek.

There was a shout from one of the pupils, who was pointing at something above my head. 'There they are again!'

Had they spotted the others? I followed the direction of the girl's finger, half expecting to see the white walls of Rigpa Gompa rising overhead, Lama la, the Dharmapalas, *Dad?* He'd been there. He'd been standing right over me...

But it was just old Gatley House.

Same as always.

Except with part of its roof caved in.

'You see them?' shouted the girl.

Fluttering black shapes swept up from the gaping hole left by the wrecking ball. A small colony of bats escaping into the clearing sky, circling and twisting above the upturned faces of the workmen, journalists, children and parents, then swooping away, searching for a place to roost. I tracked their little flapping wings until they returned past me. They flew through the front door and into the dark confines of Gatley House, where I imagined they would hang like so many hooks in the hall's ceiling.

Chattering voices of shock and concern surrounded Simon and me. We must have looked awful because Nurse Olive bawled everyone away while fussing over us with blobs of cotton wool and disinfectant from a first aid bag. I sat and let her clean me up, searching the crowd for Graham or Lily.

Before long, a fire engine, an ambulance as well as two police cars appeared. A collection of uniformed men spent half an hour in conversation with Mr Culter, the clipboard guy and Mr Taylor, who kept pausing proceedings to check on Simon. The workmen knew an early clock-off when they saw one and switched off the engines of their machines.

An hour after that, Mr Culter herded the pupils back on to the school bus along with their home-made posters. He stopped at the door, looked at me and then Miss Nuttall. When he saw the governor was busy scribbling something down in her note book, he offered me another dip of the head before disappearing after his students into the bus.

The newspapermen sloped away to get their stories in for the afternoon news. The police presence expanded and when Nurse Olive allowed them, they came to speak with Simon and me.

When the police finally gave us a break, the sun was already casting long shadows across the overgrown lawn, flashing in golden bursts where the old pond appeared through the tall grass.

Simon hadn't eaten for two days, except for the butter-tea Rabjam had served. And once I'd had the blood cleaned from my forehead and my hands bandaged, it was Simon who looked most at death's door. The police let his dad scoop him up into the ambulance.

Just before the doors shut, Simon gave me a weary smile, raised his hand, and waved his fingers at me.

An arm snaked around my waist. 'You're an idiot, Esta Brown.'

'You think I impressed Miss Nuttall?'

Mum grimaced. 'Who cares? You're a damn hero, and everyone knows it.'

'By the way. Thanks.'

'What for, love?'

'For not throwing out that last box of Dad's.'

'What?'

'Dad's box. I saw it on the kitchen table. It was... kind of a lifesaver.'

'That old thing?' She opened her mouth to say something more, but she closed it again and dust must have got into her eye, because she had to wipe it with one of her sleeves.

The blue lights of the ambulance flickered through the branches of the trees as it bounced along the muddy track. I watched until it disappeared behind the old willow tree, then frowned. Four figures stood in the shadow of its branches. They faced away from us, holding hands. 'Mum?' I said. 'Where's Gran?'

'She went back to school with the rest. Why?'

I pointed to the willow tree. 'I think she might have missed the bus.'

The lawn squelched beneath our feet. Mum moaned with each damp step. 'Is that a tin of Spam? This place is a dump, Esta, can't we just wait on the track?'

Lily looked over her shoulder as we approached. She held up an arm and jangled one-half of Graham's fluffy handcuffs still attached to it. Graham held his grandad's hand. Harry Sparks must have made his own way over here after we spoke with him at the Home. He had his head bowed towards the curtain of branches, beyond which, I knew, lay an old etched slab of stone. Gran stood to his right. She pulled a tissue from inside her sleeve and handed it to Harry. The old man took it and wiped his nose.

Mum and I stopped a few feet short and watched as Graham and Harry Sparks peeled away from the other two. Graham parted the branches like he had once done for me, and he and his grandfather disappeared behind freshly budding leaves to pay their respects to Carol Sparks.

Mum put both her arms around me, rested her head on my

shoulder and sniffed. 'Whatever happens, Est. Dad would have been proud of you today, you know.'

'I know,' I croaked.

She sniffed. 'I'm proud of you too.'

'Mum?'

'Yes, hon?'

'You're dribbling on me.'

Then she hugged me. Like I'd seen other mums hug their children. Like mums hugged their kids in movies.

Like she used to do before Dad left.

58

SNOWFALL

JULY 1986

The sun warmed my face as I stood by the window, looking out across the manicured gardens of the hospital. I refocused and watched my reflection in the glass as I pulled a brush through my hair.

Today was a special day.

Two years exactly since Dad disappeared.

Adults had a lot of complicated phrases to explain what had happened at Gatley House and what needed to happen next. And since the "Incident" the doctors insisted I stay inside, "Under Observation".

But they did at least agree with Mum that today would be a good day to make an exception. It might be "Key to the Rehabilitation Process," they'd said.

I pulled my hair into a ponytail with a purple scrunchy Mum had bought me. She'd bought a couple of hair clips to tame my fringe too. The psychologists thought that taking care of my appearance was another "Positive Step".

Anything to please.

I reached for a slim black object by my bedside table, then paused at the sound of a light knock on the door. It was followed by another knock, gentle and polite as if it were designed not to be heard. I placed the object into a small handbag. I know. But bags can be useful… just ask Graham.

A face appeared in the widening crack. 'Esta?' the nurse smiled at me. 'Ready?'

I smoothed the pale green blouse I was wearing, noticing my hand shake a little. The door opened fully, and the nurse grinned, 'You suit a skirt, love.'

I walked past her down an empty, echoing corridor that smelled of detergent and lavender.

They were waiting for me in the reception. Graham and Lily, holding hands. Simon—looking much better now—had two plastic bags at his feet. He buttoned up his Pringle cardigan at the sight of me, like he'd done with his blazer before I'd busted Hannah Piranha's nose. Behind him, lying across a couple of plastic chairs was an enormous bunch of flowers, their scent filling the room with summer.

Lily let go of Graham's hand and held hers out to me. 'Come on. They said it won't rain until evening.'

I smiled. No one was afraid of the rain anymore. They said the storm had blown out, diluting the radiation across the region to 'Safe Levels'. The weather can be unpredictable like that, apparently.

Simon lifted the bags. 'I brought sandwiches.'

I nodded. Anything was better than the food they gave me here. 'You sure you're ready?' he said.

I smiled and nodded again. I was ready. It seemed I just wasn't ready to speak yet.

Graham, Lily and Simon squeezed into the back of Mum's Renault. I sat in the passenger seat with the flowers over my knees, the bag containing my object pressing into my thigh.

No one said anything for the short drive.

Mum parked at the pub by the church and the five of us walked until we reached a roofed gateway where I paused for a moment to listen to the birds singing in the trees and a plane rumbling in the distance. *Feel the fear and do it anyway.*

'It's not a gravestone,' Mum whispered. 'It's just to have somewhere to come to remember him by and I had them add the last line like you asked.'

The headstone was slate grey with clean gold writing embossed down the front. I had to wipe my eyes to read the inscription. Even then it blurred in and out of focus. I squeezed my eyes shut and then opened them again.

MICHAEL RICHARD BROWN

August 3 1934

July 1984

Missing, presumed dead.

Loving Husband and Devoted Father

"Bound after all, by love."

I smiled. Two things existing in the same place? Happens all the time.

Husband *and* father. Duck *and* Rabbit.

Tears dropped from Mum's chin to the stone slab at our feet as she bent to lay the flowers.

I had to gulp as I pulled out the battered poetry book from my bag. I knelt next to her and placed it by the roses. I waited for her to rise. And when I was sure she couldn't hear me, I whispered:

'I'll find you, Dad.'

Gatley House was a ten-minute walk from the graveyard. The airport road had stalled in the courts while the environment agency inspected the grounds, and an argument raged about whether new homes for the bats could be found.

Graham had more luck with his wire cutters this time and we ducked under one of the KEEP OUT fences with our picnic in the plastic bags.

Grass had sprouted up around the track and driveway although I could still make out dried footprints near the toppled gate, I thought my own footprints would probably still be amongst them too and cast my mind back to the night I had hopped over to complete Simon's dare.

We climbed over the broken remains and made for the lawn. The place had settled into a lazy summer slumber. To one side, the pond buzzed with tiny insects, to the other, old tracks in the crusty earth still told the story left behind by the bulldozers.

Gatley House itself was as old and decrepit as ever, except for where the ball had torn a gaping hole through the roof and the second-floor window. A tall, metal fence had been erected around its walls now, festooned with Danger and Warning signs. The remaining windows had been boarded up. Even the basement window.

Simon reached into his plastic bag. 'Charlie drew you something by the way.'

He unfolded the sheet and gave it to me.

'I brought her down the track the other day to come and have a look.'

It was a painting of a brilliant white, shoe-box shaped building sitting in the folds of an enormous snow peak mountain. Its roof was a little dented. I held it up so I could see it next to Gatley House and tilted my head to one side. The old place didn't wobble or shift. It didn't transform into an imposing palace filled with a girl who could change her size, or one who moved with the speed of light, or an old man who could change the weather with a click of his fingers... Or Dad.

I handed the picture to Lily, lay down in the grass and rested my eyes.

I lay there, listening to the wind swish through the emerald leaves of the willow tree, inhaling the lingering aroma of gasoline and the distinctly musty smell coming from the clogged-up pond—which may or may not have contained a family of Blue Crested Newts—and, you know? Part of me didn't mind that I couldn't see any of it.

Now, as I gazed at the smiling faces of Graham and Lily and those crystal-blue eyes of Simon, for the first time since Dad had disappeared, I was content with this reality. In this moment, with these people. This was my Jewel Island.

I leaned on my elbow, watching Simon chewing grass. 'Do you think this is the duck or the rabbit?'

He raised his head from the ground, squinted at me and opened his mouth to say something, but before he did, a single dot of white drifted between us. Others followed, spiralling down like tiny feathers.

Simon stuck his hand out, caught one, and we watched it dissolve in his palm. Another landed on my nose. It was cold. Simon grinned at me. I looked up.

The midsummer sky was full of snow.

The End.

**What happened to Charlie Bullock in Gatley House?
Keep reading to find out!**

How come Charlie was wandering alone in Gatley House?

How did Esta's father come to find Charlie?

These questions and more are answered in:

Its 1984 and for Charlie Bullock, life is all about the surface detail: The clothes, the hair, the music. But when she is challenged to look beneath the surface, what lies beyond is a disturbing truth that threatens to tear her world apart and set the wheels in motion for an epic battle between good and evil.

Launching in autumn 2020

If you are interested in being an advance reader for Eyes of Mara.

Get in touch by email:
contact@rnjackson.com

A sample chapter follows.

EXCERPT: THE EYES OF MARA

The prequel to Jewel Island

R.N. Jackson

CHAPTER ONE

"They call it the murder house," Simon Taylor said, settling himself on the wall edge, his feet dangling halfway down to the thorns below. "We should go in before dad pulls it down."

Charlie Bullock heaved herself up peered down into the painful looking thicket five feet below and wondered what she was doing scrambling up walls at the age of eighteen. This particular wall of all places, with her annoying step-brother of all people.

She perched herself next to him, "It's just a rundown old building like all the others."

"This one's different," he said. "This one's got history."

"Every house's got a history, idiot."

Simon grinned at her. A big wide, stupid grin. "Not like this one, Sis." He left that phrase hanging in the still, early summer evening air. They both peered through the tangle of branches towards Gatley House. A three story detached mansion, ivy running wild up the crumbling brickwork, surrounded by trees, hedgerows. A jungle of a lawn to its front that might have once been hosted garden parties.

"Dad told me all about it," Simon said. "It was owned by this old guy and his wife. They lived here since the 1950s. He went crazy, talking about other people living with him."

"You believe anything. Dad just spreads these rumours so kids like you don't go exploring where they're not wanted."

"He went crazy," Simon continued, ignoring her. "Dad says he killed his wife. And couldn't live with the guilt. Then…" He paused and licked his lips. "Took out the floor in one of the rooms upstairs."

Charlie shook her head. "So?" Charlie asked. Trying to sound like she was bored. Trying to sound like vertigo wasn't actually making her dizzy and nauseous. She gripped the wall more tightly.

"He put a hook in the ceiling. Tied a rope to it. And… you know…" He wrapped a pretend rope around his neck tugged it and made a croaking sound.

Charlie rolled her eyes, but despite herself, she found her gaze drawn to one of the first-floor windows. Simon was enjoying this. He'd enjoy it even more if she freaked out now.

"Who does that?" she said "Think about it. You want to kill yourself, why go to the trouble of taking out a floor? Just stand on a chair and kick off it."

She didn't have time for this. Her art exam was in a week, and she still hadn't finished her portfolio. She glanced behind her and began planning how she could slide her leg back over the wall.

Visiting Gatley House had been Simon's idea. He'd said it would be the 'perfect thing' to draw for her final assessed piece: *"The heart of the thing"*

Mrs Hartley had told the class that they had to make sketches of objects that were imperfect in some way. She'd shown them things like old logs, chipped cups, rusty cutlery.

Things with character, Mrs Hartley had said.

So far, Charlie had only managed to sketch a bunch of rotten fruit. Apples mainly. They weren't even rotten, just had a few bites taken out of them.

She wasn't exactly big on imperfections. Whether it was the clothes she wore, the hair style, or the company she kept. Hence why she intended to leave Simon to his ghost stories and get home to get ready for the Pub tonight. You didn't look like Charlie Bullock without it taking at least a couple of hours in front of the mirror.

She took perfection seriously.

"Dad said he left one single beam running across the room so he could walk on it. He put the rope over his neck…"

"Simon! Enough, okay?"

"Apparently something to jump off."

"You're a sick little boy," she sighed, but a shiver ran down her spine as she imagined the old guy, mad with grief, rattling about in that dusty old mansion. Driven to jumping off into a floorless room with a rope around his…

"It's just a ghost story," she said. "And Mrs Hartley wants Still Life of imperfect things anyway."

"What's Still Life?"

"Things in a bowl. I don't think this…" she swept a hand out towards the old building, "is what she had in mind exactly."

"I bet there's loads of stuff in there you could draw. And dad said there's definitely a room without a floor."

"I wouldn't go in there if you paid me."

"Only cos you're scared," Simon said.

Charlie inspected her little brother. Fourteen years old, and right in the middle of early brat–hood. Or, she thought about her step Dad—head as round and bald as a bowling ball, gorilla arms bursting out of his work shirt—maybe this was the best it got. Maybe Simon would *devolve*, like his Dad had.

"No," she said, lowering herself off the wall, finding an edge of stone for her heel. "I don't want to go inside, because it would ruin my clothes." She jumped to the pavement. Simon followed her, smarmy grin still smeared across his face. A grin that, in Charlie's experience, nothing would peel off.

Even with the matching blonde hair, Charlie consoled herself with the thought that no one would ever mistake them for real brother and sisters. Her mum had had her before moving in with Simon's dad and they'd played at happy families for fourteen years. But surely… no one would pair them up as related by blood. He was like a different *species*.

She should just draw a picture of her family. That should fit Mrs Hartley's 'Imperfection' brief.

She waited for a couple of cars to swish past then crossed over the road. Simon at her heels like a dog.

They reached the junction of Oak Road. Just a five-minute walk to the five bedroom monstrosity her step Dad had built for them before her mum finally filed for the divorce.

It was an all-square shaped thing, with white plastering, Greek columns and even a couple of stone lions guarding the gate. Couldn't have been more different from Gatley House.

She glanced back. The tiled roof of the old building peered through the branches of the trees on the other side of the wall.

She wasn't going to admit it to Simon, but Charlie knew a bit about Gatley House and the truth was, she *was* scared of it. Always had been.

She'd walked past it for most of her eighteen years on her way into Gatley town, or to school and she vaguely remembered when someone had owned it. Ten or more years ago.

She remembered the stories people used to tell about the couple who lived there. Some retired military couple from India.

One day when there'd been an ambulance. You could see the blue flashing lights, sparking through the trees from her Primary School. There had been a hundred different stories about what had happened the next day in the playground. Even though all the adults and the newspapers had said: "heart attack".

But there had been *police-tape*. Even eight-year-olds know you don't have police tape for a heart attack.

Every day Charlie walked past over the years, she could see it, slowly sinking into the ground through neglect. A crumbling fossil, a dark relic.

And on winter days, when all the leaves were gone from the trees, if you stared at it from the right angle, its dusty windows would stare back at you.

KEEP IN TOUCH

and find out more

www.rnjackson.com

or scan the QR code:

Facebook:
rnjacksonauthor

email:
contact@rnjackson.com

Printed in Great Britain
by Amazon

45966139R00210